PHENDRIC

THE THREE LANDS

BOOK 3

A fantasy novel by

D. R. Evans

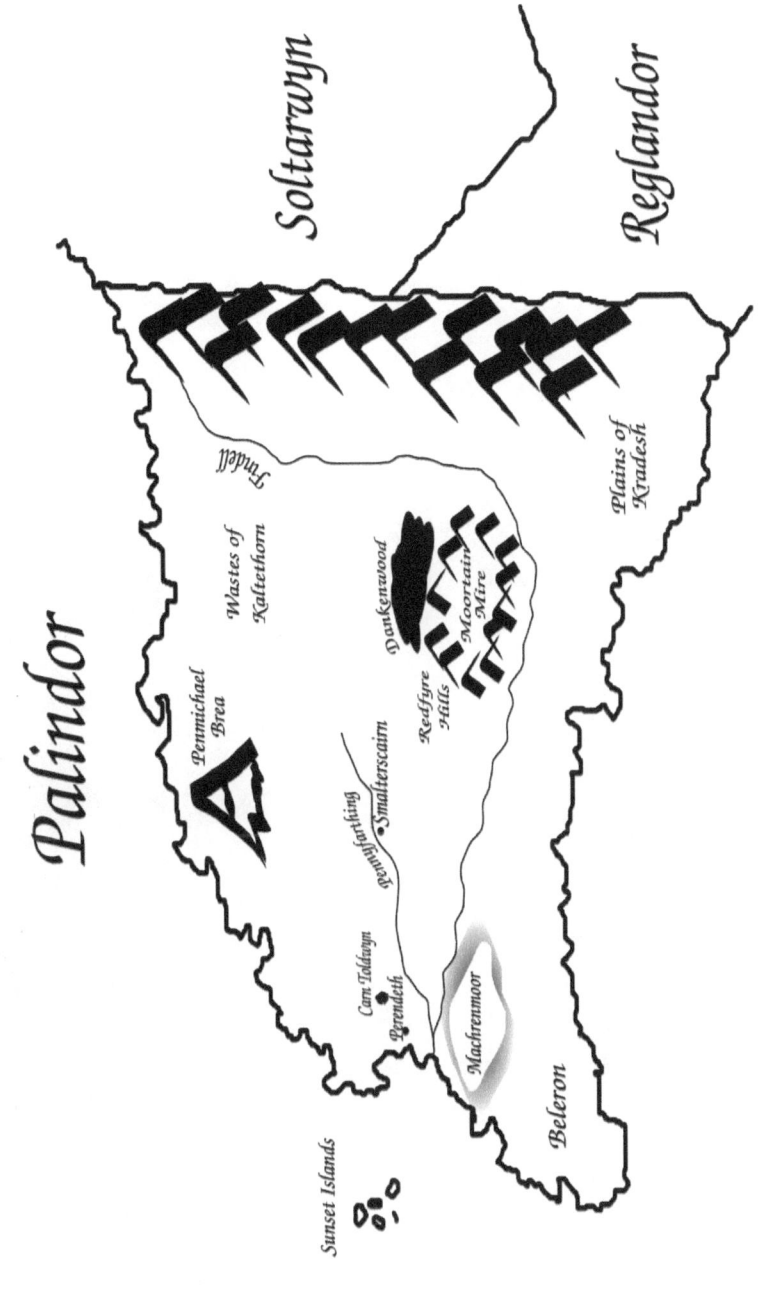

CONTENTS

Major Races of Palindor
(only the races important to our story are described here)

Dwarves. Originally underground dwellers, most dwarves now live above ground. Slightly taller than gnomes and somewhat shorter than humans, dwarves are the strongest and most belligerent fighters in the Three Lands of Abuscân. The pride of each dwarf is his (or her) battle axe. Female dwarves are only slightly less strong than males, and either would make short work of a human in combat.

Elves. There are many different types of elf, each of which is named after its most distinguishing quality. The most common elves are wood elves, who live in villages deep in woods and forests; there are also fisherelves (who live on the coasts) and even mountain elves (although these are now rare). Most elves are slightly shorter than gnomes, but are considerably leaner and more spry. They are sociable amongst others of their own kind, but considerably less so with other elves, and rarely interact with the non-elf races. Almost all elves share two great fears: tunnels and water. Only fisherelves are taught how to swim; all other elves are terrified of drowning. Only mountain elves would willingly enter a tunnel or cave.

Gnomes. The most bookish of the races, gnomes are a rarity except in Palindor. In Carn Toldwyn, Palindor's capital, they are the majority of the population. Not generally of much use in battle, gnomes are slightly shorter than dwarves. Male gnomes almost always grow long white beards. In the past, particularly intelligent and studious gnomes took an oath at a young age to become Holy Gnomes, the keepers of the ancient books.

Goblins. A race of creatures that lives underground and is rarely seen on the surface. Goblins can be quite startling at first sight, although most creatures who live on the surface will never see one. Goblins are distinguished by their long, pointed noses and ears, large eyes and dull, green-black skin. Other races tell stories about goblins to scare their children, but there is nothing intrinsically evil about goblins — they merely care little for doings on the surface. It is rumored that the treasure of the goblins far exceeds that of all other races in Palindor.

Humans. The tallest of the common races. In the earliest times, humans usually led other races into battle, and so it was decreed that only a human could be a monarch.

Hunters. Not really a distinct race, the Hunters are humans who live in the forests of Palindor. They are especially tall and strong. Rarely seen, they prefer to live solitary lives, but their skill with their longbows is unmatched throughout the Three Lands.

Major Characters

Catherine. The first High Monarch of Palindor. An elderly adult from the world of humans who first visited Palindor as a young woman.

Diana. The granddaughter of Catherine and the daughter of Michael; a strong-willed and self-centered young human.

Enwys. A young Huntress; Gwain's elder daughter.

Gwain. A Hunter.

Gwynedd. A child-Huntress; Gwain's younger daughter.

Malthazzar. The Lord of Evil and Master of Sheol. The sworn enemy of the High Lord Olvensar.

Michael. A High King and visitor from the world of humans, in which world he is the adult son of the High Queen Catherine.

Olvensar. The High Lord of Palindor.

Odrian. Initially, the first mate of the ship *Twilight Sea*; subsequently, the first mate of the *Evening Passage*. Orrian's brother.

Orrian. The first mate of the ship *Evening Passage*. Odrian's brother.

Phendric. The grandson of Drefynt, who was the last of the Holy Gnomes. An ancient prophecy foretells that the child of the child of Drefynt will be "great and saving."

Shadow. The most ruthless and powerful of Malthazzar's generals.

PROLEGOMENON

High in the dark sky hangs a sun whose harsh red brightness somehow fails to light the barren landscape below. From our vantage point on a hill high above the plain, we can see little except dark, friable, volcanic ground, riven by cracks and small canyons. Here and there are orange pools, but around them no bushes grow. The only visible vegetation is a scatter of trees — dark, stunted and gnarled — growing at random across the landscape below. The trees have adopted strange, grotesque and slightly frightening contortions. As we look out over this bleak landscape, we see no other signs of life.

At last, high above, a large bird comes into sight, its wings undulating only occasionally, as the bird glides long distances between beats. It comes closer and circles once overhead before continuing on to some unknown destination. Eventually, it disappears into the distant darkness.

Then something catches our eye. There *is* life on the plain below, and we descend the hill to investigate.

Approaching the place where we saw movement, we become aware of a foul reek that fills the air.

Hesitantly, we press onwards, until we are standing close to the object that moved. It is a large, dark, winged creature, standing vast and almost motionless, peering over a ledge into the depths of a vast Pit.

From the Pit emanates an almost tangible odor of brimstone. The very air surrounding us shimmers in small waves, carrying the odor burningly into our lungs. There is something else in the air here: everywhere in this land we expect to feel a desperation and a hopelessness; but here, standing at the very edge of the Pit, in the air that the creature breathes so deeply and, apparently, so welcomingly, those feelings are at their greatest and most terrifying. We watch and we wait, but we know that we cannot do so for long before we will succumb to the despair and, with a terrifying leap, jump forward to join the lost souls in the Pit.

There is another movement: a smaller creature approaches. The creature is dark, as is so much here, and it covers the ground in bounds, flapping small, black wings to propel itself forward between jumps. The large creature turns from its contemplation of the Pit, and observes the approaching newcomer. It blinks once, slowly, black eyelids briefly covering its red eyes. The small creature lands unsteadily and bows. It has arrived.

"Master," the small creature says.

There is a long pause, while the creature's master appears to be contemplating whether to lift the creature in its vast claws and toss it screaming into the Pit. Evidently it decides against this course of action, for eventually Malthazzar — for it is none other than he — speaks.

"You have disturbed my meditation on the souls of the lost, creature. What do you want?"

"Master, forgive me. I am only an unworthy messenger. Master, you have been absent from the castle for many days now, and the one in the dungeon has been calling for you. He says he has an idea that will please you."

Malthazzar opens his mouth and roars. We, as well as the unfortunate messenger, take an involuntary step backwards, away from the anger and bitterness and loathing that fill Malthazzar's cry.

"That vile and contemptible creature? What could he possibly have to say to me? I should have simply thrown him into the Pit, for if I had not heeded his words, I would not have been defeated."

He lapses into silence, and the messenger wonders if he has been dismissed; but then Malthazzar moves away from the lip of the Pit, unfurls enormous wings and, without another word, takes to the air.

Following as quickly as we can, we are glad to leave the terrors of the Pit behind us, at least for the moment, and before long we find ourselves entering the castle that we have had the misfortune to visit on other occasions.

We descend the narrow steps, down and yet down, until we are deep below the fortress, and there, in the deepest, darkest and most stifling dungeon, we see a gray, rat-like creature chained firmly to the slime-covered wall. The creature is difficult to see, for its shape seems constantly to change if we try to view it directly. Yet always one leg remains held fast to the wall by a fetter and a heavy chain. The creature tries to move around the cell, but it can take no more than two steps before the chain becomes taut. There is desperation in the creature's eyes.

The cell door opens, and Malthazzar steps into the dungeon. Immediately, the creature falls to the ground in homage to the lord of this place.

"Don't grovel, Shadow, it ill becomes you," admonishes Malthazzar.

"Yes, yes, whatever you say, master," says the creature as it regains its feet. It begins to hop miserably on the fettered leg.

"Why have you summoned me from my contemplation of the Pit? Do you wish to join those lost souls?"

"Master, if you desire it, send me there. But I have been chained here now for many, many suns, and while my body has been confined, I have been thinking, and I believe I have conceived a plan that will please my master."

"A plan!" Malthazzar spits out the words. "What use have I for your plans? Was it not you who suggested that I bring the High Monarchs here, thereby intervening directly in the affairs of Palindor even though Olvensar and I had agreed that neither of us would do so? If I had not listened to you, there might have been some way that I could have turned his creatures against him. But no, you advised me, and I listened to you, and here we are."

He looks forlornly around the wretched and dismal place, as if thinking about what might have been. "A plan...." He draws himself up as he speaks so that he towers over Shadow, who likewise seems to have shrunk under the weight of his master's words. And now, when Shadow speaks, it is in a very small voice indeed.

"My master, if my plan displeases you, then I beg you to throw me into the Pit, for I desire only to serve you, and if I cannot do so then my days might as well be ended."

Shadow casts his eyes to the ground, unable — or unwilling — to look at his master directly.

Malthazzar breathes deeply of the hot, still, stale air and takes a step forward. He stretches out a hand and caresses Shadow's head.

"Oh, Shadow, my Shadow," he says. "Once you were the mightiest of my generals, and now it has come to this. Come, tell me your idea. You have been chained long enough. I will listen to your plan. Perhaps this time we can defeat Olvensar."

Shadow nods skittishly. "Yes, yes, I think we can. You see, my master" — he adds the last two words quickly, for already he is beginning to forget the subservient rôle he has decided to adopt — "always before we have tried to fight the one who calls himself the High Lord directly, and he has proved himself too cunning for us. This time, I have a plan that will make it impossible for him to win."

"Go on; I like the sound of this."

"We will strike at him through those whom he loves. We will entrap the High Queen and bring her here."

"We have done that before," interrupts Malthazzar. "Do you forget that she once was in this very castle? Yet even so she escaped from Sheol."

"Yes, yes, master; I know. But this time I suggest that things will be different. Instead of keeping her here to toy with, you could simply throw her into the Pit. There is no way out of the Pit, no way at all. And by throwing one of those whom he loves into the Pit, you will hurt him in the only way he can be hurt: he will know that he has lost the very soul of one who has fought for him and trusted him. He will be beaten."

There is a long, drawn-out silence. Malthazzar weighs the words of his general carefully and, at last, he extends a claw and grasps the fetter around the creature's leg. In a single motion, he

4

snaps the annulus, which breaks into a thousand pieces. Then he lifts his head and lets out a roar of laughter.

"General Shadow, you have earned your freedom. Now, come with me, and we will plot how to bring this about...."

I The Visit

"Aw, Dad, do I really have to go?"

Michael Fowler compressed his lips to a thin line. His fifteen-year-old daughter, Diana, was seated in front of the television playing a computer game that appeared to involve the noisy destruction of a neverending stream of aliens of various shapes and sizes. His daughter had asked the question in the especially whiny voice that she knew grated on her father's ears; her eyes had not moved from the television as she had spoken.

Now she jerked the joystick to one side and pressed its red button. With a "Phizzt" that Michael thought odious and his daughter found intensely satisfying, a large brown alien was transformed into a trail of steam that slowly meandered up the screen.

"Yes, you do have to go."

Michael stepped forward and, too late, Diana realized what he was about to do. He bent down, and with a stab of his thumb turned off the power to the set. Diana sat on the floor, her back against the sofa, momentarily shocked and disbelieving that her father could be so selfish as to spoil her game. Another four aliens and she would have broken her record.

She scowled at her father, opened her mouth to speak, then looked at the expression on his face and thought better of it. She slowly closed her mouth.

"I've been telling you all weekend that we have to go see Gran this afternoon. It's her birthday and she's expecting us. Especially, she's expecting you. You're her only grandchild, Diana. She loves you, and she needs to see you." Her father's voice pleaded with Diana. "Now, please go and put your coat on."

Several retorts came to mind, but Diana knew from experience that it was pointless arguing with her father when he was in such an unreasonable mood. Well, he could force her to go with him, but he couldn't force her to be cheerful about it. Glaring, she sullenly got up and headed in the direction of the coat closet.

Michael watched the retreating figure and for the millionth time wondered where he and Megan had gone wrong.

It would have been easier if Megan had been at home this afternoon. But this weekend was their church's annual women's retreat, and as a member of the organizing committee his wife could not have escaped going even if she had wanted to. This was the third year in a row that Megan had tried to persuade Diana to join her on the retreat, and the third year in a row that Diana had steadfastly refused to have anything to do with "all your old friends," as she had indelicately put it when her mother had broached the subject.

Michael glanced out the window. The sky was overcast and threatened a cold autumnal rain before the afternoon was through. He hoped that, despite the weather, Megan was enjoying both the weekend away from home and the respite from the ongoing daily stresses of living with their rebellious fifteen year old. Michael tried to console himself with the thought that perhaps Diana would grow out of it soon. The thought came but did not stay, for it had visited him many times in the past five years. Diana gave no sign of growing out of it yet.

Diana stood in the doorway of the living room, wearing her coat now, but leaving it unbuttoned, as if to say: "You can make me wear it, but you can't make me do it up."

He nearly told her to fasten the coat, but thought better of it. Why get into another battle so soon after the last one?

"All ready?" he asked, in as cheerful a voice as he could muster. Without giving time for a reply he continued, "Let's be off then," and strode toward the front door.

Gran Fowler lived about forty five minutes' drive away in a small house in the country. Until a few years ago, she had prized her independence and the joy she found in maintaining the old house and its three quarters of an acre of lovingly tended garden. Living reasonably close to her only son and his family had meant that it was convenient for them all to get together for special family occasions while still permitting them all a healthy independence. Several times a year Michael and his family visited her comfortable, tidy home to share news face-to-face, and for Katrin Fowler to see how quickly her only grandchild was growing. In between times, she spoke with them on the telephone every week or so. It was all a very satisfactory arrangement.

But over the course of the past few years, the family gatherings had become gradually less frequent, and were less-happy affairs when they did occur.

Grandmother Fowler was not particularly elderly — today in fact was her seventy-second birthday — but her body seemed to have decided that its days were drawing to a close. Now she rarely rose from her bed, and when she did so, she merely hobbled around her cottage. It was almost six months since she had taken a step outdoors, and nearly a year since she had been anywhere farther than the garden in which she had once so delighted. There was a gardener now, an old man who came three times each week to keep the grass mown and the shrubs trimmed and the fruit picked; but, slowly and unmistakably, the once-tidy garden and trim house were beginning to fall into a state of decay.

Even in the best of circumstances, Diana hated visiting Grandmother Fowler, for she was an old woman who drank weak tea and served fruitcake and spoke to Diana as if she were still a child.

As if these embarrassments were not enough, the last couple of times Diana had been to the cottage, the old woman had made a point of taking her to one side and trying to talk to her about a strange, imaginary world that existed only inside her head just as if it were a real place. Talk of dwarves and dark knights with blooded lances, and — this always with a wistful and faraway look in her eyes — a gnome called Drefynt. A gnome! As if Diana still believed in such things. Diana wondered if her grandmother

8

was really quite right in the head. She *was* old, and perhaps she was beginning to live in some kind of childish fantasy world.

Fantasy or not, and even if her grandmother was more than seventy years old and had probably never harmed so much as a fly in her entire life, Diana, if she was honest with herself, was more than a little frightened of the old woman when she began to talk about her imaginary world. Diana had already determined not to let herself be trapped alone with her this afternoon. Even so, she wished with all her heart that she did not have to accompany her father to the old woman's cottage.

Father and daughter pulled into the gravelled driveway of Grandmother Fowler's cottage at a quarter to three. As he stopped the engine, Michael could not help surveying the house. It certainly needed a coat of paint; but, somehow, he knew that even that would not erase the rundown, ramshackle air that seemed to hang over the old cottage.

His mind, just for a moment, went back to the time years before, when he had been twelve and his mother in her mid thirties, when the two of them had fought one another in a cavernous hall in another land under the watchful and lusting eye of Malthazzar, Lord of Evil. He remembered how he had been on the point of thrusting his sword forward and killing his own mother, and how, at the last moment, it was only her steadfast look of love that had caused him to halt and to realize what he was about to do.

How was it that such a woman, a true High Queen, could be brought down to this: a lonely, weary old woman who no longer had the strength even to step outdoors and enjoy her garden?

"You all right, Dad?"

It was an uncharacteristic question from his daughter, and he shook himself from his memories as he replied, "Yes, yes, Diana. I'm fine. Just thinking, that's all. Come on, let's go inside."

He neither knocked nor rang the doorbell. Even if his mother was out of bed, it would be draining and unnecessary work for her to come to the front door. Instead, he simply pushed open the wooden door — it needed a new coat of varnish — and as soon as he was inside, called out: "Yoo-hoo. It's only us."

There was no answer. He closed the door behind them. In his hand he held a bunch of roses, purchased at a florist's on the way over. The flowers were light pink, chosen not so much for their color as for their fragrance, which was heady and strong and had filled the car for the last half of their journey and now began to pervade the hallway as they removed their coats.

He poked his head into the sitting room, saw no one, and, with Diana trailing a couple of steps behind, began to climb the stairs towards his mother's bedroom.

When he saw her, he was, for a moment, too shocked to speak. It was only two months seen he had last seen her, and in that short time she seemed to have aged several years. She was seated in bed, her back against the headboard. The curtains were only half open, and the room seemed unnecessarily gloomy. There was a stale aroma of old pot-pourri in the air, but it lasted for only a moment under the battering of the scent of the roses, which quickly filled the room with their heady bouquet. After a moment's hesitation, he moved towards his mother's bed.

Katrin smiled at her son. It was a tired, weary smile, but it was filled with all the love a mother has for her child, whether that child is one day old or middle aged and with a family of his own. She stretched out her hands and embraced him as best she could as he leaned towards her. Her grip was weak, and she quickly released him. She kissed him on the cheek. He offered the flowers.

"For you, mother. Happy birthday."

"Thank you, dear. Do they smell? I'm afraid I can't smell things very well these days."

He smiled. "Yes, mother; here, see if you can smell them." He held the flowers close to his mother's nose and she inhaled.

She nodded and gave him a wide smile that was almost a grin. "Yes. They smell marvellous. And they look beautiful."

She peered around the room. "There's a vase in the kitchen. Why don't you go put them in water and bring them back here? They'll cheer up the room. And while you're doing that, I can look at my only granddaughter. My, Diana, how you've grown. And how pretty you are. I bet you have to fight the boys off."

Diana glanced at her father as he left the room, silently beseeching him to find some way to take her with him, but either he did not understand her expression or he ignored it, and she found herself alone at the mercy of this strange old relative.

10

"Come here, Diana, I have something I want to ask you." The old woman had lowered her voice to a conspiratorial whisper, and was urgently beckoning Diana to come closer.

Hesitantly, afraid of what was to come, Diana stepped closer to the bed, until she was within touching distance. She hoped fervently that this was not a prelude to another one of the strange one-sided conversations about fantastic creatures that existed only inside her grandmother's head.

"Tell me, Diana, how well have you been sleeping lately?"

Crazy, thought Diana. *And Dad's left me in here with her.* "All right," she said, preparing to run out the room if things became any stranger.

Her grandmother looked disappointed. "Tell me the truth now. No strange dreams? Nothing about a boat and an island and gnomes and dwarves?"

There it was again, this ridiculous talk about gnomes and suchlike. Diana shook her head and took a step away from the bed. "No, nothing like that. I really ought to be going to help Dad. Back in a minute." And she turned and almost fled from the room.

The old lady sank back against her pillow. She looked puzzled. "Haven't you told her yet?" she said to the empty room. She pondered in silence for several seconds and then spoke again, a heavy sigh of understanding in her voice. "Or is it perhaps that she's too deaf to hear? What about Michael, I wonder? Has he been too preoccupied, or does he know?" She lapsed into silence until the others returned.

When Michael came back, he was carrying a tray of tea things. Two paces behind him, Diana entered with the vase of roses. After casting around for a moment, Diana moved forward, keeping her eye on her strange grandmother, and placed the flowers on the bedside table. She immediately retreated to safety behind her father, who placed the tray on the table next to the flowers. There was a teapot and two cups. He poured the tea, saying, "Diana didn't want any, but I assume you'd like a cup?"

"Yes, dear. That's very thoughtful of you."

He handed her her tea. Her hands drooped slightly as they took the weight of the half-filled cup of weak tea. He smiled at his mother. She returned the smile, then looked suddenly at Diana.

11

"Diana, dear, I had Mrs. Fotheringay buy a cake and some cookies so we could celebrate my birthday in style. They should be in the cupboard to the right of the stove. Would it be too much trouble to ask you to cut a few slices of cake and put them on a plate with some cookies and bring them up here? I would be most grateful if you could do that for us."

Michael opened his mouth to offer to perform the task, but his mother glared at him and shook her head slightly.

Diana mumbled "OK. I'll do it," and left the room.

For a long moment, neither of them spoke. The old woman put the cup to her lips and sipped the tea.

"Good tea," she said, nodding.

"I had a good teacher," Michael replied. "You wanted us to be alone, didn't you?"

"Just for a minute," his mother admitted. "Is there anything you want to tell me?"

Michael looked at the face of the old woman that his mother had become. He wondered what she was getting at. Obviously there was something she was expecting him to say. About Diana? How uncontrollable she was becoming and how worried he was that soon she might get into serious trouble? Or was it something else? He looked into his mother's eyes, which were in turn searching his own.

It was the sparkle that appeared in them that gave it away.

"You too?" he asked, almost unable to believe it.

"For the past two weeks."

The sparkle was bright. Her eyes shone so brightly that it was almost as if she was trying to hold back tears. But these, Michael knew, were tears of joy, not sadness. He discovered that his own eyes were moist, and he was grinning crazily at his mother.

"Me too," he said. "Every night, more or less the same dream. I haven't thought about that place for years now, but suddenly every night it's there. It means something, doesn't it? That I keep dreaming about it, I mean."

"Oh yes, Michael, it means something. Tell me, have you ever told anyone? Your wife? Diana?"

Michael shook his head. "No. I mean, it seemed so farfetched. I thought about telling Diana when she was a child, but it seemed so silly and pointless. What would she have thought of me if I had insisted that such a place actually exists?" A momentary doubt seemed to grab hold of him. "It does exist, doesn't it? I mean, it wasn't all just a dream that time in Cornwall, was it?"

"No, Michael, it wasn't just a dream." There was the sound of a footstep climbing the stair. "And in just a few minutes, I think you'll have proof of it. Now, be quiet, and let me handle this."

"Diana?" Michael asked in an urgent whisper. "Is she coming too?"

His mother's eyes opened wide in surprise. "But of course," she said. "I thought you would understand that. She's the whole point of the thing. She needs to be saved from herself while there's still time."

There was no time for Michael to respond before his daughter entered the room carrying a large plate on which was a small pile of sugar cookies and a couple of slices of cake. Wordlessly, Diana placed the plate on the bedside table, filling the remaining space.

"Diana, dear, there's one more thing you could do for me," said her grandmother. "There's a tree in the garden with, I think, one piece of fruit on it. Would you be so good as to go and pick the fruit and bring it up here for us all to share? It's down at the very end, in the little arbor. It looks like a peach. Would you do that for me, dear?" The grandmother smiled at her granddaughter, entreating her with her eyes.

Sullenly, Diana nodded. "OK. Sure, I'll get it. Down at the end of the garden?"

"Yes, that's right, dear. And thank you."

Diana left again. If she was honest with herself, she was glad of the excuse to get away from the bedroom and out the house. She did not like old people; they were so..., well, *old*. And sometimes they were so strange, just like Grandmother Fowler had been a few minutes ago. All that ridiculous talk about sleeping well and dreams about islands and fairies. It was about time that something was done about Grandmother Fowler, it really was.

She had reached the back door of the house and now she stood for a moment looking through the glass.

At the rear of the house was a large lawn, bordered by beds of shrubs and flowers that, during the spring and summer months, made a glorious splash of color and, in the evenings especially, produced a heady scent that invaded even the inside of the house. But at this time of year the garden looked forlorn and not a little wild. Winter was still a little way off, but the garden was already bare, with the leaves off the trees in the arbor at the far end, many of the flowers already dead, and the small plants retreating back to the ground until next spring.

As she pushed open the back door, she wondered how there could possibly be any fruit still on any of the trees, for the last fruit from their own yard had been picked more than two weeks earlier. The possibility crossed her mind that perhaps her grandmother was imagining things. Perhaps there was no fruit at all? She walked slowly across the grass, which was long and still damp from the morning's heavy dew, even though it was now late afternoon. She did not think much of the gardener if he was supposed to keep the lawn trimmed.

At the far end of the lawn was a small separated area that was almost completely cut off from the rest of the yard. A beech hedge ran across nearly the entire width of the grass, with only a single narrow gap at its center to serve as an entrance into the arbor beyond. The hedge had been recently pruned, and as she passed through the gap Diana noticed that there were piles of trimmings near the shrubs at this end of the yard.

Beyond the line of beech was an area almost completely enclosed by the hedge. There was a patch of lawn in the center, and around the edge of the lawn several dwarf fruit trees. Behind the trees to her left was the garden shed, one of its windows cracked and the whole structure looking dangerously unsafe. By the side of the shed was a compost heap, against which leaned an ancient wheelbarrow, upside down so that it would not collect the rain and turn to rust.

She cast her eyes around the damp arbor. In one corner, partly underneath the shade of a large, bare apple tree, was an old swing chair, its paint flaking and hanging slightly askew. Over everything hung an air of neglect, yet she could see that here at least the grass had been cut and the trees pruned, as if someone cared for the plants but was uninterested in the human accoutrements.

14

At first she thought that all the leaves had dropped, just as they had done at home, and she was about to turn away to return to the house and tell her grandmother that she had been mistaken about the fruit, when she saw a movement near the ground in the farthest corner of the arbor. She was startled to discover that she was not alone.

She watched as an elderly man slowly drew himself up from the ground where he had been working, tending a tree no taller than herself, which, she now saw, was the only tree in the arbor still bearing its summer mantle of leaves. Diana stepped forward as the man slowly gained his full height, which was about the same as her own.

She studied the man, obviously the part-time gardener, even as he studied her. He seemed even older than her grandmother, although not as frail. His face was lined and he sported a long whitish and unkempt beard. His clothes looked, if not exactly disreputable, at least slightly shabby, and there were large patches of brown where soil had ingrained itself into the fibers of his jacket and trousers. There were damp patches on the knees of his trousers where he had been kneeling on the damp grass to tend the tree, or whatever it was that he had been doing when he had been disturbed.

The gardener looked at her with a slight frown, which annoyed Diana. He looked almost as if he were weighing her up, that he had decided that she did not measure up to his expectations, and that the lack was entirely *her* fault. If he had said something, she would have spoken crossly to him, found some fault, told him off even. But all he did was to stand there for a long moment, his ancient eyes twinkling with a not-entirely-friendly glint, looking into her face, frowning at what he seemed to see there.

The moment seemed to stretch into a long, long time. Suddenly, Diana was desperate to break the silence; anything to distract the gardener's gaze.

"You must be the gardener," she said, thinking even as she said it that it was a remarkably stupid comment.

The old man looked around the small arbor. A hint of a smile came to his lips.

"Not a bad little place, is it?" he said.

15

"I've come looking for a piece of fruit; my grandmother Fowler sent me," Diana said, ignoring the old man's question.

The man slowly turned to look at her again. Diana found herself becoming infuriated at the slowness of the man's movements. He seemed almost to live at a different speed from normal, as if everything had to be viewed, weighed, savored and judged before moving on to the next item of business. After what seemed an age, he said, "A fruit? At this time of year?"

"It's my grandmother, Mrs. Fowler. She said there was a tree here that still had a piece of fruit on it. What about that tree behind you?"

The old man turned slowly and regarded the tree at which Diana was pointing. Diana was certain that it was the very tree that he had been working on when she had first spotted him, yet now he seemed surprised to see it there.

"Oh, aye. There's a fruit, right enough. Just the one."

Diana drew closer.

The old man was right. There was a single large fruit with the appearance of a peach, or perhaps a nectarine, hanging at shoulder height. It was strange that there was just the one fruit, but so it seemed to be; there was no trace even of any smaller, unripe fruit hanging from the narrow branches of the young tree.

The old man was still talking. He was standing directly between Diana and the fruit, making it impossible to do what she wanted, which was to pick it and leave the old gardener to his work.

"It's only a young tree. Mrs. Fowler planted it this spring. She grew it from seed, you know."

Diana did not believe it for a moment. The tree, admittedly young, had obviously been planted at least several years ago. She wondered why the old man was telling her something that was so obviously untrue.

"She's a very special lady, that grandmother of yours," the gardener added gratuitously.

Diana sighed inwardly. He was just as bad as her grandmother. Obviously he was about to begin a long monologue on what a wonderful person her grandmother was. Well, she'd soon put a stop to that. She brushed past the gardener and grasped the fruit

16

with one hand, gave a quick twist of her wrist, and felt the weight of the peach or whatever it was come away from the tree.

The fruit now safely in hand, she said shortly, "Thank you. I've got it now," then turned and walked away towards the arbor's entrance.

She did not know what it was that caused her to stop at the gap in the beech hedge but something prompted her to do so, just before she left the arbor. She halted and turned to look back at the corner from which she had just come, and it was several seconds before she could believe her eyes. The old man had vanished. Without a sound and with no way of leaving the arbor other than the gap in the beech hedge where she was now standing, he seemed to have completely disappeared. And the tree in the corner, which moments before had been leafy and green, now stood brown and lifeless.

Obviously, she had made some sort of a silly mistake: the gardener and the tree must be hidden behind some larger tree. She began to retrace her steps.

As she approached where she had spoken with the old man, she found her heart inexplicably racing. She had not been mistaken, she was certain of it, even though what she was now seeing could not possibly be true. The tree from which she had plucked the fruit not a minute before was now bare and desiccated. She lifted a hand to it and bent a twig. It snapped drily. The tree was dead.

She looked around, then called out, "Gardener? Where are you?"

The only reply was the sudden motion of a squirrel darting across the grass.

She walked slowly across to the shed at the far side of the arbor, which was the only place where the old man might have hidden. But the door was locked on the outside with a big, heavy padlock. She peered through the cracked window, but inside there were only a few garden tools. A moist, stale, slightly moldy odor hung over the little hut: it had not been used for many months. She looked down at the fruit, large and firm in her hand, then one last time at the empty arbor.

Michael and his mother heard the sound of Diana's footsteps taking the stairs two at a time as she raced upstairs. They paused in their conversation and Diana burst into the room, breathing deeply, as if she had run all the way from the bottom of the garden.

She thrust the fruit at them. "Here. Take it," she said. There was a challenge in her voice, as if she were daring them to accept the offering.

Her father gently took the fruit from her hand. Suddenly oblivious to both his mother and his daughter, he turned the fruit around, inspecting it. He looked at his mother with an enquiring expression. He caught the faintest hint of a nod in return.

His mother smiled, then began to talk to Diana.

"My dear, you are all out of breath. It's all right. You didn't need to hurry. We could have waited."

"It... it...."

Diana stopped, suddenly unsure what to say. How could she tell them that the gardener had completely disappeared almost while she watched, and that a tree went from life to death in only a few moments? She couldn't. If she said anything, she would sound as crazy as her grandmother did when she began to go on about her dreams.

Diana shook her head. "It doesn't matter," she mumbled.

Her grandmother gazed at Diana for several seconds. Diana tried to hold her gaze, but found that she couldn't.

Diana thought: *She knows. I don't know how she knows, or how much she knows, but she knows something about what went on out there.*

For a moment, just for the barest flicker of a moment, she wondered if perhaps her grandmother was not crazy after all. But she quickly quashed that thought. Obviously, the whole thing had been a big mistake. There must have been some other way out of the arbor, and the old gardener had decided that he had done enough work for one day and had chosen that moment to depart. And the tree? Well, she must have just made a mistake, that's all. She must have been confused. The tree from which she had picked the peach was still there, it had to be; it was just that she had looked in the wrong place and seen that old dead tree instead. That's all, nothing to it.

She lifted her gaze from the floor. Her grandmother was still looking at her. Moving no more than the tiniest fraction of an inch, the old woman shook her head, as if telling Diana that what she was thinking was wrong.

"Cut the fruit, dear. You can use the cake knife," Grandmother Fowler said to Michael. "If you cut it into thirds, we can all have a piece."

"I don't want any," Diana said.

Michael picked up the knife and began to cut through the soft flesh of the fruit.

"My dear, just to please an old woman, just this once. That tree is unique, and I think you'll find that its fruit is unlike any you've ever tasted. Please do try it, just for me."

Diana's father had finished cutting the fruit and now it lay exposed in three parts on the tray next to the tea things. It still looked like a peach, except that there was no stone in the center of the orange-yellow flesh.

"No stone," her father said, obviously surprised.

"No, Michael. I didn't expect one, did you? After all, no more fruit will be needed after this one."

Diana looked in puzzlement at the others. She could not escape the feeling that there was something going on here about which she knew nothing, but her grandmother knew everything, or at least most of it, and her father was dimly groping his way toward understanding. She felt as if she were a character in a play but, having begun the scene well enough, all the other characters seemed to be reading lines from a different script. It was an eerie and thoroughly unpleasant feeling. Or maybe the others were simply crazy.

"Here, dear. Do have a slice." Grandmother Fowler pointed at one of the slices, then took one for herself. Diana's father did the same. Diana decided that there was no point in arguing. She lifted the last piece, looked at it briefly, then popped it into her mouth.

She opened her eyes wide in surprise, for the flavor caught her completely off guard. It was not that it was not pretty much what she had expected, for the fruit definitely had a flavor reminiscent of a peach or a nectarine; it was the unexpected intensity of the flavor that was so astonishing. The fruit tasted so strongly that it

19

seemed almost to explode in her mouth. She felt as if for the very first time she was tasting fruit the way it was *supposed* to taste.

She chewed on the fleshy slice, closing her eyes so as not to be distracted from her enjoyment of the flavor. She savored every morsel, every tiny swallow. She ran her tongue around her lips to catch every last drop of juice.

Suddenly, the room was cold. She shivered as a breath of wind touched her cheek. The quality of the light through her closed eyelids changed. The air smelled strangely of salt, as if she were close to the sea. She opened her eyes, and for a long, long moment, she did not move. She closed her eyes tightly, then opened them once more. But it was still the same.

Her mouth fell slack as she surveyed the island on which she was standing.

II The Island

It was the kind of thing that completely shatters one's understanding of the way things are. Diana, fifteen years old, knew what was possible and what was not. And what had just happened fell firmly in the latter category.

One moment, she had been standing in the bedroom of her ailing grandmother, savoring the flavor of the peach-like fruit, and the next... well, the next moment she had opened her eyes because of a sudden chill wind and discovered herself to be, not in the gloomy bedroom with the scent of roses cloying the air, but instead standing atop a small promontory that was almost completely surrounded by calm, clear, blue water.

The sky was also blue, paler than the water, and dotted with clouds, one of which was covering the sun. Even as Diana tried to take in what had happened, the cloud moved away, the sun shone out, and the coolness that had made her shiver was replaced by the mellow warmth of an Indian summer afternoon.

She was not alone. Standing not far away were two people.

One of them she recognized instantly as her father, although he was dressed in a way that she had never seen before, and seemed to be standing taller and more sternly than was his habit. He was dressed in some kind of leather tunic with matching leather trousers. Around his waist was a belt that was closed by a large buckle, in the center of which was a red stone that reflected the sunlight brightly. On his feet were a pair of moccasins. Most unsettling was the fact that at his side hung a scabbard, and sheathed inside the scabbard was a sword.

The other person was a woman. She was as tall as Diana's father, and had long, flowing hair that was even darker than his. The woman was dressed similarly to her father, in a leather suit, over which was draped a maroon cape that was held in place by a clasp at the neck. A belt similar to her father's was at her waist, except that in her case the stone in the buckle was white. She, too, wore a scabbard from which the hilt of a sword protruded.

Diana took a hesitant step towards the pair, and was immediately aware that her own attire was different from what she had been wearing just moments before. She was dressed similarly to the others; the only difference — and one that inexplicably annoyed her — was that she wore a narrow belt with a simple wooden buckle. Then she noticed that there was a second difference: unlike the others, she carried no sword. This annoyed her even more.

But there were more pressing questions than why she was dressed slightly differently from the others.

"What happened?" Diana asked.

It was some time before either of the others replied, for they were engrossed in surveying their surroundings.

The promontory on which they stood was attached by a low, sandy isthmus to what appeared to be an island, one of several that seemed to be scattered nearby. The part of the island on which they were standing was a small but steep hill, on whose top they stood, the ground falling away in all directions towards the sea. The promontory was almost circular, and in all directions except towards the larger portion of the island the shoreline was no more than a couple of dozen paces distant. The only sand to be seen was on two narrow beaches, one on each side of the isthmus.

Three other small islands were visible, but all rose steeply from the sea and their tops were higher than the hill on which they were standing, and so were hidden from view. The islands were much smaller than their own, scarcely as large as the promontory, and appeared to be completely surrounded by low cliffs.

22

The sea was almost a dead calm, with just the faintest of ripples undulating across the surface.

It was the woman who finally answered her question, although not in a manner that pleased Diana.

"We're in Palindor," she said. There was a frown on her face as she looked around. "At least, I *think* we're in Palindor," she added, somewhat less certainly.

With a start, Diana realized that the woman was her Grandmother Fowler, although now she seemed scarcely older than her father, and all signs of frailty had disappeared.

"Gran?"

The woman looked at Diana and then laughed a loud, wholesome, joy-filled laugh. Diana decided that if this woman *was* Grandmother Fowler, she was the most ungrandmotherly person she had ever met.

The woman regained control of herself. "Yes, I suppose you could call me that. But here they call me the High Queen Catherine. And this" — her grandmother indicated Diana's father — "this is the High King Michael. Be careful" — she dropped her voice as if she were revealing something confidential — "he's known as the High King of War, so you don't want to get on the wrong side of him."

"But where is this? What did you call it? Paladin? And how did we get here? And what about these clothes?"

"Questions, questions. Not Paladin. Palindor. Your father rather foolishly decided not to tell you anything about this place when you were growing up. I tried to explain to you, but I suspect you thought I was rambling like a foolish old woman. After all, who could possibly believe in a world populated by elves and dwarves and goblins and gnomes? I know that *I* didn't believe it, even after I had been here several days the first time. But" — and here she looked at the narrow isthmus that joined them to the rest of the island — "I'm not exactly sure where in Palindor we are. It's not somewhere I recognize, and there aren't many places I haven't been. Still, it's good to be back." She made no effort to keep the pleasure from her face.

Diana listened to this with her jaw becoming ever more slack. Now she spoke again. "Wait a minute. This doesn't make sense.

You mean to tell me that this is that place Gran used to tell me about? And that you're my Gran, even though you don't look a bit like her."

"Appearances can be deceptive, Diana. That's an important lesson to learn. As I said, here I am addressed as the High Queen Catherine, and your father is the High King Michael. You'll have to get used to it; I'm afraid that 'Gran' and 'Dad' won't be sufficient."

Diana looked first at the woman who called herself Catherine, then at her king-father. "Then I'm the High Queen Diana?" she half asked, half announced.

Michael opened his mouth to say something, thought better of it, and closed it once more.

Catherine ignored Diana's question and opined, "I think we're on an island. It doesn't look very large, but it seems to be getting late in the afternoon and we probably don't have long to explore. Come with me, everyone." And without waiting for a reply she began to stride down the slope in the direction of the isthmus.

The others followed. They all stopped when they reached the twin beaches of the isthmus, which were separated by a narrow strip of green couch grass in which grew clumps of bluer, spiky marram. The water that lapped against the sand was transparent blue. On a hot summer day, it would have been very inviting. Michael dipped his hand into the water and immediately withdrew it.

"Cold," he said. "We don't want to go swimming, that's for sure."

They began to explore. It was not a very large island, although they soon realized that it would take an hour or two to explore it thoroughly. It was shaped roughly like an egg, with the small promontory sticking out into the sea at the sharper end, which Catherine declared to be roughly southward after glancing at the position of the sun in the sky.

The western and eastern sides of the island were quite different in character. The eastern side was heavily wooded with evergreens, but the western side was almost bare of trees. A ridge ran roughly north-south along the center of the island, dividing the two halves. Over much of the island the trees peeked a little way across the ridge on to the western side, but then they quickly ended and were replaced by grass and clumps of heather from which small, flat, granite boulders obtruded. Here and there were stunted trees, their branches crazily asymmetric, pointing to the east as if they were continually being blown by a violent westerly gale.

Several streams tumbled down the western side of the island, apparently bubbling up from underground springs. Much of the western shoreline was taken up by a narrowing beach, the continuation of the beach that began at the isthmus.

The coast on the eastern side, apart from the small beach at the isthmus, comprised a swath of grass that ended in a drop of a few feet down to the level of the water.

After exploring for a while, they realized that the day was drawing to a close. They were close to the northeastern end of the island, and they quickly agreed that they would be unable to complete a circumnavigation of the island before sunset.

The woods here came down nearly to the water's edge, and they had been carefully walking in single file along a strip of grass between the wood and the water. Now they gathered into a small group and surveyed their surroundings.

They had a good view of several other islands. Some of the islands were similar to theirs, with gently sloping hills and even, here and there, what looked like the pale mark of a beach, but most were like those they had seen at first: small skerries or islets incapable of supporting so much as a single full-grown tree.

Catherine shielded her eyes and peered into the distance.

"The Sunset Islands," she suddenly announced.

Michael turned, shading his eyes and following her gaze. After a few moments, he decided that he could see something too, almost lost in the haze that clung to the northeastern horizon: a single point where the sun seemed to reflect off some bright point that floated above the darker haze that clung to the horizon. "Penmichael Brea?" he asked.

Catherine nodded. "I think so. And if that's Penmichael Brea, then we must be on the Sunset Islands. I don't think they're inhabited, are they?"

"I don't know. I don't think they were in our day; but who knows how long we've been away?"

"That's right," agreed Catherine, "I was forgetting. Time runs differently here." There was a tinge of disappointment in her voice.

"I don't know what you two are talking about," interrupted Diana, "but this place is certainly inhabited. Look, there's smoke," and she pointed southward across the wooded slope behind them.

Sure enough, a thin column of blue smoke was percolating its way upward into the late afternoon sky. The trail was almost perfectly straight, and it seemed almost to glow as it caught the rays of the lowering sun.

Without another word, Diana set off through the wood in the direction of the smoke. Catherine and Michael hesitated by the shore for a moment.

Michael voiced the thought that both shared. "It could be dangerous." Instinctively, his hand dropped to the sword at his side.

Catherine nodded. "It could be. We don't yet know much about this place. Did you notice? She's not armed."

"Nor does she wear the belt of a High Monarch. We'd better go with her. She might need our protection."

"All right. I just wish we knew a bit more about what we're supposed to do now we're here."

Diana was by now out of sight, although they could hear her as she pushed her way through the undergrowth. Michael began to hurry after her. After a moment's hesitation, Catherine followed.

They found the source of the smoke easily enough. There was a dell about halfway up the side of the hill on the eastern side of the island. The wood stopped at the edge of the dell, inside which the trees were replaced by a patchy, flowering, long-stemmed grass. A stream trickled down the higher, westernmost side of the dell and disappeared into the ground on the eastern side beside a small outcrop of dark rock. In the very center of the dell was a small, single storey, roughly thatched cottage. At the closest end of the cottage was a chimney, and it was from this that the thin column of smoke rose.

Much of the ground next to the cottage was covered by flowering shrubs, which combined to produce a spectacular, colorful display even in the shadowed light of the late afternoon. Catherine could not immediately identify any of the shrubs. Scattered around the edge of the dell, and climbing the slopes to the wood, were a number of dwarf fruit trees, many of them heavily laden.

The cottage was a tiny affair, constructed not particularly well from the granite stones that the three had observed scattered over much of the island. A couple of windows were visible on the east-facing wall, as was a central door. The windows were protected by shutters, which at the moment stood open. The northern wall of the cottage, the one on which the chimney had been built and which directly faced them, had neither window nor door. Against this wall leaned a round boat, a kind of coracle, its bottom facing outward. On the ground beside the coracle was an oar.

There was no immediate sign of life apart from the smoke rising from the chimney. But the cottage was surely inhabited, for at the far end, where the stream passed closest to the building, was an area where the ground had been carefully turned and planted with crops. Catherine could make out beans and squash and what looked like a row of potato plants.

For some time, they looked at the cottage and listened intently for some indication that its occupant was nearby. The front door hung open, so the person who lived there could not be far away, but they detected neither movement nor sound.

Eventually, Diana said, "Well, I'm going to see if there's anyone home." She plunged down into the dell and began to walk towards the cottage.

"No, wait!" called Michael, but it was too late; Diana was already approaching the building. Catherine and Michael exchanged glances, and wordlessly followed the headstrong girl.

Diana paused at the closest window and looked inside. For a moment she could see nothing. The inside of the cottage was dark, and it was difficult to distinguish one shadow from another. Then something moved. For several seconds, she peered into the darkness, trying to make sense of the shape she could see. It moved again. Then it spoke.

"You're early. You're not supposed to be here until tomorrow."

Diana realized that while she had been having difficulty seeing inside the cottage, the person inside had evidently been afforded a perfectly good view of herself.

27

Now that he had spoken, she began to be able to distinguish him from his surroundings. He seemed to be a small man, cleanshaven, and seated cross-legged on the floor. He rose to his feet while she was studying him, but this added little to his height, for his legs were extraordinarily bowed. He was attired in a bluish tunic and breeches that were a sort of dirty brown. On his head he wore a red cap that looked more than a little ridiculous. He walked to the open door and stepped out of the cottage just as Catherine and Michael arrived.

Now that he was fully visible, it was obvious that he was a very small man indeed. Standing in the doorway no more than a few paces away, Diana could see that he reached no higher than her waist. He looked first at her, and then at Catherine and Michael.

"I'm sure it was tomorrow you were supposed to come," the strange little man said with doubt now in his voice as he looked at Diana.

He turned his attention to Catherine and Michael and as he saw their belts he frowned and then gave a little shrug.

"But perhaps I made a mistake," he said. "I do sometimes, you know." Then, remembering his manners, he continued, "Oh, I'm terribly sorry, your Highnesses; I do apologize for not welcoming you properly."

He made a funny bow; at least, he tried to do so, but his legs were so bent that in order to bow he had to contort his body in a most peculiar manner, with legs bent and feet pointing outwards, and his head leaning forward and downward so that it was almost touching the ground. He looked in imminent danger of tumbling forward head-over-heels. It was all Diana could do not to laugh at the peculiar little man.

"Welcome to my humble abode," he said.

Diana had noticed, much to her annoyance, that he seemed to be speaking only to the others and that if she was included in his remarks it was only as a sort of appendage. The little man straightened. At least, he straightened from the waist up, his legs remaining widely splayed.

"I must apologize to you both" — the word "both" was not lost on Diana — "for the state of disarray of both myself and my

28

cottage. I was not expecting you until tomorrow. Please, do come in." He stood to one side and gestured for them to enter.

Diana, who had been rendered first speechless by the comedy of the funny little man, and then angry by his reference to "you both", was the closest of the three to the open door. She swept past the man and haughtily strode inside.

The man said in a low voice, "I apologize, Your Highnesses. I know well enough who you are. But what is the name of your ill-mannered servant?"

Unfortunately, he had not lowered his voice enough, and Diana, even though inside the cottage, heard his words.

Before either Michael or Catherine could respond, she stormed out and stood in front of him.

"How dare you, you little man?" she shouted, bending down and holding her face less than an arm's length from his. "I am no servant. And I've been inside your ruin of a hovel. I wouldn't go back in there for anything. It's nothing but a ramshackle old hut. Certainly not fit for a High Queen like me."

She turned to Catherine and Michael. "You can stay if you want, but I can tell you right now that it's not worth going inside. I'm going to find somewhere more fitting, even if it's only a cave."

Holding her head high, she stormed away. She clambered up the side of the dell and, in moments, disappeared into the wood.

"Oh dear," murmured the little man, quite taken aback by Diana's outburst. "Now I've ruined it. What was it I said? Why did she claim to be a High Queen? She's not, is she? Isn't she just your servant girl?"

"Well...," began Michael.

Catherine shook her head. "No, she's not a High Monarch. At least, not yet — if ever. But neither is she a servant girl. She just doesn't understand yet about the way things are here. Now, my little friend, you do us great honor by inviting us into your home, but you have yet to tell us your name."

"What?" the little man suddenly blushed. "Oh, how remiss of me. I do most earnestly beg Your Highnesses collective forgiveness. My name is Glandryth. I am a simple fellow, and I apologize for my clumsiness and seeming stupidity. I'm not very used to visitors."

Glandryth. Somewhere, Catherine was sure that she had heard that name before, but she could not place it. She frowned in concentration. It was no good; she could not remember.

"Now, please," continued Glandryth, "do come in and I'll make us all a refreshing cup of tea. Will your companion return, do you think? Or perhaps we should search the island for her? The sun will set soon and it will be dark before long."

"I think that perhaps we should leave her alone for a while; give her a chance to think things through. If she hasn't returned by the time we've finished tea, then we can think about looking for her," said Catherine.

Glandryth led the High Monarchs inside. The building was divided into rooms by crude walls constructed from granite rocks just like those of which the house itself was made. The front door led directly into a large room that occupied more than half the available space at one end of the building. Two doorways led into other rooms: a kitchen and a bathroom, Catherine guessed. There was a straw palliasse in one corner of the large room. Sconces hung around the walls, although none of the torches were yet lit for the evening.

A log fire burned in a grate at the far end of the room, filling the air with the aromatic scent of burning pine. There was little furniture: a small table hugged the far wall, with two rough chairs pushed under it; a spinning wheel stood close to the table; a pair of wooden rocking chairs were near the fire, one on either side of the hearth. None of the chairs was large enough to seat a human comfortably. A finely woven mat covered much of the packed earth floor, except for a small area near the fire and a border around the edge of the room. On the floor near one of the chairs was a garment, which evidently Glandryth had been in the process of sewing, or perhaps repairing, when he had been disturbed.

Catherine walked to the garment and promptly sat down cross-legged beside it. She patted the mat beside her, motioning Michael to join her.

"A cup of tea would be both welcome and refreshing, master Glandryth. And we both thank you for your hospitality. This is a small island, and there is no way off it?"

"Not apart from my coracle."

"In that case we need have no concern about leaving our companion to wander alone with her thoughts for a while. She can't go far, and it would be best for her to be alone while she considers the consequences of her actions."

Catherine lifted the garment on the floor beside her. It was a cloak. In the firelight it was difficult to determine its exact color; blues and reds seemed to ripple through the cloth. But there was no mistaking the quality of the weave; the cloak was finely woven and would prove to be both durable and waterproof when it was finished. "Did you weave this? You are very talented, master Glandryth."

The little man looked embarrassed. "The talent is not mine, Your Highness. The High Lord bestows talents on us all; the talent is really His." Then, with a twinkle, he added. "But even so I thank you for your kind words. Now," he said abruptly, "the tea."

He disappeared into one of the other rooms and emerged moments later carrying a large pot of water, which he attached to a tripod that was installed inside the grate. The pot hung freely, rocking gently above the burning logs.

While Glandryth was performing this chore, Catherine had examined the mat on which they were seated. Like the cloak, it was finely woven and durable. Unlike the cloak, which was unpatterned (even if she could not decide what its color was) the mat was imbued with countless intricate patterns. It must have taken even a talented weaver many years to complete.

"The fire is hot and the water will boil quickly," said Glandryth, interrupting Catherine's thoughts. "Please forgive me; if I had not made a mistake about the day, I would have been watching for you and had the tea ready when you arrived."

"How did you know we would be coming?" interjected Michael.

"He told me. Oh! I forgot! He left a message for you. It's most important, he said, that you all understand that none of you is to leave the island. You are all to remain here until he returns."

"Who told you? The High Lord?" Michael asked.

"The High Lord? Oh, no; I haven't seen him in a very long time. No, it was..."

"I know who it was," interrupted Catherine, for she had finally remembered where she had heard this little man's name, and at the memory, she felt a tingling frisson of anticipation.

The last time she had heard Glandryth's name, she was in a chamber deep under the Mountains of Mourn, near the eastern border of Palindor, a prisoner of the colony of goblins who dwell far underground in that region. A little furry creature who subsequently had become a great friend had rescued her. She remembered telling the creature (rather rudely she realized in retrospect) that she had never seen anything like him before, and in his reply he had mentioned "my friend Glandryth."

"It's the dablik, isn't it?" she said.

Glandryth nodded. "Yes. He's the only one who visits me nowadays. Not that I'm complaining of course. If I wanted company I would go and live on the mainland. No, I'm perfectly content to live here with just the occasional visit from my friend to keep me company and share the latest gossip from the Three Lands."

Catherine discovered that her eyes were watering at the memory of the times she had shared with the dablik. She was so pleased to discover that he was still alive. That was one of the problems about coming to Palindor: one was never quite sure how much time might have passed since one's last visit, and one had to be prepared for the shock of discovering that friends who were in their prime when one left had become old or even died in one's absence. But she recalled now that the dablik didn't seem to have aged at all between her first two visits to Palindor, even though they were many hundreds of years apart.

She thought wistfully of her friend Drefynt, the last of the Holy Gnomes, who had aged and withered between those visits, so that he was feeble and old when he died just before the confrontation between herself and Michael in the Great Hall at Dynas* Carn Toldwyn. Perhaps, then, the dablik and his friend Glandryth aged more slowly than other mortal creatures. But in any case she was glad that the dablik at least was still alive, for when they met there would be much to talk about.

---

* *Dynas* is the Palindoric word for *castle*. This encounter is recorded in *Shadow*.

She looked at the two chairs pushed under the small table, then at the two rocking chairs. The thought that the dablik had spent many hours in this very room, rocking in front of the fire and sharing convivial conversation with Glandryth, made the strange furry creature seem suddenly close. She blinked back incipient tears. In a way, she felt almost as if she had returned home after a long journey in foreign parts.

The water in the pot began to boil, and Glandryth removed the pot from the fire. He poured the water into a container in which was a small pile of crushed leaves. The sweet and tangy aroma of flowers and spices immediately wafted through the room.

A cool breath of air entered through one of the windows.

"The wind will likely pick up now. It usually does around this time of day," said Glandryth. "When it begins to get dark I close up the shutters, but I think there's plenty of time for tea before that will be necessary."

"I think I'd better go in search of Diana," said Michael, a worried look on his face.

"Tea first, searching for wayward children after," said Catherine in a voice that brooked no argument. "It'll do her good to be by herself for a while."

Diana scrambled up the bank. It was not easy to climb out of the dell while holding her head high to preserve what remained of her shattered dignity, but she did a creditable job. "Ill-mannered servant" indeed. Just what sort of place was this where people called her such things?

As she reached the lip of the dell, she glanced back at the cottage, to see who was coming after her. She paused in amazement, unable to believe the all-too-evident fact that no one was running after her to try to persuade her to come back.

Well, if that was how they wanted it!

She turned away and stomped off into the wood. Never had she been treated so condescendingly, and by such a silly little man with such impossibly bowed legs. Why didn't one of the others force him to apologize? At the very least they could have run after her and apologized for him. But no, even that seemed to be beneath them.

"Huh! If that's how much they think of me, I'll show them," she mumbled. "I'll just stay out here as long as it takes. I'm certainly not going back there, begging them to take me back. High Monarchs indeed. I'll show them I'm as good as they are." And with a disdainful toss of her head, she stomped and blundered her way deeper into the wood.

She soon realized that her behavior was a mistake. There was nowhere to run, nowhere she could hide on such a small island. The only sign of life they had seen on the entire island was the little man's cottage, so there was no one to whom she could go for comfort and succor.

The eastern side of the island was already in shadow and a breeze was beginning to spring up. Before long it would be evening and unless she could find somewhere warm and safe for the night, Diana knew that she would eventually be forced to return to the cottage.

But of course they were counting on exactly that. They expected her to come crawling back with her tail between her legs. Well, she wouldn't do it! So there!

There remained only the northwestern quadrant of the island to explore. From a distance, the western side had looked almost bare, but perhaps there would be a warm cave or somewhere else where she could pass the night in relative comfort. She began to walk up the hill to the ridge that bisected the island. She was beginning to feel hungry, and she wished she knew whether the big red berries that hung from the bushes that grew in the shade of the evergreens were edible. But she dared not try one in case it was poisonous. She began to hurry forward, concentrating on climbing so that other thoughts could not distract her.

She topped the ridge and, within a few strides, the trees suddenly thinned and she stepped out on to an open, boulder-strewn area of short grass.

She halted and looked across the unexplored portion of the island to the sea beyond. A strengthening cold wind struck her full in the face. She shivered.

How long would it be before darkness fell? Not much more than an hour, perhaps even less.

She looked around for somewhere where she might be able to spend the night.

Between the place where she was standing and the shoreline there were only a few twisted, weather-beaten trees. The sparse, clumpy grass reached all the way to the shore. Some distance to her left, she could see the yellow of the sand on the western side of the isthmus. There was no sign of a cave or anywhere else where she might get comfortable and stay warm for the night.

She could see several other islands nearby, mostly to the north and northwest. A couple of the more distant ones looked almost as large as this one, although their coastlines seemed much rockier and she could see thin white lines of surf where the sea, which was beginning to be stirred by the wind, broke against rocks.

The closest island dropped sheer into the water that surged around its cliffs and created creamy white pools that looked dangerous even at this distance. She considered trying to swim to one of the other islands, but dismissed the thought immediately. Not only was the water icy cold, but there were probably strong currents in the channels between the islands. Whatever else she might do, swimming away was not an option.

A sudden movement caught her eye.

A two-masted ship in full sail slid gracefully into view from behind the closest island.

The ship was painted a dark gray, almost black; its sails were colored similarly. A flag hung from the top of the aft mast, fluttering desultorily. The flag was also black, bordered by a wide maroon margin.

Diana could see people moving around on deck, but from this distance it was impossible to see any detail. As she watched, it became apparent that the ship, if it maintained its current heading, would pass close by her own island.

The ship came closer, and she began to make out details. She could see that the people on deck were all wearing striped smocks and blue trousers, and most wore little red caps. One sailor pointed towards her island, at a place not far from where she was standing. She followed the line of the finger and saw a little

35

stream that crossed the beach and debouched into the sea. The ship began to change course, heading now for the stream.

Another vessel, similar to the first, came into view from behind the same island. It changed course to follow the first ship. A few moments later, the first ship lowered its sails and Diana heard a rattle of chains as it dropped anchor. A third ship sailed into view from behind the same island.

One by one, the other two ships anchored alongside the first. The sun reached the horizon. The three vessels had apparently found a safe harbor for the night.

Aboard the ships, there was a bustle of frenetic activity. The wind began to freshen as the sun dipped below the horizon. Diana crouched for protection against the chill wind. She watched as a small rowing boat was dropped over the side of the closest ship. A name was painted on the ship's transom, but it was too far away to be legible.

A second rowing boat appeared from behind the trio of dark ships. The dinghy contained three sailors: one who was rowing and two others who sat in the rear of the boat. The rest of the boat seemed to be filled with something that she could not make out.

For a moment, Diana wondered what was occupying the boat; then she saw barrels being lowered carefully into the other dinghy, and realized that that was what filled the boat that was now making its way towards the beach. A third dinghy appeared, similarly laden. She watched as the boats made for the beach and landed next to one another, close to the stream.

From each dinghy, the sailors who had not been rowing splashed noisily ashore, carrying between them a barrel slung beneath an oar. They walked to the stream and knelt there, taking it in turns to place the barrel under the surface of a small pool.

The sky began to darken, and Diana surreptitiously moved closer in order to watch the sailors at work. As the last barrel was being filled, one of the sailors stopped and stared directly at the place where Diana crouched. He pointed straight at her. She had been seen.

Unintimidated, she stood and began to make her way down the hillside to the place where the men had now stopped working and awaited her arrival. She walked as casually as she could, aware of the sailors' gaze.

"Evening, miss," one of the sailors greeted her as she approached.

He accompanied his words with a low bow and a wide sweep of his arm. The others nodded politely and doffed their red caps respectfully.

"Sorry, miss. We didn't know the island was inhabited, or we would have asked your permission. We needed water, you see. We have come on a long voyage and for the past week have been living on reduced water rations. I hope you don't mind that we took your water."

"Mind?" said Diana. "Of course I don't mind. And in any case, it's not my water. I don't live here."

"Oh, I misunderstood. My apologies again, miss. We did not see your ship. But forgive me — I have not introduced myself. My name is Orrian. I am first mate on the ship *Evening Passage*, the flagship of our little fleet."

Diana was charmed as much by the sailor's obvious sincerity as by his politeness. Here was someone who knew how to treat her, manifestly unlike that obnoxious little bow-legged man who had called her a servant. An idea came to her and, without giving it a second thought, she began instantly to put it into practice.

She inclined her head towards Orrian. "My name is Diana," she said, "and I have no ship. In fact, I'm stranded here and I've been wondering how I might leave this island."

Orrian appeared to consider this for some time while the other sailors stood around waiting for him to respond. Eventually, the first mate said, "Well, miss, if you would be interested, I could take you aboard the *Evening Passage* and see if the captain would permit you to travel as our guest. I cannot speak for the captain, of course, but I am sure that, in the circumstances, we could carry you as a passenger until we make landfall. That is, if the captain considers it safe."

"Safe?"

"Aye, miss. These are wild and uncivilized parts, and Captain Malliss might think it safer for you to remain here than to journey with us to the Lands of Abuscân which, if reports are to be believed, are ruled by violent and vicious people. There may be fighting when we arrive, and, if you'll forgive me saying so, a battle is no place for a lady such as yourself." He smiled at her, then quickly continued, "But if you would not mind waiting, we will return to the ships with our cargo and then come back and row you out to the *Evening Passage*. I would not ask you to wait, but it would be unladylike, I am afraid, to ask you to sit on these barrels. Besides which, you can see how low the rowboats are riding, and to add another person might be dangerous. With your permission then?"

"Yes, certainly. I'll just wait for you here."

"Good. We will return shortly."

And with that the sailors took their places on the dinghies, which now looked in imminent danger of sinking. Straining, the rowers began to pull at their oars and the dinghies moved ponderously away from the shore.

The sky continued to darken while Diana waited. Here and there, stars appeared, although the sky was becoming more cloud-covered by the minute. The clouds scudded quickly overhead, driven by an energetic wind that now began to reach down to the ground. Diana wrapped her arms around herself and began to walk in small circles in an attempt to keep warm.

Lights were lit on board the ships, and she could just make out the bustling activity as the barrels were loaded aboard. A shadow detached itself from the mass that was the *Evening Passage*. It was a dinghy, moving rapidly closer. Flecks of white showed where the oars bit into the sea, and it was not long before, with a scrunching sound, the keel of the rowboat ran aground on the sandy beach.

The boat contained only two people: a burly rower and the first mate, Orrian. Orrian jumped into the water, waded wetly through the waves that were beginning to break against the sand, and then pulled the boat a little way up the beach. He held a hand out towards Diana.

"Do you think you can make it?" he asked. "I could carry you if you like."

Diana was in two minds about the sailor's proposal. On the one hand, it might be pleasant to be carried by a sailor who obviously thought of her as a lady; on the other, she wanted to him to be in no doubt that she was independent and quite capable of looking after herself.

"It's all right," she decided. "I don't mind." And she stepped forward and clambered aboard.

She sat at the seat that ran along the rear thwart. Her feet, which were clad only in leather moccasins, already felt as if they had been held against blocks of ice, for frigid seawater sloshed around the bottom of the boat and had soaked the moccasins as she had made her way to her seat. She struggled not to let the pain of the unexpected cold show on her face.

She must have succeeded, for the first mate looked at her first appraisingly and then approvingly; then, with a grunt of exertion, he pushed the dinghy away from the shore and jumped aboard. He, she now noticed, was wearing tall sea boots which, no doubt, were waterproof. She could have kicked herself for not accepting his offer of assistance, but of course it was much too late to do anything about that now.

For a few moments she remained facing the island, but the rower, who had remained silent and unmoving since the dinghy had beached, now expertly turned the dinghy and began to row towards the ship that lay at anchor not far away.

It was at this moment that Michael walked out from the shadow of the trees, looking around for some sign of Diana. He immediately saw the dark shadows of the boats at anchor near the isthmus and, after a moment or two, he spotted the dinghy that was being rowed rapidly away from the beach. It was several seconds before he realized that the brown smudge seated with its back towards him was his daughter.

He cupped his hands to his mouth and shouted, "Diana! Diana!"

But the freshening wind grabbed at the words and dragged them away to be lost in the trees behind him; Diana gave no sign of having heard his shouts.

He began to run down the hill, but after a few strides he tripped over a low boulder and fell heavily to the ground. He was vaguely aware of having banged his head painfully as he fell, but the only thought in his mind was to stop the boat from taking Diana away. He picked himself up and ran on, shouting, but to no avail. By the time he reached the beach, the dinghy had reached the closest of the ships and the two shadows had merged.

In the darkening dusk, he could make out no details of what was happening on the anchored vessels. He stood at the water's edge, shouting Diana's name into the wind.

There was no obvious response, although it was impossible to tell whether that was because he was too far away to be heard or because he was being ignored.

He turned away, and his knees suddenly buckled underneath him. Lifting his hand to his face, he discovered that he was bleeding profusely from a wide cut on his temple. Clumsily, he regained his feet and began to stagger back towards Glandryth's cottage.

III The Evening Passage

The crew dropped a jack-ladder down the side of the boat, and Diana clambered awkwardly up it. Several pairs of arms helped her aboard the *Evening Passage*.

She landed on the deck and looked around. The *Evening Passage* was not a large ship and most of the crew were on deck. She counted twelve sailors, all men, dressed in striped blue and white smocks and blue trousers. Some were bareheaded, but most wore the red sailors' caps she had seen from the shore. Orrian was dressed identically to the others, with no obvious sign of his rank. All the sailors seemed quite young, and they were all tall and burly. Remembering Orrian's words about the possibility of hostile natives, she recognized that the ship's crew would be quite capable of putting up a good fight if it became necessary.

The sailors seemed friendly, and they greeted her politely while Orrian came aboard, climbing the jack-ladder behind Diana. After every man had greeted her in turn, Orrian ordered them back to work while he gave Diana a tour of the ship.

The *Evening Passage* was smaller than she had thought from a distance, but evidently it was quite seaworthy, for it was obvious that this was a working vessel that had come on a long journey. The varnish on the deck, as well as the dark paint that covered her superstructure, was worn and faded, and here and there patches of bare wood showed through. A thin layer of salt seemed to cover everything, further lightening the dark paint. The boat had a comfortable air, as of a vessel that worked hard and knew its worth.

The *Evening Passage* had a low fo'c's'le and a somewhat higher poop, atop which was a lookout. A complicated pattern of ropes criss-crossed in the air. High on the foremast was an empty crow's nest. From the aft mast flew the flag she had seen earlier.

Because of the black paint, it would have easy to conclude that this was a dark and gloomy ship, but it was obviously not so. Aided perhaps by the obvious enthusiasm of the sailors, Diana got the impression that, to the contrary, this was a happy vessel.

"You'd probably like to see your cabin," said Orrian, his words intruding on her thoughts.

He led her forward towards the fo'c's'le, which had two entrance doors, one on each side of the deck. He seemed to take it for granted that she would be staying.

After a momentary pang of uncertainty whether she was doing the right thing, Diana followed Orrian, who opened the fo'c's'le's starboard door and stood aside to let her enter.

"The second door on the starboard side, miss. Mind the step as you go in."

She found herself in a short, cramped passageway. It was no more than half a dozen paces to the second door on the right, which she opened and then passed through into the cabin beyond.

The cabin, like everything else she had seen so far, was small, but she immediately fell in love with it. Unlike the drab gray-black color of the hull and superstructure, the cabin was painted in a soft pastel blue. The air carried a faint aroma of pot-pourri which, strangely, did not seem out of place.

A bed ran the length of the far wall, which bent slightly to accommodate the curvature of the ship's hull. There were two small portholes above the bed, each with a diminutive golden drape that could be slid across to cover the glass.

Small oil paintings of the *Evening Passage* were scattered around the walls. There was a tall dresser against the forward bulkhead near the foot of the bed, with a leaf that was extended to form a small desk. Next to the dresser was a closed wardrobe. In one corner was a basin, with a ewer half filled with water standing in a pair of rings that, Diana guessed, were designed to keep the ewer from falling over and breaking during a storm. The bed was covered with a maroon coverlet that seemed to shimmer in the light from the lamps that were affixed to the walls. The cabin seemed so perfectly suited to her that it was almost as if she had been expected.

"Dinner will be served shortly in the messroom, miss, and the captain will talk to you then," the first mate said from the doorway. "I will call you myself. In the meantime, I am afraid that I have other duties I must to attend to. Please feel free to rest, or to wander around the ship. There are clean clothes in the wardrobe. Just ask if there's anything else you need." And with that, the sailor quietly closed the door, and Diana was left alone.

Diana wanted to call after him, to thank him for everything, and to ask if there was anything she should know about the captain, but Orrian had gone before she could open her mouth.

For some time she just stood, looking around the small cabin, drinking it in. She noticed that the boat was rocking slightly on the swell. The wind was still freshening, and was now beginning to gust, and the boat's motion was increasing to match it. She wondered if there might be a storm in the night. If so, how would she fare? She had never been on a ship before, and the possibility of being on a small vessel during a storm, even if safely anchored and close to land, was not particularly pleasant. She hoped that she would not disgrace herself by being sick.

She crossed to the wardrobe and opened it, and nearly cried out in delight. Hanging in a neat row were a series of garments, glistening colorfully in the flames from the lamps.

One by one she removed the clothes and held them up to the light. They were very different from one another, but all beautiful, each in its own way. Most were trouser suits of one sort or another, but at one end of the rack were a couple of magnificent dresses more beautiful than anything she had ever seen before. They were the kind of dress one might wear to a grand reception or evening ball. She lifted one of them out of the wardrobe and saw to her delight that it looked like it would fit.

She locked the cabin door and then quickly removed the leather suit she had been wearing, along with the unpleasantly wet moccasins, and changed into the dress. It fitted perfectly, and even though the only mirror in the cabin was a small affair of burnished brass above the washbasin, Diana knew that she looked more beautiful than she had ever done before.

She examined the other clothes on the rack. Most were what might be termed working clothes: trousers and tunics, yet made of the finest and softest material, and embroidered with intricate designs that must have taken years to complete. She lifted an attractive suit of maroon and brown from the rack and decided that it too would probably fit. She changed out of the dress and put on the suit, which was soft and thin, yet surprisingly warm. The colors shimmered in the lamplight. Diana giggled with delight.

There was one suit unlike all the others: at the end of the rack was a suit of dark metal links. She lifted one sleeve and rubbed her hand over the metal. The links were tiny and hard. This suit, it was obvious, was designed for battle.

In one corner of the wardrobe was a stand with several little slots, in each of which was a pair of shoes. She found a pair that matched the suit she was wearing and put them on. She was not surprised to discover that they were a perfect fit. Like the suit, the shoes were soft and supple, and she hardly knew that she was wearing them. The design worked into the maroon leather matched the one that was woven into the suit. She knew, even without benefit of a good mirror, that she looked stunning.

There was a knock on the door. Unlocking it, she saw Orrian standing in the passageway.

"Ah, good; you have found the clothes. Your size, I hope?"

"Yes," mumbled Diana, suddenly struck by the odd circumstance that clothes such as these had been aboard a ship that seemed to be crewed only by men; but before she could ask anything about this peculiarity, Orrian continued, "Dinner is served, if you would be so good as to join us."

He bowed and gestured for Diana to follow him as he turned and led the way outside.

The messroom was at the opposite end of the ship, below the poop. Orrian and Diana descended a companionway and then passed through a doorway and into a large room; probably, Diana decided, the largest on the ship.

The messroom was nearly filled by a long table that ran almost its entire length and around which were a dozen or more chairs, nearly all of them now occupied. There were two entrances: the one through which she and Orrian had entered, and one at the far end. The smell of food cooking filled the air, and Diana decided that the door at the far end must lead directly to the galley.

There were just three empty places at the table, all at the far end: one on each side, and one at the very head of the table. Orrian took the seat on one side, and gestured for Diana to sit in the one opposite, leaving only the seat at the head of the table unoccupied.

There was a chorus of greetings from the men: "Good evening, miss," "Glad to have you aboard," "Welcome aboard, miss," and Diana felt herself blushing as she nodded politely to the sailors in return. Then a silence fell around the table, and almost immediately Diana heard the sound of a firm tread on the companionway down which she and Orrian had descended.

A moment later, there entered the room the last thing that Diana expected.

She was tall and dark, and there was a smoldering fire in her eyes that betrayed a strength and power that could be confined only with difficulty. She was also undeniably beautiful. As she entered the room, the men noisily pushed their chairs back and got to their feet. As applause broke out, Diana realized that she was the only person still seated and, eyes still glued to the magnificent woman who now strode past her to stand beside the chair at the head of the table, she clumsily got to her own feet, applauding with the others.

The woman was attired in a suit similar to those Diana had seen in the wardrobe in her cabin — although, Diana thought as the applause began to die down, none of the suits in her own cabin could possibly be *quite* as grand as the one that this woman wore. And even if they were, Diana knew that she could never have worn anything that would have half the effect that this woman had.

It was several moments before Diana realized two things: first, that the woman must be the captain of the *Evening Passage*; and second, that alone of all the people in the room, the woman was armed, for from a belt around her waist hung a scabbard from which extended the jeweled grip of a sword.

The captain glanced around the table, looking at the men rapidly, one by one, in clockwise order beginning with Orrian. Her eyes at last alighted on Diana, immediately to her right.

The captain's eyes seemed to pause on her for a moment, and in that moment Diana felt as if her very soul was laid bare for inspection. Oddly, for it was hard to see how one could ever forget that feeling, it seemed like there had been someone else, and quite recently too, who had performed the same trick of weighing her entire life at a single glance, but before she could remember exactly where and when that might have been, the captain's eyes had slid away and she had, with a slight inclination of her head, given permission for everyone to be seated.

Diana sat down along with the crew and almost immediately the door opened and a sailor entered bearing a tray. A delicious aroma filled the room, and Diana's mouth began to water. The sailor placed the tray before the captain.

"Ma'am, the cook sends his compliments and begs me to inform you that he believed a celebration to be in order now that we are so close. And we have fresh water, too."

"Thank you, sailor. My compliments to the cook, and tell him that his efforts are appreciated."

The sailor bowed and departed, returning moments later with a second tray, which he placed near the foot of the table. Sailors started to help themselves and, as soon as the captain had taken the first bite of her food, began to tuck in. Friendly conversation commenced all around the table and it was not long before the meal was in full flow.

Diana began to wonder how she should begin a conversation with the captain, but she need not have worried, for the captain soon turned to her.

The captain smiled, exposing perfect teeth, and said, "Good evening, miss. I am Captain Malliss, mistress of the fine ship *Evening Passage* and also of the other two ships that comprise

46

our small fleet. I understand from my first mate that you were stranded on the island at which we replenished our barrels, and that you would be willing to accept passage on my humble vessel."

Diana nodded uncertainly.

"Good, then that is settled. I hereby officially welcome you aboard. You approve of your cabin, I hope? It is next to my own. If there is anything you should want, please do not hesitate to call on me."

"Thank you, Mistress Malliss; that's very good of you."

The captain leaned forward conspiratorially and said quietly, "You should call me 'captain,' otherwise it is bad for discipline."

She smiled at Diana.

"Oh, yes, I'm sorry, captain. Thank you. It's a beautiful cabin. I'm afraid that I tried on some of the clothes. My own were wet, you see."

"Of course, of course. I see that they fit you perfectly."

For a moment, Diana wondered just *why* they had fitted so well, for the captain was much taller than she, but Captain Malliss continued speaking, and Diana had no time to dwell on the puzzle.

"You are welcome to them. What is the point of fine clothes if they simply hang in a wardrobe? No; much better for them to be worn. And they will certainly flatter you better than those poor clothes you were wearing when you came aboard. And now, my dear, you have quite forgotten something."

For an anxious moment, Diana wondered what the captain could possibly mean.

"Your name, my dear. What is your name?" the captain prompted.

Diana relaxed. "Diana, captain."

"Diana! Oh, how beautiful! Such a perfect name, and it suits you so well. Diana. Yes, so much better than... yes, well, never mind. Such an apt name. Well! Glad to have you aboard the *Evening Passage*, Diana. You are welcome as long as you wish to remain."

"Thank you, captain. Thank you very much. I do have one question, though."

"Certainly. Ask, and I shall do my best to answer."

"Where exactly are you bound? And to what purpose? Your first mate said something about it perhaps not being safe?"

"Ah, yes." Captain Malliss nodded in an understanding way, although her smile remained fixed firmly on her face. "We are bound for a place known as Palindor, which is one of the Three Lands of Abuscân. This is my second journey there, and I would be less than honest if I did not tell you that my first visit, which was merely a brief exploration, was not an entirely pleasant experience.

"In fact, Palindor is a most primitive and uncivilized place. However, it is quite pretty and, on the whole, if it were not for its inhabitants, it might even be rather pleasant.

"Earlier explorers brought back stories of mountains of gold and mythical beasts, but I saw no sign of such things during my brief stay there. However, we have come to see for ourselves whether such things exist and whether perhaps this land of Palindor might be worth further visits."

She leaned forward and continued in a low voice so that no one could overhear. "Quite frankly, my dear, I am sure that once we've arrived we'll find nothing very strange at all about the place. I've heard too many tall tales about unexplored lands to be taken in myself. But it will be a bit of a disappointment to the crew, no doubt, when they discover that this land of Palindor is no different from anywhere else."

"And how long will it be before we reach Palindor?" asked Diana. It could not be far away, for she had seen for herself the smudge on the northeastern horizon shortly before they had discovered that wretched man's cottage.

"Not much longer at all," replied the captain. "It is but a short distance from these islands. In fact, the mainland was spotted from the crow's nest this afternoon. But I wanted to replenish our water supply before reaching Palindor itself, because it is quite possible that the inhabitants will be hostile and may not permit us to refill our barrels; so when we saw the stream on the island on which we found you I thought it wisest to fill our barrels promptly."

The boat gave a sudden lurch that caused several pairs of hands to reach out quickly to stop crockery from sliding off the table.

The captain nodded to herself. "Ah! The breeze is freshening as I hoped it would. We will weigh anchor later this evening and continue our journey overnight. By tomorrow we should reach the mainland, and then we shall all see for ourselves what this fabled land of Palindor is really like."

IV An Attempted Rescue

Michael staggered through the doorway of the granite cottage, whose interior was now lit by flickering flames coming from torches in the sconces attached to the walls of the living room, as well as by the steady glow from the low fire in the fireplace.

Catherine was deep in conversation with Glandryth. She had quite lost track of the time, and considerably more than an hour had passed since Michael had left to go in search of Diana. Catherine experienced a momentary pang of guilt as she realized that Michael had taken much longer than either of them had expected to find Diana and talk her into returning for the night. She should have gone with him.

But the guilt was driven from her mind as soon as she saw Michael. He leant weakly against the doorjamb for support; his face was caked with dried blood, his clothes were filthy, and pieces of twigs stuck out of his hair, as if he had fallen several times in the wood and been either unwilling or unable to tidy himself up.

Catherine scrambled to her feet.

"Michael, what happened? Are you all right?" Before Michael could reply, she turned to Glandryth and said, "Glandryth, he's injured. Get some water and some herbs."

Catherine dashed across the room and gently supported Michael, easing him through the doorway. Once he was inside, she let him collapse gently on the floor, where he sat with a bemused look on his face. She examined his head while he tried to explain what had happened. His words were slurred, and Catherine had to listen carefully to understand what he was saying.

"I was running and I fell over. I'll be all right. I think it's just a cut, that's all. But it's Diana: she's gone."

"Gone, gone where?"

In the light of a nearby torch, Catherine tried to remove some of the caked blood in order to investigate the cut underneath. Glandryth appeared from the kitchen, carrying a bowl of cold water and a fine cloth.

"The herbs are diffusing; they will take a while, but you can use this to clean his face."

He hurried back into the kitchen.

Catherine dipped the cloth in the water and began to wipe away the blood. Michael was speaking, but she paid no attention, concentrating instead on the job of cleaning his face. She became happier as she proceeded. There was only one obvious cut, on his left temple, and although deep, it had already closed. His nose had also been bleeding, but that also had stopped.

"Quiet now," she said. "Let's finish with this and then you can tell us the whole story from the beginning."

Glandryth returned, carrying another small bowl in which herbs were suffusing. Catherine dipped her cloth in the bowl and began to wipe it over Michael's cut. He winced as she touched the wound.

"It's all right. It'll help you feel better," she said.

She continued working, and soon she was satisfied that she had done everything she could. He had lost quite a lot of blood, and she hoped that the loss of blood rather than any real damage was what accounted for his evident weakness and confusion.

"Something to help him sleep?" she suggested, and Glandryth nodded and returned to the kitchen, from which he emerged moments later with a handful of leaves that he took to the fire and dropped in the kettle that hung above the flames.

"Now, Michael, tell me again. What was this about Diana being gone?"

Michael told the story in his slurred, tired speech. It took him some time, because he had to think carefully about each word.

Several times he stopped as if confused and only continued after prompting from Catherine.

"There were three small ships lying at anchor on the western beach near the isthmus. It was getting dark, and I couldn't see very well, but they seemed to have sent a rowboat for Diana. I saw her being rowed back to one of the ships. I shouted, but she was too far away. I was running towards the beach when I fell and cut my head. By the time I got there, the rowboat had already reached one of the ships. I shouted as loudly as I could, but I couldn't make myself heard. As far as I know, she's still there."

"Here, drink this."

Glandryth offered Michael a mug of hot liquid which he had poured from the kettle. Michael grasped the mug and sipped it. He grimaced.

"Come on, Michael, drink it up. It'll do you good," encouraged Catherine, and Michael had a sudden memory of himself as a young child being nursed by his mother after a bout of some childhood disease.

He took another sip of the bitter, scalding liquid.

"Did she go voluntarily, do you think? Or did it seem like she might be a prisoner?" Catherine asked.

"I don't think she was a prisoner," he said at length, although there was uncertainty in his voice. "There were only two other people in the rowboat as far as I could see. She was at one end, with her back to me. Then there was the person who was rowing, and one other at the front of the boat.

"Her hands or feet might have been bound, I suppose; I wouldn't have been able to see that. I should have shouted louder. I'm sure I could have made myself heard if only I had tried harder. I should have swum out to the ships, but it was too far, and the water was too cold, and I'd hurt my head."

He shook his head, regretting his failure.

"Now, now. Try not to worry yourself. There's nothing we can do about it now. Maybe she's just spending a few hours on the ships. We can go over there in the morning and talk to her then. We'll soon get it all settled."

The lids of Michael's eyes suddenly seemed very heavy. He was having a hard time concentrating on what Catherine was saying. He opened his mouth, but coherent speech was beyond him and even he could not understand the words that issued from his mouth.

"But what if she is a prisoner and the boats leave in the night?" was what he tried to say; but it came out too slurred to be understood. Suddenly he longed to lie down and sleep.

He sagged forward, and Catherine and Glandryth together laid him out gently on the floor. He could still hear the two of them talking, but he was too tired to join the conversation.

"It's a potent sleeping draught, Your Highness. I hope that was all right," he heard.

"Certainly, Glandryth; best thing for him. He's confused, and I'm not sure how much of his story we can rely on. In any case, we'll sort things out in the morning. My only real concern is that the dablik quite clearly told you that we were all supposed to stay on the island until he arrives, and I'm not at all sure that being on board a ship anchored nearby is the same thing.

"But if we were to go chasing after her, I don't see how that would help. That would mean that none of us had obeyed the dablik's instructions, which would only make things worse. Michael would realize all this if he were thinking straight. Let's let him sleep, and then we'll see what tomorrow brings."

He heard no more as a deep sleep overtook him.

When Michael awoke, the room was dark, except for an orange-red glow cast by the embers of the fire. He was slow to wake, and for some time he simply lay on the hard floor, trying to rid himself of the desire to go back to sleep.

He could hear the sound of breathing and, concentrating carefully, he could distinguish the sound of two people asleep elsewhere in the room. He looked around, and in the glow from the embers he made out the shadowy forms of Catherine and Glandryth stretched out on the floor near the center of the room and in one corner respectively. There was a third sound, that of the wind, blowing gently against the shutters.

Quietly, Michael stretched his aching muscles. He got carefully to his feet and peered around in the gloom, making sure that Diana had not returned. Satisfying himself that there were just the three of them, he stole quietly to the door. He opened the door, scarcely daring to breath, hoping that it would not squeak. Soundlessly, he slipped outside and closed the door behind him.

Outside, the moon was full and high in the sky. Everything he could see — the house; the forest; the vegetable garden; even the stream that gurgled through the dell — was lit with the silvery light of the moon. It was the kind of night on which, if such things had actually existed, he would not have been surprised to see a ghost steal silently from the forest and into the dell, intent on mischief.

He was standing in the lee of the building, but he could see the tops of the trees swaying, and the sound of the wind was accompanied by the continuous burdened creaking of many branches moving backward and forward in the breeze.

He began to climb out the dell. He had formed no real plan of action, but the first thing he had to know was whether the ships were still at anchor on the other side of the island.

Michael was fully awake now, the chill of the wind and the exertion of climbing helping him shrug off the last of the sleep, and he began to climb quickly through the forest towards the point on the far side of the ridge where he could look down on the ships.

He reached the ridge and then, moments later, stepped out the forest and on to the grass of the western side of the island. He immediately saw the three ships outlined in silver on a dark sea, still anchored not far from the shore. The sound of the ships carried on the wind: the creaking of timbers and the snapping of hawsers as they rocked to and fro on the swell of the sea. He contemplated the ships for some time, wondering what to do.

He knew that Catherine was right, that he really should not leave the island. But on the other hand, he was worried about Diana. After all, what if she was a prisoner of the people on the ships? And even if she were there willingly, what if the boats set sail before Catherine and he had a chance to talk to Diana?

Someone needed to see her, to try to persuade her to return to the island or to rescue her, whichever was necessary.

If the water had been warm, he might have considered swimming out to the boats, for the distance between them and the shore was not great, but he remembered how cold the water had been when he had simply dipped his hand into it that afternoon, and he knew that the cold would quickly exhaust him if he tried to swim any distance.

He was almost ready to give up until morning when he remembered the coracle that leaned against the side of Glandryth's cottage. Of course! How could he have been so stupid? It would not be easy to paddle the coracle against the westerly wind, but it was not very far, and he was feeling strong and invigorated after his deep sleep. He was fairly sure that as long as the wind did not worsen he could reach the boats safely. He turned and hurried back towards the cottage.

The coracle was quite small, obviously built by Glandryth for his own use. This was good, for it meant that it was easy for Michael to carry, and also that the wind would not have much surface to catch on once it was in the water. He heaved the coracle on to his shoulder, picked up the paddle that lay on the ground nearby, and set off back across the island.

It did not take long to reach the isthmus, although even in that short time the wind had freshened. He stood at the water's edge, contemplating anew the distance to the ships.

Small waves were now breaking at his feet and he wondered if he really was strong enough to paddle all the way to the boats. He had just about decided that perhaps it would be better after all if he were to wait until morning when he heard a sound that filled him with alarm. It was the sound of people talking: the wind was carrying the sound of voices from the boats.

He could not tell what they were saying, but the voices were quickly joined by several others. Sounds of movement began to come from the ships. Then oil lamps began to flare out, adding a yellow cast to the moon's silvery illumination of the ships, which suddenly looked impossibly distant.

Without further thought, he tossed the coracle into the water, threw himself into it, and began to paddle furiously.

He moved quickly away from the shore, but it was hard work as the westerly wind kept trying to push the little craft back towards the island. He gritted his teeth and tried to set himself a steady rhythm: lean forward to the right; drop the paddle in the water; pull steadily back; then repeat the actions on the left side of the coracle. A lot of his effort was wasted as the coracle, lacking a rudder, kept wanting to spin instead of move forward. That, combined with the wind, which began to veer as it continued to freshen, made progress frustratingly slow.

There could be no doubt now that there was activity on the ships. Lanterns swung to and fro, and he could make out the shadows cast by the crew as they moved around on the deck of the closest ship. He tried to paddle faster, but he was beginning to get tired now and the wind was blowing more strongly, and his extra efforts simply seemed to make the boat spin faster instead of hurrying it forward.

A different sound came from the closest ship: a heavy, slow, steady movement as of something heavy being dragged against wood. It was several seconds before Michael realized that it was the sound of an anchor being weighed.

Now he began to feel desperate. He paddled even harder. He looked back and was gratified to see how far behind him the shore now was. Looking forward, he persuaded himself that the closest of the ships was really not so far away. Just a little longer, and a little more effort.

Now there was another sound: the sound of grunts from men who were exerting themselves, pulling heavily as slowly the sails began to be raised. And as soon as he heard that, Michael's stomach sank, and he admitted to himself that he was going to be too late. He glanced back once more towards shore. He was more than three quarters of the way to the closest ship. He dug his paddle in even harder. Perhaps he would not be too late after all.

The closest boat loomed above him, and the bottom of the sails that now were rising to the top of the masts were hidden by the high gunwale. He redoubled his efforts, but even as he did so the ship began to move slowly through the water.

He called out, then dropped the paddle on the floor of the coracle and cupped his hands around his mouth: "Ahoy!" he shouted as loudly as he could. "Ahoy! Ahoy!"

But the men on the boat did not hear him; or, if they did, they ignored his shouts, and the ship began to gather speed as it slid out of the harbor. Within moments, the second ship, which had been hidden behind the first, also began to move, and, seconds after that, the third followed suit.

Michael watched helplessly as the three vessels moved away. Under other circumstances, it would have been a beautiful and mesmerizing sight, the three ships coming under full sail, the white chop of the sea being split by their bows into creaming, phosphorescent "V"s, the entire tableau bathed in the full clear light of the moon shining high above. But instead of awe Michael was filled only with a silent despair.

He remembered the words he had heard Catherine speak before he had fallen asleep: "The dablik quite clearly told you that we are to remain on the island until he arrives." And now one of their number had left the island. It did not bode well.

But his despair lasted only a very brief time, for he suddenly realized that he himself was in danger. He had been so engrossed, first in trying to reach the ships before they weighed anchor, then in simply watching them as they pulled away under full sail, that he had not realized how much the wind had veered as it freshened.

The coracle now was being pushed in a south-easterly direction. He realized with a sudden anxiety that on this course he would be blown past the island altogether. He lifted the paddle from where he had dropped it and thrust its blade into the water.

It was getting difficult to paddle. Not only was he tired, but the wind was driving the waves into short, choppy graybeards, and steering the coracle in the tightening sea was nigh impossible.

Desperation seized him. The silvery band of land was slipping past at a terrifying speed. It would not be long before the island fell behind altogether.

The coracle hit a high whitecap, and a spill of water arched over the side and into the boat. It was like an omen, and Michael suddenly knew that, paddle as he might, he was not going to get back to the island.

He tried, of course, stabbing the paddle desperately at the water and trying to make headway, but it was no use. In only a short time he passed by the promontory at the south end of the island. And beyond that, there was only open water.

He looked back with despair at the island that was already beginning to look small and insignificant.

He turned to face east, just as the coracle smashed into another wave. The wave broke over him and soaked his clothing.

Michael began to shiver, despite the warmth of his exertions. He stopped paddling and instead began bailing with his bare hands. Another wave splashed over the side of the little craft, and he realized that he was in danger of drowning if he could not keep the craft reasonably empty of water. And then a miserable cold rain began to sweep sideways across the sea, driven by the wind and soaking him further, if that were possible.

The water in the bottom of the coracle slopped around noisily, and it began to seep into the leather of his clothes. He could feel the biting cold of the water as it seeped higher up his legs. And with every wave that broke over the side, the little craft rode a little lower in the water, making it easier for the next wave to do the same.

Until now, he had not really been worried. He was being blown south-eastward, and somewhere off in that direction was the mainland of Palindor. It would be only a matter of time before the wind blew him ashore. But as he pondered this, yet another wave added itself to the water slopping around in the coracle. If the wind continued to strengthen, the boat would soon be swamped — and if that happened he would never live to reach dry land.

V *Phendric*

Everyone agreed that Phendric, son of Benglubber, son of Drefynt, was an odd gnome, even by the standards of his unusual family.

He had seemed normal enough as a child, but shortly after the death of his father* Phendric began to display the first signs that he might not, after all, have escaped the family's curse of unorthodoxy.

Always a rather bookish gnome, he began to acquire an apparently insatiable interest in old books and matters concerned with the old days when Palindor was founded. He spent weeks and months poring over the tales and stories in the books in the library at Dynas Carn Toldwyn.

In years gone by, this would have been taken as a good sign and encouraged by parents, for it might have led to the youngster eventually becoming a Holy Gnome; but in these more enlightened times such an interest was deemed, if not exactly unhealthy, then at least somewhat unusual. If his mother had been a little less busy, perhaps she would have tried to guide the young Phendric's interests towards other pursuits, but she was so occupied with the farm that she had little time for such thoughts. Consequently, as time went on Phendric's appetite for books and the learning they provided only increased.

---

* Recounted in *Shadow*.

When he became old enough, he began to travel, first around Palindor, and then, like his father's sister Sherna before him, in the distant lands of Reglandor and Soltarwyn.

His travelling had a definite purpose: to search out the oldest manuscripts and learn more about Palindor, Toldwyn, and, most of all, about the High Lord Olvensar himself, for it gradually became clear to Phendric that the history of the Three Lands was like a great tapestry on which a gigantic motif was being woven, and that the guiding hand behind the shuttle was that of the High Lord himself.

Phendric absented himself from Palindor for years and then decades at a time as he taught himself to read the old scripts and began to understand the nature of the High Lord.

He returned to Carn Toldwyn one last time, shortly after his mother's death. He sold the family farm but, having no great use for money, gave the proceeds away and retained not even enough to provide himself with a room in one of Carn Toldwyn's inns. He preferred instead to live in a clearing in the forest east of the town.

He spent a long time studying the ancient manuscript that his father had been translating at the time of his death. Whether Phendric could translate the manuscript no one knew, for by now there was no one else in Carn Toldwyn who was interested in such matters. Certainly Phendric committed no translation to paper; if he did translate the book, then the exercise occurred entirely in his head.

One day, he did not appear at the castle library as was his daily custom, and it soon transpired that he had left Carn Toldwyn. This was slightly more than a hundred and fifty years ago at the time of our tale, and people had by now completely forgotten about Phendric, the peculiar grandson of the last of the Holy Gnomes.

Phendric was now living in the southeastern portion of Palindor, in a part of the forest that once had been called Dankenwood. Once, Dankenwood had been a dark and frightening place, but now it was no different from the rest of the thick forest that covers much of the Third Land.

He lived in a small hut in a clearing, and led a solitary life. Often, a year or more would pass between his conversations with other creatures, for few passed that way.

Phendric was content in his solitude. Books cluttered his hut, and he spent his days reading, learning, contemplating the ways of the High Lord, and trying to translate some of the more difficult of the old volumes that he had acquired on his travels. He rarely travelled nowadays, for he was beginning to reach that age when home is preferred to elsewhere. In any case there was no reason to leave his cabin, for everything he desired was close at hand.

His life was simple, and filled with hours of contemplation. He never thought of himself as a prayerful gnome. In fact, gnomes in general are not a particularly prayerful lot, not at all like the sages of old, despite the attribution "Holy" that many of the wisest of gnomes have been given — the word was used to signify wisdom and a sense of apartness rather than anything spiritual.

Phendric had never seen a vision, never claimed any special revelation from the High Lord, certainly never seen the High Lord face to face as had his grandfather. He spent hours of each day in quiet contemplation of the world around him, and over the years he had developed the habit of considering daily some great truth.

He ate mostly vegetables, augmented by occasional meat brought by a passing Hunter, and cheese from the goats that wandered the area near his cabin. He pored over his books, lived in peace with his surroundings, and generally was more than content with his lot.

One morning, Phendric awoke with a feeling of unease that stubbornly refused to yield to the chores of the day. He could not put his finger on the source of his disquiet, but despite the distraction offered by his books, as the day progressed he found that he could not shake an increasing sense of anxiety. By bed-time, he felt an overpowering sense that it was time to leave his comfortable existence in Dankenwood.

Next morning, he arose at daybreak. He packed a simple lunch of bread and cheese and began to walk southward through the forest.

It was not long before Phendric reached the edge of the forest. He stepped out into the golden sunlight of the warm autumn day, and began to climb the slope of the nearest of the Redfyre Hills.

He halted at the top. It being by now almost noon, Phendric settled comfortably on the grass and unpacked his lunch.

As he ate, his eye wandered over the vista spread out before him. Away to the east towered the Mountains of Mourn, marking the eastern boundary of Palindor. To the north the forest stretched until it reached the distant red-brown haze that marked the Wastes of Kaltethorn. Beyond that, hidden by the haze that shrouded the Wastes, lay the sea. In the northwest, the solitary peak of Penmichael Brea stood like a lone sentinel, towering high over the surrounding forest.

Over in the extreme northwest was the Great Sea, glistening brightly in the sun. Almost directly to the west, he could just make out the high, flat moorland of Machrenmoor. Beleron was hidden behind a hill; then the coastline curved back towards him so that not far away to the south was the sea, separated from his vantage point only by the Moortain Mire, the far side of the ring of Redfyre Hills, and the Palindor forest that stretched almost as far as the coast.

Off to the southeast were the plains of Kradesh and beyond them, on the far side of a low chain of hills, lay the River Chân, marking the boundary between Palindor and Reglandor.

It was a peaceful day, and the sun seemed to shine especially warmly on the Redfyre Hills. As he finished his lunch, a desire for sleep stole over the gnome, and his eyelids began to grow heavy. He lay on the grass and soon he was asleep.

As he slept, he dreamt.

He dreamed that he was floating upward. He looked down and saw himself, asleep on the grass with a look of peaceful contentment on his face. He began to rise higher and higher, so that soon his sleeping form was lost to view and the whole of Palindor lay spread out below him, as if he were seated on a high cloud, looking down on the Third Land.

"Beautiful, is it not?"

"Yes, it is," agreed Phendric, without turning to see who had spoken.

"And yet it is spoiled."

"Spoiled, my lord?"

"Look to the west, gnome."

Phendric turned to the west and saw, far away on the horizon, farther even than the Sunset Islands, a dark cloud, brooding and massing. He watched the cloud for some time, and even as he watched, it became darker, and larger, and closer.

"What is the cloud, my lord?"

"It is your destiny."

And suddenly Phendric was chilled with a terrible certainty that the cloud represented something larger, and more powerful than anything he had ever imagined.

He woke.

While he had been sleeping, the sky had clouded over and rain was now beginning to fall.

And Phendric the gnome began to tremble.

A strange thought came unbidden to Phendric's mind: *The cloud can hide the sun, but it can't destroy it. Eventually, it is the cloud that will be destroyed, and the sun will shine on. Tomorrow, the cloud will be gone, and the sun that is now hidden will warm the land once more.*

He shaded his eyes and looked to the west, trying to see if a dark mass truly brooded there, but he could see nothing except the gray pall that filled the sky.

He got to his feet and began to walk westward.

VI Landfall (1)

As soon as Diana awoke, she knew that something had changed. It took her several moments to run through the events of the prior day, concluding with the meal with Captain Malliss and the crew and then, finally, her return to her cabin, where she had changed into a nightgown of silk and lace and gone directly to bed.

The cabin was as she remembered it, but even so there was something different. Last night, the motion of the ship had been a barely noticeable bobbing up and down on the gentle waves of the shallows close to the shore. This morning, the ship was heeling over and a steady *thump, thump, thump* reverberated through the planks of the hull. With each *thump*, the entire ship trembled slightly, as if it were being pounded by a gigantic rubber mallet.

The ship was under sail.

She looked out the porthole above her bed. The starboard side of the boat was heeled over close to the water, and she could see nothing but dark water on which bubbles and white trails floated rapidly past in the direction of the ship's stern.

Diana got out of bed and dressed hurriedly in a suit not unlike those she had seen the sailors wearing yesterday; then she hurried on deck.

The sharp tang of the salt air caught at the back of her throat. The deck sloped at such an angle that walking was impossible

unless she kept a constant grip on some part of the ship's superstructure. Out here, the rhythmic sound of the ship as she
pounded through the waves was all but lost in the sounds of the
wind whipping through the rigging and tugging at the full sails
and the urgent squawking cries of the gulls that flew just aft of
the stern of the *Evening Passage*.

Yesterday, the sky had been clear and the sea a serene blue;
today a strong, chill wind blew lazily from the north and the
sky was a leaden overcast; the sea through which the *Evening
Passage* was forcing her way was white-capped and sullen, the
waves parting reluctantly for the three ships on an eastward reach.

Diana crossed the slanting deck to the port rail, which was
high above the churning sea. She stared out across the water
to the north, where a coastline lay not far away. The land was
low and tree-covered. Where the land met the sea was a line of
cliffs, at the foot of which the sea pounded itself into angry white
breakers. Here and there, white fountains of spray betrayed the
presence of rocks some distance out from the shore; she hoped
that the helmsman was taking them a safe distance from the land,
for the ship would surely be destroyed if it were to hit a rock at
this speed.

Several sailors were on the deck, some watching the coastline
like herself, others eyeing the billowing sails. The sails of the
Evening Passage were dark gray; possibly they had once been
black but now were faded; around their borders was a maroon
stripe, mirroring the colors of the flag that fluttered proudly from
the top of the aft mast.

The first mate, Orrian, stood behind the wheel in the center
of the ship. Suddenly he called out: "Ready to change course,"
and, moments later, he spun the wheel so that the ship veered
and heeled over even more, the starboard railing coming close to
the surface of the sea for several seconds before the ship returned
closer to the vertical. Diana watched a rock pass by the port beam
no more than a dozen paces distant. Once it was safely past, the
Evening Passage resumed her course parallel to the coast, but a
little farther out.

Orrian called out to Diana: "Breakfast is in the messroom
where we ate last night. We didn't want to wake you."

"Thank you," Diana called, but there was no response from Orrian other than a quick gesture of acknowledgment with his hand as he returned his attention to his task.

Diana walked unsteadily along the port side of the ship, keeping a firm grasp on the rail, until she came level with the companionway. Timing her movements carefully, she let go the rail and dashed across the deck and down the steps.

The messroom was empty except for the captain, who was just completing her meal. She called out: "Breakfast for the passenger," and as Diana took her seat a sailor entered from the galley bearing a tray covered with fruit and bread. He placed the tray in front of Diana, bowed, then made his way back to the galley.

"Did you sleep well?" asked the captain.

"Yes, thank you, Captain Malliss. Never better. We're near to land, I see. Is it Palindor?"

"Yes. We're looking for a harbor. As soon as we find one, we'll anchor and go ashore and explore. Maybe we'll try to talk to some of the natives. We passed a few farms earlier, but there were no gaps in the cliffs where we could have attempted a landing. Are we still sailing past forest?"

"Yes."

The captain nodded. "I thought so. I think it's all forest from now on. Still, there are probably villages hidden in the trees, so maybe we'll be able to find some natives and hear what they have to say for themselves. You're welcome to join the shore party if you'd like, although I'm afraid that I must insist that you be armed if you do."

Diana looked dubious, and the captain continued, "But of course we can see how you feel once we're ready to go ashore. You can always stay behind on the ship if you don't want to take any risks."

The boat suddenly heeled violently as it turned hard to port, and Diana's hand flew out to prevent the food from sliding off her tray. From above came the sound of running feet as sailors scurried to obey orders. The rhythm of the waves against the ship suddenly changed, becoming altogether gentler, and the ship came close to the vertical.

"Ah!" exclaimed the captain. "I warrant that Orrian has found somewhere to shelter."

Her words were confirmed not a minute later, when a sailor hurried down the companionway and stuck his head through the messroom doorway.

"Captain, we are about to anchor."

The captain nodded in acknowledgment and, moments later, the boat turned to head into the wind and the sound of luffing sails could be heard above shouts as the men hurried to lower them. An anchor was played out at the bow. A second anchor was dropped from the stern and, suddenly, the boat was anchored, bobbing up and down gently on the waves.

"If you will excuse me?" said Captain Malliss and, with a nod and a smile, she arose and went on deck.

Diana bolted what remained of her food and hurried after the captain. All three ships were anchored close to the shore, which here formed a wide bay sheltered from the northerly wind. Tall cliffs rose to the west and the east, and to the north a wooded valley opened out into a narrow beach of pale yellow sand. At the eastern end of the beach, a narrow spit protruded some distance from the shore.

The *Evening Passage* and one of the other ships, the *Twilight Sea* (according to the name painted on her transom), were anchored more or less in the center of the bay. The third ship, the *Dark Sky*, was anchored near the spit. Aboard all three ships there was a lively bustle as sailors hurried to complete the job of tidily ending their voyage. Ropes were coiled, stays fastened tightly around cleats, sails stowed, and the rowing dinghies dropped from their davits at the stern of the *Evening Passage* and the *Twilight Sea*.

Members of the crew began to appear on deck dressed no longer as sailors but as soldiers. As Diana watched, sailors went belowdecks, returning minutes later in suits of gray chain mail that glinted metallically in the weak sunlight. At his side, each sailor wore a stubby scabbard from which protruded the hilt of what was, presumably, a dagger. Diana remembered the mail suit she had seen hanging at one end of her wardrobe, and wondered if it too came with a weapon.

Soon, she and the captain were the only splashes of color amidst the crowd of gray mail suits. The captain looked up at the aft mast, where the flag was fluttering in the stiff breeze. She smiled to herself. Diana saw that identical flags were flying from the aft masts of the other two ships.

"All right, men," said the captain when all had gathered before her. "Your orders are simple. I want no trouble unless the natives start it. If they fight, you will fight back, but otherwise you are to keep your weapons sheathed. Remember, although these are believed to be a vicious and hostile people, we must give them the benefit of the doubt. Do not attack unless you yourselves are attacked first. Travel in pairs. Try to discover if there are any towns or villages nearby, then return here and tell me how you were treated. That is all. You may go."

The sailors formed into a straggly line, with much pushing and shoving, for all seemed keen to be among the first to set foot in the unexplored land. A jack-ladder was dropped over the side near the stern and the first soldier began to descend to the dinghy below.

From one of the other ships, Diana heard a sound that seemed out of place. It was the sound of horses clip-clopping on a wooden deck.

Sure enough, on the *Dark Sky*, anchored next to the spit, a gangplank had been thrown out and one end now rested on the deck of the boat while the other was on the sandy spit. And on deck were three large, dark horses.

One by one, the horses were led down the gangplank by men dressed as knights. Their armor was strangely black, and seemed to swallow the sunlight. Diana shivered, as if the air were suddenly chill.

The horses seemed unafraid of the narrow path down which they had to walk to reach dry land, and it was not long before all of them stood on the land, cropping the narrow strip of couch grass that grew along the top of the spit. The knights gathered in a group and appeared to discuss something, but the discussion was soon over, and one by one they mounted their horses with easy, fluid motions.

In single file, they began to walk along the spit in the direction of the valley. Diana watched the knights cross the beach and disappear up the valley without so much as a single glance behind them.

The first dinghies had now reached the shore. The soldiers got out of the boats and waited in small clusters on the beach while the dinghies were rowed back for their next load of passengers.

Captain Malliss appeared at Diana's elbow.

"So, would you like to go with them, my dear?"

"Isn't it dangerous? You said yourself that it might be, and I see that all your men are armed."

"True, but it is only a precaution, just in case. One can never be too careful when exploring a new land. You heard my orders to them. I don't really expect trouble, but it is better to be safe than sorry. There is armor and a dagger in your wardrobe if you wish to join them. You are welcome to go with my men. My first mate, Orrian, would be glad to have you explore with him. Unless, of course, you are afraid, in which case, you are perfectly free to remain here with me."

It was this final comment that decided Diana. Until the captain had intimated that perhaps it was fear that prevented Diana from joining the crew, she had been quite prepared to remain on board until the men returned from their reconnaissance. But Diana did not want the captain to think that she was afraid.

"I'll go put on the mail," she said, and hurried away to her cabin.

She returned a few minutes later dressed in a suit of dark-linked mail. At her side hung a scabbard. She withdrew the blade from its scabbard, testing its balance and sharpness. The dagger was surprisingly light, the blade narrow and flexible. It glinted dully in the overcast.

"Over here, miss," a soldier called, and she hurried toward the jack-ladder. The two remaining men in line stood back to let her climb down the ladder and take the last place in the dinghy. The oarsman began to row towards the shore. Glancing back at the *Evening Passage*, Diana could see the captain conversing with Orrian as they leant on the rail and watched the dinghy heading for the beach.

"What do you think, General Shadow?" the captain asked the mailed figure at her side.

"I think, my lord, that before long she will be fighting alongside us, and then the first part of the trap can be sprung."

A grin suffused the captain's face.

"My thoughts exactly, general. Now, join the others and make sure that everything goes according to plan."

The figure at her side gave a slight bow, then left the railing and joined the two remaining soldiers as they waited for the dinghy to return for its final trip.

VII First Blood

Gwynedd the Huntress was closing in for the kill. She had seen the spoor at dusk the day before, and rather than risk losing the animal in the darkness she had made camp for the night next to the fresh trail.

Gwynedd was not a particularly good Huntress; she admitted that to herself, for she knew that she was young and inexperienced. This was to be her first winter hunting alone, without either her father or her mother to help her in tracking and killing the animals that would keep her alive over the coming months.

Only six weeks before, father, mother and daughter had come together in one place for their semi-annual meetings at the time of the equinox to decide Gwynedd's status.

There was no fixed age for the child of a Hunter to spend its first winter alone, and so graduate from "child" to "Hunter." Most children were thirteen or fourteen years of age when they became Hunters, but some waited as long as eighteen, and it was not unheard of for a child to become a Hunter even as young as ten, although it was many, many years now since that had happened.

Gwynedd was thirteen, and no real shame would attach to her if she remained a child for another year, or even two. But she was a direct descendent of the great Aramis, and so she was expected to become a Huntress at a younger age than most.

Heth, her mother, was quite happy to delay the inevitable for another year. But Gwain, her father, who was of the line of Aramis and Anthelron, was adamant that Gwynedd's time had come.

Heth said, "Gwain, please let us wait one more year. Remember what happened to Enwys. I could not bear to lose our second child as we lost the first."

"Look at the skies, Heth, and tell me what you see," replied Gwain.

Gwain and Gwynedd had hunted together all summer, and Gwynedd, as she lay listening to the conversation while she pretended to sleep, knew that in that time he had formed a high opinion of his daughter's skills. She was sure that her father felt she was ready.

Heth was silent for a moment, but eventually she had to admit it. "A good winter: few storms, rather mild."

"And how was the winter in which we lost Enwys?"

"Cold and snowy."

"Many died that year, even experienced Hunters."

"But even so, she is young. One more year will not harm her."

"She is thirteen, Heth. I was a Hunter when I was eleven and you became a Huntress at thirteen. Enwys was but nine years old. I am sorry, Heth. I made a mistake. I misjudged Enwys' abilities. But I do not believe that I have misjudged Gwynedd's."

There was a long silence. Heth stared into the fire, remembering. Gwynedd too tried to remember her sister. She could not remember much, just a strong, tall girl who could fell a deer at the age of nine almost as well as Hunters twice her age. It was six years ago now that Enwys had spent her first winter alone. She had never been heard of since. Her body had never been found.

"Heth," said Gwain with a note of pleading in his voice, "you know that this will be a good winter for a child to become a Hunter. Next winter may be hard, with much snow and cold. This winter will be easy. The hunting will not be difficult. There will be few dangers, for the bears will remain high in the mountains. And don't forget that I have hunted with her all summer. She is young, but not so young that she cannot be a Huntress. She is skilled. Perhaps not so skilled as some at her age, but it is her time, Heth. I have watched her carefully these past months, and she is a child no more. Whatever we might prefer, we must release her to prove herself. Next spring, she should wear the badge of a Hunter."

Gwynedd hoped fervently that Heth would agree to let her hunt alone this winter, so that next spring when they came together at equinox, they would confer on her with pride the right to wear the little white cross that would mark her as a Huntress.

Heth tried one last time. "If she were my child alone, Gwain, I would keep her with me for another winter. She is young, and not particularly strong for her age. My sister became a Huntress only in her sixteenth year, yet now she is recognized as one of the greatest of living Hunters."

Gwain himself, of course, was understood by all to be the best Hunter alive, but he had to agree with Heth's words, for her sister Lystra was indeed reckoned to be one of the great ones.

For a moment, Gwynedd wondered if Heth was going to stand against her father, but her mother continued, "But she is your child too, a child of the line of Aramis, and it is not my place to disagree with my daughter's father. Tomorrow, Gwynedd may leave us as a child, and I trust to the mercy of the High Lord that when we return to this place next equinox, she will be a child no more, but a true Huntress."

Gwynedd was barely able to suppress a squeal of delight. She wanted to rush out and hug her parents. But that, she realized, would have been the action of a child, not a Huntress. So she remained resolutely still, and silently thanked the High Lord for her mother's words.

The next day, after a brief farewell, Gwynedd mounted her horse, Sage, and walked the animal with as much dignity as she was capable out of the clearing. She did not look back at her parents. That, too, would have been the act of a child.

That was six weeks ago now.

In those six weeks, she had learned more than she had ever thought possible. At the equinoctial meeting, had she been asked her opinion (which she was not), she would have said without hesitation that she was ready to winter alone. The last three winters had been exceptionally mild, just as the harbingers promised for the upcoming season: the signs in the skies and the movements of the animals both portended another easy winter, so there was little danger of freezing or being caught in a deadly snowstorm. Food should be plentiful and easy to catch. And had she not just spent half a year with her father hunting the small summer animals that lived in the southeastern portion of the Third Land, learning the skills of tracking and of shooting accurately, quickly and silently?

But as the days turned to weeks, Gwynedd began to realize that she had much yet to learn. In winter, most animals hibernated. If a Hunter was lucky enough to find a burrow or small cave where some small creature slept, the kill was quick and easy, and provided enough meat for a day or two. But most Hunters went for the larger game in winter, because one or two large kills provided enough meat to see a Hunter through until springtime. But the larger animals were much more difficult to find.

The lessons she had learned at her father's side were valuable in their way, but they were summer skills and of limited use in winter. Her mother, with whom she had spent the last three winters, was an expert tracker of large game, especially deer, and from her Gwynedd had learned much, but after six weeks alone Gwynedd was beginning to wonder if she had learned enough.

Three times in those weeks she had come close to catching a deer only to lose the trail when the animal crossed a stream. On one other occasion, she had even caught sight of her prey, only to have it take fright at some too-fast motion as she nocked an arrow to her bow. She had loosed the arrow, but it had missed — something that she was glad that neither her father nor her mother had been present to witness, for it would have made her the butt of comments for many days — and the deer, which would have sustained her for a month or more, had darted into the trees and she had never seen it again.

She had stayed alive these six weeks by eating autumnal fruit and nuts and by catching the occasional rabbit or squirrel. But this was no way for a Huntress to live, and if she did not begin to do better before winter was far advanced she knew that she would begin to weaken, which would slow her reflexes and so diminish further her chances of catching large prey. And even if she did survive the winter, she would feel obliged to refuse the Hunter's cross at the spring equinox, for to accept without being worthy would be to dishonor the name of her ancestor Aramis.

These thoughts were weighing heavily on her mind when she spotted the deer spoor in the damp, muddy forest floor late in the afternoon. She dismounted from Sage and studied the spoor. It was fresh, no more than half a day old. The deer that had made it she judged to be a female of two summers. The doe was travelling alone, moving slowly in a southerly direction. Gwynedd made a promise to herself that this time her prey was not going to escape. Before tomorrow evening she would make her first big kill of the winter.

She halted for the night at the place where she had discovered the spoor. She slept fitfully, eagerly awaiting first light. There was a light rain in the night, accompanied by gusting winds, and more than once she got up to check that the animal's spoor was in no danger of being obliterated.

At last, the pale light of the new day appeared in the east. She arose and reexamined the spoor closely in the early morning light. The rain had only partially obscured it, and the spoor was still easy to read. The deer had passed this way not long before dusk last night. It would have settled somewhere for the night and now was probably not more than an hour or so ahead of her. With luck, she would catch the animal before noon. She mounted Sage and began to follow the trail.

It was a gray day, of the kind known as a "Hunter's friend," and that pleased her, for it meant that there was less danger that the deer might be scared by a stray reflection from the metal tip of an arrow as she fitted it to her bow.

She trailed the animal for much of the morning. She found where it had spent the night easily enough; the animal seemed to have arisen early and moved south without delay. Every now and then, Gwynedd dismounted and examined the spoor. There was no doubt that she was closing on her prey.

As morning drew to a close, she estimated that she was no more than a few minutes behind the doe. For the hundredth time, she checked her bow and quiver and the dagger at her waist. By next winter, the dagger would be relegated to a scabbard at her ankle, and at her waist would hang the broadsword of a Huntress. Now that she was close to her first real kill of the winter, she knew that she would survive the season and go on to be recognized in years to come as a great Huntress.

The sound of a bird crying with alarm startled her. She chided herself for daydreaming. The deer was not hers yet. But it could not be long now. In a very short while she would have to dismount and stalk her prey on foot. Her stomach tightening with excitement, she kept her eyes firmly on the spoor.

She was eyeing the ground so intently that at first she did not see the mounted rider blocking her path. It was Sage that first noticed the ominous figure. The horse halted so suddenly that Gwynedd momentarily lost her balance. As she recovered herself, Sage whickered and took a step backward.

Gwynedd looked around, worried that she had approached the deer too closely and that she and Sage had startled the animal, wasting the morning's work. But she saw at once that the cause of Sage's reaction was something altogether more ominous than a defenseless doe. Completely blocking the narrow forest track was an enormous black horse on which sat a tall figure in black armor.

For several seconds, riders and horses eyed one another. Sage took another step backward.

Gwynedd had never seen such a rider, nor such a horse, before. A lance hung from the saddle of the beast, and from the waist of the armored figure hung a large, black scabbard.

The black rider kicked his horse gently, and slowly the massive animal began to move forward. Sage stepped backwards again.

"There, there, Sage; it's all right," Gwynedd said quietly, patting her horse and trying to reassure the frightened animal.

But Sage refused to be placated. For every step that the black horse took, Sage matched it. But the stride of the stranger's horse was much larger than Sage's, so the distance between the two gradually shrank until it was no more than ten paces.

The knight made a throaty sound and his horse halted. Gwynedd reassured Sage again, and after a moment he too came to a stop.

"Who are you?" asked the black knight.

His voice was deep and chilling. The forest all around suddenly fell quiet. Gwynedd shivered.

"Gwynedd," she replied.

Her voice was a croak. She cleared her throat and tried again.

"Gwynedd, Child Huntress of the forest of Palindor, at your service."

For what seemed like a long time nothing moved; then the knight dismounted. He walked towards Gwynedd.

Sage began to step backward once more. The knight halted and slowly drew his sword.

Gwynedd was frozen with fear. The blade of the knight's sword was even blacker than his armor. Where she expected to see the gleam of metal there was only a darkness that seemed to swallow all the light that had the misfortune to fall on the blade.

"You are my prisoner," said the knight. "You will come with me."

He took another step closer. And now, at last, Gwynedd found herself able to move.

"No I won't," she shouted, and she pulled tightly on the rein to turn Sage around, ready to flee back the way she had come, all thoughts of the doe forgotten.

The knight took one last step as her horse turned. The knight drew back his sword and plunged it deeply into Sage's rump.

Instantly, the horse crumpled to the ground. Gwynedd was thrown forward as the horse's legs folded underneath it. She turned to look at her horse as she scrambled to her feet. Her beloved Sage was laid out on the ground, staring forward out of sightless eyes. Dead.

It had happened so quickly that it took a moment for Gwynedd to understand that her beloved Sage was truly dead. She watched, horrified, as the knight pulled his sword from Sage's body. Gwynedd stared in disbelief. There was no blood on the weapon, which remained as blackly sinister as ever; neither did any blood flow from the small gash in the horse's rump.

The knight looked from sword to Gwynedd.

Gwynedd screamed, and fled into the forest.

She did not know for how long she ran. All she knew was that she ran as quickly and for as long as her legs and her lungs would let her. She pushed herself onward until eventually, after what seemed like an age, she could continue no farther, and she slumped against a tree while she caught her breath.

The only sounds she could hear were the usual sounds of the forest: a couple of birds twittering not far away; a high-pitched melody from a songbird high in the sky; the scurry of a squirrel jumping from one tree to another; the soft rustle of a light wind caressing the trees.

Gradually, she recovered.

She held her breath and listened intently, but heard nothing to suggest that she was being chased. There was a small circle of bushes nearby, and wearily she pushed into their center, then she dropped down to the ground so that she would be out of sight should the knight pass by.

Slowly, she became calmer; her mind began to work again, and she started to take stock of her situation.

Her first thought was that she needed to get away from here. Her second was that, apart from dagger at her side, she now was unarmed, for the quiver of arrows on her back was useless without the bow that was attached to poor Sage's saddle. And she had no food at all now; what little she had had was in the saddle bag.

The closest settlement, an elf village, was the better part of a day's walk to the west. But in her haste to escape she had run southeast, so that now the fearsome warrior was between her and safety.

She decided to wait until nightfall, when she would try to make her way westward and hope that the knight was not....

She held her breath, for she had heard the sound of muted conversation not far away. She thought she heard a girl's voice. Whoever it was was coming closer.

She strained to hear the words of the conversation, but was unable to make them out. The voices stopped, but their owners were close enough now for their progress to be clearly audible. They kept coming closer. Suddenly, through a gap in the bushes, she caught sight of movement. And then the movement stopped.

Someone — a man, not the girl — said, "Wait! There's someone near here."

Gwynedd held her breath, not daring to call out, for through the tangles of the twigs she could see the color of the clothing worn by the intruders: it was black.

The moment stretched out. *Surely, they'll move on*, Gwynedd thought. But the intruders remained motionless, listening as intently as she.

"I'm sure there's someone here somewhere," the man said, and then the bushes through which Gwynedd was peering moved. A man dressed in dark mail had parted them and was staring directly into Gwynedd's eyes.

Gwynedd scrambled to her feet even as the figure pushed its way forward through the bushes. Dimly, she was aware that there were two of them: behind the man was an arrogant-looking young woman only a couple of years older than Gwynedd herself. Both were dressed in dark mail, and both wore small scabbarded blades at their waists.

Gwynedd was fast, and she moved without conscious thought. A Huntress has to be able to live not only by wits and skill but by the speed of her reflexes, and Gwynedd knew instinctively that she could draw her own weapon and strike before the man coming towards her would have time to draw his dagger.

In a single motion, Gwynedd rose, drew her dagger and lunged forward, holding out the weapon before her. She thrust toward the one place that was not protected by the tightly woven chain mail. Her blade sank into the man's neck. He let out an agonized scream as the lethal point went home.

The knife went too deep, and Gwynedd immediately realized that while she had killed the man, she had also lost her knife, for the dagger twisted out of her grip as the man fell under his own weight. Gwynedd jumped to one side as the man's momentum carried him forward even as he fell to the ground, blood throbbing from the severed artery at his neck.

After a single moment of hesitation, Gwynedd turned to flee.

Diana watched in disbelief as events unfolded at an appalling speed. She and Orrian had been walking all morning, and her feet were beginning to tire. It was a long walk back to the *Evening*

Passage, and she had just asked whether they might turn around soon, for the forest, at least in this area, seemed to be uninhabited. He urged her to continue for a while yet, and she was wondering how much longer it would be before Orrian might agree to turn back, when her companion halted without warning and raised his hand.

"Wait!" he said. "There's someone here."

She held her breath, listening intently. What had Orrian heard? A twig breaking? The sound of someone's voice? A footstep nearby? Try as she might, Diana could hear nothing other than the forest sounds that had accompanied them all morning.

Orrian frowned.

"I'm sure I heard someone," he said.

He moved towards a low circle of bushes at the side of the path.

The rest happened so quickly that Diana barely had time to take it in.

Orrian must have seen someone, for he suddenly plunged forward, as if intending to apprehend someone. Over his shoulder she saw a young girl dressed in green getting hurriedly to her feet.

Orrian stepped towards the girl, opening his mouth to speak, doubtless to reassure her that they meant no harm. In a movement so quick that it was almost invisible, the girl in green lunged forward, a knife suddenly in her hand. The blade buried itself in Orrian's neck and his legs folded under him. The girl let go of the knife, and Diana saw with horror that the girl must have severed an artery — blood was everywhere.

Filled with anger, Diana drew her own dagger and pushed through the bushes, following the path that Orrian had made. The girl turned to flee. She would surely have escaped, for she moved more quickly than Diana had ever seen anyone move before, but in turning she caught her ankle on an exposed root and, after flaying the air for a moment, she sprawled forward on to the bush through which she was trying to escape.

Diana caught up with her, and thrust her blade forward with all her strength. It broke through the girl's clothing, punctured her skin, then sank in all the way up to the hilt.

But the girl was still moving, still struggling to get to her feet. Diana let go of the knife, which was now buried in the girl's back.

Astounded, Diana watched as the girl kept going even as a ghastly red stain began to spread across her tunic.

In a few moments the girl was gone.

Diana looked down at the friendly sailor who had accompanied her on their simple mission of exploration. There was no doubt that he was dead. Blood drenched the body and the surrounding grass. Diana turned away and was violently sick over a bush. Then she fled the foul place, heading back the way they had come, desperate for the safety of the *Evening Passage*.

For a long time nothing moved in the little circle of bushes. Then Orrian's body seemed to flicker and dissolve and turn dark gray, absorbing into itself the drying blood that covered both it and the surrounding vegetation. Gradually, a gray shape emerged. The details of the shape changed from moment to moment, but one thing did not change: on the creature's face was a wide yellow grin.

Shadow opened his mouth and let out a single malicious laugh. Then, in the blink of an eye, he was gone.

VIII   The Dablik Arrives

Catherine was the first to wake. She had slept well, although at one point she had had a strange dream in which a tremendous storm had arisen and blown Glandryth's cottage high into the sky, only to land safely atop Machrenmoor on the mainland of Palindor, near the quoit that marked the underground tomb of Toldwyn, the founder of the Third Land.

Gathered around the quoit was a crowd of her friends from her earlier visits to Palindor: the Holy Gnomes Trondwyth and Drefynt, and Drefynt's wife Lorin, and their daughter Sherna, along with several others. In the dream, they seemed to be standing around, just waiting for something to happen.

She asked what they were waiting for.

"Toldwyn's return," said Drefynt. "Look," and he pointed off to the north, toward the town of Carn Toldwyn.

Catherine's gaze followed his finger and she saw the figure of Malthazzar, enormously magnified, straddling the distant castle.

Malthazzar spoke to Catherine: "You cannot kill me, Catherine. Even your sword Scalmyùt can do me no harm."

Then a veritable swarm of dark creatures spewed forth from Malthazzar's mouth and landed not far from the quoit.

"Fight! Fight!" urged Sherna, drawing a sword.

There was more of the dream, but when Catherine woke she could not remember what happened next.

The whole thing was surreal and nonsensical of course. Not only were all the creatures by the quoit dead, but Catherine had long ago sworn never to raise her sword in anger. She still carried Scalmyùt, but she knew that she could never again use it against another creature, even one as loathsome as Malthazzar.

Even the reason that her friends had given for being on Machrenmoor made no sense. There was a myth that one day Toldwyn, the founding warrior of the Third Land, would rise from his grave to defend Palindor, but Drefynt had once told her that it was no more than a story and had no basis in any prophecy he had ever read.

Ridiculous though it all was, Catherine woke with a burning, angry feeling that was somehow connected with the dream. Her inability to remember how the dream had ended only added to her sense of frustration and anger.

She sat up and blinked in the gloom of the cottage.

The fire had gone out overnight and the only light came from a couple of feebly glowing embers. For a long while, Catherine simply sat on the straw, hugging her knees, trying to rid herself of the emotions that the dream had engendered.

There had been a storm in the night — she vaguely remembered hearing its howling moan as it had whipped through the branches and around the cottage. The noise had almost woken her, but not quite, leading instead to the beginning of the dream that had so upset her. The storm had died down now. As she listened, she could hear a faint pattering sound: a light rain was falling on the roof.

There was a movement in the far corner of the room: Glandryth was getting up. A few moments later, he flung open a shutter and a gray daylight invaded the room; along with it came a cool, rain-sodden breeze.

"I'll make the fire; we'll need it today," said Glandryth.

Catherine was about to offer to help, when her eyes strayed across to the place where they had left Michael sleeping last night. Her eyes opened wide in surprise.

"Michael! He's gone!" she exclaimed.

They rushed outside and stood in the drizzle, calling his name.

"I hope he hasn't left the island," said Glandryth with a worried look. "The dablik would be very displeased if Michael has gone as well."

There were no replies to their shouts, and together they moved away from the cottage, climbing the hill while they both continued to call Michael's name. The rain seemed to absorb their cries, so that no matter how loudly they shouted, they had the feeling that the sound penetrated almost no distance through the sodden air.

They climbed over the ridge that divided the island. Reaching the edge of the wood, they looked down at the angry sea on the western side of the island.

There was no trace of the ships that Michael had described the night before. All they could see were sharp, white-peaked, continually-moving hills of wind-driven water.

"He said they were anchored out there," said Glandryth, pointing roughly to the place where the ships had been. "Could he have swum so far?"

"I doubt it," said Catherine, "The water was very cold, and he said last night it was too far to swim."

The idea struck the two of them at the same moment. "The coracle!" They turned as one and ran back to the cottage.

They saw instantly they reached the dell that Glandryth's little home-made vessel was missing, as was its paddle.

"He took the coracle but never brought it back. In this sea...." Catherine dared say no more.

They were both thinking of the angry, gray sea, in which it would be dangerous madness to venture out in a coracle. It would be swamped in a very short time.

"Look," said Glandryth, and Catherine's spirits suddenly rose. It was true that there was no sign of the coracle and its paddle, but Glandryth was pointing to the chimney of the cabin, from which was spiraling blue-gray smoke. Someone had lit a fire in their absence.

"Come on," he urged, and together they ran down the slope towards Glandryth's cottage.

The dablik was tired after his journey from Penmichael Brea. He was also angry at himself, for, unlike Glandryth, he had kept careful track of the days, and he knew that the three humans should have arrived on the island yesterday, the night of the second full moon following the autumnal equinox.

But he could hardly be blamed for being late, for how could he have foreseen the circumstances that caused him to lose an entire day?

He had had, of course, every intention of being with his friend Glandryth when the humans arrived. After all, it was not every decade that the High Lord appeared and gave him such an important task. And it was easy to persuade himself that it *was* an important task, for the High Lord had not been seen in Palindor for many hundreds of years, not since he had suddenly appeared at that fateful meeting in the Judgement Hall in Dynas Carn Toldwyn when Queen Catherine and King Michael had last been in Palindor.

The dablik had been minding his own business a couple of days before the equinox, enjoying the fruit that weighed down the trees on the upper reaches of the Mountains of Mourn in the eastern part of Palindor. It was going to be a record crop this year, and the dablik was making the most of the fact.

Although the dablik preferred to travel and to sleep underground in the vast network of tunnels that stretched below the surface of the Three Lands, he had to venture on to the surface to eat, and this time of year was his very favorite, with so many fresh berries and nuts from which to choose. The summer had been extraordinarily mild; indeed, the weather for the past couple of years had been better than any he could remember, with wet but mild winters, and warm, slumbrous summers, and in consequence shrubs and trees were heavily laden with ripening fruit.

The dablik was particularly partial to two kinds of fruit. One was the blueberries that grew in profusion on the western slopes of the Mountains of Mourn and could be picked for several weeks around the time of the autumnal equinox in mild years, before the first snows came. The other was much rarer: a drupe halfway between a blackberry and a raspberry, but larger and tastier than either. This berry had no Palindoric name, for the dablik was the only creature who knew that it grew in Palindor*. So the dablik thought of it by the name that the farmers of northeastern Soltarwyn had given it: the cuzzleberry.

Even in Soltarwyn, cuzzleberry bushes had never been widely cultivated, for the bushes fruited only after a full year of perfect weather, and although most of the farmers of that land kept one or two bushes for their own use in the occasional year in which fruit formed, there was no money to be made from them, for the berries were too few and the weather too unreliable for the cuzzleberry to become a cash crop.

Apart from the farms in northeastern Soltarwyn, there was only one other place where the cuzzleberry grew: in a protected corner on the northern slopes of Penmichael Brea, the solitary peak in northwestern Palindor. This year, the dablik reminded himself daily not to forget to visit the place a month after the equinox, for the cuzzleberry harvest, like that of the blueberries, promised to be better than any he had ever known.

But one day just before the equinox, the dablik was pattering down a tunnel in eastern Palindor on his way to his lunch of blueberries when he rounded a corner and saw that his way was blocked by an old man who leaned on an ancient staff and looked for all the world like a wizened and weathered gardener.

The dablik skidded to a halt, almost colliding with Olvensar.

The High Lord smiled. "In a hurry, dablik? I understand that the blueberries are especially good this year in the hidden valley where once the healer and the seer lived. And don't forget the cuzzleberries. They are coming along nicely. Another six weeks and they will be well worth a visit."

All of a sudden, the dablik was no longer in a hurry. A calmness had fallen over him, and a certainty that whatever good things he was hurrying to would only improve if he remained here awhile with the High Lord.

"Do not worry, good dablik," continued Olvensar. "I will not keep you long, but I have an errand for you. Would you do something for me?"

---

* Apart, perhaps, from Treadlong the Traveller, who seemed to have visited everywhere in the Three Lands.

"Of course. For you I would do anything."

The High Lord paused, looking at the golden creature with those eyes that bored right through a creature and saw into its very spirit.

"Hmmm..., I remember that when you were a youngster I sometimes had to chide you for making rash statements. I was hoping you had learned something in the centuries since then. Never make a rash promise, master dablik, for one day you might have cause to regret it."

The dablik's gaze dropped to the ground at the rebuke. He knew that the High Lord was right, of course: there were some things that he would not do, even for the High Lord.

"I am sorry, my lord. I will do my best to remember what you say."

"Of course you will. Now, I have a simple task for you. When you have tired of blueberries, I would like you to visit your friend Glandryth in the Sunset Islands, and inform him that at the time of the second full moon after the equinox he should be prepared to receive three visitors. I ask in my name that he give them shelter and welcome. I would like you also to be there to greet them, and please be sure that Glandryth impresses on his guests that they are not to leave the island until you have joined them. Do you understand all that?"

The dablik nodded. "Yes, my lord," he said. "But if I might be so bold as to ask: who exactly are these visitors?"

"Two of them you have met before, and one of those is an old friend."

The High Lord smiled broadly at the dablik, who guessed: "The High Queen?"

"You spoil my fun by guessing," Olvensar said with an indulgent smile.

The dablik's own face burst into a grin. "Then I shall certainly be sure to be there when they arrive. But what happens once they are here? Then what?"

"Then we shall see what we shall see. Don't be so inquisitive, my young friend. Life would not be very interesting if one always knew what came next, would it?"

The dablik considered this for a moment, then said with perfect seriousness, "No, my lord. But it might be much simpler."

The old man chuckled. "Be off with you. Go to your blueberries. And mind that you don't forget the task I have given you. Now, I shall keep you no longer from your important assignation with lunch."

And with that the old man stepped to one side, into the very rock of the tunnel itself, and simply disappeared.

The task, as Olvensar had promised, was a simple one. At least, the first part of it had proved to be so. After the constant diet of blueberries had become a little too much even for the dablik, he had headed westward and crossed underneath Palindor and the Great Sea until he reached Glandryth's island, where he delivered the message from the High Lord.

By this time it was some four weeks past equinox. The next full moon was not due for nearly two more weeks, and so, after giving Glandryth the message, the dablik had set off once more under the sea, this time heading for Penmichael Brea and the cuzzleberries.

The cuzzleberries were even better than he had expected. The only problem was that they were so inaccessible.

The tunnels that criss-crossed underneath Palindor boasted hundreds of entrances, mostly in the form of what appeared to be small caves in the hills that dotted the Third Land. In most of Palindor one was never more than an hour or two's journey from a tunnel entrance, but there was one place where entrances were rare: on the slopes of Penmichael Brea.

In fact, there were only two entrances on the mountain. One was on the southern side, in a cave that long ago had been the home of the hermit Terafin but which now was empty and unused. The second entrance was a crack in the rocks on the northern side of the mountain. The cuzzleberries grew in a glade about two hours from this crack.

For the better part of a week, the dablik feasted on the bountiful crop. As the moon waxed towards full, he reluctantly left them to the squirrels, so he would not miss his appointment with the High Queen.

But he had a shock when he reached the crack that led to the tunnels: it was now occupied by a bear. The dablik tried to edge his way past the animal, but the bear had other ideas. As far as it was concerned, the cave was its property until spring.

So the dablik had no choice but to make his way around to the south side of the mountain to Terafin's old cave, and enter the tunnels by that route.

The detour cost him a day. When he arrived at Glandryth's cottage early in the morning of the day following the full moon, it was deserted.

"Glandryth? Your Majesty?" he called, but there was no reply.

But the door of the cottage had been left open, so they couldn't be far away. The dablik made up a fire — for it was a chillsome, drizzly day — and settled into a rocking chair to await the return of Catherine and the others.

IX The Cottage in the Goyle

Gwynedd had no idea how far she ran, then stumbled, then, eventually, dragged herself forward. She was so frightened that at first she lost all sense of pain, and simply ran as quickly as she could from the dreadful place where the people dressed in black had ambushed her. It was some time before she even realized that she was wounded.

She had run perhaps half a thousand paces before, quite suddenly, the pain in her back hit her. She stopped and leant on a tree for support, gasping. She tried to feel her back with her hand, but she could not reach the place where the pain originated. But her hand when she withdrew it was covered in blood.

Gwynedd tried to carry on, but managed no more than another hundred paces before she began see dark spots flickering in her eyes. She stumbled and crashed to the ground. She tried to crawl forward, but dragged herself only a few more paces before her arms gave way.

Gwynedd looked around, trying to get her bearings, wondering if perhaps she was close enough to some woodelf village that she might be able to drag herself to a path where she might be found. But she was lost. Suddenly, the forest that was normally her friend seemed an alien and dangerous place.

She tried to move, then to call out, but the pain was too great for either. The most she could accomplish was a mournful moan that would not have been heard ten paces away. She closed her eyes, trying to concentrate and keep the pain at bay, but it was no use. The pain overwhelmed her, and she lost consciousness.

Her father found her less than an hour later.

It was hardly a coincidence, for Gwain had been following Gwynedd ever since he and Heth had agreed to let her hunt alone.

Gwain was never more than a day behind his daughter. He carefully examined all her tracks. The campfires in particular told him much. Although it was now six weeks since he had seen her, he knew that Gwynedd was having a difficult time of it. He was trailing her quite closely now, for he was worried that if the weather turned unpleasant Gwynedd might quickly find herself in serious trouble.

He came across last night's campfire at midmorning, as he usually did. He knew that it was several days now since she had eaten meat, and he was wondering if he could not simply meet her "accidentally" in the forest and suggest that they move eastwards together.

But to his delight he saw, close to last night's encampment, the spoor of a young doe. The spoor was from yesterday afternoon, and Gwynedd must have discovered it last night as the light was beginning to fade. Probably she had made an early start this morning, with the intention of killing the animal before midday, so she would have enough time to strip the meat from the carcass before nightfall.

An hour later he stopped again to examine the tracks.

Next to Sage's tracks, he saw the widely spaced footprints of his daughter, obviously running for all she was worth in the opposite direction. Gwynedd's tracks left the trail and plunged into the forest. For some reason, Gwynedd had dismounted a short distance ahead and then run back the way she had come, only to plunge off the track and into the forest. Whyever would she have done that?

91

He commanded his own horse, Peregrine, to remain where it was while he followed Sage's hoofprints. His hand on the hilt of his broadsword, Gwain began to move softly forward.

At the next corner, he stopped and drew in his breath in astonished horror. There was a confused jumble of tracks on the ground; but all thoughts of reading the tracks were driven from his mind by the sight of Sage stretched out before him, almost blocking the path. The animal was dead.

He listened intently. The only sounds came from the forest birds: a clear indication that whoever had done this thing was now gone. He hurried forward to examine Sage.

The animal lay stretched out in an unnatural pose, its eyes open, staring sightlessly forward along the ground. But most worrying of all was the horse's hindquarters, where the sleek brown hair had turned a dirty gray.

He walked to the rear of the beast, and there, in the left rump, he saw a patch where the animal's hair was positively black. Centered in the blackest area was a narrow slit, as of a wound made by a broadsword — except that from this wound no blood had escaped. Indeed, there was no sign of blood anywhere.

"A Dark Knight," he whispered in horror.

For a moment, he was rooted to the spot. Then he turned and fled back to the place where Peregrine was quietly nibbling grass. Without a word, he clambered back into the saddle, then unsheathed his sword and began to guide his horse through the forest, following his daughter's trail.

He soon reached a place where there had been some kind of a struggle, one in which his daughter had been injured.

Now he gave no consideration to the noise he was making as he followed Gwynedd's trail. The trail was fresh, less than an hour old, and it was obvious that she could not have run very far, for there were plenty of red drops on the ground marking her path.

He reached her ten minutes later, lying unconscious beside the trunk of a tree.

"Gwynedd," he shouted.

There was no response.

Gwain jumped out of the saddle and ran to her side. He felt her pulse and turned her over to look at her face, ignoring for the moment the hilt of the blade that protruded from her back.

She was in a coma. Her pulse was weak, and she was pale and shivered in her sleep. Not good. She did not even groan when he moved her. He wondered if there was any hope.

Placing his hand on the hilt of the dagger, with infinite care he removed it. He gave one glance at the blade before discarding it: the blade glistened metallically in the gray daylight. That was something — at least it wasn't a Dark Knight's weapon. The wound began to bleed, and he ripped off part of his tunic to use as a pledget to staunch the flow.

He examined Gwynedd more carefully. She had lost a lot of blood, and the blade must have been thrust into her body with a vicious strength, for it had broken a rib and had in all probability punctured a lung. That Gwynedd had been capable of running at all was a testament to her fear, for her pain must have been truly appalling.

He touched her wound, trying to elicit a response. She let out a barely audible moan. Good. At least she had not lost so much blood that she was incapable of feeling pain. He replaced the bloody pledget with a clean shred of his tunic.

Gwain racked his brains. His daughter was alive, but unless he found someone skilled in the healing arts, Gwynedd was going to die before the day was through.

Where could he take her? In the old days, there had been healers scattered throughout the land. But they had all died long ago. There was no one these days with skills to match the Old Ones. There was only one creature alive who might be able to save his daughter: the strange gnome called Phendric, who some called a Holy Gnome. But Phendric lived in the old cabin that had once belonged to the Master of Dankenwood, which was more than a day's ride from this place.

Where else could he take her? The answer came reluctantly: there was nowhere. But he could not just stand by and do nothing, for then Gwynedd would surely die. Carefully, then, he lifted his precious daughter and laid her on Peregrine's back, binding her into position so that she would not fall off. Then he took the bridle and began to walk.

The nearest village was Riverford, a woodelf hamlet that lay a day's walk to the west. It was not a foregone conclusion that anyone in Riverford would help — even if Gwynedd survived the journey — for it was a small, tight-knit community of taciturn wood elves who were as likely to ignore the presence of the sick human as they were to tend her. But it was all he could think of. So with a heavy heart and a stream of entreaties to the High Lord to permit his daughter live, Gwain led his horse with its comatose burden through the forest.

After a little while, they emerged on to the coastal plain. Here the wind was chill and strong, and carried the tangy, biting smell of the sea, which to Gwain's nostrils was a strange and unpleasant scent that overpowered his normally acute (for a human) sense of smell. Under ordinary circumstances, he would have turned away and regained the safety of the forest with its comfortable, friendly scents and meandering paths; but now he needed to make good time, so he lowered his head into the breeze and continued walking the horse as quickly as he dared, stopping every few minutes to examine his daughter.

She was failing. Every time he checked her pulse it was weaker. But he was doing everything he could. With tears welling in his eyes, he continued moving westward.

As the sun was beginning to fall toward the horizon their way was blocked by a deep V-shaped wooded valley of the type known locally as a goyle.

The goyle scarred the coastal plain from north to south. He stopped momentarily at its edge and peered down the slopes. He was momentarily angry, for it would delay them to drop down into the goyle and then climb the far side. But his anger lasted only a moment, for there was nothing he could do to change the situation. He began to lead Peregrine carefully down the slippery slope, still wet from a morning shower that must have passed this way.

He was more than halfway down the side of the valley when he spotted a ramshackle building nestled on the valley floor. It was quite alone, and seemed out of place, for despite its tumble-down appearance, it was set in an immaculate garden of beautiful flowering shrubs. The stream that ran through the goyle on its way to the sea passed through the garden, close by the house. A path to the house crossed a small wooden bridge over the stream. Rags of smoke came from the chimney, only to be torn apart by the dying breeze from last night's storm.

Gwain shivered as the sun dropped below the opposite rim of the valley. He stopped and felt Gwynedd's pulse. It was several seconds before he was sure that the pulse was still present. Her face was ashen.

There was no choice. Another hour, perhaps less, and Gwynedd would be dead. If nothing else, the house would be warm and probably safe, and there would be food, and surely whoever lived there could not deny shelter to one so desperately close to death.

He kissed his daughter gently on the cheek. Her skin felt cool. Gwynedd was dying. He prayed: *Please, Lord Olvensar; take me if you must, but save my daughter.* And with that forlorn thought, he led Peregrine towards the bridge across the stream.

The house was poorly built and in an even worse state of repair. The chimney from which smoke issued listed dangerously to one side, looking as if it must collapse in the next storm. Indeed, the entire edifice looked dangerously as if it would crash to the ground were a good strong gust to come roaring down the goyle.

The garden was a stark contrast. The grass was trimmed and borders of shrubs and flowering plants gave a dazzling display more appropriate to spring or early summer than late autumn. As he crossed the bridge, Gwain noticed that rocks had been placed in the watercourse, creating a friendly burble as the water flowed over them.

Reaching the building, he rapped smartly on the wooden door. He was dismayed, but hardly surprised, to see that the door was splintered and hung crookedly, affixed to its frame by a single hinge near the top of the door.

He stepped back and waited to see who would answer his knock.

The answer was not long in coming. The door was opened tentatively, and Gwain had to lower his eyes, for it was not a human who had opened the door, but a middle-aged, nervous female elf — although the house was obviously designed for humans.

The elf's eyes opened in horror as they flitted from Gwain to the burden on his horse.

Gwain bowed and began to introduce himself: "Good afternoon, mistress. Gwain, Hunter of the forest of Palindor, at...."

The elf rushed past him and started to pull at the cords that bound Gwynedd to the horse.

"Yes, yes, yes. All that can wait," said the elf. "I've been waiting for you all day. Although I didn't know what I was supposed to do when you got here. It's obvious now, of course. Do hurry up and help me with these cords. Did you tie them? I'm not very good with knots. She looks very sick. Can you move her? I'm the only one here right now. Oh, I do hope she's not too far gone. When mistress Harsforn returns, she'll know what to do. I have a bed ready in the parlor. Can you carry her?"

After this burst of disjointed sentences, the elf let go of the cords in exasperation and started to examine Gwynedd without actually touching her while Gwain began to untie the knots.

"Hurry," the elf continued. "There's not much time, there really isn't. You should have got her here sooner. Why did you delay? Anyway, you'll have to lift her. I'm not strong enough. But we've got to get her inside where she'll be warm and comfortable. What were you thinking of? You didn't even put a blanket over her."

The talkative elf, who had not even given her name, looked accusingly at Gwain, who, now that the knots were untied, simply stared at her.

"I'm sorry. I didn't think. I...," he said.

"Never mind. Time enough for recriminations later. If necessary. Which they usually aren't. Come along now. Take her down and follow me. Be very careful with her."

Be very careful, Gwain thought. *How could I be otherwise? She's my own flesh and blood.*

But he said nothing. Instead, as gently as he knew how, he eased Gwynedd off the horse and into his arms. How fragile she looked, and how precious, like a child's doll. With a sinking feeling in the pit of his stomach, he realized that she looked as if she had no more life in her than the same child's doll. Tears began to well in the Hunter's eyes, and he blinked quickly to clear them away.

The elf, amazingly, had stopped talking and now led them through the canted doorway and into the building.

The interior was ill-lit, and it was several moments before Gwain could make out anything at all. There were few windows, and those that did exist were small. This, added to the darkness that came from being situated at the floor of the wooded goyle, and the dark wood that seemed to be the principal decoration inside the house, gave the building a gloomy air that was quite at odds with the surroundings outside.

Gwain stood, blinking in the hallway, listening to the deep rhythmic ticking of a long case clock coming from somewhere nearby. There was a wide doorway to his left, through which the elf hurried. He followed into the room beyond.

The clock was in a corner of this room: a tall timepiece with a pearl-colored face informed him incorrectly that the time was a little before noon (or, possibly, shortly before midnight).

"Put her here," ordered the elf, and Gwain saw that a sofa had been prepared for just such a sick visitor. A pillow was at one end and blankets were tucked underneath the cushions of the seat. The elf watched while Gwain placed his daughter on the makeshift bed and covered her with the blankets.

"Look after her for a minute," said the elf, disappearing back through the doorway.

Gwain looked down at Gwynedd. Her breathing was regular, but very shallow, and her face — what he could see of it in the gloom — looked paler than ever. He could hear the elf moving not far away.

The elf returned almost immediately, carrying a steaming poultice that filled the air with an odor that was simultaneously sweet and bitter.

"Turn her over so I can put this on the wound," the elf ordered.

Gently, Gwain turned his daughter and pulled the blankets down and then lifted her tunic so that her back was exposed. For the first time, the elf touched Gwynedd. She lightly examined the wound, although it was a mystery to Gwain how the elf could see properly to do her work. The elf nodded, seeming to be satisfied, then gently laid the steaming poultice on the caked blood. Gwynedd spasmed as the poultice was applied, and a sudden cry escaped her lips. Then she settled once more. Quickly, the elf bound the poultice in place with thin leather thongs.

When she had finished, the elf looked up and seemed surprised to see Gwain still standing nearby.

"Haven't you gone yet?" she asked.

Then she put her hand to her mouth and suppressed what looked and sounded like a giggle — which Gwain thought in the circumstances was one of the most insensitive things he had ever witnessed.

He was about to admonish the elf when she continued, "Oh, silly me; I forgot to tell you, didn't I? You're to follow the goyle down to the beach. They'll be waiting for you there. Don't forget to take your horse, you'll need it. Don't just stand there gaping. There's no time to waste."

The elf turned away and began to stroke Gwynedd's cheek, while murmuring something under her breath that Gwain could not quite catch.

The Hunter's head was full of questions, but for now he recognized that the elf was doing all she could for his daughter. Never mind that he did not know the elf's name; nor that he had no idea how he and Gwynedd could possibly have been expected; nor that he longed to know what the prognosis was for his daughter; nor that he wondered who could be waiting at the end of the goyle. His daughter was being cared for by someone who seemed to know enough about the healing arts that there was at least a shred of hope that she might be saved. That was all he really needed to know. Without a word, he stole from the room.

As dusk began to fall, he mounted Peregrine and they set off down the goyle.

X Landfall (2)

Michael soon discovered that if he continually shifted his weight
so that the coracle rode up and down the waves instead of trying
to pound its way through them, much less water splashed aboard.
But it was hard work, watching out for the incoming waves and
timing his rocking so that the boat tipped at exactly the right
moment, and he soon began to tire. And even when he got it
right, still some water found its way into the boat, and with each
added splash the coracle became heavier, sank lower, and became
harder to control.

Rain-filled clouds scudded across the sky from north to south,
hiding the stars as they flitted overhead like enormous shadows,
dropping their burden of moisture as they went. The moon, when
he could see it, was full and high in the sky, and it lit the seascape
with an eerie glow that served only to emphasize Michael's solitude
when it disappeared again. Phosphorescent spume and spindrift
scudded across the wavetops. The wind gusted noisily as it skidded
over the wavetops and around the coracle. And all the time the
coracle was pushed southward, away from Glandryth's island.

Long before dawn, Michael was exhausted, but still he kept
rocking the coracle and bailing the frigid water with his bare
hands.

The wind had veered and then backed in the night, blowing him around the southwestern peninsula of Palindor — the area known as Beleron, famous for its fertile fields and productive farms. As the false dawn began in the east, the rain finally stopped, and Michael could discern the shadowy mass of the mainland of Palindor not far away to the north.

He looked around, but all he could see was the coastline and the breaking waves. Overhead, the last of the morning stars were visible through ragged gaps in the overcast. In the west, the moon was about to set. There were no other vessels in sight: the black ships had long ago disappeared into the night.

Every muscle in Michael's weary body ached, crying out for relief. The waves now were short and choppy; steep, pointed escarpments had replaced the rolling hills of yesterday evening.

Suddenly, Michael realized that he could hear waves crashing against cliffs.

The coast was very close. The cliffs stood high above him, and at their base was a line of deadly surf.

He had been driven into an inlet, and the sea here was gray and forbidding, and shadowed by the tall cliffs.

The wind swirled around inside the little cove, and pushed the coracle closer to the cliffs. The currents seemed to conspire with the wind. The coracle was almost impossible to control as it began to spin haphazardly in tiny whirlpools, then to slide up and down mountainous waves shaped by the rocks that lay not far below the surface. All the time the coracle moved closer to the deadly surf. The sea became confused, the incoming waves crashing into those that had reflected from the granite cliffs, so that they interfered with one another, here creating a mountain of water, there a deep valley between peaks. The coracle slid down into a valley, then rose high up a mountain before crashing down into the next valley.

Michael began to fear for his life. If the sea were to pound him against one of the rocks, either those at the base of the cliffs or those that lay in wait just under the surface of the seething sea, he would be instantly crushed and quickly drowned. But he barely had time to consider this prospect before the disaster he had dreaded actually happened.

A massive incoming wave moved shoreward to meet the reflection of a similarly gigantic wave that had passed under the coracle moments before. The coracle dipped into a valley and then shot upwards as the two waves met precisely underneath the flimsy boat. At that moment there was a strong gust of wind. Michael, who had been thinking about the rocks, did not have the coracle balanced correctly and the wind flipped the coracle over. Michael was plunged into the icy sea.

After a moment, his head broke the surface. A strong undertow pulled him first this way, then that. The coracle was floating upside down, just out of reach.

He tried desperately to swim to the boat. He touched it, but there was nowhere to gain a purchase. The wind caught the coracle and began to drive it away. Moments later, the coracle was lifted from one wavetop to another, and then was thrown forcibly into the cliff just as a wave thudded into the shore. It was instantly smashed.

Despair clutched at Michael, for he realized that he would be next. A wave broke near him, and along with its spume he was pushed closer to the cliff. His foot touched a hidden rock, then, as he turned to face another incoming wave, he received a mouthful of white foam. Choking, he was thrown against another rock, crushing muscles in his shoulder.

His hand brushed against something in the water beside him: the paddle from the coracle.

He fell across the paddle and kicked hard. The sea pushed him suddenly to the left, and then to the right, the currents near the cliff pulling him in all directions.

Another current took hold of him, and he found himself, still clinging to the paddle, being swept out the cove. The current took him around a point, and now not far away he could see a small beach of golden sand. On a fine day he could easily have reached the beach in a minute or two; but now — tired, cold, tossed in all directions by the whimsies of wind and wave, dragged down by his clothes, one shoulder in agony — he knew that the task was beyond him.

His head was buried by a wave. Choking, he tried to keep his head above water. Then he was picked up and thrown bodily against a rock, lurking just out of sight below the water level. His face crashed into the rock with sickening force, and as the next wave lifted him, he saw dimly that the water was now tinged with red. He was pounded against the rock a second, and then a third, time.

He closed his eyes.

He stopped struggling. The water seemed suddenly to become calmer, and now that he was no longer fighting it, it was oddly pleasant to let it have its way.

He was so tired, and so cold, and surely just a moment's sleep would do him good.

Michael was washed ashore close to the point where a stream crossed the beach and debouched into the sea. He lay unconscious amongst the seaweed and the flotsam of the storm. The coracle came ashore here also, ripped to shreds, its wooden seat smashed into driftwood, the wooden ribs of the boat snapped like matchsticks. But Michael did not see it.

The cove remained in shadow all day, the tall cliffs keeping the weak, cloud-covered sun at bay. The wind died down, and the gray sea receded with the tide, leaving behind a line of seaweed and driftwood. After a while, the tide began to come in again. Seagulls came and pecked at the flotsam, but they stayed away from the motionless human near the western end of the beach. It was late afternoon before anything other than the scavengers moved on the beach.

"Well, here he is, but where's your Hunter?"

"I don't know. I thought he'd be here by now. Maybe he's been delayed. He's coming, though. I'm sure of it."

"Well, that's all very well and good, but in the meantime, what are we supposed to do? We can't move this one; he's too big."

"Can't you treat him with something? Then we can wait for the Hunter to arrive."

"Treat him? What he needs is a bed and a warm bath. The ointments I brought aren't going to help him much. Probably make him worse instead of better. I thought you said he was going to be wounded."

"Well, he is, isn't he?"

"Of course not. Rocks did that. I expected knives or spears. Quite a different thing. What I brought would probably do no good at all. I wish you'd told me properly what to expect so I could have brought the right salves."

"Well, I couldn't help it. All I saw was the blood. Do what you can...."

"Listen. Is that a horse?"

Two old women stood next to Michael, one on either side of his outstretched form. One of them now knelt and extracted something from a bag that she carried over her shoulder. She looked at Michael as if evaluating him. He had a deep gash on his left temple, and another on the right cheek. His clothes were ripped to shreds and here and there she could see a bloody wound on his torso. She did something to his face with her hands and then began to spread an ointment over his forehead. His breathing relaxed and became deeper.

The old woman looked up as the sound of a horse moving down the goyle became clearer.

"He's coming, Iadron," she said.

The woman called Iadron had a worried frown on her face.

"What's the matter?" the other continued. "It's the horse you said would be here. You should be pleased. You got it right for once."

But Iadron just shook her head and then touched the other's shoulder and motioned for her to move away from the form at their feet.

"Quick, Harsforn! It'll be here in a moment and it mustn't see us."

"Wha...?" said Harsforn as Iadron pulled her towards the end of the beach.

"Quick!" Iadron repeated in an urgent whisper, "There's no time to argue. Just hide!"

The two old women slid behind a rock just as a horse stepped out of the goyle and on to the sand.

It was large and black, and in the saddle was a figure dressed in black armor. The knight, after pausing for a moment to survey the scene before him, slid out the saddle. He strode across the sand to Michael. For some time he looked down at the body; then he knelt down and suspiciously ran his gauntleted hand across Michael's temple. In his sleep, Michael shuddered. The knight straightened and looked around, slowly scanning the beach.

A squawking seagull flew overhead, then circled and landed on the rock behind which the two old women were hiding.

The knight turned to regard the human at his feet. Then he slowly drew his sword, considered the body, and laid the tip of the blade against the flesh of Michael's neck.

"If you don't come out, I'll kill him."

Harsforn looked at Iadron. Iadron shook her head. "He'd only kill us as well," she whispered. "It's best this way."

The knight waited, but the only reply came from the seagull, which gave a raucous cry, lifted itself into the air, and glided expertly out to sea.

The knight pressed lightly on his sword, just enough to break the skin of Michael's neck. Then the knight lifted the sword and resheathed it. After one more glance around the beach, he returned to his mount and climbed into the saddle. A few moments later, he disappeared back up the goyle.

For a long time, nothing moved.

At length, Iadron murmured, "I think he's gone," and with infinite slowness she peeked around the edge of the boulder. She stood up. "It's all right."

The two old women left the safety of the rock and returned to Michael, but Harsforn let out a cry of dismay, for the High King's neck was turning gray.

Gwain heard the sound of the horse from some distance away. He reined Peregrine to a halt and listened intently, reading the sounds. They matched the deductions he had made from the track beside the stream: a horse and its rider had come out of the forest and followed the stream toward the sea. Now they were returning up the valley.

It was a large horse, and carrying a heavy load. *Two people?* the Hunter wondered. Then another possibility occurred to him: *a Dark Knight.*

Gwain made a clicking sound with his tongue against the roof of his mouth, and Peregrine halted. Making no sound that could have been heard ten paces away, Gwain dismounted. He made a tiny sibilant sound, and as he led his horse off the path and behind the closest shrubs the horse was almost as silent as its master.

The bushes stood at almost head height, and the Hunter crouched behind them and motioned Peregrine to kneel at his side. They waited.

The other horse and its rider drew near and, without breaking stride, passed the bushes. Gwain peered after the retreating forms as they continued up the goyle.

He felt a tingle of fear and his muscles instantly tightened as if preparing for a fight.

He had never seen one before, of course; who now living in all Palindor had? But a Dark Knight could hardly be mistaken for any other creature. Was this the same Knight who had attacked his daughter's horse? And was it now returning to the cottage to kill his daughter? He made a motion commanding Peregrine not to move, and then silently slipped out from the bushes and began to follow the Dark Knight.

The Knight followed the stream for only a short distance before forking to the right up a small path that led steeply up the side of the valley. Gwain halted at the junction. The Dark Knight apparently had no intention of visiting the cottage. Gwain breathed a sigh of relief, then turned and retraced his steps to the place where Peregrine still lay concealed.

Remounting, he set off once more following the stream downhill. After a couple of minutes, the goyle opened out on to a small sandy beach with high cliffs on both sides.

Two old women were standing over an object at the line of flotsam that marked the highest point of the morning tide. He dismounted and led Peregrine towards the old women. They were both short, very wrinkled, and dressed in clothes whose best days had been long ago. Neither of them spoke as he approached.

It was only as he halted in front of the women that he realized that the large object beside which they were standing was a man, lying awkwardly on his side on the weed that was already beginning to reek. The man was either dead or very close to it, for blood was caked over several wounds, and his face was as pale as Gwynedd's. On the side of the man's neck was an evil-looking gray patch.

One of the women shot the other a look of triumph. To the Hunter she said, "So you arrived at last. Quick, now, he's too heavy for us to lift. Put him on your horse and bring him back to the cottage as quickly as you can."

The other woman shook her head. "I'm not sure it will do much good." Gwain was unsure whether she was speaking to him, to her companion, or merely to herself. "Time is moving along quickly, and it's been many a year since I've treated a cut from a dark blade."

"And if we stand here talking about it, it'll be another year before we get him home. Stand aside, Harsforn, and let the Hunter do his job."

Gwain, however, did not move, for he had recognized Harsforn's name. He looked at the woman curiously. "You can't be you Harsforn the healer," he said.

"If you say so."

"I mean... I meant to say... are you Harsforn the healer?"

"What of it if I am?"

"Nothing; it's nothing," he said, but as he turned to lift the comatose human, his heart was lighter than it had been for some time, for Harsforn the healer and her sister Iadron the seer featured in the story of his ancestor Aramis and the first visit of the High Queen to the Third Land. According to that story, Harsforn had healed the High Queen after she had accidentally cut herself on a dark blade — and if Harsforn could heal such a wound, then surely there was real hope for his daughter Gwynedd.

He bent down and swept away the seaweed that was draped across the man's unmoving form. And received another shock. For the man was wearing a belt buckled by a metal clasp in the center of which was a dark red stone. He turned to the women.

"Do you know who this is?" he asked.

"Of course we know. Just get on with it," snapped Harsforn.

And Gwain bent to his task, suddenly aware that he was involved in something great and important. Only direst need could have brought the High King Michael back to Palindor. First the Dark Knight, and now the High King. Something deep and mysterious was surely happening here.

But he had no time to ponder such matters, for the old women were already walking away in the direction of the goyle. He lifted Michael on to his horse and bound him securely.

"Follow us," called Iadron as they disappeared into the valley.

Gwain hastened after them, leading the burdened Peregrine. He soon caught up with Iadron, who was walking more slowly than her sister.

"You're quite correct," she said. "That is Harsforn. She once treated the High Queen Catherine, you know, when she was cut by a dark blade."

"Don't talk such rubbish," riposted Harsforn over her shoulder as she turned a corner ahead of them. "I never even saw the High Queen. All I did was give that gnome — what was his name? I don't remember. Doesn't matter anyway — all I did was give him a hæmony salve to treat the wound. Obviously it was a light wound, much lighter than this one, otherwise she would never have recovered."

"Then you must be Iadron, the seer," said Gwain.

"You've heard of me. That's nice."

"I am overjoyed to make your acquaintance, for my name is Gwain, and I am of the line of Aramis, who once also had dealings with the High Queen Catherine. The story of how you helped her is well known to me. And am I to assume that the cottage that lies ahead is yours?"

"Assume what you like. But yes, it is where we live."

"And you know that this person whom the Dark Knight wounded is the High King Michael?"

"The High King? Oh, yes, of course it's Michael. And I also know that you've brought a sick child to the cottage. At least, that's what you were supposed to do."

"I did. It's my daughter. She *is* very sick, but with ordinary wounds, not those caused by a dark blade. Do you think Harsforn can save her?"

"Oh, pooh! That is a simple matter. Old though we are, that won't be beyond her. Why, I wouldn't be surprised if I could do it myself."

There was a disbelieving cackle from around the corner ahead.

"Just how old are you, ma'am? If you don't mind me asking."

It was now Iadron's turn to cackle, and she called to Harsforn: "He asked how old I was, dear."

"Younger than I am, young man," called Harsforn.

"By but a few minutes," Iadron amplified. "We are twins. Not that you'd ever know it to look at us. Between you and me, I'm not sure that she's up to saving this one," she confided. "She's rather out of practice. When she first started as a healer, we saw many wounds caused by dark blades, but there's not a lot of call for that skill nowadays."

"Where was that? There are few records of dark blades in Palindor."

"Will you two hurry up and stop chattering?" called Harsforn, hurrying ahead even faster.

Iadron threw Gwain a wry smile, and then closed her mouth firmly and hastened after her sister.

When they reached the cottage Gwain removed King Michael from his horse and installed him on a makeshift straw bed in a corner of the same room as Gwynedd. As he carried the High King into the room, Gwain was relieved to see that his daughter was breathing deeper and more easily than at any time since he had found her.

Harsforn examined Gwynedd while Gwain was settling Michael. She said, "No danger there, though it will take a while to heal. Well done, Esterin," she added to the elf who hovered nearby.

Then the healer turned her attention to the High King, whose neck had darkened noticeably even in the short time since Gwain had first seen it.

"Well, since I'm not much use here, I'll go make some tea," said Iadron to no one in particular, and she left Esterin and Gwain to watch while her sister examined the comatose High King.

XI On Deck

Diana, even though she ran all the way from the place where Orrian had been killed, was the last of the shore party to return.

"Quick! Take me aboard. I must speak to the captain," she panted to the sailor standing beside the waiting dinghy.

A few minutes later, she was in the captain's cabin aboard the *Evening Passage*, explaining what had happened.

"It was completely unprovoked, Captain Malliss. Orrian was just going to ask her if there was a village nearby, but the woman — no, she wasn't even a woman really, she was no more than a child — she pulled a knife from somewhere and simply threw herself on him. He never stood a chance; his neck was slashed before he even realized what was happening. The child turned to run away; I don't think she had realized that there were two of us, and I managed to stab her in the back. My dagger stuck, but she seemed hardly to notice. She pushed her way through the bushes and that was the last I saw of her."

"You examined Orrian? He was really dead?"

"Oh, captain, if you'd been there you'd have known for yourself there wasn't any doubt. It was horrible."

At the gruesome memory, Diana had to close her eyes; she swallowed hard to stop herself from retching.

Captain Malliss nodded grimly. "I am sorry to say that I am not completely surprised. Orrian is the third of our crew to have been lost to the barbarians. You are the last to return, so I am at least grateful to know that there will be no others. Come, Diana, I must speak to my men."

Diana followed the captain on to the deck.

"You, sailor; hail the *Twilight Sea* and the *Dark Sky* and tell their crew that I wish to see them all gathered on deck here in half an hour. And inform Orrian's brother Odrian that his twin is dead and that he has been promoted from first mate of the *Twilight Sea* to first mate on my own ship. Now, Diana, if you will excuse me, I have much to think about."

Half an hour later the combined crews of the three ships were gathered in small groups on the deck of the *Evening Passage* discussing the day's events in subdued voices. There was general agreement that a response was called for. Diana discovered from one of the sailors that all three of the deaths had been from unprovoked attacks similar to the one that had killed Orrian. She was approached by a sailor from the *Twilight Sea* who introduced himself as Orrian's twin brother, Odrian. Diana expressed her sympathy.

Odrian replied grimly, "If I know Captain Malliss, the people of this land will soon learn to mend their ways. When she sets her mind to revenge, things can get very unpleasant for those who have wronged her."

An expectant hush suddenly fell on the gathering, for the captain had stepped on deck from the fo'c's'le. She looked grim as she stood by the gunwale and turned to face the sailors. In her hand was a furled sheet of paper.

The captain began to address them.

"The inhabitants of this land are obviously aggressive, and they need to be taught a lesson."

A loud chorus of agreement came from the sailors.

The captain unfurled the sheet she had been holding.

"Here is a rough map that I made on my first expedition to Palindor." She held the map up so that all could see it.

"We are roughly here," the captain continued, stabbing at a point off the southern coast. "And the capital of Palindor, a small, unfortified town called Carn Toldwyn, is here."

She stabbed midway along the western shore.

She paused. The captain's eyes roamed over her crew. Every sailor made an effort to look more warlike than the others. Diana discovered that she was frowning as belligerently as the rest of them.

In a loud, measured voice that carried far across the water, Captain Malliss said: "I propose that we sail to Carn Toldwyn and take it by force."

The shouts of acclamation that greeted this plan were deafening.

XII Under the Great Sea

Glandryth and Catherine approached the cottage quietly. Their elation at the sight of the wisps of smoke rising from the chimney was quickly tempered as Catherine tapped Glandryth on the shoulder and pointed to the wall where the coracle had been. The wall was still bare.

"Perhaps it's not Michael," Catherine whispered.

Glandryth frowned, then hurried forward across the grass to the front door. He opened the door and peered inside. Suddenly, he ran forward and disappeared into the cottage. Catherine followed at a more circumspect pace; she stood in the doorway for a moment, then let out a cry of delight and followed Glandryth inside. Rushing across the room, she hugged the large mouse-like creature with golden fur who had just raised himself from the rocking chair.

The dablik tried to extricate himself and hide his embarrassment at the boisterousness of Catherine's greeting. But Catherine neither noticed nor cared, and simply hugged him all the tighter.

"Dablik!" she exclaimed, "it's so good to see you again. You haven't changed a bit."

"It's been a long time," said the dablik, "but indeed it is good to see you again, Your Majesty." He paused. "But where are the others? The High Lord distinctly said that there would be three of you."

"Oh, dablik! There are. Or rather, there were. Michael and his daughter Diana were with me. Oh, how shall I put this?" Catherine gathered her thoughts before continuing.

"Diana, who is rather headstrong, went off in a huff last night. Michael said that he saw her being rowed out to some ships that were anchored on the other side of the island. We think that sometime in the middle of the night Michael took Glandryth's coracle and went to join her. When we got up this morning there was no trace of any ships, or of the coracle, or of Diana or Michael. We've scoured the island looking for them. They've all gone."

The dablik frowned and shook his head. "This is not good, not good at all."

"Dablik, do tell us what's going on. Glandryth said that you've seen the High Lord. Where is He? Why are we here? The last two times I've come to Palindor, it was because the Third Land was in great danger. Is it in danger again? And why haven't I seen the High Lord myself?"

The dablik wearily regained the rocking chair and offered the other to the High Queen. She declined the offer (the chair would have been uncomfortably small) and instead sat expectantly on the floor.

"Would you make us some tea, friend Glandryth?" asked the dablik. "Then I'll tell you both what I know. Which, I am afraid, is not very much."

Glandryth hurried to the kitchen and returned with a bag of blackberry leaves. In a short while the soothing aroma of blackberry tea filled the small cottage.

Catherine waited expectantly for the dablik to begin, but he just rocked thoughtfully and refused to be drawn until the tea was poured into three stout mugs and he had taken his first sips of the scalding liquid.

"It's different this time," he eventually began. "The High Lord appeared to me one day as I rounded a tunnel in eastern Palindor, not far from the place where I first met you, Your Majesty. He gave me two messages, only one of which concerns you." There was, after all, no reason to mention the cuzzleberries. "I was to come here and tell my friend Glandryth to expect you along with two others. You were to arrive on the second full moon after the autumnal equinox, which was yesterday. He told me to make sure that you remained here until I returned.

"I intended to be here yesterday, to greet you when you arrived, but I was unavoidably detained elsewhere." The dablik hurried on, hoping that no one would ask the reason for his tardiness, for he felt more than a little guilty that he had been stuffing himself on cuzzleberries instead of attending to the High Lord's business. "So here I am, a day late, and two of you already missing. I wish He'd give me a bit more of a clue about what we're supposed to do now."

"It's His way though, isn't it?" offered Glandryth. "You know: to start you off and then let you get on with it. Sort of like a story, really. It's only when you get to the end that you realize how much of a hand He had in everything. At the time, you sort of feel swept along and as if everything is totally out of control. You notice all your own mistakes and not the much larger pattern that He is weaving.

"The trick — if trick is the right word, which I'm not exactly certain it is — is to keep on trusting Him and asking Him for guidance. My experience is that if you do those two things, you won't go far wrong. It seems to me that if He didn't leave strict instructions, then that means you should just think of something reasonably sensible to do, and then get on with it. At least," he concluded, realizing that he was sounding rather preachy, "that's my advice."

"What do you mean: '*you* should just think of something sensible to do?' What about you, Glandryth? You're involved as well," said the dablik.

"Me? Oh, no; I'm not involved at all. I've lived on this island for a good long time now and I'm just about settled in. I'm perfectly happy just to continue the way I am, thank you very much. No adventures for me, I don't think. No, you are the adventuresome ones. If you want my advice, you'll leave here and get across to the mainland and see what's happening there. My guess is that once you arrive you'll soon discover exactly what the High Lord has in mind for you."

114

"But how could we get to the mainland?" asked Catherine. "Come to that, how did...? Oh, I see. There are tunnels even out here, aren't there?"

"Yes, there are," affirmed the dablik. "This is where they end, at least in this direction. The mainland is only a day or so away. We could be in Beleron this time tomorrow, and at the quoit or in Carn Toldwyn the day after that."

Catherine nodded. "So where have you just come from? Why weren't you here when I arrived?" She very nearly added: "Because then all three of us could have been met and taken to Palindor as Olvensar no doubt intended."

The dablik looked suddenly forlorn. "I see that there is no escaping. I suppose I have an admission to make. I was gorging myself on berries on the slopes of Penmichael Brea. It's my own fault I'm late. I'm sorry."

Catherine hurried to move the conversation forward, for she did not like to see the normally cheerful dablik look glum. "Well, never mind that now. What's done is done. Come on, old friend. I think Glandryth's suggestion is an excellent one, and there's no time like the present. If Glandryth will permit us to take our leave, with thanks for his hospitality, let's go now and make our way to the mainland."

She downed the last of her blackberry tea.

"Wait a minute," said Glandryth, rising from the other rocking chair, in which he had seated himself to drink his tea, "and I'll put some food and water in a pack for you. You won't find much food while you're travelling under the sea. And I know how the dablik always underestimates how long others take to move around in those tunnels of his. If I remember rightly, the journey from the mainland took me a good half a day longer than he predicted."

He disappeared into the kitchen while the dablik meditatively finished his tea at a more leisurely pace.

"What happened after Michael and I were last here?" asked Catherine. "I asked Glandryth, but he said that he takes no interest in events beyond the the island."

"Nothing much," said the dablik. "Shortly after King Michael left Pirren Glanwyn to invade Palindor there was a rebellion and the cousin of the old king was crowned in his place. There has been peace among the Three Lands ever since. Olvensar almost never appears any more, and gradually He seems to be being forgotten, or at least relegated to some poorly defined and lesser rôle. The whole situation is not a lot better than it was when you first came here.

"There haven't been any actual edicts against Him, of course, but He just seems to have become a part of history somehow. A lot of the youngsters seem to be completely ignorant about the High Lord, regarding Him as a sort of mythical being who was around at the time of the founding of the Third Land, along with Toldwyn and Sam Ironhand and the others. They seem to think of Olvensar as a sort of magical servant of Toldwyn's. Just about as wrong as you can be, of course, but that's often the way of history, isn't it?"

"Were you there?" asked Catherine. "At the beginning, I mean. When Palindor separated from Reglandor?"

"Beginning? Why, may the High Lord bless you. That wasn't the beginning. There was a lot before that."

"All right you two," interrupted Glandryth. "Here's a pack for Catherine. You'll just have to fend for yourself, my friend," Glandryth added with a smile, "unless, that is, the High Queen is willing to share with you."

He thrust forward a finely spun pack that glistened in a multitude of colors in the firelight. Catherine hefted it on her back and it instantly adjusted itself to the contours of her body. It was without doubt the most comfortable pack she had ever worn.

"Now, be off with the two of you. Go with my blessing and, I pray, that of the High Lord also. And you, my friend, be sure to return and tell me all about your adventures."

The dablik smiled. "I'll do my best, Glandryth, as always."

They did not embrace, but Catherine could not mistake the look that was in their eyes as they took their leave of one another.

Catherine and the dablik left the cottage, and as they began to climb the side of the dell the High Queen said to her companion, "You really love him, don't you?"

"Glandryth? Of course. He's a good friend. The best. You mustn't misread his reluctance to be involved, you know. He may be small, but he was once a great warrior. He thinks a lot.

Where most creatures want to rush in and fight, or run away, or just *do* something, Glandryth sits and thinks and then eventually comes up with the perfect plan for the situation. He's put many a warrior to shame in his time."

The two looked back at the cottage as they reached the lip of the dell. Glandryth was standing at the doorway. They returned his wave. Then they turned and disappeared into the wood.

The entrance to the tunnels was near the northernmost part of the island, in the shadow of a tall, lichen-covered boulder. The dablik plunged into the shadows without a moment's hesitation, but Catherine paused and took several deep breaths.

Until this moment, the thought of crossing under the wide channel that separated the Sunset Islands from the mainland had engendered no particular fear, but now that the moment had arrived she was gripped by an icy dread.

The memory of her last journey in the tunnels under the Mountains of Mourn, when she had become lost and captured by goblins, irrationally gripped her.

She took a long look around, suddenly aware of the brush of the salt-laden breeze against her cheek, the gray-blue limpidity of the sea, the dull autumnal sky in which hung a weak midmorning sun. She suddenly thought of the High Lord and whispered an urgent prayer: "Give me the strength to do this, Olvensar." Then she forced herself to turn away from the breeze and the sea and the sky and to step into the shadowy cave into which the dablik had plunged.

The tunnel angled steeply downward. The air was still and heavy, and she noticed patches of dark green growth on the walls. She hurried forward. The tunnel soon levelled off; she turned a corner and, up ahead, she could dimly make out the form of the dablik waiting for her to catch up.

Suddenly her heart beat faster, and an attack of claustrophobia threatened to overwhelm her. She closed her eyes, and reminded herself that Olvensar had once told her that he would be with her always.

She told herself that there was nothing to worry about: the dablik would be with her all the way to the mainland, so it was impossible for her to get lost or to be captured by goblins this time. She swallowed, opened her eyes, and began to walk forward.

The tunnels under the sea were quite different from those under the mountains. These tunnels were straighter and taller, and branched infrequently. As the pair left Glandryth's island behind, Catherine felt her equanimity returning.

The air in the tunnel smelt strongly of brine. Underlying the briny odor was a less agreeable hint of something rotten, as if seaweed was decaying not far away. Trickles of water came through invisible cracks in the roof and walls, and ran down the sides of the tunnel to join a small rivulet that ran along its floor. Catherine's shoes quickly became sodden and began to chafe, so she removed them and hung them around her neck. The walls now were almost completely covered with a slimy green growth, half seaweed, half moss.

The dablik padded onward a short distance ahead, stopping frequently to check that Catherine — slowed by being barefoot — was following. They stopped once for food. It was impossible for Catherine to find a comfortable position in which to eat. She had to crouch in the tunnel rather than sit, for the only place to sit was in the trickle that ran down the center of the tunnel floor. The flow of the water told her that they were still going downward, although not by much. After eating, Catherine reshouldered her pack and the pair set off once more.

Catherine lost all track of time. The day wore on monotonously, nothing much changing, except that her feet became raw and she began to long for a bowl of hot water in which to soak them.

At length they came to a point where the tunnel widened slightly, just enough for her to be able to sit down and lean against the wall without being forced to sit in the cold trickle of water. They halted. Catherine was exhausted, although the dablik looked as fresh as ever.

She asked: "How much farther? I'm not sure how much more of this I can take today."

"We're about a third of the way there. If we put in a full day tomorrow, we'll be on the surface early the morning of the day after. But you're right, you look all in. Get some rest. If I'm not here when you wake up, just give a call and wait for me. I won't be far away."

Catherine was too tired to argue. As long as she had been walking, it had been easy to keep putting one foot in front of the other; but now that she had stopped, it was impossible to keep her eyes open. In moments, she had lain down on the hard rock, using her pack for a pillow, and was fast asleep.

When she awoke, she panicked momentarily before remembering where she was. She was just about to shout for the dablik, who was probably exploring one of the occasional side tunnels, when he padded silently into view and greeted her cheerily: "Good morning. Ready to go?"

They fell into the same pattern as the day before: the dablik running on ahead, then pausing for Catherine to catch up.

They came to a place where the tunnel opened out into a large chamber, the bottom of which was hidden by a pool that almost deserved to be called a lake. There were many tunnels opening on to the chamber, and all except one angled up and away from the chamber, so that they filled the lake with a dozen or more dribbles of water. One tunnel angled downward, and water from the pool trickled away down it.

The air here was pungent, and the walls of the cavern were covered in greenish brown weeds that glowed eerily.

They stood at the edge of the pool. "We're about half way," said the dablik. "You see over there?" He pointed across the pool to the opposite shore, perhaps a dozen strides away, where the largest of the other tunnels angled upward, "That's where we're headed. From here it's all uphill to the mainland."

It struck Catherine that they must be far below the sea, and the thought triggered a small shiver of fright. The dablik seemed not to notice. He stepped out into the pool.

"Don't worry. It's not very deep. You can paddle across."

Catherine followed. At its deepest point, the water barely came over her knees, and she soon reached the other side. They continued on their way.

By the time that they stopped for the night, Catherine was exhausted. Her joints ached and her feet were worn to an almost bloody rawness.

The place where they had halted was a small chamber a few paces down a small side tunnel. The chamber was just large enough to accommodate the two of them. Catherine stretched out on the ground using the pack as a pillow and fell asleep even more quickly than the night before.

The dablik looked down at Catherine as she slept, and felt a surge of pity for the High Queen. It occurred to him that she would appreciate a gift of fresh berries when she woke. He padded out of the chamber and turned towards the mainland.

After a while, he reached a place where the dribbles down the walls of the tunnel ceased, and the soft green mossy weed grew no more. He was making good time. It would not be long now before he was on the surface, for there was a small tunnel not far ahead that led steeply up to a rocky outcrop not far from the southern coast of Beleron.

He turned a corner and almost fell over in amazement.

The dablik knew every tunnel under the entire land of Palindor. This was not a boast, it was simply a fact. If he had been placed blindfolded in a tunnel selected at random, and if the blindfold were then removed, the dablik, after a few moments to look around and sniff the air, would have been able to tell you exactly where he was.

Most of the underground labyrinth never changed. There were but few places in which new tunnels were being dug. In the east, under the Mountains of Mourn, goblins still dug the occasional new tunnel, although their workmanship was poor and generally they preferred to mine the older levels that had already been excavated; away in the northwest between Penmichael Brea and the coast there was a colony of kobolds whose shallow tunnels were frequently extended but which did not reach down to the deep rock that required extensive quarrying skills; finally, and deepest of all, far under the sea off the coast of Palindor lived a colony of goblins whom he had discovered many centuries ago, but whom he had never again had cause to visit. In these few places new tunnels were being dug, but everywhere else the tunnels remained the same from century to century. And every one of those tunnels was known to the dablik.

And so for a moment he was stupefied when he turned a corner under the Beleron coast and saw a new tunnel.

It was new, but it was not fresh. In fact, it looked no different from any other ancient tunnel. He approached it cautiously and ran his paws over the edges of the entrance. The inspection confirmed his suspicion: the tunnel was old, just as old as the one through which he had been hurrying. He stepped back, tilted his head to one side, and pondered this development.

The tunnel gave every appearance of having been here for a very long time indeed. But if that were so, then how had he never seen it before? There could be only one answer: somehow, the entrance had been rendered invisible. And that smacked of something distinctly out of the ordinary. He pondered the dilemma before him: should he investigate the tunnel, or should he ignore it, at least for now, and carry on with his plan of getting fresh fruit for Catherine?

It was a difficult decision. His natural curiosity battled with the need for haste, for it would not do to be exploring strange and mysterious tunnels under Beleron when Catherine awoke. He decided on a compromise. He would ignore the tunnel for now, but if it were still here when he returned from collecting berries, and if he thought there was time, he would investigate a little way up the tunnel.

He turned away and hurried off at full speed towards the surface.

The tunnel was still there when he returned a couple of hours later with a two large pawfuls of berries wrapped in a tasty leaf. He had been half hoping that the mysterious tunnel would have disappeared in the interim, but there it still was. He looked at it for a few moments, then placed the berries at the tunnel entrance and nervously (for he had a feeling that he really should not have left Catherine for so long) he began to pad along the new tunnel.

The tunnel seemed little different from any other, except that no side tunnels branched off it, and it was much straighter than most. Instead of winding its way through the softest rock, it simply plunged forward in an almost-straight line.

Its course was northeastward, and it climbed slowly with a slight incline. If it held to its course, it would surface somewhere on Machrenmoor.

The dablik began to hurry even faster. It was beginning to get late. He had not meant to leave Catherine for so long, but now that he had begun this journey, he was reluctant to leave it. But the tunnel continued onward, its course essentially unchanged, and he was still deep underground when he decided that he simply had to turn around. Catherine would be waking soon, and she would be worried if he was not close by. The dablik was already afraid that even if he ran all the way back at full speed, he would not be back before she woke.

So, sniffing the dry air of the tunnel one last time and deciding that there was a distinctly musty odor that in his haste he had not noticed before, the dablik turned and rushed back the way he had come.

He ran the whole way back to Catherine.

As he approached the chamber where he had left her, he paused to listen for the sound of worried cries, but was comforted to hear only silence. She must still be asleep.

He halted at the entrance of her chamber, ready with apologies should they be necessary.

He looked inside.

His mouth fell open and he dropped the berries. For where he had left Catherine sleeping peacefully there was now only her pack, battered and opened, its contents strewn around the floor of the chamber.

Of the High Queen herself there was no sign.

XIII Invasion

Myfanwy looked out the window of the small thatched cottage on the southern outskirts of Carn Toldwyn. She examined the sky for a considerable length of time before announcing her decision to the two youngsters at her side.

"Yes, I suppose it will be all right."

Instantly the peace of the cottage was shattered by whoops of joy from Mafik and Maflen. Mellow, her husband, contributed only a silent smile.

Mellow, Myfanwy, Mafik and Maflen enjoyed picnics, and they made a point at least once each week, whenever the weather was good enough, of travelling some distance from Carn Toldwyn to some place where they could be alone and share a time of family togetherness.

"Where shall we go?" Myfanwy asked her husband.

Mellow considered the question just as if it it were an issue that had been brought before the Ruling Council, of which he had long ago been elected leader. "Mellow by name, mellow by nature," creatures said of him, and the fact was no less true for its frequent repetition.

It was late in the year; they shouldn't go too far in case the weather changed.

"How about Perendeth?" he suggested. "It's been a while since we've been up there, and I dare say the place will be deserted today."

The decision was applauded by the youngsters. Perendeth was a favorite, and they had not picnicked there since spring.

Myfanwy turned away from the window and tried to calm the excited youngsters. "Now, children, breakfast first, then I'll need your help packing the things," she said in a vain attempt to try to install some order into the household.

At last, and not without having to threaten to change her mind about allowing the picnic, breakfast was over, and the three of them repaired to the kitchen to fill the hamper.

"I'll get out of the way," said Mellow, and he selected a pipe, put on an overcoat, and went out into the chill morning air.

There was a touch of frost on the ground where it was shadowed. Mellow lit the pipe — a gnomish habit that he had acquired somehow long ago — and began to saunter along the paths that meandered through the neighboring cottages, exchanging greetings and sharing smalltalk with his friends and neighbors.

When he returned, the children were being chivvied into their overcoats, and panniers of food were already hanging at the side of the family's donkey.

"All set then?" he asked.

"Yes!" the children cried.

"Where are we going again?"

He peered around vaguely, as if he were an aged dwarf whose memory was failing.

"Perendeth," the children screamed.

"Perendeth? Again?" He scowled. "Weren't we just up there this spring?"

"That we were," Myfanwy affirmed.

"How about somewhere different, like Toldwyn's Quoit?"

"Perendeth!" shouted Mafik, unsure whether his father were seriously suggesting that they picnic in such a bleak and forbidding place.

"Daddy!" said Maflen, more sure that his father must be joking.

Mellow laughed and sighed heavily in mock defeat.

"All right, then, have it your own way. Perendeth it is. But I hope you don't expect me to go running around in those eerie old tunnels."

The children giggled at the thought of their staid old father running anywhere. Exchanging a grin with his wife, Mellow took the donkey's bridle and the family set out toward Perendeth.

They arrived about an hour later, the children laughing and running on ahead and playing games of catch, the parents sedately leading the donkey. The family crossed the lush green grass to the place where the ancient barrows stood.

The wind blew gently from the north, and Mellow and his wife found a suitable place to lay out the picnic in the lee of one of the barrows. They had a good view of the lowlands of Beleron and the southern portion of the Great Sea, which stretched into the distance. A hazy patch of greenish brown — the Sunset Islands — smudged the western horizon. Laughing, the children disappeared into the tunnels underneath the barrows.

After a while, they reappeared, and sat still just long enough for lunch before they hurried off again towards the old tunnels. Mellow leaned against the soft grassy incline of a barrow and closed his eyes for, as he put it, "just a moment of relaxation."

He was woken by an insistent tapping on his elbow.

"Huh? What?" he said grumpily. It had been a very pleasant nap, but much too short.

"Look, Mellow," said Myfanwy.

He followed the direction of her pointing finger. Then he bolted upright and rubbed his eyes.

Edging northeastwards along the northern coast of Beleron were two ships in full sail. They were still some way away, but the sight filled him with dread. It was obvious that the ships were making for the twin mouths of the Findell and the Pennyfarthing, which lay not far to the south of Carn Toldwyn and were hidden from view by a low hill.

Mellow jumped to his feet and ran to the edge of the cliff, where he watched the ships for several minutes. Never had he seen such a thing. Palindor boasted few boats, none of them used in this part of the Third Land, and all were small and suitable only for inshore fishing. The vessels that were now moving ominously along the Beleron coast were magnificent seagoing craft capable of travelling great distances. They could never have been built in Palindor.

As if that were not bad enough, their coloring was even more frightening. If such craft ever were to be built in Palindor, they would be gaily painted, with bright reds and yellows and blues and greens, and the sails would either match the parti-colored hulls or be the brightest white. But these ships looked distinctly menacing as they edged closer. The hulls and even the sails were dark. Against the blue of the sea, they looked black.

Flags fluttered at the aft masthead of each craft. They were too far away to be clearly visible, but one thing was obvious: they, too, looked evilly dark. These, the boats seemed to be saying, were no pleasure craft — they were weapons of war.

The ships did not deviate from their courses. At this rate, it would not be long before they were at the mouths of the rivers.

"Get the children and go back to Carn Toldwyn as quickly as you can. I'll see you later," Mellow said to Myfanwy, who had come to stand at his side.

"Where are you going?"

"Those ships look like they are heading for the mouth of the Findell. If they are, I want the Ruling Council to be there when they arrive."

"Do you know what they are, then? They certainly don't look very friendly."

"Trouble, that's what they are," Mellow replied grimly, and after a last lingering look at the encroaching vessels, he turned and strode quickly away downhill in the direction of the town.

Aboard the *Evening Passage* it was a glorious day. All trace of the storm of two nights before had disappeared. The sea had calmed and was now merely a gently undulating swell passing lazily underneath the hull; the ship rocked gently from side to side with a motion that was more comforting than threatening.

The *Evening Passage* and the *Twilight Sea* had spent most of yesterday tacking eastward in tandem along the southern coast of Beleron, anchoring for the night not far from the westernmost point. Early this morning they had rounded the point and were now, as the day turned into afternoon, sailing on a close reach along the northern coast of the peninsula, to the place where the captain's map showed a river debouching into the sea.

The black flags with maroon lists flew crisply from the aft masts, pointing south towards the gently rolling farmland of the Beleron peninsula. Diana was on the deck of the *Evening Passage*, leaning against the starboard railing, watching the low-lying farmland glide past.

The only sounds were the wind whistling through the rigging and the breaking of the waves against the ship's bow. The sun shone down on the slowly changing pastoral scene before her. Here and there among the fields, Diana could see cottages. Occasionally, she could distinguish individual farmers as they worked in the fields, bringing in the last of the harvest.

If Diana saw any tension between the idyllic scene passing before her and the deadly attack by the armed girl in the woods, it did not show in her face. She felt relaxed and as peaceful as the countryside at which she was looking.

"Enjoying the view?"

Diana turned and saw Captain Malliss approaching, matching her slow gait to the gentle roll of the ship. The captain joined Diana at the rail.

"It doesn't look like they'll be much trouble," said Diana.

"No. Peaceful-looking lot, aren't they? Still, they gave us a hard enough time in the woods. But I dare say that once they find themselves caught between us and the knights they'll see the foolishness of their ways soon enough."

The captain's plan was simple. The sailors would take the *Evening Passage* and the *Twilight Sea* around the coast, anchor near the mouth of the river that split the western coast in two, then land and march northward toward the town that was the capital of this place. The knights from the *Dark Sky*, meanwhile, would converge on the same point from the east after riding through the forest. Later today when the sailors and the knights converged on the town, it would be without warning.

So far, everything was going according to plan, and by late afternoon they should be in Carn Toldwyn. Diana looked at the position of the sun in the sky, then at the speed at which the land was moving past, and then, finally, at the low-lying point that marked their destination.

"Wondering if we'll make it today?" asked the captain.

Diana nodded.

"Don't worry; we will. Are you going to join us in our triumphant march through the town?"

"If you'll let me."

"My dear, it would be an honor. But you had better get dressed for it. I've left a new knife to replace the old one on your bed. A word of warning: don't touch it; if your skin is once cut by such a blade, you will almost certainly die. It is a lethal weapon. Remember that when you draw it."

"Is it poisoned?" asked Diana, an odd mixture of horror and glee on her face.

"You could say that," the captain replied. Without elaborating, she moved away to talk to Odrian, who was at the helm.

Diana waited for a few minutes, watching the land slide past. She glanced forward and noticed that now the mouth of the river was quite close. Many of the sailors on deck were attired in their dark mail suits, preparing for the march into town. Time to get dressed. She left the railing and hurried to her cabin to prepare for the invasion.

She saw the knife immediately. It lay, small but dangerous-looking, in the center of the bed. Gingerly, she lifted the weapon and looked at it with curiosity.

The blade did not shine like ordinary metal. Instead it was the blackest black that she had ever seen, darker than the darkest coal. It was impossible to see the contours of the knife, for there was no reflected light to give any clues where they might be. She put her left hand forward to run her thumb along the blade's edge, then stopped, remembering the captain's warning. She withdrew her hand hurriedly. It would be stupid to be poisoned by her own weapon. Carefully, she replaced the blade on the bed and opened the wardrobe.

When she returned to the deck a short while later, she saw that the rest of the crew were now changed and had congregated near the center of the deck. She wondered if the others' weapons were like her own, or if they were ordinary metal blades.

But she had little time for speculation, for, within moments, the order was given to lower the sails and Diana realized that they had reached their destination.

On the south side of the river the land rose to form a forbidding treeless moor. She could just make out some sort of a monument on the highest point, but it was too far away to make out any details.

There was a burst of activity all around as the sails were lowered and the anchors dropped. From the *Twilight Sea* came similar sounds. Within a short time, the two boats were anchored side by side not far from the shore, and the dinghies were in the water and filling with armor-clad men ready for the first trip ashore.

On the shore a crowd was beginning to congregate. The arrival of the ships had obviously not gone unnoticed, and the crowd that had gathered to watch the disembarkation was growing by the minute.

The crew of the *Evening Passage* sorted itself into three groups, corresponding to the three trips that the dinghy would have to make until almost all the crew, except for a skeleton lookout, would be ashore. Diana and the captain — who had strode on deck moments after Diana clad in a mail suit similar to the others — would be on the final trip.

Diana watched as the first dinghy rowed ashore and the crew disembarked on the southern bank of the river, opposite the place where the crowd had gathered on the northern shore.

The dinghy returned and took the second group of passengers ashore. Then it came back and took the final group, including Diana and the captain.

The crews of the two ships gathered together on the southern shore. There were twenty three of them. As yet, there was no sign of the knights, but the captain seemed unperturbed that they had not yet appeared.

The river was quite wide, and Diana now observed that this place was actually both the confluence of two rivers — a larger one to the south, a smaller to the north — and also their combined mouths. There was a path near the place where the crews had gathered, and the path led directly to the only visible means of crossing the rivers: a narrow bridge that had obviously been constructed to permit the farmers of the southwestern peninsula to transport their wares northward to the town that, according to the captain's map, lay a short distance to the north, behind the low hills that hugged the northern bank.

Diana looked at the crowd gathered on the northern shore. Here and there she saw the flash of a weapon. She estimated that more than a hundred were gathered on the opposite shore. Twenty three against more than a hundred. Did Captain Malliss really know what she was doing?

"You will remain here," said the captain, addressing the mail-clad crew. "You and you will accompany me," she continued, nodding first at Odrian and then, much to her surprise, at Diana herself.

Diana looked around, sure that what she had taken as a nod in her direction had been intended for someone else. But there was no one standing nearby.

"Yes, you, Diana. Are you not related to those who called themselves High Monarchs of this place?"

Diana had forgotten that. It seemed so long ago now, but it could not have been more than... but there was no time to finish the thought, for the captain continued imperiously, "Come on, woman," then began walking towards the bridge, with Odrian scurrying at her heels to keep up.

Diana followed.

The captain stepped on to the bridge. At the halfway point she stopped and put out her hand so that neither Odrian nor Diana could pass. The three stood, waiting and watching the crowd in front of them.

After some time, a group of five detached themselves from the crowd and made their way towards the bridge. More people were joining the crowd all the time, and Diana estimated that there were at least a hundred and fifty of them now. But what a motley group they were compared to the militaristic and dangerous-looking formation that stood on the southern shore.

These people — if "people" was the right word — were of all shapes and sizes. A few of them were tall; none, though, quite as tall as the captain. But many were short, stunted people wearing strange caps and tunics. Some of the men sported full white beards; others, the more belligerent-looking ones, some of whom sported axes stuck in their belts, had dark hair and heavy eyebrows from under which they seemed to be glowering. Although they looked undisciplined, they also looked like they would be a formidable rabble in a fight. It was not a happy thought.

The five who now made their way across the bridge (with difficulty, for no more than two could walk abreast) were themselves a motley collection.

The one in front — the others followed in two groups of two — was of the short, dark-haired belligerent type, although Diana was quick to notice that this specimen did not appear to be armed. The two immediately behind him were more normal in appearance, and were slightly taller and considerably older than Diana. Of the pair bringing up the rear, one was a white-haired man with a full beard and a long red cap that, Diana thought, made him look perfectly ridiculous, and the last was a very small, lithe, jumpy sort of a creature who seemed to bounce backward and forward, taking several steps to every one of the others' as if he (or she, it was impossible to tell which) was incapable of proceeding at a normal pace. None of the group appeared to be armed.

This strange group came to a halt, the closest of them, the stumpy, dark-haired one, barely an arm's length in front of the captain.

Captain Malliss was the first to speak.

"You are?" she asked imperiously.

The dark-haired one gave a grave bow and then stood as straight as he seemed able — which was a pointless exercise, partly because he seemed to be permanently stooped and partly because even if he had been capable of standing straight he would not have reached much higher than the captain's waist.

"My name is Mellow, dwarf of Carn Toldwyn. On behalf of the Ruling Council and the inhabitants of Carn Toldwyn and Palindor, I greet you and welcome you in peace."

A short bark that might have been either amusement or exasperation escaped the captain's lips, while Diana pondered the fact that "dwarf" was exactly the right description for the strange, stocky man.

"I am Captain Malliss, and you will lead me to your castle," the captain said peremptorily.

For a moment, the other said nothing. Then a twisted scowl came to his face. "I'm sorry," he said, "I don't understand."

"Dwarf Mellow, it is perfectly simple. We are here to invade your land and to avenge our fallen comrades. Now, get out of the way, or I will give orders to have you removed by force."

The dwarf looked behind him and saw that the other members of the Ruling Council were as nonplussed as he.

Mellow said, "I'm sorry; I'm afraid there must have been some mistake. To what fallen comrades do...."

The captain interrupted him. "Odrian; teach him a lesson."

The first mate drew his dagger. Diana noticed with a tinge of surprise that the blade glistened like ordinary metal in the lowering sun; she had more than half expected that, like the blade she had been given, it would be made of the dark substance that seemed to swallow light.

Mellow took a step backward. Odrian stepped wordlessly forward and with a sudden motion thrust the dagger forward and into the dwarf's body. Mellow looked down in amazement at the red stain that appeared on his breeches. Odrian withdrew the blade and stepped back, taking his position just behind the captain.

Mellow clutched at his chest and suddenly looked faint, an expression of horrified disbelief on his face. The two people who stood directly behind him moved forward and helped him to stand upright. Then they began to lead him, tottering, back across the bridge. Captain Malliss followed close behind, with Odrian behind her. After a moment's hesitation, Diana followed. Behind her, the first crewmember stepped on to the bridge and began to cross.

As quickly as that, it was all over.

The crowd on the northern shore drew back to let the members of the Ruling Council tend Mellow.

"Someone with healing skills! Quickly!" the jumpy one called out, and a wizened, gray-haired woman with a bag over her shoulder tottered out of the crowd to assist Mellow, who was now white-faced and groaning.

The captain and her entourage swept past the crowd to the accompaniment of a subdued hissing and began to walk along the track towards Carn Toldwyn.

A few minutes later they entered the town. They walked through the southern neighborhoods and began to climb the slope towards the castle. Eyes stared at them from behind the colorful curtains that adorned the houses lining the road. But no creature showed itself until they swept into the courtyard of the castle itself.

Even though the castle was rarely used, there remained by custom a pair of dwarves who stood guard at the entrance. The dwarves, though armed with heavy axes, were more for show than otherwise, for the position was by common consent filled by old dwarves who wished for one last honor before they died. Because of this, the burdens on the guards were not great, and the pair usually sat at a small wooden table underneath a porch that had been especially constructed to keep the weather off, close to the entrance of the keep. Most of the time the guards played cards or chatted; indeed, it was not an uncommon sight for one or the other to be seen nodding quietly of an afternoon, sleeping off his lunch.

Today the two were a pair of old friends, Yerrin and Duggen, who were in the middle of a friendly game of dominoes when Yerrin looked up and saw a gaggle of strangers clad in dark mail striding into the courtyard, led by a tall woman who looked for all the world as if she owned the place.

The dwarves noisily scraped their chairs as they stood. Yerrin stepped forward, brandishing his axe in as threatening a manner as he knew how.

"Halt!" Yerrin said. "Who are you? And what business have you in Dynas Carn Toldwyn?"

Theoretically, the same question was supposed to be asked of every creature who desired access to the keep, but in practice this was the first time that the dwarf had ever issued the challenge.

Somewhat to his surprise, the tall human and her entourage did indeed halt. He waited for a response, which she seemed in no hurry to give. As he waited, he and Duggen, who now had extracted his own axe and stood with visible nervousness just behind Yerrin, heard the sound of hooves on the cobbles of the road leading up to the castle. The sound came closer, and shortly there rode into the courtyard three large knights riding black stallions and dressed in the darkest armor that either dwarf had ever seen.

The knights clattered across the courtyard and came to a halt beside the tall woman.

Now the woman spoke. "I am Captain Malliss, and I order you both to stand aside," she said in a voice that echoed off the walls.

The two dwarves exchanged glances and grasped their weapons more tightly.

"I cannot let you pass until you tell me what business you have in Dynas Carn Toldwyn," said Yerrin.

The captain made a small gesture with one hand, and one of the knights dismounted. Without a word, the knight drew his sword and then stepped forward to stand in front of Yerrin.

Diana, who with Odrian was standing immediately behind the captain, observed that these knights, who surely were the same ones who had disembarked from the *Dark Sea*, were armed, like herself, with weapons whose blades sucked in all the light that fell on them.

She watched in horror, unable to avert her eyes as the inevitable happened.

"The captain told you to stand aside."

The knight's voice was quiet and rasping, yet in the silence that had fallen on the courtyard it seemed to ring out as clearly as a shout. Surely, Diana thought, the dwarves would stand aside now? But neither dwarf moved. Instead, the one who had issued the challenge drew back his battle axe, ready to strike at the knight.

"State your business," the dwarf said. After the knight's voice, the dwarf's sounded insubstantial and impotent.

"This is my business," said the knight and then, with a speed surprising for one so massive, the dark blade sliced the air in an arc. It sliced through the dwarf's armor as if it were no more than a linen tunic, and buried itself in the dwarf's side.

The knight withdrew the blade effortlessly and the dwarf collapsed to the ground. With a cry, the other dwarf lunged forward, his battle axe flying toward the knight.

The knight stepped to one side and the axe clanged harmlessly against his armor. The knight thrust with his sword, and the weapon penetrated the dwarf's armor and sank into his soft belly. The knight withdrew the blade and the second dwarf joined his companion, lifeless on the ground.

The knight turned to the captain and offered a deep bow. Without a word, Captain Malliss strode past the bodies and through the doorway into the castle.

XIV Prisoner

Something woke Catherine.

She had been dreaming about being back in Glandryth's cottage, where she was, for some inexplicable reason, seated at the spinning wheel trying to spin a long scarf from some material that kept changing color. Into the dream had intruded a sound that did not fit: the sound of metal clinking lightly against metal. It was not loud, but it was very close, and was enough to wake her.

She held her breath, waiting intently for the sound to repeat. She had almost decided that it had been merely a part of the dream when she froze, her blood suddenly chill.

It *was* metal clinking against metal. It wasn't heavy or ponderous, but the opposite, as of something — or someone — hurrying towards her, carrying a light chain, or garbed in chain mail, making a clinking noise with every hurried step.

The sound stopped at the mouth of her chamber. She saw a young human woman with a light fetter around her left leg, and a chain that dragged over the floor behind her and disappeared into the darkness. Catherine squeezed against the wall, hoping that the woman would not turn to look inside the chamber.

The woman looked into the chamber, and their eyes met.

Whatever Catherine might have expected to see in the eyes of the chained woman — anger, defiance, hatred — was not there;

there was only a kind of despairing hope. The woman rushed into the chamber.

"Quick, quick! Give me your weapon."

The woman was even younger than Catherine had first thought. Her clothes were ill fitting and of a strange design. She was unhealthily thin, with a wan look in her eyes; her face was almost preternaturally pale. The woman held out her hand for Catherine's sword.

"Please, the weapon," she pleaded. She lifted her leg to exhibit the ring around her ankle. "They'll be here soon. Hurry, please, hurry!"

Catherine drew Scalmyùt and without hesitation struck at the chain near the point where it joined the fetter. The sword cut through the thin metal effortlessly.

"Thank you, oh thank you. Now hurry, or...."

The young woman turned at a sudden sound. Catherine looked up from the broken chain lying at her feet to see something that she had hoped never to see again.

Clustering around the entrance, so that it was impossible to escape, were five goblins. Four of them were armed with pikes; the fifth held the other end of the chain that Scalmyùt had sliced. The pikes were lowered and pointed threateningly towards the two humans. Only the sight of the unsheathed Scalmyùt seemed to give them pause, and they hovered uncertainly at the chamber entrance.

"You cannot escape," said the goblin who was holding the chain. He coiled the chain and held it lightly in one hand, while drawing a dagger with the other. "You are trapped, both of you. There are too many of us to slay."

Catherine looked at them, wondering how many she could kill before falling herself, then she shook herself, remembering her promise never to use a weapon in anger. She sheathed her sword.

"I will not use my sword in anger, no matter what the provocation," she declared.

The young woman looked at Catherine in horror, and she lunged to try to draw Scalmyut from its sheath. Catherine turned so that the sword was beyond her reach.

"No! I made a vow to the High Lord, and I will not break it. I will trust Him to look after us."

One of the goblins made a hissing sound and then two of them entered the chamber, their pikes held carefully in front of them, making short stabbing motions.

"Both of you come with us," the one with the chain said, "and the king shall decide what is to become of you."

For a moment the young woman looked like she was going to cry, then she glared at Catherine. Prodded by the goblins' pikes, she started to leave the chamber.

"You too," said a goblin, stabbing lightly at Catherine. The point of the pike penetrated her tunic and pricked her, and Catherine in turn glared at the goblin.

"There is no need for that. I shall come quietly."

She followed the young woman out of the chamber.

The goblin who had pricked her looked down at Catherine's pack, which was still on the floor where she had been using it as a pillow. He opened it and upended it, so that the contents fell out. He selected a few berries and stuffed them in his mouth; then he made a sound of disgust and kicked at the rest of the food. He turned and followed the others from the chamber.

They walked in single file back towards the small lake, the young woman first, followed by a pair of goblins, then Catherine, then the last three goblins. All the goblins kept their pikes lowered, but they were unnecessary; the woman strode forward down the tunnel at a good pace, her head high, as if she was pretending that the others did not exist.

They did not halt until they reached the watery chamber, where they all gathered at the water's edge.

"You know the way," said one of the goblins and he made a motion with his pike. The young woman began to wade through water towards the tunnel that carried the water away from the pool. The others followed.

Soon after they left the chamber, they took a dry side tunnel and followed it for a long time. Catherine took the moccasins from around her neck and put them on. Oh! what a relief it was to walk once again on a cushion of soft leather. She tried to strike up a conversation with the young woman, but the latter steadfastly ignored her, and Catherine soon gave up the attempt. Every now and then, they stopped to rest, but only Catherine seemed not to resent the halts.

As always in the tunnels, Catherine lost track of time. After a while the tunnel began to twist and to turn, and there was a sudden increase in the number of side chambers. They passed a large chamber from which the hiss of goblin conversation emanated.

By the time that they reached their destination, Catherine was nearly faint with weariness. She looked up and caught the young woman gazing at her with a look of unmistakable hatred.

The air was hot, almost unbearably so. This, combined with its heavy stillness, made it hard to breathe properly, and Catherine found herself laboring over every breath.

"You wait here," said one of the goblins to the young woman. "You come with us first," he said to Catherine. "The king must decide what to do with you."

Two of the goblins remained with the woman, while the other three now pressed Catherine forward down a tunnel whose walls glittered yellowly. The tunnel was not long, and soon she found herself standing in a medium-sized chamber in which the same glittering material — obviously some kind of gold — abounded.

Weapons of silver and gold hung on the walls. In the very center of the room was an enormous throne of gold, seated on which was a goblin clad in silver and gold armor.

Her captors pushed Catherine forward.

She bowed before the goblin king while the one who had carried the chain said, "The other human tried to escape, Your Highness, after her chain was broken by this one's sword."

"Remove her sword and scabbard," ordered the goblin king, and before Catherine could protest, her belt was undone and the weapon and its sheath removed from it.

"What have you to say for yourself, human?"

Catherine regarded the king defiantly. "I could have used my weapon against your soldiers, but I refrained from doing so. I could have killed several, perhaps all of them, yet they are all alive and unharmed. I plead mercy for myself and the other human. Let us go. We mean you no harm."

The goblin king opened his beaked mouth and let out a series of rasping sounds that Catherine interpreted as laughter.

"No harm? Why, you foolish creature. These are our tunnels. What could you possibly have gained by attacking my soldiers? You would have been caught and it would only have gone all the worse for you when you came before me. If you chose not to attack, it was only because you recognized the futility of resistance."

She looked at the goblins who were standing around and obviously enjoying her predicament. They were just as she remembered them: small creatures with pointy ears, glabrous skin and large red eyes. They wore light chain armor, and most of them carried pikes. They crowded around the walls of the room, wrinkling their noses and keeping their distance. A couple of them stepped forward and prodded her experimentally with pikes, but none of them spoke.

"And what is this I see around your waist? A most interesting jewel. Guards, remove her belt."

"Jewel? Did someone say there is a human here who wears a jewel in her belt?"

Catherine turned towards the entrance of the throne room and saw an ancient goblin, his skin thin and papery, with a wisp of a white beard and eyes that stared whitely and without sight from his skull, leaning against a metal staff. Unlike all the other goblins, this one was dressed not in mail, but in a garb of white that served to accentuate the paleness of his skin. Next to him stood a much younger goblin, normal in every respect except that he too was garbed in white. The young goblin, she noticed, held out a protective and supportive hand which grasped the elder one by the elbow.

"Holy One," said the king, "there is a new human here, found by my soldiers when the other human tried to escape."

The old goblin mumbled something inaudible and began to advance unsteadily towards Catherine, his way guided by the younger one at his side. The pair halted before Catherine.

"What have you to say for yourself, human?" the old one asked in a voice that was barely a whisper.

"As I was explaining to the king, I could have used my sword to protect myself and yet I chose not to. I have sworn before the

High Lord never to use my sword as a weapon, and I will not do so, even at the cost of my own life."

The old one made no reply to this noble speech. Instead, he held out his hand and touched her. He was hunchbacked and could barely reach above her waist, but he felt the jewel in the center of her belt buckle, his fingers, delicate for all their age, tracing out the incomprehensible cyphers forged into the metal of the buckle surrounding the white jewel.

"Sit," he commanded, and Catherine found herself obeying without giving the matter thought.

The goblin traced his papery hands gently over her face.

When he seemed satisfied, he asked, "And what were you doing in the tunnels, human?"

"I was travelling from the Sunset Islands to the mainland of Palindor, Holy One."

The old goblin nodded. "Yes, an easy route. One that even a human might navigate." Whether he was speaking to himself or to Catherine was not exactly clear.

"That belt," he continued, "is it yours?"

Then, before Catherine could respond, the old goblin replied to his own question: "I'm getting slow in my old age. Of course it's yours. No one else could wear that belt, could they?"

Catherine looked around, but the old goblin's voice was so low that she was sure that his words had not been audible to anyone else.

"It is my belt. And you are right: no one else can wear it."

"I have finished with her," the old one said, more loudly.

The king said, "Put her weapons with the weapon store, and remove her belt and place it with the jewels. Take her to the island for now. I will consider what to do with her later."

As the guards stepped forward, the old one leaned forward and spoke quietly to Catherine. Afterwards, she tried to be sure of what she had heard, but the old goblin's voice was all but inaudible, and the sound of the approaching guards smothered his words. What Catherine thought he said was, "Trust me; I'll do what I can." But there was no time to ponder the meaning of his words, even if she had heard them aright, for she was pulled to her feet and quickly taken away by the goblin soldiers.

She was led through a maze of tunnels until she reached an enormous chamber, larger than any she had seen before. It was far too large to have been dug by goblins, or indeed by any creature: it was a naturally occurring cavern, far underground.

Water lapped at Catherine's feet, stretching as far as she could see into the distance and glistening strangely in the dim light from the roof high above her head. She felt a breath of torrid air wafting over the underground lake. Her feet sank slightly into a dark sand that formed a kind of beach.

"Your belt," said one of the guards, holding out a claw-like hand.

Catherine hesitated. The belt was the mark of her rank, and she was loath to surrender it. But what else could she do?

The goblin said, "I can take it from you by force if you would prefer."

She unbuckled her belt and handed it to him.

"Now, you will get in the boat with us," said the goblin, and for the first time Catherine noticed a small rowing boat not far away, drawn up on the dark beach.

She clambered clumsily inside and sat in the bow. The boat was made of metal, its shell adorned by the intricate carvings that commonly embellished the work of goblins. Two goblins joined her in the vessel. One lifted the metal oars that lay in the bottom of the boat and fitted them to the rowlocks. The other sat in the rear of the boat, opposite Catherine, his pike at the ready.

The goblins seemed nervous. Either they could not swim or there was something in the water that frightened them.

Two of the soldier goblins pushed them off, and they began to row across the lake.

Catherine tried to gauge the size of the lake, but it was an impossible task. The ceiling glowed dimly high above, but whether it was thirty feet away or two hundred was impossible to tell. Similarly, it was impossible to judge the distance to the far side. The only feature she could see was a low, dark mass that hugged the water ahead of them, partially obscuring the dim glow of the far wall.

It was some time before she realized that the dark mass was growing larger and that it must be their goal.

The oars splashed steadily — the goblin who was rowing was both clumsy and slow — until suddenly the goblin in the rear called out, the rower stopped, and they glided forward until the metal boat crunched against another dark beach.

Now that they had arrived she could see that the dark mass with which they had collided did in fact glow, but more dimly than the vault above.

"You will get out," said the goblin with the pike. "Food and water will be brought to you. You will be told when the king has decided what to do with you."

Catherine hesitated.

"Go on," the goblin urged. "You will be safe. It is an island. There is nothing here that will harm you."

The goblin leaned forward threateningly and leveled his pike. Clumsily, Catherine disembarked.

The water covered her ankles. It was cool, but far from cold. Under her feet she could feel the sand of the beach.

The goblin who had been rowing applied himself once more to the oars. The boat was soon lost in the gloom of the cavern, although for some time Catherine stood in the water, holding her moccasins, listening to the sound of the oars' clumsy splashes growing fainter.

Eventually, she clambered up the slope of the dark beach, on to the island itself.

"So they've brought you here as well. May the High Lord have mercy on us both," a voice said out of the darkness.

XV A Healing

The dablik looked at the mess.

"Goblins," he said, detecting a hint of their characteristic slightly sour, briny odor.

Without his aid, Catherine would never be able to escape. But there was something else to consider. He wavered indecisively.

The new tunnel was calling him like a lodestone. There was something important and mysterious and deep about that tunnel — for he of all creatures knew that a tunnel cannot suddenly appear in that manner, and he burned with curiosity to know what lay at the far end. He suspected that the tunnel led not to some ordinary cave somewhere on Machrenmoor, to but a very special and holy place, the holiest in all Palindor.

If his suspicion was right, then it was obvious what he should do. Catherine would be safe enough as a prisoner of the goblins. She was in no real danger. Whereas, if he was right about the tunnel, things were afoot the like of which had never before been seen in Palindor.

He looked around the chamber around one last time. Then, his mind made up, the dablik began to retrace his steps back to the mainland.

144

It would have been easy for a deep gloom to have descended on the cottage in the goyle, for it was clear even to someone as untutored in such matters as the Hunter Gwain that the two people who were spread out on settles in the front room were very sick indeed.

He spent hours watching as Harsforn and Esterin busied themselves preparing salves and poultices while Iadron produced innumerable cups of tea.

Michael's wounds seemed much more serious, and Harsforn's ministrations were directed more towards him than they were to Gwynedd, who now slept peacefully on the settle, her breathing deep and regular. His daughter was attended mainly by Esterin, and it was only natural that the Hunter and the elf began to strike up something of a friendship.

It was now late evening, and Esterin had suggested that since there was nothing more that she could do right now for Gwynedd, she and Gwain might as well leave Harsforn to work in peace. So they had retired to a small bench at the far end of the garden, some distance from the cottage and close to the stream.

The night was clear and cold. The Hunter and the elf were bundled warmly against the evening chill.

For some time they sat without speaking, the elf looking up at the stars, the Hunter listening to the musical sound of the water burbling over the rocks in the stream bed.

"You needn't worry," said Esterin after a while. "Your daughter will recover. She is well out of danger."

"Thank you," said the Hunter. "I don't know if I can ever thank you enough. She was going to die, wasn't she? When I arrived, I mean."

"It looked that way, yes. But nothing happens that the High Lord cannot turn to good somehow. Even if she had died, it would have been important for you to remember that."

"Easy to say. But sometimes I wonder. I already lost one daughter, and the thought of losing the only child left to me..., that is very hard."

The elf said nothing. For a while the silence was broken only by the sound of the stream and the occasional hoot of an owl somewhere in the woods on the slopes above them.

"Tell me about Iadron and Harsforn," Gwain said. "And yourself as well. I have heard of them, of course. My family had dealings with them, long, long ago."

"What is there to say? They are the reason I am alive today. I was born in a cave in eastern Palindor, in a cave in which the seer and the healer were then living*. My father was a fisherelf from Palindor, my mother a woodelf from Reglandor. The story is long and complicated, but the seer and the healer saved my mother's life while I was yet in the womb.

"I grew up in Reglandor, close to the Fire Mountain, but as I grew older and passed from child to adult, I began to feel sure that the High Lord was telling me that my place was here, with Harsforn. I thought that my parents would object when I told them that I wanted to come to Palindor to find her, but instead they accepted it as if they had known all along that one day I would have to leave them and search for Harsforn.

"I found her eventually. When I arrived at their cottage, Iadron opened the door, and before I could say a word she called out to Harsforn, 'She's here. I told you she would come today.' And a strange feeling of having come home settled over me.

"That was all many years ago. I am apprenticed to Harsforn, and she is teaching me much. But sometimes I catch Iadron watching me, as if she knows something about me that even I do not know. But whenever I ask her about it, she refuses to say anything and simply offers me another cup of tea." The elf laughed. "They're a strange old couple, but I love them... I love them very much indeed."

Silence fell once more. Eventually, Esterin said, "Come. It is getting late. Let us look in on Gwynedd one last time, and then we must get to bed."

Candles were burning in the front room. As the Hunter and the elf entered the room, Harsforn was looking at the dark patch on Michael's neck, muttering despairing imprecations while her sister looked on, wringing her hands.

Harsforn turned to Iadron. "My dear, there is nothing more I can do. There is something more deadly at work here than I

---

* For more details, see *Shadow*.

have ever seen before. A dark blade is a dangerous weapon, and to have the skin punctured in such a way is not good, but even so by now he should have begun to respond to the hæmony. Yet the darkness keeps spreading. His breathing is strong for now, but by morning I am afraid it will all be over."

"I know," said Iadron. "I see as much in your face. But there must be something more to it than that. After all, why did I see him in a vision if we weren't meant to save him?"

Harsforn shrugged. "I know not. All I know is that I have failed the High King."

The silence that followed Harsforn's statement was broken by a rap at the front door. Everyone looked at everyone else, frowns on their faces, as if to say: "Who could be knocking at this time of night?"

Esterin went out into the hallway, closely followed by Gwain, who surreptitiously placed his hand on the hilt of his sword.

Esterin opened the door.

On the threshold stood a gnome, his clothes travel-stained, a look of strained fatigue on his face. There was a tiredness in his voice when he spoke.

"I heard someone say they have failed the High King," he said, indicating the open window of the front room. "That may or may not be true, but most assuredly you have not failed the High Lord."

With this odd pronouncement, he walked past Esterin and Gwain and into the front room. He passed Iadron, Harsforn and Gwynedd without so much as a glance, and stopped by Michael's head.

For some time he gazed at the High King without speaking. Everyone watched him, but only Harsforn, who was the closest, could see the peculiar expression on the gnome's face.

For a long time, the gnome did not move.

"I have done my best for him," said Harsforn, "but I cannot stop the spread of the darkness."

The gnome nodded as if in agreement, or perhaps understanding, but did not reply.

The silence dragged on.

"A cup of tea?" suggested Iadron.

That at last seemed to drag the gnome from his reverie. He turned and smiled.

"I've lived alone too long and am quite forgetting my manners. I'm sorry. Yes, a cup of tea would be most welcome. And I must apologize for barging in like this. I am sorry if I am intruding. I have walked a long way, and I am very tired. A cup of tea would be most refreshing, most refreshing indeed."

"My name is Iadron, and this is Harsforn," said the seer.

"And I am Esterin."

"And I am Gwain, Hunter of the forest of Palindor. This poor creature" — Gwain indicated the form on the other settle — "is my daughter, who has been wounded, but whom Harsforn and Esterin are tending."

"She will recover," said Harsforn, partly to Gwain, partly to the gnome.

The gnome bowed as the introductions were made. "And my name is Phendric, gnome of the place that was once called Dankenwood. I thank you for your hospitality, and would be most grateful if you would permit me to stay the night. Don't worry about finding me a room; I would be most happy to remain here with the High King."

Harsforn was about to say something when she noticed that Iadron was staring at the newcomer with wide eyes. Harsforn could see nothing odd about him, except for the obvious fact that such bookish creatures were rarely seen in such a state of disarray.

Then, as if she had made her mind up about something, Iadron turned and disappeared in the direction of the kitchen. Harsforn tried to concentrate on Michael's wound, but the look on her sister's face bothered her, and it was only a few moments before she made an excuse and followed Iadron to the kitchen.

"What is it?" asked Harsforn. "Did you see something?"

Iadron nodded. "Yes, but don't ask me what."

"What do you mean?"

Iadron shook her head. "Not now." There was a sparkle in her eyes and an expectant look on her face.

"Don't be silly. I'm your sister. You can tell me."

"Not this time. Come on, pass me a cup for the gnome."

When they returned to the front room, Phendric was seated cross-legged on the floor beside the settle on which Michael slept. Harsforn gave Michael's neck a cursory glance as she handed Phendric his tea. She blinked, and peered more closely at the neck. She frowned, for she was certain that the patch of gray had stopped spreading.

She looked curiously at the gnome as he drank his tea. Had he done something to her patient while she had been in the kitchen? Or were her own medications at last beginning to take hold? She could not tell.

Suddenly the clock in the corner struck eleven — although its hands, as always, stood at a little before twelve — surprising everyone, for surely it had been but nine o'clock only a short time before. Esterin excused herself for the night, and Harsforn realized that her own eyelids were heavy, and she heard herself saying goodnight to the others. Moments later, Iadron too bade everyone good night. Wearily, the seer and the healer followed the elf up the stairs and to bed.

Gwain had barely heard the clock strike, for his eyelids had been heavy with sleep for some time, and now he finally succumbed even as he sat on the floor, his back against the settle on which his daughter slept. The candles began to gutter and, one by one, they went out.

Who can say what happened that night? That Phendric was the last to remain awake there can be no doubt. Whether he remained awake all night, and whether he applied any medications to the High King or simply sat with him all night can never be known, although the latter seems the most likely.

In any case, Gwain was woken shortly before dawn by a hand gently shaking his shoulder. His first thought was that he could not remember the last time he had slept so deeply. As he came fully awake, he felt a surge of strength, as if he was prepared for anything that the day could possibly have in store for him. It was only as his eyes focused on the face of the gnome who was gently shaking him that he recollected the events of the day before, and a heaviness settled on his heart.

"Come, we must be leaving," the gnome was saying in an urgent whisper.

It was some moments before Gwain realized that someone else was standing in the shadows at the far end of the room, near Michael's settle. He wondered who it could be, and what had lent such urgency to the gnome's voice. He got to his feet and looked down for a moment at where his daughter lay asleep.

"I can't leave; my daughter is ill," he said.

"She is not ill. She is wounded, that is all. And as the healer said last night, she will recover. Harsforn and Esterin will see to that. But we have no time to waste, we must be going or we shall be late."

"Going? Where? Late for what?" Gwain's voice rose in confusion and not a little anger.

And then he stopped, for the first light of the false dawn had now entered the window and touched the face of the one who stood at the far end of the room. Now Gwain realized that the settle on which the High King had lain last night was empty.

"The High King must be taken to Machrenmoor, and I must go with him. But he is tired, and so am I, and we need your horse. Lead us there, and by the time you return to this place your daughter will be restored to health."

For a moment, Gwain opened his mouth to argue. Then he closed it again. He nodded and asked, "What about the others: Iadron and Harsforn and Esterin? What will they think when they find us gone?"

"They will understand."

And with that tenuous assurance, Gwain nodded and walked to the doorway. Phendric and the High King followed, and as the first light of the new day struck the top of the ridge above the goyle, the three began to make their way up the western side of the valley, Gwain leading Peregrine, astride whom sat the gnome and the High King.

Harsforn was the first downstairs in the morning, and she immediately went to the front room to examine her patients. She gasped in surprise.

Iadron, coming down the stairs behind her, asked: "What is it, dear?"

Harsforn turned to her sister. "They've gone. All of them except the child."

Iadron nodded to herself. "It was he, then. I thought it had to be."

"Who? Who was who? You're speaking in riddles, old woman. Do you know where they've gone? What happened to the High King? He couldn't possibly have recovered so quickly." A gruesome thought struck the healer. "Or is he dead?"

"Oh no, my dear, I don't think so. It was the gnome, you see; couldn't you see there was something about him?"

"Something about him? I'll say there was something about him. A strange one, that gnome, appearing from nowhere like that, long after sunset, and barging in like he owned the place and understanding exactly what was happening without being told. I just wish someone would tell *me* what's happening, that's all."

"I expect we'll find out in good time. In the meantime, you should be thankful. What did he say his name was? Phendric? Well, it's as good a name as any, I suppose."

"What are you babbling about now? Has the whole world gone mad?"

"Don't you remember what I once said, my dear? Don't you remember that that nice scribegnome Meldor wrote it all down just before he took himself off to found the Order of Holy Gnomes when Palindor was just being established and Toldwyn was on the verge of winning the War of Founding?"

"You mean... that *that*...? that *he*...?"

"That's right my dear. Phendric is the one who will be great and saving. I'm sure of it. He is the one whom I saw in my vision all those centuries ago. But I wonder...."

"You wonder what"

Iadron looked hard at her sister.

"I wonder if he knows?"

XVI On the Island

Catherine experienced a moment of fright at the unexpected sound of another voice coming from just a few paces away. The goblins had said that there was nothing here to harm her, but they had made no mention of the fact that the island was already occupied. She had assumed, obviously mistakenly, that she was alone. So when a voice spoke out of the gloom, she nearly fell backward into the lake in fright.

"Sorry, I didn't mean to startle you," said the voice. There was a movement, and out of the grayness came the young woman whose chain Catherine had severed.

"And I suppose I need to apologize," the woman continued. "I'm sorry. You've no idea what it's been like to be trapped here all this time by myself. When I saw you it was the first real chance to escape I've ever had. I don't suppose there'll be another."

She appeared to be on the verge of tears.

Catherine put an arm around the woman's shoulder. "Now, now. Don't cry. There are two of us now. Look at me. I'm not downcast, am I?"

The woman shook her head. "But you don't know what it's like to live here like this...."

"Hush. Don't worry. Now, tell me, who are you, and what exactly is this place?"

"Time enough for that later. Time! There's time enough here for anything." She sniffled back incipient tears. "Come along and follow me; there's a place that's not bad near the center of the island."

The island was not large; Catherine quickly discovered that she could walk all the way around the beach that marked the shoreline in only a few minutes. The beach was a narrow strip of dark sand, but most of the island was covered by a gray, fine-grained soil in which strange plants had taken root. They had large, soft leaves and pliable, springy wood. The woman had worn several paths across the island through the plants. Near the center of the island she had constructed a small bower, inside which was a bed made of the large, soft leaves.

The woman said, "We must make you a bed like mine. It's easy; you just pull the leaves off the plants and put them on the ground. The soil isn't hard, and these soften it even more. You can use the largest leaves as a kind of blanket" — she indicated a pile of large leaves next to her bed — "although there's no way of sewing them together to make a proper covering. The plants don't provide food, and there's no water on the island, but the goblins bring food and water across twice a day by boat. They just leave a box on the shore and take away the box from last time. Here's the box they left me. I was wondering why it has so much food; now I know."

She gestured towards an ornate box. Catherine opened it. Inside were two large bowls containing unidentifiable slops, a couple of small hunks of goblin bread, and a large metal canteen. She wrinkled her nose in disgust at the slops.

"You'll get used to it after a while," the young woman said. "You'll have to, otherwise you'll starve."

Catherine closed the box and replaced it on the ground. "So will you tell me now? Who are you? And how did you get here?"

A faraway look came into the woman's eyes.

"I should be sorry, of course. But I'm not."

"What do you mean?"

"For you. I should be sorry for you, that this has happened to you. But I'm not sorry. I can't be. It's been so long now without anyone to talk to..., I'm sorry; I'm going to cry...."

153

And before Catherine could move to comfort her, the woman had burst into tears.

Catherine settled herself by the woman's side and put her arm around her shoulder.

"There, there. I'm here now. But, please, what is your name?"

The woman wiped her eyes on the sleeve of her tunic and sniffed back the tears.

"Enwys," she said. "And thank you; I'll try not to cry."

"Now, Enwys, tears are nothing to be ashamed of. You've been here by yourself for a long time; but now you have me to talk to. And I have you to talk to. We won't be lonely, and there's lots to talk about, isn't there? I don't know where we are or what might become of us. But you can tell me what you know, then maybe we can think of how we might get away from here."

Enwys looked as if she were going to burst into tears again. She shook her head. "No. You don't understand. You can't escape from here. These are goblins, and no one has ever escaped from goblins."

"Did they tell you that? Because if they did, I can assure you that it's not true."

"But everyone knows that you can't escape from goblins."

"I assure you, it's been done."

"How do you know?"

"Because I have done it myself."

Enwys looked at her incredulously. She shook her head.

"You're lying. Everyone knows that no one can escape goblins."

Catherine removed her arm from around Enwys' shoulder, and looked her sternly in the eye.

"In the first place, young Enwys, you need to understand one thing: I never lie. Do you understand that?"

Enwys nodded.

"And in the second, it is quite true that it is no simple matter to escape the clutches of goblins, but with the High Lord's help I have done it once, and, when the time is right, He will show us how to do it again."

"He will? Do you really think so?"

"I'm certain of it," said Catherine firmly. "And in a little while I'll explain why I'm so certain. But now I want to hear about you:

who you are, how you came to be here, and everything you know about our captors. My experience of goblins is that they are not unkindly creatures if you approach them the right way."

Enwys nodded and, still fighting to hold back her tears, began her story.

"What you say is true: they aren't unkind. They feed me as well as they can, and they do try to look after me. They just don't seem to understand how much I miss the surface. I've given up talking about it to them. Whenever I used to bring up the subject, they would say: 'The surface!' and shudder, and then say: 'No, you can't really want to go there. We've heard stories of what it's like, although we can't really imagine the horror of looking up and seeing no comforting rock over one's head. Just... nothing.' You could hear the horror in their voices. They don't seem to understand how much of a prison this is."

"But why won't they let you go?"

"They say I know too much, and I would lead an army into the tunnels to steal their treasure. I used to keep telling them that I wasn't interested in their treasure, but they seemed as incapable of understanding that as they are of believing that I really would like to go back to the surface. They insist that the moment I'm free I'll bring an army of surface creatures into the tunnels to steal their gold. Mostly they seem to be afraid of dwarves. They have a story of a battle fought long ago in which dwarves nearly wiped them out, and forced them to live much deeper underground than they used to."

"Have you ever seen their treasure? Is there really that much of it?"

Enwys nodded. "Oh yes. And they add to it all the time. They are continually mining, and their workmanship is second to none. It's almost impossible for them to construct anything plain or simple. That box that they bring our food in, that's about the simplest thing that I've ever seen them make, yet it would take a human half a lifetime to make something nearly as delicate. So, you see, they keep me prisoner, even though of course I am no real threat to them."

"But how did you get here? Surely you weren't using the tunnels to cross from Palindor to the Sunset Islands?"

Enwys looked at Catherine quizzically. "I don't know what you're talking about. Is that where we are, somewhere under the Great Sea to the west of Palindor?"

"I think so, yes. At least, that's where I was when you found me."

"A long way from home, then." Enwys sighed. Seeing the quizzical look on Catherine's face, she continued, "I've never really been in western Palindor; it was always a bit too domesticated for us. I was a Huntress. Or, rather, I was nearly a Huntress. Oh, it's all so long ago now."

"Never mind, dear. Take your time. I'm right here to look after you if it all gets too much."

"Thank you. You are very kind. And you'll tell me your story as well?"

"Yes, of course I will."

Enwys seemed strangely comforted by the promise, and continued her tale.

"I was the child of Hunters, and a member of the most distinguished family of Hunters in all Palindor. My father was Gwain, of the line of Aramis" — if she had been looking at Catherine when she said these words, she would have seen Catherine's start of surprise, but instead she was looking sightlessly into the vegetation around the bower, her thoughts long ago and far away — "and my mother was Heth, of a family well known for its hunting skills.

"It is the custom of Hunters that when the parents think a child old enough, the child is left to fend for itself for a winter. Historically, children of the line of Aramis tend to be tested in this way earlier than those of most other families. In my case, my father and mother thought I was ready for my freedom when I was only nine years old.

"Despite my youth, I thought I was a good and competent Huntress and was perfectly capable of surviving on my own. So I was relieved that the autumnal signs indicated an easy winter ahead, which meant that my parents would have no excuse not to let me winter by myself.

"The season started well. I hunted on the western slopes of the Mountains of Mourn, a place where bear can often be found, and within six weeks I had killed enough meat and gathered enough nuts and berries to see me through the winter. So for the rest of the winter I was more or less left to my own devices. I decided to spend it exploring the slopes. A Huntress, you understand, must know her land better than any of the creatures with whom she shares it.

"Winter passed uneventfully, although much more harshly than the portents had predicted, until one day I made a mistake while hunting a snow cat above the snow line not long after the solstice.

"I had been so busy trailing the cat most of the day that I hadn't noticed the signs in the sky, and as the afternoon wore on I suddenly realized that a storm was about to begin and there was no chance that I could get down the mountain and into the forest before it started. I began to search for shelter. As the clouds massed, the upslope wind began to get colder and damper and the first flurries began to fall. I realized that the storm was going to be a bad one and might last for several days.

"This was of little concern insofar as food was concerned. Although I did not have much in my pack, a Hunter's real concern is always water, and that is one thing that's always available where there is snow. I was more worried about staying warm, for I had brought no warm gear to sleep under, expecting the trip to take no more than a single day.

"Just as the blizzard began in earnest, I found a cave in the mountainside. It was deep, but I didn't explore very far, since there didn't seem any reason to do so.

"I slept that night near the entrance. Next day the storm continued with, if anything, even greater ferocity. Becoming bored, I began to explore the cave.

"Even now I don't know how it happened. I was certain that I marked every turn I took, for the tunnel that the cave became as it burrowed into the mountain began to branch and divide, and I didn't want to lose my way. But somehow it wasn't long before I turned to retrace my steps and discovered that I was lost.

"For a while, I wandered around at random, hoping that I'd come across one of the junctions I had marked, but the passages all looked the same, and tunnels branched and angled upwards and downwards at random. Every time I chose a tunnel that seemed to head up towards the surface, I would soon find that I was instead moving downwards, deeper into the mountain.

"Well, you can imagine how I felt after a few hours of that. I'm afraid that at one point, Huntress though I nearly was, I simply sat down and cried. Then I got up and wandered around some more, but for all the progress I made I might as well have been wandering around in circles.

"I had a little food in the pack, but I carried no water and was beginning to feel thirsty, so I ate most of what I had, and then I fell asleep.

"When I awoke, I was more thirsty than ever. I ate a little more food, hoping that the moisture it contained would quench my thirst a little. Then I set out once more wandering the tunnels.

"I don't know how long that continued, but at last I stopped and listened carefully, for I was sure I could hear the sound of running water. Without my really noticing the change, the tunnels through which I was travelling no longer had the appearance of a natural cave, but seemed more as if they had been purposefully mined. They ran straighter, with fewer branches, and it began to be easier to go in the direction I wanted to go, which was towards the sound of the water.

"I made a couple of mistakes and had to backtrack a little, but it wasn't long before I stepped out the mouth of a tunnel and on to a ledge which was wet from the spray of a small waterfall that fell down a steep cliff. Gratefully I drank from the waterfall. It was warm and tasted of iron and salt, but at least it was liquid. Anyway, I stayed there and ate what remained of my food and drank some more from the waterfall, unpleasant though it was, and then slept once more.

"When I awoke I had a shock, for I immediately saw that I was no longer alone. Nearby stood three creatures that I know now to be goblins, but at the time were unknown to me.

"I remember being frightened, for they looked ferocious and carried pikes, but I was not as scared as I might have been, because I realized that having finished my food I wouldn't last long, and it was obvious that I would never find my way back to the surface without help. So in some way I was relieved to discover that I was not the only inhabitant of the tunnels. I thought that perhaps the creatures might be able to lead me back to the surface. At the very least, surely they would feed me, so it could be only a matter of time before I escaped the tunnels.

"How wrong I was! The goblins talked for a short while among themselves, apparently unsure what to do with me. Eventually, they decided to take me to their king, although they kept talking about 'not making the mistake we made with the last human,' which I could make no sense of.

"Anyway, they prodded me with their pikes and marched me through a maze of tunnels, until we reached the place where they lived. I was taken to the royal chamber, where I met their king.

"The king made it clear that they would give me food and drink, but they had no intention of helping me to find a way back to the surface, although it was obvious that they knew of at least one such way.

"He really didn't seem very interested in me, although it was some time before I discovered the reason. They left me free to roam the tunnels and I could have escaped at any time if only I had known the way back to the surface. But I didn't, and after a while I became a sort of fixture in the goblin colony. Nowhere seemed to be barred to me, and I soon discovered their treasure store, and watched them mining ore and minerals, and watched their artisans as they crafted gold nuggets and etched beautiful gems.

"Down at the lowest part of the colony were the furnaces, where ore was converted to metal. These furnaces, I soon discovered, were busy all the time, and they seemed to be turning out large numbers of weapons and vast quantities of chain mail, which was of a light and delicate quality that I had never seen on the surface.

"Slowly it dawned on me that the goblins were preparing for a battle, and in my naïveté I assumed that that meant that they would be travelling to the surface, and perhaps then I would have a chance to escape, for they really seemed ambivalent about my status as a prisoner, and I am sure that had I been able to find a path to the surface they would not have objected to my leaving. But perhaps, in retrospect, I misunderstood their attitude. Perhaps they were ambivalent simply because they knew there was no way for me to escape.

"Anyway, I stayed with the goblins for some indeterminate period of time. Of course there is no day or night down here, and it was so long ago now that my memory might be playing tricks. It seemed like several months, but it might have been only weeks, or perhaps even a year or more. But one day, everything changed.

"I awoke one morning — not that I could tell whether it was really morning on the surface, of course — to the sounds of shouting and the clash of metal on metal. Goblins were running around in consternation. All of them were dressed in chain mail and most were carrying weapons. I realized that the colony was under attack. It was some time before I understood that the attackers were another group of goblins, who seemed intent on reaching the treasure room and stealing the treasure from 'my' goblins.

"Well, for a while, all I saw were goblins from my colony running around, then I began to see wounded goblins making their way past the small chamber I had been given as my own, and after a while it became clear that my goblins were losing the battle. Not long afterward, I saw the first of the attacking goblins. There was little difference between the attackers and those I knew, except that the attackers seemed a little smaller and quicker, lighter on their feet, and their chain mail was not quite as well made and was a shade less gray than the mail of my own goblins.

"The attackers passed my chamber in ones and twos. Some of them looked my way and seemed to regard me with interest, but they were too busy to bother with me.

"I hesitated to go out into the tunnels, for fear of being caught up in the battle, so I stayed where I was, waiting for the fighting to end, for the thought had come to me that perhaps these new goblins might be willing to guide me to the surface. It was strange, but at the time I didn't wonder how my colony had come to be attacked. I had always assumed that there was just one way to reach the colony, through the cave on the surface.

"After a while the only goblins I saw were from the attacking forces. My goblins had lost. I was wondering what to do when a small group from the victorious army strode into the chamber and ordered me to follow them. I was herded into a group with a couple of dozen goblin prisoners and we were addressed by one of the attackers who was obviously of high rank.

"'You will be marched back to our tunnels,' he said. 'You will be given food to eat and water to drink, so you will not starve. Do not imagine that you can escape, for you will be well guarded, and anyone who tries to escape will be killed. And in any case' — and here he let out a sibilant laugh — 'you will be too burdened to be able to go very far very quickly.'

"Then we were taken to the treasure chamber. We were given packs to wear. I, being larger than any of the goblins, was forced to carry two packs, despite the fact that the goblins were stronger than I. The packs were then filled with treasures taken from the mound in front of us. Even though we were all laden, we carried away no more than a quarter of the mountain, but it seemed enough to satisfy the invaders. We began to make our way slowly through the tunnels, guarded by the invading army.

"It wasn't long before I began to stumble with the weight of the treasure I was being forced to carry. At first, the goblins thought I was feigning fatigue, and they prodded me with their pikes to try to make me keep walking at the same speed as everyone else.

"One of the goblins who had been taken prisoner tried to intervene on my behalf, telling our captors: 'That creature is a human. She is from the surface, and is weak, despite her size. She should not be made to carry more than one pack.'

"At first, our captors ignored him, but eventually I fell over and was simply too tired to get up no matter how many times they prodded me. One of the guards turned to the goblin who had spoken and said: 'Then you may carry one of her packs.' The poor creature nodded as if he had expected this development and soon we were on our way again, he now the one slowing us down as he struggled with two of the heavy packs.

"I don't know how long we walked in this manner, but it was for many days. Gradually I realized that the colony in which I had been a prisoner occupied only a small part of a vast system of tunnels that runs under much of Palindor.

"No one offered any help to the poor goblin who was carrying my second pack, so we evolved a system where we shared the extra weight, taking it in turns to carry the second pack.

"Eventually, after what seemed like many days, the tunnel we were in began to go steadily downward, even deeper underground. The air became distinctly warmer, and our captors, who until now had been marching with a grim and humorless determination, seemed to become more friendly and buoyant. I decided that we must be coming close to the end of our journey, and I soon discovered that I was right.

"After another couple of rest periods, we began to see other goblins, attired normally, not for war, and it wasn't long before we arrived in a large chamber and were told to drop the packs we had been carrying. A gaggle of goblins peered at us from tunnels adjoining the chamber, interested no doubt to see both the treasure and the prisoners that had carried it from the losing colony.

"We were taken away, leaving the treasure behind, and confined in a group of small chambers for a day or two. Then we were taken from that place and addressed by the goblin who seemed to be the leader of the army. He said, 'The king has decided that you are to be freed, with the exception of the human; you are free to join our society and work with us. We will not stop any goblin who tries to leave, but we warn you that the journey back to the mountains is long and tortuous and it is unlikely that anyone who chooses to leave the colony would survive and find his way back to his home. You will find life here to be comfortable, but the choice of whether to stay or not is up to each individual.'

"There were mutterings around me, but I was not listening, for I was too busy wondering what fate they had planned for me.

"I soon found out. I was brought to this island, and shortly afterward the king himself came to speak with me.

"'You present us with a problem,' he began.

"'How so? I mean you no harm,' I said. 'I was a prisoner of the goblins before. Am I now to continue to be a prisoner? All I ask is that you show me a way back to the surface so I may join my own kind. Would you not wish the same if you were held on the surface as a prisoner of humans?'

"He seemed to consider this argument for some time, but eventually he said, 'I am afraid I cannot let you go. For here we are more exposed to attack from the surface than is the colony from

162

which we took you. It's true that here we are deeper underground, but the journey from here to the surface is easy and if we were to release you it would be a simple matter for you to lead an army back here to steal our treasure. No, I am sorry, human, but I am responsible for my people and I cannot release you. However, there is something that perhaps I can do for you in return for a service you can render us.'

"I was suspicious of this, and remained silent while he made his proposal.

"It seems that goblins are partial to the soft fruits that grow on the surface. All they eat here is a kind of gruel made from the ground leaves of plants such as those on this island, so I suppose it is hardly surprising that they think of berries as an exquisite delicacy.

"But, of course, as a rule they dare not venture out on to the surface, simply out of fear. Occasionally, a goblin will venture out and return with a fruit or a few berries in order to prove his worth as a warrior, but that brings back enough only for that goblin and the king, who automatically receives half of anything found on the surface. The proposal that the king had for me was simple: I was to go out on the surface and bring back berries for them. In return they would see that I was given a quarter of whatever I brought back with me.

"I was not interested in a quarter share of anything, but I thought that the arrangement would give me an opportunity to escape, and so I agreed. But it turned out that I was mistaken, as you yourself saw. The goblins fashioned a long, light chain, which they attach to a fetter around my ankle every time we leave the colony. So although I can move with some freedom, still I am bound to them by unbreakable links.

"You can imagine my frustration when the time came to go to the surface and they attached the fetter and chain. All my hopes were instantly dashed, for of course I had no hope of ever breaking the chain without a tool of some kind. And so began my work for the goblins.

"At this time of year, I make frequent trips to the surface. There are several exits that the goblins know about, and probably many more besides, because it soon became apparent that the goblins don't know every tunnel in the system, and they use only a few of the largest ones, like the one in which I found you. That was where I was going when I came across you: to the surface to pick berries from a valley which I think is somewhere near the base of Machrenmoor, although it's hard to be sure, because they let me out only at night, and never for very long.

"The goblins stay in the cave while I pick the berries. You probably noticed that they were all wearing empty packs. We fill the packs as quickly as we can, and then return to the colony. Usually, I spend a couple of hours on the surface. This year especially the harvest is plentiful, and I have lost count of the number of trips we've made.

"We have a system now. I know the way well, and I usually go on ahead, so I can spend a couple of extra minutes breathing the fresh air and enjoying the sky before the goblins catch up and shout from the cave that it's time to begin work.

"You can imagine how I felt when I saw you in that chamber. I couldn't believe my luck. At first I just wanted to give you a message to take back to the surface, to tell people that I'm still alive, hoping that maybe someone could mount a rescue. Then, when I saw that you were armed, I realized that this was the best opportunity I'd ever had to try to escape. I thought that if we could only get rid of the chain, there was a good chance that we would be able to duck down a side passage and hide.

"As you know, I was mistaken." At this, the Huntress lowered her head dolefully. Eventually, she concluded: "Anyway, that's my story. Now, how about you? How did you come to be in the passages?"

Catherine paused for a long while, wondering how much she should tell the Huntress. If she told her the entire truth, would the Huntress believe her? Would it be better simply to tell some of the truth, but not all of it?

Eventually, she decided that to refrain from telling everything was no different from telling an untruth, so she began her tale with a simple declaration.

"My name is Catherine; I am a High Monarch of Palindor."

Her companion's shock was obvious even in the gloom of the bower, but she did not interrupt while Catherine told her story.

It was a long while before Catherine finished, and when she did both she and Enwys were nodding with tiredness. It was obvious that the Huntress had many questions, but it was also clear that the time for sleep had long past, so Catherine refused to say any more and insisted instead that questions could wait until the morning.

Too tired to argue, the Huntress yawned and lay down on the bed of leaves. Catherine too lay down, and she barely had time to construct a silent prayer for help before she too was asleep.

XVII A Warrior's Return

The dablik was in a hurry, and when the dablik was in a hurry he could move through the tunnels very quickly indeed. Partly he was driven by simple curiosity, partly by a fear that if he were too late he might miss something momentous. Partly, too, was an anxiety that when he returned to the spot at which the new tunnel had appeared he would find that it had vanished. And so he ran at full speed on all fours back to the point where the new tunnel had appeared.

When he reached it he was out of breath. The tunnel was just as he had left it. After catching his breath, he entered the tunnel.

He wondered what lay at the other end. The longer he walked, the more sure he became of where the tunnel was leading. But what would he find when he got there?

Far above his head, the sun arced into the sky and began to fall toward the western horizon. On Machrenmoor, the late-afternoon stillness was disturbed by movement. A horse was crossing the eastern part of the moor. On the horse's back were two creatures: one human, one a gnome. The horse was led by another human, clad in the green of a Hunter, out of place on the gray moor. The Hunter led the horse across the high, flat moortop towards the stones of Toldwyn's Quoit.

From a distance, the quoit looked like a giant milkmaid's stool. It comprised three squared columns of granite supporting a large, flat, table-like slab of the same rock, erected on the very highest point of the moor. As they approached the quoit, the sun dropped behind it, silhouetting it blackly against the orange of the setting sun.

The final zephyr of the afternoon died away, leaving the air utterly still. Not even the song of a bird broke the stillness of the ending day. The only sound was Peregrine's rhythmic plodding.

As they reached the quoit, the sun dipped below the horizon. There was a breath of chill air, and Gwain shivered. They halted.

There was a small outcrop of rock close by the quoit, and Phendric and Michael dismounted and took shelter in the lee of the boulder against the chill breeze that now sprang up. Gwain glanced northward toward Carn Toldwyn. Most of the town was hidden by the moor's bulk, but the northern reaches, and especially the hill on which the castle stood, were visible in the distance

"What's that flag?" asked Gwain, pointing towards the castle.

From the highest tower a large black flag caught the final scattered westerly rays. The maroon of the flag's border looked like blood. But the others ignored his question, for Michael had discovered something among the rocks behind which they were sheltering.

"Look, there's a passage here," he said.

And indeed, among the shoulder-high boulders was a low, narrow passage that curved quickly downward, apparently leading underground.

Phendric considered the passage for several moments, then plunged into it. Michael, after a moment's hesitation, stooped and followed the gnome.

Gwain watched the others disappear and then, with a final frown at the flag flying from the castle, followed after them.

The narrow passage twisted a couple of times, then opened out into a short tunnel. At the far end was a yellow light, as of a candle burning. Phendric led the way through the tunnel, and they almost immediately found themselves in a wide, low chamber.

Hanging on the walls were several sconces, in which torches were burning, providing the light that they had mistaken for a candle. There was one other entrance to the chamber: a low, dark hole in the far wall. The chamber was empty, except for one thing: a table made from a single slab of granite filled the center of the chamber.

And laid out on the slab was a human.

"This is a holy place," whispered Gwain.

"All places are holy places," said Phendric, so quietly that he could barely be heard by the others. "But you are right, Hunter. This is indeed a holy place."

Michael moved to stand beside the rock slab, his hand on the hilt of his sword.

He looked down at the person laid out on the slab.

It was a youngish man, perhaps in his mid twenties, possibly even younger. The man had long, blond hair and was dressed in a light mail armor that reflected the yellow flames of the torches. On one side of the man lay a sheathed sword, its scabbard worn leather, showing that the weapon had been well used. On the man's other side was a small shield with an intricate design of gold on a green background.

Gwain said, "You know where we are, don't you?"

"No," replied Michael.

"We're under the quoit. Look up there."

Gwain pointed to the ceiling directly above the slab. In the packed earth of the chamber's ceiling was a single square block of stone — the same block that lay under the center of the quoit.

"This is Toldwyn's tomb."

"Then that...."

"That's right," said a strange voice. "That's Toldwyn."

Phendric, Gwain and Michael all turned at the intrusion. From the low hole in the opposite wall a creature emerged. It was smallish and rodent-like, with golden fur, quivering whiskers and dark eyes that wore a serious expression.

"I know you!" declared Michael.

The creature bowed towards Michael, and then to the other two in turn.

"Indeed you do," the creature said. "I am the dablik, and it seems to me that it is no coincidence that has brought us together in this place at this moment."

"What do you mean, creature?" asked Gwain.

"I mean that I arrived here by means of a tunnel that, though it seems old, is in fact new. And you have arrived here from the surface by means of a passage that, though you found it with no difficulty, yet has never before been discovered even though many people have visited the quoit above our heads. There is something deep going on here, something very deep indeed.

"Yon gnome speaks the truth when he says that this is a holy place. It has long been known that the ley chamber in which Toldwyn was laid to rest is the holiest place in all Palindor. Look around and answer me this: how are these torches still lit if they have been burning ever since the body of the warrior Toldwyn was placed here after his death?"

While the dablik had been speaking, Phendric had edged nearer to the body on the table. Now he interrupted.

"After his death? It seems to me that Toldwyn is not dead; he merely sleeps. Look: he breathes."

And as if to confirm the gnome's words, the man on the table emitted a long sigh, as of someone disturbed from a deep and peaceful sleep. The sound echoed around them, and the flames of the torches, despite the fact that no wind could possibly have found its way into the chamber, suddenly wavered, projecting grotesque moving shadows on to the walls. For a moment, they were all distracted by the flickering shapes. When they returned their attention to the center of the room, the man on the slab had risen on to one elbow and was blinking his eyes.

He sat up and rubbed his eyes. A long, tired moan escaped his lips. Then he surveyed the chamber.

"Who are you? Where am I?" he demanded.

Michael stepped forward and stood before him, their eyes level.

"The question is: who are you?"

For a second, there was no reaction. And then a fire suddenly blazed forth in the man's eyes. He dropped a hand to his scabbard and in a single move drew the sword from its sheath and jumped to the floor. Michael stepped backward, his hand at the hilt of his own weapon, ready to draw it if necessary.

"Who am I?" the man roared. "Who am I? Do you not recognize Toldwyn, founder of Palindor? And if you do not recognize me, surely you recognize my sword Den-yowŷnk, slayer of Dark Knights? Who are you and these creatures" — he disdainfully included the others with a wave of Den-yowŷnk — "to disturb my sleep?"

The sword glistened brightly in the yellow glare of the flames. He looked around belligerently, challenging them. His gaze returned to Michael.

"I am Michael, High King of Palindor, and we should not be fighting like this."

Toldwyn looked surprised, then suspicious.

"Michael? The High King?"

"I am he."

Toldwyn's eyes dropped to the buckle of Michael's belt. "Your Majesty, forgive me," he said, inclining his head.

"There is nothing to forgive."

"Then have I slept so long?" Toldwyn continued, incredulity in his voice. He appealed to the others: "Tell me; how long have I slept?"

"Long enough," replied Phendric. "The High Queen Catherine has come and gone twice and has now come a third time. The High King Michael, as you see, stands before you. This very evening as the sun set, not many minutes ago, this good Hunter espied a black flag edged with maroon flying over the castle in Carn Toldwyn. Yes, you have slept long; but your time is now come."

"A black flag? Over the castle? The castle then, it has been completed?"

"Aye; untold centuries ago. But it is occupied by the enemies of Palindor."

"Then there is no time to lose. We must fight," roared Toldwyn with a shout that echoed around the chamber.

The flames of the torches guttered perilously.

Toldwyn had returned.

XVIII Occupation

It was a grand feeling to walk the streets of Carn Toldwyn and
see the inhabitants step back in fear.

Captain Malliss and her soldiers had walked into the town
only yesterday, yet already the inhabitants recognized who was in
charge. The black and maroon flag flew triumphantly from the
highest tower.

The castle had plenty of rooms for the soldiers, including Diana.
The town's inhabitants had been pressed into service as servants.

Diana had been allocated a room in the northern tower. It
was the very picture of what she might have expected a room in
an ancient castle to look like. The windows were slits, providing
a protected place from which to fire arrows into the courtyard
below. The walls were rounded, forming the outer wall of the
tower. On the walls hung a mixture of paintings of battle scenes
and ancient weaponry. Above the head of her bed was a pair of
enormous crossed swords that were so large that Diana wondered
if they were merely for show, for surely no one could wield them
as weapons. A chain and mace hung on the wall to her right. To
her left was a shield on which was painted an intricate golden
design on a forest green background.

A small basin was in what would have been a corner if the
room had had corners, and a desk sat under the widest of the

windows. That window faced due north and looked out over the verdant Palindor forest.

The morning after the crew had taken over the castle, Diana jumped out of bed, quickly washed and dressed, and went in search of food. She was ravenous.

Breakfast was served, as supper had been, in the Great Hall. Most of the soldiers were already present, being served by the inhabitants of the town. Some of these were human, but most were small, strange-looking women with rotund bellies and serious faces. The aroma of freshly baked bread filled the hall, and Diana's mouth began to water. She was about to take a seat near the center of the enormous table that ran almost the entire length of the room when she saw that the captain, at the head of the table, was beckoning her.

There was an empty seat on the captain's right. Odrian was seated on her left. The captain gestured for Diana to take the empty chair. An old woman wearing a blue apron and a white bonnet, looking for all the world like some character from a child's book, appeared at Diana's shoulder and placed before her a plate of syrup-covered pancakes.

"I trust you slept well," said Captain Malliss, leaning forward so that her words could be heard over the hubbub of conversation.

"Yes, thank you; like a baby."

"Good. Now, as soon as you have finished breakfast, I would be grateful if you would join me in the throne room. You and I and Master Odrian need to discuss something."

The captain attacked a pancake. Diana helped herself to a glass of water, then began to eat.

The captain departed soon afterward, but Odrian remained behind, waiting while Diana ate her fill. When she had finished, Odrian accompanied her to the throne room, which was a small room on the opposite side of the castle. Though small, it was decorated in a grand style, with soft, richly embroidered tapestries on the wall, interleaved with small daggers of exquisite design. The throne itself was golden, and raised on a low dais.

When Odrian and Diana entered, the captain was standing at one wall, examining a painting. She beckoned the newcomers to join her.

172

"Tell me," she asked Diana, "what do you think of this?"

The painting depicted a battle in which a man clad in silver armor was leading a troop of creatures, many of them not identifiably human, against an armored force. There were several things in the picture that caught Diana's attention.

The first was the man who was leading the charge. Although he was dressed in a kind of silvery chain mail, his head was uncovered and she could see that he was surprisingly young. She wondered who he was. The inscription underneath the picture was in a script she could not read.

"What's the picture called?" she asked.

"Toldwyn and the Battle of Carn Toldwyn," the captain replied.

"Toldwyn? Is that the Toldwyn for which the town is named?"

"Yes. Actually, I believe that the town takes its name from the hill on which this castle is built. The hill is named after the young man because this was where he met his end. At least, so goes the local superstition."

There were other things in the picture that piqued Diana's interest. One was that the standard borne by the flag bearer at the extreme left edge of the picture and the design on Toldwyn's shield both appeared to be identical to the blazon on the shield in her room. But strangest of all was that, apart from the two obvious sides about to engage in battle, there was a lone individual in the picture who was peeking out from the forest that formed the picture's backdrop. This individual was apparently watching the battle that was about to take place. And that person was dressed in black armor, and sat astride an enormous black horse, just like the knights from the *Dark Sky*.

"Interesting picture, is it not?" Captain Malliss asked.

Diana nodded.

"You know what it tells us, though?"

Diana shook her head, unsure of the point that the captain was trying to make.

"It confirms what should have been obvious the moment we set foot inside this castle. The picture tells us that although we walked into this castle yesterday with barely a drop of blood being shed, this land has a history of violence and battle. Yesterday, they were unprepared for us. Today, they will begin to work out a strategy to fight us. Tomorrow, or the next day, or next week, we will find ourselves with a fight on our hands."

"I suppose so."

Turning from the picture, the captain continued, "And the reason I wanted to see you two alone is that I want you to be the ones who prepare our side to lead that fight."

"Us? But you hardly know me," protested Diana.

"True, but don't look so shocked. The men respect you. More importantly, *I* respect you. You have demonstrated that you know how to fight even when the need to do so is sprung upon you with no warning. What more do I need to know? Anyway, the point is that since you are not a member of my crew, I have no right to order you to do anything. Listen to my plan, and tell me if you accept. If you refuse I will not think the worse of you. Agreed?"

Diana nodded hesitantly.

"All right. Here's my plan. Odrian will be the commander of my regular forces. The men are used to taking orders from him, and his orders will be obeyed without question. But I need someone else, for a different job. What I really need is a spy."

"A spy, captain?"

"Yes. When they launch their attack, it will be much easier for us if we have some idea of when it is coming and what form it is going to take. And, as I have just said, you are not a member of my crew. Therefore, if you appear to be a turncoat, the locals are more likely to believe it of you than of any of my men.

"What I suggest is this. We establish you in their eyes as one of my principal lieutenants. I shall appoint you deputy to Odrian. Then you will spend some time in simply walking the streets of Carn Toldwyn, so that everyone sees you. At some point it will begin to become clear to us who the leaders of the opposition are — I suspect that that dwarf Mellow or some other member of the Ruling Council will have a hand in it — anyway, when the time is right, you will go to the leaders. You will tell them that I mistreat you and do not trust you and do not recognize your abilities. It's an old story, but common enough for all that, and they will believe it, if only because they will want to.

"Having apparently changed your allegiance, you will ingratiate yourself with them, learn their plans, their strengths and their weaknesses. Naturally, you will report all this back to me. Then, when they make their attack against us, we will be ready.

"What I'm asking is not without danger. I am aware of that, and that may be reason enough for you to deny my request. But I tell you honestly that you are the best person for the job. So, Diana, what do you say?"

Diana found herself agreeing even before she had really considered the magnitude of the assignment. This was something! To act as a spy in the enemy's camp. To be trusted with such a delicate and dangerous mission. How satisfying it was to be recognized as capable of such a daunting and demanding task. And the captain had chosen *her*; *she* was the captain's first choice for the job. In fact, the captain had as much as said that she was the *only* choice. At last she was among people who understood what she could do.

"Wonderful!" said the captain. "Then I suggest we begin the subterfuge immediately. Go out and walk the streets. And don't be too nice to those you meet. The first thing to do is to establish yourself as someone in authority under me. Your apparent dissatisfaction with me can come later."

With a smile on her face and a spring in her step, Diana left the throne room.

Captain Malliss grinned broadly at Odrian. "Well, General Shadow, what do you think?"

"I think, my master, that things could not be going better."

XIX Across the Lake

Catherine slept uneasily, her dreams filled with troubling and slightly frightening images from years before, when she was trapped with the goblins under the mountains.

She made noises in her sleep, sometimes shouting so loudly that she woke Enwys. After the third such occasion, Enwys stayed awake for some time, watching her new companion thrash around on her palliasse of leaves. Enwys remembered the nightmares that had haunted her own dreams for months after she had been captured. Then her own fear that she had lost her one chance to escape returned, and tears streamed down her face.

Eventually, they both must have slept, for when they woke they could hear the sound of a boat not far away.

"That'll be our food," said Enwys.

They hurried down to the black sand of the narrow beach, Enwys carrying the box that had held the food they had eaten the evening before. The boat was quite close, limned against the dim glow of the rock. It held two goblins. Enwys placed the box on the sand and retreated a few steps.

One of the goblins ordered them to stand clear and, moments later, the metal shell crunched against the black sand.

The humans watched while a goblin unloaded a small box from the boat, exchanging it wordlessly with the one on the beach. He pushed the boat out from shore and climbed in. It was all over in a matter of seconds. The rower leant to his oars, and in a short while the humans were alone again.

They ate breakfast. The gruel and goblin bread were augmented by a small jar of some kind of fruit paste, presumably prepared from berries that Enwys had brought from the surface. Enwys smeared the paste on the dark, heavy goblin bread with the aid of one of the leaves, and Catherine followed her example. It tasted good, although distinctly gobliny. The water tasted slightly of rust, but otherwise seemed good.

Catherine asked something that had been bothering her for a while.

"Why can't we just swim across the lake? It's quite a long way, but the water is warm.... Does something dangerous live in the lake?"

"I don't know. But that's not the reason. You'll think me stupid, but I'm sorry. I can't swim."

Catherine pondered this a moment. "I could teach you," she offered. "It's not hard."

Enwys shook her head. She looked close to tears. "You'll think I'm a baby, but really I'm not. Maybe it's easy for you. You're a High Queen. But I'm just a Huntress. I've never heard of a Hunter who could swim. I thought about it when I was first left here; I even started to wade into the water once, but when the moment came to try to take my feet off the bottom, I just couldn't bring myself to do it. I'm sorry. I'm just too scared."

Privately, Catherine was certain that with patience she could teach Enwys to swim. But that would take a while. Maybe there was a faster way to escape.

"If I could get us safely across the lake, do you think that you'd be able to get us back to the surface without any help?" she asked.

"But how are you planning...?"

"Never mind that. Just suppose that right now we were both standing on the shore over there. Would you be able to lead us to the surface?"

"I know the way easily enough. That's not hard. But the colony never really sleeps. There are always goblins scurrying around in the tunnels. We'd be quickly caught unless we were very careful. They can smell humans even when they can't see us. To be honest, I really don't think we'd get very far."

"Isn't there any special time when the tunnels are reasonably empty? Some sort of gathering that most of them go to?"

"Nothing that I know of. But perhaps if we are quiet, and try to get away during the period when I'm normally asleep, we might be able to escape. I don't know."

"All right, then," said Catherine, "We have to try. Here's what I have in mind. At a time when they expect us to be asleep, I will swim across the lake to the place where the boat is beached. If I can reach the boat, it should be a simple matter to row it back here. Then I could pick you up and row you across the lake. Then it would be up to you to try to get us to the surface. What do you think? Might the plan work?"

Enwys considered Catherine's proposition for a long time. Eventually, she nodded doubtfully. "Yes," she said eventually. "It *might* work. If we can stay hidden. But can you really swim so far?"

"I think so. It's not really that far, I don't think. The gloominess of the cavern makes it seem deceptive. I'm more worried about whether there might be something living in the water that would enjoy me for lunch, but I think I have a way to test that. Anyway, you're sure that you know the way to the surface if only I can get us to the shore?"

"Oh, yes. I'm sure of that. Just as long as we can stay hidden."

"Well, we'll just have to be as quiet as we can and trust to the High Lord for the rest."

"But what's your plan for seeing whether it's safe for you to swim across the lake?"

"Simple. I'm going to swim around the island a couple of times and see what happens."

Enwys looked at Catherine with awe in her eyes. "You truly are a High Queen, aren't you?"

"It's the only way to make sure it's safe. Come on. No time like the present."

She got up and walked to the water's edge. Enwys followed silently.

Catherine took off her shoes and stripped to her undergarments. Then she tentatively walked out into the water.

The ground sloped steeply, and within only a few steps the water reached her waist. Quietly, for she knew how well sound carried over water, she bent her knees and lowered herself until only her head was above water. She began to swim in a languid, silent breast stroke.

Swimming in the lake was unexpectedly unnerving. The water looked black and mysterious, and she kept telling herself that it was only water and nothing more dangerous or unpleasant than that. She forced herself to taste it: it tasted unpleasantly of iron salts, but seemed harmless enough.

She swam close to the shore, barely out of her depth, while Enwys followed her on the beach, watching carefully. Once, to conquer her own fear, Catherine dived under the surface and swam a few strokes underwater. Everything was blacker than a moonless night; there was no difference between swimming with her eyes open and with them closed.

A little farther on, she began to wonder how deep the water of the lake was. Treading water, she said to Enwys, "Don't worry, I'm just going to try something." She swam directly away from the island for a couple of dozen strokes to reach deeper water.

She dived straight down and swam as deep as she could, until her eardrums hurt and her lungs ached, but still she had not touched bottom. The lake was much deeper than she had thought.

Breaking the surface, she said, "I'm coming in now. It seems safe."

The rest of the day passed uneventfully. They talked occasionally of their respective pasts, but both had their minds on the coming night, and their conversations quickly drifted off into nothingness.

The goblins in the boat delivered more food and water, then left.

When it was time to go to sleep, neither felt tired. Catherine was worried that once they went to sleep they might not wake up before the boat arrived in the morning. They needed to be gone long before then, otherwise their disappearance might be discovered and they would be quickly caught.

"How long will it take us to reach the surface?" she asked.

"It's a long way. It takes us an entire day to get there and back when the goblins take me. It must be at least five or six hours each way. The goblins can travel faster than us. They could probably do it in two or three hours."

"Then we'll need to have four hours' lead to be sure they don't catch us."

There was silence for a while, then Catherine asked, "Are you tired?"

"No."

"Then maybe we should just get it over with. Let's go now."

They walked to the shore. They listened intently, but could hear only the sound of the blood in their ears. Catherine stripped to her undergarments.

"May the High Lord be with you," said Enwys.

She looked embarrassed for a moment, as if unsure whether she should embrace Catherine, who was, after all, a High Queen. While she hesitated, Catherine hugged her and said, "Don't worry; I am in no doubt that the High Lord will be with both of us."

Catherine entered the water. She leaned forward and began to swim. She did not look back.

After a couple of minutes, Catherine began to realize that this was going to be more difficult than she had anticipated. It was gloomier than she had expected, and it would be easy to lose her way, for there was nothing to identify the place where the boat lay.

After a while, though, she saw the narrow line of the beach ahead. It stretched away in both directions until it eventually merged with the dim glow of the cavern walls.

She had nearly reached the beach when suddenly she stiffened in horror. Something had brushed against her leg. She remained motionless for a moment, and felt another touch against her foot.

Panicked, she struck out hard for the beach.

Now was the very time when she should have been most quiet, but her fear drove her to swim as fast as she could, regardless of the noise. As she neared the shore, she felt thin tentacles reaching up and clutching at her body. She put her head down and swam at full speed.

She swam straight into the beach, scraping her stomach. Even now she could feel something touching her legs. She struggled to her feet and, gasping, climbed out on to the sand.

She turned and looked back at the lake, wondering if whatever it was that had been trying to grab her might follow her on to the beach.

It was several moments before she realized that something was floating on the surface. It looked like tentacles.

Then she realized.

With an explosion of relief, she reached out and touched a tentacle. It moved away at her touch, then drifted back as she withdrew her finger.

She didn't know whether to laugh or cry. She had been frightened by weed, that was all. She let out a *phew!* of relief.

Catherine scrambled to her feet and cocked her head, listening carefully in case the sounds of her frenetic swimming had attracted attention.

She heard nothing. The beach seemed to stretch only a short distance to her right before it ended. She was almost certain that the boat was therefore to her left. She began to walk in that direction.

She saw it soon enough: a metal shell pulled up on to the sand. There was no sign of a guard. For a moment, she wondered if perhaps the goblins removed the oars when they left the boat, but then she saw them, lying in the bottom of the shell.

She pushed the boat out on to the water and then, as quietly as she could, clambered aboard. She began to paddle away from the shore. After a couple of minutes she decided that she was far enough from the shore to risk rowing. She fitted the metal oars into the rowlocks and began to row steadily towards the dark shape that was the island.

It did not take long to reach it. She beached the boat and scrambled ashore. Enwys was waiting next to Catherine's clothes, and while Catherine got dressed Enwys boarded the boat.

They had to hurry now, in case the goblins discovered that the boat had gone. Catherine got back into the boat.

As she refitted the oars, she whispered, "I didn't hear anything. It sounds pretty quiet over there. I think there's a chance we'll be able to get away without being noticed."

Then she bent to the oars and began rowing back towards the shore. They soon reached it. She let the boat drift the last few paces into the beach. It landed with barely a sound.

They pulled the boat out of the water. As Catherine was replacing the oars in the bottom one of them slipped and a metallic clatter pierced the silence, echoing around the cavern. They held their breaths, fearful that the noise would bring an armed goblin.

But nothing happened, and now Enwys took the lead, whispering urgently, "Follow me."

It was quickly obvious to Catherine that her companion did indeed know her way to the surface, but she also realized just how difficult it was going to be to get away undetected.

The fear that they would be heard was replaced by another, for the silence of the lake had been exchanged for the disconcertingly close sound of goblins scurrying through nearby tunnels. Goblins deep in conversation passed close by every few moments.

Progress was slower than Catherine had hoped, for every time they heard goblins approaching, Enwys pulled her into the closest chamber until the danger had passed. But no sooner would they return to the tunnel and continue on their way than they would hear more goblins approaching and have to dive into another chamber.

They carried on in this way for some time, sometimes escaping discovery only by moments.

"We're nearly at the edge of the colony," whispered Enwys after what seemed like an hour or more of this perilous dodging in and out of tunnels and chambers. There were now fewer chambers and branching tunnels, and they were both beginning to think that they were going to escape without incident when they heard the sound of goblins approaching down the tunnel up which they were travelling. It was a noisy group, and one of them must have told a joke, for they heard the loud sibilant laughter that is so characteristic of goblins.

Catherine and Enwys looked around in sudden fear, for the only entrance where they might hide was a chamber a short distance ahead, near the bend around which the goblins would appear at any moment. Catherine ran forward, beckoning Enwys urgently to follow. Catherine dived into the chamber, Enwys immediately behind her, only a moment before the goblins turned the corner.

And at that moment Catherine realized with horror that the chamber was already occupied.

On the floor lay a family of goblins. All were asleep, but if Catherine had taken one more step, she would have trodden on the father of the family. The humans dared not take another step, and so they pressed themselves against the wall, hoping that none of the goblins in the tunnel would look in their direction.

Catherine watched the backs of the goblins as they passed. It was the very last one, a youngster carrying a pike that had been specially shortened for him, who stopped right at the entrance to the chamber and said, "Papa, what's that smell?"

The young goblin swiveled to look into the chamber, his nose wrinkling as he tried to identify the unusual odor. His eyes met Catherine's.

He shrieked: "Papa! It's a surface creature."

The youngster drew back in fear, leveling its pike at the humans.

The goblin sleeping at Catherine's feet began to stir and mumble hazily.

"Run!" Catherine shouted.

She dashed out the chamber, dodging the youngster's pike, and began to run in the direction of the surface. Behind her, the entrance was blocked before Enwys had taken so much as a single step. A full-grown goblin gave chase to Catherine and caught up with her before she had taken ten more steps.

"Halt!" he shouted harshly, stabbing with his pike.

Catherine stopped. The two humans were unceremoniously herded together as a surprised goblin father looked out of his bedchamber and asked what was going on.

The goblins seemed to be unsure what to do with the humans.

"I caught them, didn't I? I smelled them first," said the youngster.

"That you did," agreed one of the adults. "Now, why don't you go tell the captain of the guard what you've done. We'll wait here and keep a careful eye on the two of them."

The young goblin scampered away.

The adults kept their distance, as if they were half afraid that the humans, even though unarmed, would somehow fight their captors. But it was an unnecessary precaution, for one look at Enwys was enough to tell Catherine that her companion was on the verge of tears.

The captain of the guard arrived quickly, with a stern and commanding expression on his face and three other goblins in tow. He frowned at the humans.

"Are you the same humans who are supposed to be on the island in the lake?"

Catherine nodded, and the captain looked at her quizzically, obviously wondering how they could have escaped. Evidently, he failed to solve this puzzle, for eventually he shook his head and said, "Come with me."

The two humans were led away, surrounded by goblins.

They were held in a chamber for a short time while the captain sent someone to the island to determine if these really were the humans that were supposed to be safely marooned. When the news came back that apparently they were, his manner became brusque. Catherine and Enwys were herded from the chamber and through a maze of tunnels until they reached the king's throne room.

The room was empty. A small group of particularly vicious-looking goblins placed themselves between the prisoners and the room's one entrance.

"What'll they do with us?" Enwys asked, the first words she had spoken since their capture.

Catherine put her arm around Enwys' shoulder.

"Don't worry," Catherine replied. "We'll be all right." She wished that she could sound more sure of herself.

There was a movement near the door and the soldiers parted to permit the king to enter. The king barely glanced at the humans as he strode across the room and seated himself on the golden throne.

There was a long and uncomfortable silence while he peered at them. Catherine met his gaze without flinching; Enwys stared at the floor.

At length, the goblin king spoke. "You are the humans whom we have fed and supplied with water, and given a private place to live?"

Neither answered. Catherine began to realize that perhaps the goblins looked at their captivity in quite a different manner than did the humans.

"Answer me!" the king commanded, his eyes flaring red.

"We are those humans, Your Majesty," said Catherine, lowering her eyes meekly to the floor.

"Is this then how you repay our hospitality? By trying to escape? You were trying to escape, were you not?"

"We were, Your Majesty," admitted Catherine.

"How did you do it? My soldiers inform me that the boat is still on the beach, and yet here you are. How can that be?"

"I swam across the lake, Your Majesty. Then I took the boat and returned to the island for my friend."

"Swam?" The goblin king looked puzzled. "Swam? What does this word mean: 'swam'?"

"Sir?"

The interjection was tentative, from a feeble voice, as of a very ancient creature.

Catherine turned to see that the old, blind goblin dressed in white was being led into the throne room. He leant on his staff and moved slowly. He looked older and more frail even than the last time she had seen him. By his side, and supporting his master discreetly, was the young acolyte. As before, both were unarmed. A silence fell on the throne room as the old goblin shuffled forward until he was standing beside Catherine. He addressed the king.

"Perhaps I can be of assistance, Your Majesty. Swimming is a capacity that some surface creatures possess. It is a means of propelling oneself through, or across the top of, a body of water. Perhaps you were told tales of such things when you were young. On the surface there are many places like our lake...."

"But without a sky?" the king interrupted.

185

"Without a sky," agreed the blind one, and the king visibly shuddered at the thought.

"And there are creatures that have the ability to travel across these bodies of water by a means that I do not fully understand but which is called 'swimming.' Until now I was unaware that humans had this capacity but, apparently, they do."

"Not all of them," interjected Catherine. "With humans it is not a natural behavior, but it can be learned. Many humans never develop the ability to swim, for most do not need it."

"But you know how to... what was the word?" said the king.

"Swim; yes, Your Majesty, I know how to swim."

"And this is how it is that although we left you on the island without a boat, yet you now come to be on the shore?"

"Yes, Your Majesty."

"This presents us with a difficulty, for it does not please me to confine you both more securely, yet I see no other way. If you are determined to leave us, then it is the only way to prevent you from doing so."

"If I might make a suggestion?" It was the blind goblin who had spoken.

"Of course, Holy One," said the king.

The old goblin turned to face the humans. "Would you be willing to promise not to escape if we returned you to the island?"

"What foolishness is this, Kalingroth?" interjected the king. "Such a promise is worthless. They will simply agree and then escape as soon as the opportunity presents itself."

"I am sorry to disagree with Your Majesty, but I think not. Would you do that? Would you break a promise?"

His blind eyes rested on Catherine, and she knew that somehow he knew that she would not lie.

"No, I could not do that. But neither can I promise not to try to escape. We are creatures of the surface, not of this place. We belong there, not here."

"And if you were to escape, would you bring others into our tunnels to steal our treasure?"

"No. I willingly make that promise to you."

"And you?" the sightless one turned to face Enwys, and Catherine wondered how he knew where she was, for she had been silent ever since he had entered the chamber.

Enwys said, "I don't care about your treasure. All I want is to go home."

"Enough of this foolishness," said the king. "I have no interest in your empty promises. You will be returned to the island and there you will be chained to stakes so that you may not leave that place except under guard. That is my decision. I have spoken."

"No!" shouted Enwys.

One of the soldiers stepped forward and pushed his pike under her nose. "Be quiet," he commanded.

"No! I will not be quiet! This isn't fair. We've never done you any harm, we...."

Two strong goblins grabbed Enwys' arms and dragged her, still shouting, from the chamber.

Catherine watched after her and as she did she so was startled to hear the old goblin speaking in undertones that were inaudible to anyone else because of Enwys' shouts.

"Be patient," the old one said.

Catherine had no time to think about this, for she too was now gripped by strong goblin hands and hustled towards the entrance.

Her last sight as she was led from the throne room was of the old goblin supported by his staff, the acolyte by his side, watching her as intently as if he were fully sighted.

XX Convocation

"What can we do?"

It was Shán, one of the two human members of the Ruling Council, who asked the question that was on everybody's lips.

The entire able-bodied population of Carn Toldwyn was at the convocation, which was being held on the flat ground just north of a rise south of the town.

Lookouts were posted to warn of the approach of any of the invaders, but the latter seemed to have no interest in the meeting, although they must have known of its existence because shortly after sunset the streets of Carn Toldwyn had been filled with creatures hurrying southward.

The five members of the Ruling Council were present: the human brothers Shán and Talrynth, the elf Woodruff, the gnome Dibgrín and the leader, the dwarf Mellow. They were seated at the front of the convocation, facing northward, towards all the others. Behind the mass of gathered creatures they could see the town itself, dominated by the castle, its black and maroon flag flapping desultorily in the drafts that occasionally stirred the evening air. Mellow, his torso bandaged, sat in the center of the group.

A waning moon was rising in the east and cast the landscape in a silvery gray light.

"Let's review the situation," said Dibgrín. "Mellow was the first to warn us that two ominous-looking ships had been sighted coming up the Beleron peninsula, making for the mouth of the Findell. Wondering where they might be from and what they wanted with us, many of us, including the entire Ruling Council, went to observe them as the crew disembarked.

"We gathered on the northern shore of the Findell even as they did the same on the southern. There were few of them, fewer than thirty."

He was interrupted by a young gnome in the front row who shouted out: "Twenty three; I counted them."

"Twenty three," Dibgrín continued. "But though they were few, they were dressed in a dark chain mail and had, I think it is safe to say, a menacing air about them. Speaking personally, I didn't like the look of them at all.

"Anyway, we had a hurried discussion, and decided that as your representatives, the Ruling Council should greet them and try to determine the reason for their presence. Their leader, a tall woman who looks like a human but is taller than any human I have ever seen" — there were murmurs of agreement at this assertion — "walked on to the bridge over the rivers, along with two of her crew. She halted at the midway point, evidently waiting for a deputation to greet her. This we did. The five members of the Ruling Council, led by Mellow, advanced across the bridge and stopped in front of her.

"At this point there was a brief conversation, which culminated in the captain of the ships, who calls herself Captain Malliss, imperiously stating that her crew was here to subjugate Palindor. Of course Mellow tried to protest this, and that was when he received the wound that he carries this evening."

Mellow smiled wanly; in the moonlight, he looked particularly pale and weak.

"The rest of us helped Mellow back to shore and watched helplessly as the soldiers from the ships swept past. From what we have been told, they then proceeded to take possession of the castle, after killing the two guards.

"Some of you have been forced to wait on them in the castle. Do you have anything to add?"

There were shakes of heads and calls of "They're a mean lot," and "No good will come of this," but nothing substantive was added to Dibgrín's recitation.

Shán thanked Dibgrín and then turned to the crowd and repeated his earlier question.

"You've heard what has happened, so now we are faced with the question: what are we to do?"

"Fight," shouted someone in the middle of the gathering, and the syllable was immediately taken up and repeated as a kind of chant, growing in volume until the sound must have echoed off the hill before them and reflected back into Carn Toldwyn itself.

Indeed, it did exactly that, for, standing on the highest tower of the castle, the captain and her first mate peered across the intervening moonlit town to where the glimmer of lights showed that the meeting was taking place.

The captain turned to Odrian. "Well, General Shadow. It seems like they want to fight us. How quaint. But it can do us nothing but good."

"Yes, master," agreed the first mate. "And one wonders how they think they can be anything more than a minor annoyance."

"One does indeed. But we must not permit ourselves to be distracted from our true purpose here. Has there been any sign of the High Monarchs as yet?"

"No, master. But they are around somewhere, I am sure of it."

"Oh, I *know* it, Shadow, for I feel their odious presence in the land. There are others here whom our enemy loves, and perhaps we can trap some of them too. But we must not be too greedy. If I can get just one of them, the High Queen perhaps, then the High Lord will have to admit defeat. They are out there somewhere, and it won't be long before they begin to make themselves known. And when they do..." — the captain smiled — "...and when they do, then we spring the trap."

Shadow laughed, and the captain joined in: a loud, mirthless laugh of a long delayed and now imminent victory over an enemy never before bested.

On the hill to the south, Mellow raised a hand, and gradually the chanting subsided.

"Fight!" He echoed the chanted word. "I understand the sentiment, and, indeed, I think all of us on the Ruling Council agree with it."

The other members nodded.

"But the question is: how can we fight them effectively? We outnumber them manyfold, but it is a long time now since the citizens of Palindor went to war. Most of our homes have weapons, but none of us are skilled in their use, save only a few of our dwarves. Our invaders appear to be experienced in battle, and they will not easily be bested.

"But there is something else, something worse; something that is both worrying and puzzling at the same time. We have heard tell that mounted warriors suited in black and riding large black horses have been seen around town. Can anyone confirm this?"

A dozen or more hands shot up, to the accompaniment of cries of affirmation.

A frown appeared on Mellow's face. "Such creatures sound like the Dark Knights of old, who were present when Palindor was first founded and then were seen briefly during the period when the High Queen Catherine first visited us. And if Dark Knights are present, then perhaps there is little point in fighting, for our enemy commands forces greater than any we can muster."

A hubbub arose at these words, and Mellow gestured for silence. "Derwent, please come forward and tell us what the books say about Dark Knights."

Silence fell as a middle-aged gnome with a salt-and-pepper beard stepped from the crowd.

The gnome bowed respectfully towards Mellow, then turned and looked over the crowd. He shuffled nervously, and when he spoke, it was in a voice that was difficult to hear. For the duration of his speech, no sound came from the crowd, so intent were they on his soft, weedy voice.

"My name," he began uncertainly, "is Derwent. I am a gnome." At this there was a titter of laughter from some, because of course he was a gnome. Derwent looked embarrassed, and tried again. The laughter quenched itself.

"I am interested in the archives that are kept in the castle, and I have studied the folk tales maintained by the different races that inhabit Palindor. As you know, the detailed history of the Third Land was lost in the great fires at Perendeth, where the original library was maintained by the Holy Gnomes. But some of our earliest history can still be pieced together, partly from stories, partly from the books written by the Holy Gnome Drefynt in the latter part of his life, and partly from those fragments of some of the books in ancient script that have been translated.

"My own special interest has been the stories told by the Hunters about the period of Palindor's founding, along with some of the tales of sages and necromancers told by the few still living who call themselves wizards."

At the mention of this last word, a feeling of awe descended on the gathering, for all knew that scattered here and there around the Third Land was a handful of members of an ancient race that, even though long ago fallen from its days of glory, still maintained mysterious powers and a long memory of greater days. Most ordinary creatures, if they were honest with themselves, were more than a little frightened of wizards, and many would have preferred to believe that they no longer existed. Derwent's words were an uncomfortable reminder that such a belief was mere wishful thinking.

"I cannot say that I understand the details, for I certainly do not. But as you all know, the High Lord Olvensar was in some way responsible for the founding of this, the Third Land. You also know that the High Lord still lives, or at least we think that He does, and that He occasionally (but rarely) intervenes in circumstances here. The last time that He is known to have been seen was, of course, at the clash of the High Monarchs at Dynas Carn Toldwyn when Drefynt's son Benglubber was killed*. You also know that at that time not only the High Lord but also His enemy, the creature Malthazzar, was present.

"It is this Malthazzar, whom some call the Evil One, who controls those known as the Dark Knights. The Knights are Malthazzar's élite warriors. They brandish swords that have the power not only to kill, but to remove the spirit of a person and condemn it to whatever fell place Malthazzar inhabits.

---

* An event recounted in *Shadow*.

"Do not ask me for more details, for I have none. Was Malthazzar created by the High Lord? And, if so, to what possible end? There are myths that the Dark Knights once fought on the side of the High Lord and then for some reason they changed sides to fight with Malthazzar. But is there any truth behind these stories? Why, indeed, has Olvensar never completely destroyed Malthazzar? Does he not have sufficient power? These are all questions to which I have no answer. Indeed, these were questions that even the Holy Gnomes, with access to much greater resources than I, could never answer fully, although, of course, there were many theories.

"But I can tell you this: that whenever the Dark Knights have appeared in our history, it has been to do the bidding of Malthazzar, and if they are here now, then Malthazzar also is here, or at least close by. We know that Malthazzar can assume human form, for once he appeared as the unfortunate Queen Cerebeth, so it is possible, indeed it is my personal opinion that it is likely, that the one known as Captain Malliss is none other than Malthazzar.

"I can also tell you that in the early days, when magic abounded in Palindor, it was possible to stand against the power of the Dark Knights.

"There is one story I have heard in which the warrior Toldwyn stood against a Dark Knight and vanquished him. But the weapons of those days have long disappeared and today's weapons would, I believe, have no more effect on a Dark Knight than would a stalk of fresh grass.

"Do not ask me for advice, for I have none to offer. But I do warn you of this: if Dark Knights truly walk the streets of Carn Toldwyn, then the power of Malthazzar is here, and we need to take that into account before we decide how, and indeed whether, to fight the invaders. That's all I have to say."

He bowed to the Ruling Council and hurried back to his place in the crowd, glad that his ordeal was over.

Mellow spoke into the gloomy hush that had fallen.

"You see that the decision of how to fight the intruders is not an easy one. We should fight these intruders, yes. But with what means, and how to do it? These are not simple matters. For now...."

"Intruders!" A lookout shouted. "Coming this way."

The crowd turned as one. Approaching was the woman who had been with Captain Malliss when Mellow was injured. Behind the woman were two large horses on which sat knights in armor that refused to reflect the moonlight. Those who had privately disbelieved the rumors of Dark Knights were suddenly forced to reconsider their opinions.

The crowd remained deathly silent as the trio approached. The newcomers halted when they reached the crowd. The woman spoke.

"Captain Malliss orders you to disperse. Go back to your homes."

Someone in the middle of the crowd shouted, "Who are you to order us around?" It was quickly taken up by others. "Who are you?" "You can't order us." "Go away and leave us in peace."

The woman raised her hand for silence. "My name is Diana," she said. "It is a name you would do well to remember. Captain Malliss has appointed me to act in her stead wherever I go in this land, under only herself and her second-in-command, Odrian. With the help of these Knights I intend to ensure that the peace is kept. Now, you will all return to your homes. This meeting is over. Go!"

For a few moments, no creature moved, as if a battle of wills were about to take place. What would Diana and the Dark Knights do if no one obeyed them?

It was Mellow who broke the impasse. Slowly, he got to his feet. His head hanging disconsolately, he walked around the crowd and, casting a sideways glance at the intruders, he passed them and continued towards the town.

Others began to follow. In only a short time, only five remained behind: the four other members of the Ruling Council and the gnome Derwent. Derwent approached Diana.

"Tell me, where do you come from?" the gnome asked. The nervousness that had been so evident when called on to talk in front of his friends and neighbors was absent now that he stood before creatures who were the very forces of evil.

Diana looked at the strange, stunted man with the peaked hat and the straggly beard.

194

She snapped, "Go away, little man! You too," she added, gesturing towards the others who remained. "I could have you all killed for disobeying my command."

"If you won't answer that question, then perhaps you would tell me this: what is your purpose here?" persisted the gnome.

Diana's hand went to the hilt of the dagger at her belt, and slowly she drew the weapon. The gnome's eyes followed the motion. He started in surprise. A dark blade. The stories maintained that such blades could be wielded only by the Dark Knights themselves. Yet now he saw with his own eyes that a mere human could also wield the dark power. The stories were wrong.

"Go! or I'll use it," Diana warned.

The gnome backed away. To the others, he said, "Come, let us leave this place."

Together, they passed the invaders and headed into town.

XXI Kalingroth and Treneere

It was the morning after their abortive escape, and Catherine and
Enwys were back on the island in the lake.

Neither had slept well. Enwys had cried for more than an hour
before succumbing to a restless sleep. Catherine had found her
mind replaying the events in the throne room, trying to remember
everything that had happened. She had a niggling feeling that
she was missing something important.

Each of them now had a ring around her right ankle. The
rings were attached by long, fine chains to a post that had been
placed near the center of the island. Fine though the chain was,
it was enormously strong, and Catherine soon realized that it
was pointless trying to break it. For her part, Enwys had simply
looked at it and then continued crying.

Now they were both awake. Catherine was fingering the chain.
Enwys was sullenly watching her.

"It looks like it should be easy to break, doesn't it?" said
Enwys. "But it won't break, I can assure you of that. Don't think
I haven't tried. Out on the surface where I can't be seen, I've tried
everything I can think of. Smashing it between stones, rubbing
against sharp rocks — nothing works. It takes a sword like yours
to break it. There's nothing we can do. We're trapped."

Catherine could see that if she allowed Enwys to continue in this vein, it would not be long before the tears were flowing again.

"Tell me about the blind goblin," she said, partly to take Enwys' mind off their predicament, partly because she genuinely wanted to know. "He's obviously important. He interrupted the king and the king didn't object."

"But the king didn't believe him. If only he had let us make that promise, we might still have had a chance of escaping."

Catherine was horrified. "Surely you wouldn't go back on your word?"

"Wouldn't I? I don't know. I don't see why not. Oh, I'm so confused."

Enwys sniffled, and Catherine quickly interrupted to stop the tears that were about to begin.

"Tell me about the goblin. Why is he so different from all the others?"

"I don't know much about him. He's some sort of advisor. I know more about the one that goes everywhere with him, the young one who helps him walk. His name is Treneere, and he's the gnome who helped me when we were captured and brought to this place. I think that the old one is some sort of a holy goblin, if there is such a thing. The king calls him the Holy One. His real name is Kalingroth, but they don't seem to use it much. Treneere will take his place one day, I suppose. But I really don't know much about it."

"Listen," said Catherine. "I think they're bringing our food."

Because of their conversation, the boat had almost reached the beach unheard. Now Catherine stood and hurried to the beach. The fetter around her ankle was loose and the chain very light, so that it would have been easy to forget that it was there were it not for the irresistible tug when she reached the end of its range. The goblins were already leaving the day's box of supplies when she reached the beach.

"Thank you," she said, but the only response was a miniscule bow from one of the goblins. He clambered back into the boat with the empty box. Catherine watched the boat disappear into the gloom of the cavern.

How long, she wondered, would this continue?

The day passed unhappily, with Enwys sporadically bursting into tears, and Catherine watching silently and praying to the High Lord. The hours passed slowly and uneventfully, except for the brief return of the boat late in the day. Eventually, tiredness fell on them both and they fell into a deep sleep.

Catherine slept dreamlessly, except for once, when the sound of oars splashing nearby seemed so real that she wanted to get up and investigate. But the splashing seemed to pass by the island without stopping, and she soon returned to her dreamless sleep.

Shortly after they awoke, the goblins delivered more food and water.

They ate and drank a disconsolate breakfast. Enwys was still uncommunicative, and even Catherine was beginning to despair.

Catherine tried to think of some way to lift their spirits, but there was nothing to say. She still wondered why the old blind goblin had urged her to be patient. What had he meant? Had she heard him right? What was his name again? Kalingroth.

And then her heart skipped a beat. Surely it could not be.

That was what had been bothering her: the goblin's name. Kalingroth. She had heard that name before. It was the name of a goblin who had befriended her when she had been a prisoner under the Mountains of Mourn. But it couldn't possibly be the same goblin. The Kalingroth whom she had known was middle-aged even then, and goblins had rather shorter lives than most surface creatures. And in any case, her Kalingroth was just an ordinary goblin, living in the tunnels under the mountains, not a holy creature attached to a colony somewhere in western Palindor.

But it was an unnerving coincidence.

She was just about to say something about this when she heard a distinct splashing coming from the lake. For some reason, the boat was returning.

She and Enwys went to the beach, but it was some time before the boat arrived, for it was being rowed even less expertly than usual. When it finally came into view through the gloom she was surprised to see the very goblin about whom she had just been thinking. Sitting in the rear was the old goblin Kalingroth, and doing his best at rowing was Treneere, who had once befriended Enwys and shared the burden of the extra pack with her.

"About to land, brace yourself," said the Treneere quietly, and Catherine saw Kalingroth grip the side of the metal shell tightly. He need not have worried, for the boat was hardly moving, and it was with only the slightest of shudders that it beached and came to a halt.

Catherine watched as Treneere helped Kalingroth to disembark. The old one wrinkled his pointed snout of a nose and then turned in the direction where she and Enwys were standing.

He said, "You're here, then?" just as confidently as if he had been able to see them.

"Indeed, we are," affirmed Catherine.

"Permit me then to apologize for the way you have been treated, Your Majesty. I have tried to persuade the king to release you and the other human, but I am afraid that he takes a different view of surface affairs than do I."

Kalingroth paused for a moment, as if unsure what to say next.

Then he continued, "Treneere, please be so good as to return the items."

The young goblin reached into the bottom of the boat and withdrew two items that made Catherine's heart soar.

"Forgive us for being so long, but it was quite difficult for my young assistant to sneak into the treasure room and obtain these so that they might be returned to their rightful owner."

Treneere held the objects out towards Catherine. She took the belt and buckled it around her waist.

"Is she wearing it?" Kalingroth asked.

"She is, master," replied Treneere.

The old goblin smiled knowingly.

Catherine shook her head at the remaining item that Treneere was holding. It was the sword Scalmyùt, sheathed in its scabbard Scelberon.

"I don't want those. My days of fighting are over."

"Forgive me for saying so, Your Majesty," said Treneere. "But your fetters...."

Catherine looked down at the chains that snaked across the ground, back towards the center of the island.

Enwys stepped forward, a sudden glint in her eyes. "If you won't, I will."

199

She was about to tear the sword and scabbard from Treneere's hand when Catherine shouted "No!", stopping Enwys in her tracks.

The sound of the monosyllable echoed off the roof of the cavern and slowly died away.

"I thank you for all your help, Enwys," said Catherine. "But that sword is for a High Queen."

She took Scalmyùt and Scelberon from Treneere, fastened them around her waist, and then slowly drew Scalmyùt. Despite the gloominess, the sword's blade seemed to glitter with a light of its own. She brought the sword down on the chain at the place where it joined the fetter around her ankle, and immediately the ring split open. She stepped out of the ring and then freed her companion with a single purposeful stroke. Resheathing the sword, she bowed to the goblins.

"My companion and I thank you for your assistance."

Kalingroth gestured towards the boat. "Now, Your Majesty. If you would be so good as to accompany us, it is time we were leaving."

"Leaving? Where are you taking us?" asked Enwys suspiciously.

"Taking you? My dear human, we are in no position to take you anywhere. Rather, we merely ask that you accompany us to the far side of the lake, where there is a passage that my acolyte has located and which can be followed all the way to the surface."

"We would be honored," said Catherine.

Enwys said nothing, but she regarded Kalingroth suspiciously as Catherine got into the boat. Catherine gestured for Enwys to join her, and she did so with obvious reluctance. The two goblins embarked. The water lapped nearly at the gunwales.

Catherine took the oars over Treneere's protests that such a mundane task was beneath her dignity. She began to row.

It was farther than she had expected, and it was some time before Treneere called out, "Nearly there, Your Majesty," and Catherine glanced over her shoulder to see that they were approaching another beach of dark sand.

"The way from here to the surface is simple," said Treneere as soon as the humans had disembarked. "You see that tunnel? Turn to your left and follow it as far as it will take you. Eventually you will come to a point where it joins another tunnel. Turn right there. You will travel a short distance, and then take a left fork. If you follow that tunnel as far as it goes, it will bring you out at the chamber where the water gathers under the Great Sea. From there the fastest way to the surface is the third tunnel on your left. All you need do is follow that one until it reaches the surface."

"I know that tunnel," interjected Enwys excitedly. "Once we get to the chamber, we're almost home."

"Kalingroth," Catherine said. "I must thank you for your help."

The old goblin nodded, but his sightless eyes were not on her. They were staring blindly at the rock wall of the chamber.

Catherine continued, "But I must ask you, why did you do it? And what will become of you?"

There was a long silence. Enwys tugged at Catherine's sleeve. "Does it matter?" she whispered. "Come on, let's get going."

"Yes, it matters very much," said Catherine, for she could see a glistening trail of tears trickling down the goblin's face.

Eventually he said, "I suppose it is asking too much to know whether you recognize my name?"

"At first I didn't," replied Catherine. "But just before you came to rescue us, I remembered where I had heard it before. It belonged to a goblin I once knew, a long time ago. Was that one of your forefathers?"

Kalingroth shook his head.

"It was a very long time ago, and far away at the other end of the the Third Land. I did not know who you were then. But I do now, and I have been waiting for your return ever since." His voice was so low that he might have been talking to himself.

"But...." There were suddenly so many questions that Catherine did not know which to ask first.

The goblin said, "You tell her, Treneere. I cannot."

"Do we have time?" asked Treneere.

"There is time. After such a long wait, there is time; and if there is not, then the High Lord will cause time itself to stand still. Tell the tale, good friend."

And so Treneere told his master's story.

"As you doubtless are aware, Your Majesty, goblins are not as a rule a particularly spiritual race. We tend to keep to ourselves and let other races get on with whatever it is that they get on with. Give us some good rock and strong arms and a good vein to mine, and we are generally content. We rarely have dealings with surface creatures, partly because our paths almost never cross, and partly because we have no interest in their doings.

"Generally, we live full, and for the most part content, lives. We have our stories and traditions about the way that everything came into being at the will of the High Lord, but the name of the High Lord is used but rarely in goblin culture. In fact, in our traditional ceremonies it is used on only two occasions: at the accession of a new king and at the ceremony for the death of a king. But generally we have no real cause to think about the High Lord and so we mostly just get on with the weave of our lives without bothering too much about whether they form part of some greater tapestry.

"And our lives, even though we habitually carry arms, are generally peaceful. But occasionally, very occasionally, something upsets the equilibrium. Sometimes, one goblin colony will invade and steal treasure from another. It does not happen often, for the ways of the deep tunnels are difficult to remember, and to lead an invading army safely through the tunnels and then back home again is a challenge fraught with danger. But still, it sometimes happens.

"Even more rarely, a goblin will become convinced that he (or she, although there is only one recorded instance of a female making this claim) has seen a vision and spoken with the High Lord. Such goblins are automatically accorded the status of Advisor to the King, and they are permitted greater latitude in their conduct than ordinary goblins, and have access to the king at all times. They wear white to distinguish themselves from other goblins, and they are forbidden to bear arms for the rest of their life.

"Your Majesty, I know from my master that you have been in the hands of goblins once before. Long, long ago, several generations ago now, you somehow stumbled into the hands of the colony under the Mountains of Mourn. That is the same colony into which I was born and raised, and also the one in which your friend Enwys was imprisoned when she became lost in the tunnels.

"As Enwys may have told you, not long after she joined us, a party of goblins from the colony where we now reside raided us. They took several of us prisoner, along with a goodly portion of our treasure, and brought us here.

"The last raid before that one was long ago, shortly after Your Majesty was in our colony. My master was captured during that raid and brought here, just as Enwys and I were centuries later.

"In those days my master was neither more nor less than an ordinary goblin, just as perhaps you remember him (for I see that you age in a manner quite different from other creatures). It was on his journey here as a prisoner that he experienced a vision of the High Lord. I cannot give you details, for I do not know them, and my master will not speak of them, but I do know that when the High Lord spoke to him, he gave my master both a task and a promise.

"The task was that one day he would be called upon to serve you — and I believe that it was at this time that the High Lord specifically said that you were a High Queen, a fact that was unknown to the goblin race before then.

"The promise was that his life would be lengthened so that he might live long enough to see this day and to aid you.

"Because of the tradition of our race, my master immediately became an Advisor to the King here, even though he was originally from another colony. He has advised well over the years, but his faith was tried sorely as the years passed and nothing happened.

"He became old, and then more than old, and blind, and then less than blind. He has lived nearly four times as long as is normal for a goblin, and as you can see he is now ancient and very, very tired. But he never gave up expecting you. When I was captured and arrived from Mourn, the High Lord came to me in a dream and told me that it was my task to look after Kalingroth, which it has been my burden and my delight to do these last few years. I owe my master everything, for although I saw the High Lord in a dream, and was thus entitled to wear the white robe, even then I still did not really believe that the High Lord was anything more than some sort of myth. But now... now I know better.

"The High Lord has revealed much to my master in recent weeks, and I have seen for myself that what my master said was to be has come about...."

The younger goblin's voice trailed off, and Catherine looked at Kalingroth, who was nodding his head slightly in the rear of the boat. His tears had stopped now, but the ancient goblin looked more frail than ever, and Catherine feared for him.

With a sudden flash of insight, Catherine asked Kalingroth, "There is more to come, isn't there? Something you haven't shared with Treneere."

After a long pause, Kalingroth replied wearily, "Yes. Yes, there is. For, you see, the High Lord has told me that the help I have given you and the other human will cost me my life and the life of one whom I love dearly."

"You and Treneere," said Enwys.

Catherine asked, "This escape, no others know of it?"

"No," said Kalingroth. "And when we return the king will be angry, and in his anger he will kill both myself and my acolyte. I know this to be so, for the High Lord came to me just last night and told me these things in a dream."

Kalingroth looked blindly at Treneere. "Go with these humans and leave me here. It is the only way you can save yourself. I know that it will be frightening to be in a place where there is no sky of rock, but I beg of you now, as one last favor to your master, go with them, for it is your only chance."

"Oh, master, master, how can you ask such a thing?" Treneere scrambled towards Kalingroth so that the boat rocked wildly. He embraced the old goblin tightly. "Of course I cannot leave you. I could never leave you."

"But you have heard what I have said. I kept that from you, but I shouldn't have done so. The High Lord himself told me. If you remain with me, we will both die."

"Perhaps, but I have no fear of death. I would fear more what I had become if I were to leave you now. You said that to go with these humans is the only chance I have to save myself. But you are wrong, my master. The only chance I have to save myself is to be with you until the end. And that is where I shall be: by your side, to the very end."

Treneere turned to the humans. "Now, go! We have been here long enough. You remember the directions I gave you?"

"Yes," said Enwys.

"Then leave this place and hurry to the surface. May the High Lord bless you both."

Enwys was already turning to leave.

Catherine said, "I would wish you His blessing also as a benison, but He has already blessed you greatly, even unto death. I pray, though, that one day we shall meet again."

She stared for a long moment at the two goblins, then she turned and hurried after the Huntress.

XXII Retaliation Begins

An uneasy air hung over Carn Toldwyn. The town's inhabitants were uncertain. Was some sort of opposition going to be organized? Or was the Ruling Council going to wait to see what happened next before making a move?

The Ruling Council members themselves were unsure how to answer these questions. After breakfast, they met in Mellow's house to discuss the situation. Mellow looked tired as he sat in his armchair looking at the others.

Mellow's wife Myfanwy was stationed at the window, and his older son Mafik was at the rear of the house, ready to warn them in case Diana or another invader approached the house.

But matters were about to be taken out of the Ruling Council's hands.

Opinions in Carn Toldwyn differed widely as to what the invasion meant and what, if anything, was to be done about it.

The majority of the inhabitants of Carn Toldwyn are gnomes, and the typical gnomish response to the unexpected has always been to wait to see what happens next. And so in many gnomish households the general opinion was that the most prudent course was to wait and observe events as they unfolded, especially given the dangers that were involved if the gnome Derwent was right that Malthazzar was involved. The name of the High Lord, normally rarely used, was heard frequently now. "If Malthazzar is here, then the High Lord cannot be far behind. This is Olvensar's battle, not ours. He will find a way to save us," was a typically gnomish reaction to the invasion.

There were others, mostly dwarves, who felt that the invasion was perhaps not all bad. It was far from proven that Captain Malliss was really Malthazzar, and it had to be admitted that, until the ships had arrived, defenses had been sorely lacking. The captain was accepting volunteers to join her band of sailor-soldiers, and not a few dwarves had opted to join them. These dwarves were now being trained by Odrian and represented the beginnings of a resurrection of Palindor's army, an army that would dissuade the kings of Reglandor and Soltarwyn from casting glances towards the west.

And in other houses, yet another conclusion had been reached.

Hewyn was a dwarf, and justly proud of the fact that his ancestor Kettering of Soltarwyn had fought alongside Toldwyn himself and been part of the guard of honor at the coronation of Yndlarn I, the first king of Palindor. Perhaps the fact that he was young and unmarried also contributed to Hewyn's conclusion about the invasion, for it is always easier to risk one's life when one knows that no one else cares greatly whether it is preserved.

But whatever the reason, Hewyn, who had remained silent throughout the convocation, failing even to join the general chant of "Fight! Fight!", had left the meeting with only one question in his mind: how could the invaders be turned out of Palindor?

Hewyn's cottage was in the northeastern quarter of the town, halfway up the hill and almost in the shadow of the castle. He worked as a stonemason, helping to maintain the castle. For a week now he had bided his time, waiting for the Ruling Council to produce a viable plan of resistance.

Just last night he had accosted one of the Ruling Council's members, Dibgrín, and asked him when the first blow would be struck. Dibgrín's prevaricatory response had caused him to turn away in fury, and he had hurried home, angry that a whole week had passed without any decision being made. As far as Hewyn could see, there was no choice: the invaders simply had to be fought with any and every means at their disposal. It made no difference whether Malthazzar or Dark Knights or anyone else was involved — the creatures of Carn Toldwyn had to stand against them.

He stomped through the streets angrily, and when he arrived at his cottage, he locked the door behind him. If no one else would do the job, he would do it himself.

The first target was obvious: beginning with her supercilious and peremptory ending of the convocation south of town, the human who called herself Diana had paraded around Carn Toldwyn almost as if she were a queen of Palindor. She, then, would be the first to feel the edge of his battle axe.

As in the homes of almost all dwarves, an axe hung over the mantelpiece in Hewyn's living room. Indeed, in the last few days, all over Carn Toldwyn dwarvish battle axes had been taken from their mounts and tested for sharpness, usually for the first time in centuries.

Hewyn now did likewise and, like the others, he immediately discovered that the blade had no edge worthy of the name, time having worn it to a dullness.

There was no question of getting it sharpened. For although there were nearby several dwarves with forges, the mail-clad soldiers had ensured that those forges were now used only for the manufacture of tools and not for the sharpening of weapons.

Hewyn replaced the axe above the fireplace and grimly left the living room and climbed the stairs to his bedroom. But he was not going there to sleep. Instead he pushed the bed to one side, exposing a brass ring embedded in one of the floorboards. He pulled, and the floorboard lifted reluctantly.

Underneath was an object wrapped in cloth. Hewyn carefully lifted it from its hiding place and replaced the floorboard and the bed. Then he went to the window and carefully made sure that the curtains were tightly closed. He returned to the bed and unwrapped the object.

It was an axe. He tested the blade, not with his thumb, but with a single hair of his beard, which he pulled out and then let fall gently across the edge of the axe. The axe cut the falling hair in two and Hewyn knew that in his hand he held the weapon that would strike the first blow against the invaders.

Carefully, he rewrapped the axe and placed it on the floor beside his bed. Tomorrow, the blade would be proven in battle.

Hewyn had but a hazy notion of the origin of the weapon that lay at his bedside that night. Had he known that the axe had been forged by the very first Samuel Ironhand, he would have felt even more secure about his decision to fight.

In the Old Days, when Palindor was being founded by Toldwyn, Yndlarn and the others, there lived a reclusive old human by the name of Samuel Ironhand* whose weapons were imbued with deep power.

Over the centuries, most of these weapons were lost or destroyed, or their power simply faded away. There were, however, a few exceptions. One of these was Scalmyùt, the sword of the High Queen. Another was Toldwyn's sword, Den-yowŷnk. The last that concerns us is Hewyn's battle axe. Like all weapons created by Ironhand, the battle axe had a name, Tewlladher, which can be translated into the modern tongue as "Killdark." It was one of the few weapons ever forged over which the High Lord himself offered a blessing, and thus one of the few that could withstand the power of a Dark Blade.

But none of these truths, or at least only the vaguest perceptions of them, were known to Hewyn that night as he slept. He knew merely that the blade was old and powerful, and had been in his family for a long time.

Hewyn slept deeply that night, and he awoke late the next morning, the daylight already filtering through the curtains and lighting the bedroom.

After breakfast he hid Killdark under the bed and then left to reconnoiter the town.

The streets were unnaturally deserted. Here and there a creature hurried past on an errand, but mostly the streets were empty. Most of the creatures Hewyn saw were gnomes with harried, hunted looks on their faces, as if they were uncomfortable at being outside at all.

---

* For more about Samuel Ironhand, see *Palindor*. A fuller account of the original Samuel Ironhand can be found in *Tales and Histories from the Early Days of the Third Land* by Partrin the gnome and *A History of Abuscân, Volume Five: The Third Land Founded* by the historian Bullwhistle of Soltarwyn.

It was midmorning before he saw the first of the mail-clad invaders — the human who called herself Diana, striding down the road from the castle as if she owned the place. She was accompanied by a mounted Dark Knight, whose horse walked a pace or two behind the woman.

Hewyn watched as the pair passed. Diana did not even glance in his direction. The Dark Knight turned his head, but it was impossible to be sure what he was looking at, for behind the narrow slits of his visor it was impossible to discern the Knight's eyes. The pair continued down the hillside.

It was shortly after that that he saw the first armed dwarf.

It was Brinning, a dwarf who also lived in the northwestern corner of town, not far from the castle. Brinning was walking down the street with an axe openly stuck in his belt. He was accompanied by his wife, Dhurlyn, who was carrying an empty basket. From the looks of them, they were on the way to buy groceries.

As they drew closer, Hewyn observed that Dhurlyn was also armed. Hewyn recognized the two brightly colored decorative axes that usually adorned their mantle. He had little doubt that the axes would be useless in a fight, for whoever heard of true battle axes with handles that were brightly and intricately painted? And doubtless the blades were no sharper than the axe that hung over his own mantle. But that hardly mattered, for simply by wearing them the dwarves were making a statement.

"Greetings," Hewyn called.

Brinning and Dhurlyn returned his greeting and halted.

"I see you are armed," Hewyn continued, pointedly.

"No law agin' it, is there? A creature is free to wear a weapon, ain't he?" replied Brinning in the broad brogue of southwestern Beleron where he and his wife had been raised.

"Aye, that's true."

"Then mayhap you want to be thinking on taking that axe down from where it's hung all these years and putting it to a more useful purpose."

"I don't suppose you've been able to get your axes sharpened?"

"'aven't tried, not yet. Thought I'd sneak out tonight and 'ave a talk with old Firren who runs the forge up north aways an' see if we could send some custom 'is way. Rumor is that these 'ere Dark Knights and the captain an' all is only really interested in Carn Toldwyn. The rest of Palindor is still as free as a bird."

"So it might be possible to smuggle out some weapons and get them sharpened?"

"Aye, so I've 'eard."

The sound of hooves on cobblestones interrupted them. Diana and the mounted Dark Knight rounded a corner and came into view.

Diana spotted the dwarves and approached angrily.

"What do you mean by that? Are those weapons you two are wearing?" Diana called as she neared the dwarves.

"If it please your Honor," said Dhurlyn, performing a little curtsey — and Hewyn almost laughed out loud, for the battle axe was a most incongruous adjunct to someone who, without it, presented the very picture of a harmless, middle-aged, motherly dwarf about her daily shopping — "'tas always been true that dwarves an' suchlike 'ave been able to wear axes around town. It don't signify nothing."

"Well it does to me," Diana snapped. "Take those axes off, right now."

Brinning intervened: "Begging your pardon like, Your Honor, but by whose authority exactly is it that you be asking?"

Diana stared disbelievingly at the effrontery of the dwarf who had questioned her.

"By the authority invested in me by Captain Malliss, if you do not remove those weapons this instant, I shall be forced to command my companion to remove them from you."

"Please, Your Honor, we don't mean no 'arm," began Dhurlyn, but the Knight's horse took a step forward and the Knight slid his sword from its scabbard.

The pale sunlight was swallowed by the drawn blade and the two armed dwarves looked uncertainly at one another. Suddenly, the blade swept down. There was a clatter, and Dhurlyn looked down to see that the tip of the dark blade had sliced through her belt, and the decorated axe had fallen to the cobbles.

Dhurlyn looked up in horror at the Dark Knight, aware that had she made the slightest motion towards him, the blade would have pierced her clothing and punctured her skin.

Without a word, Brinning removed the axe from his belt. He held it out to Diana.

"'ere, take it," he said.

Diana took the axe, then picked up the other from where it had fallen.

"Henceforth weapons are forbidden."

Diana turned away. For a long moment the Dark Knight looked down on the three dwarves, then he followed Diana.

Eyes blazing, Hewyn stomped away from Brinning and Dhurlyn without a word. He had had quite enough of this.

He returned to his house and went upstairs. Retrieving Killdark from under the bed, he balanced its weight in his hands.

It was many years since Hewyn had practiced with an axe, and even then it had not been a serious matter, merely sparring for the games that were held occasionally. This was a heavy axe, and would be an unwieldy weapon in hand-to-hand combat. This axe was designed principally for throwing. But to throw an axe accurately required much practice, and that could be done only outdoors and over a period of many days.

But Hewyn was determined to make the best of it. Someone had to strike the first blow against the invaders, and what he had just witnessed made him determined that it would be he who struck that blow. He stuffed the axe into his belt, adjusted its position so that it was properly balanced, then walked out the room, down the stairs and out the house.

The streets were even emptier than they had been. He walked from one end of Carn Toldwyn to the other, from his house near the castle to the bridge across the Pennyfarthing, and in all that time he saw only four other creatures on the streets: three gnomes and a human. All of them gave him a wide berth.

At the bridge he halted and for some time stared silently at the river that flowed underneath. Then he turned and began to make his way back towards the castle.

He went along the western side of the town, but even here, in a residential area normally busy with gnomes going about their business or passing the time of day in idle chat, no one was out of doors. He climbed the hill towards the castle. Halfway up the hill he halted, hearing at last the steady *clop-clop-clop* of a Dark Knight's horse.

Around a corner came Diana and her Dark Knight. At the sight of the two of them, Hewyn changed his plan. It was not Diana who had threatened and scared Brinning and his wife this morning — it was the foul creature who took his orders from her. It was time that the Dark Knight swallowed some of his own medicine.

Hewyn stanced firmly, his feet spaced for balance. He slowly removed the axe from his belt.

Diana and the Knight approached until they were some half dozen paces from Hewyn. They halted.

"It is forbidden to wear a weapon," Diana said.

"I'm not wearing it," replied the dwarf.

His left hand gently tossed the haft near the blade, so that the head of the weapon rose half a hand's breadth in the air, then fell back. He repeated the motion. His right hand firmly held the wooden haft near its base.

"Then it is forbidden to wield a weapon," Diana said.

Hewyn continued to heft the axe while appearing to consider her words. Eventually, he said. "I do not recognize you. Are you a member of the Ruling Council? I don't remember you being elected to that position."

"Do not bandy words with me. You know who I am. I am Diana, and I order you in the name of Captain Malliss to yield that weapon to my Knight."

"Ah, *your* Knight, is he? Well, Diana, I have news for you. Some of us would rather fight than be reduced to slavery."

"I'll give you one more chance. I order you one last time: surrender your weapon to my Knight."

For a long while Hewyn simply stood, and stared, and continued hefting the axe. The dull thud as it repeatedly landed in his hand became monotonous.

"I think not," he said at length. "I am a free dwarf of Palindor, and I take orders from no creature. However, if the Knight desires

213

my weapon, he is welcome to try to take it from me. But perhaps it is not he who wants it. Perhaps it is you?"

"Take it from him," Diana snapped.

"Shall I harm him?" asked the Knight.

The question surprised Hewyn, for until now he had not considered the possibility that these creatures from the netherworld might be able to talk.

"Do whatever you want. I care not," she said.

The Knight drew his sword.

XXIII Reunion

Catherine and Enwys left the old goblin and his young acolyte and
began to hurry through the tunnels as Treneere had directed them.
Catherine tried to put out of her mind the price that Kalingroth
and Treneere were going to pay for helping them escape, but
several times in the first few minutes Enwys had to urge Catherine
to make haste.

With a sigh, Catherine reconciled herself to the fact that there
was nothing she could do for the goblins and tried to put their
fate out of her mind.

The tunnel was exactly as Treneere had described it. They
hurried along, spurred on by the thought of what would happen
to them should the goblin king discover their escape and send his
soldiers after them.

Every now and then, they stopped to catch their breath, listening intently for any sound of pursuit. There was one thought that
comforted them: that a goblin army racing through the tunnels
after them would be audible for a long way. The tunnels remained
empty and silent, and as soon as they had recovered their breath,
they hurried onward.

After a while, they arrived at the chamber in which the water
accumulated, and now for the first time they were faced with a
real choice, for there were many exits from this chamber.

They stood on the edge of the pool and looked across the water at the tunnels.

"Treneere said that the third tunnel to our left is the fastest way to get to the surface," said Catherine.

"Yes, but after coming this far we don't want to get caught. Perhaps we should go another way?"

Catherine was unsure. On the one hand, she wanted to be on the surface as quickly as possible, because once they reached it they would be safe from pursuit. On the other hand, there was still the possibility that they would be captured if the goblin king sent his soldiers after them.

"How long would it take to reach the surface if we went some other way?" asked Catherine.

"Anywhere between a quarter of a day and maybe a day and a half, depending on which route we took. The one I know best takes us some way south and is quite a long way. It's where the best berry bushes are."

"I've been thinking. What if the goblin king gets Treneere or Kalingroth somehow to tell him what directions we were given? It might be a good idea to take a different route. So let's take the way you know."

With that agreed, they waded through the water and hurried along a tunnel on the far side of the chamber.

Neither of them wanted to stop to sleep, but it was not long before they had to rest for a while. They took it in turns to nap while the other listened for pursuers. They heard none.

Refreshed, they hurried on.

After a while, they began to smell an earthy odor. Then they turned a corner and Catherine, who was in the lead, abruptly stopped, for the dull glow of the rock walls suddenly gave way to blackness. The earthy smell became stronger, but with it there was something else — a sort of tang that she could not immediately place.

"Just up ahead; there's a sharp turn to the left, and then we'll be out," said Enwys.

Catherine let Enwys take the lead. Catherine shivered as a cool breeze wafted past. There was a patch of light gray just ahead, and in that patch glinted pinpricks of twinkling white light.

A few more steps, and they were standing at the entrance of a cave, looking up at the cool, cloudless Palindor sky.

For a time, neither spoke. Catherine heard a sound from her companion, and it was several moments before she realized that Enwys was sobbing.

"I didn't believe I'd ever get away," said the Huntress through her tears.

Catherine was not sure what to say. She had been *almost* certain that the High Lord would show them a way to escape. But, now that they were actually standing on the surface once more, she had to admit that, deep down, even she had had her doubts after they had been recaptured.

"Thank you, Catherine," said Enwys, the sobs receding. "Your Majesty, I mean," she amended, for during their imprisonment there had seemed little point in titles, but now that they were free, it suddenly seemed inappropriate to call a High Monarch by anything less than her due.

"Well, where do we go from here?" Catherine asked.

They were standing in a small, screened-off area on the side of a hill, their view of the valley below blocked by dense bushes.

"The first thing we do," Enwys said firmly, "is to get something to eat and drink. There should be berries on these bushes unless there's been an early frost, and there's a stream not far away at the bottom of the hill. We're somewhere near the south coast, although I've never been sure exactly where. In fact, I didn't even realize that the goblin colony was under the Great Sea until you told me. I imagine that we're somewhere on the Beleron peninsula, but we'll know for sure when it gets light. First things first, let's get something to eat."

So the two fell on the bushes, discovering to their delight that the thin branches were weighted down with large, sweet, juicy smoothberries that quickly assuaged their hunger and took the edge off their thirst.

"Let's get away from the entrance just in case the goblins come after us; then we can rest," said Catherine when they had eaten their fill, for now they had begun to feel the full brunt of their tiredness.

Enwys led the way around the screen of bushes. Catherine caught her breath at the placid beauty of the sight that greeted her eyes.

A short distance to the south lay the sea — that was the source of the tang in the air, Catherine now realized; the stars glistened off its smooth surface so that it looked almost as if they reached down to the very mouth of the valley below.

They were about halfway up the western side of a steep V-shaped valley. Enwys stood breathing deeply of the briny air.

"Fresh air," she said, "and all this space." She gestured to include everything around them.

She embraced Catherine in a bear hug. "Thank you. Oh, thank you! I could never have done it without you."

"Yes, well," said Catherine, embarrassed at this display of gratitude, "let's find somewhere to rest before I fall asleep on my feet."

"Right," agreed Enwys, and she began to lead the way down the wooded hillside.

At the foot of the valley a stream burbled over rounded stones on its way to the sea. On either side of the stream was a swath of grass. They found a nook between a tree and a boulder and, within moments of lying down, both were fast asleep.

They awoke late. The sky had clouded while they slept, and the sun shone weakly through the veil that now hid the sky.

Enwys sniffed the air. "Snow. Or possibly rain. Something, anyway, unless we're lucky. In an hour or two."

Enwys stopped, realizing what she had done, and laughed out loud. "All this time and I still remember how to read the signs."

"Of course," said Catherine. "Once a Hunter, always a Hunter. You can put the past behind you now. You're home again."

Catherine noticed that Enwys' attention had been engaged by something on the ground. She was on her hands and knees, rubbing a finger over a small patch of grass.

"What is it?" asked Catherine.

"Hoof marks. Horses have passed this way. Some time ago now. Several days, maybe a week. Nothing since."

"Well, we should be getting going as well, I suppose. Which way should we go?"

Enwys pointed upstream. "The other way just leads to the sea; but there must be something this way."

They walked for a few minutes in silence — Catherine because she was wondering what to do next, Enwys because silence is the way of the Hunter — when they rounded a tight meander and halted. A short distance ahead on the opposite side of the stream stood a ramshackle cottage surrounded by a lush lawn and a beautiful display of flowers. It quite took Catherine's breath away.

A thin trail of smoke rose from the chimney, but there were no other indications that anyone was home.

They looked at one another. Neither spoke, but the same question was in both their minds: should they make themselves known or should they pass by without stopping? A little way ahead a path crossed a small wooden bridge and led towards the cottage.

There was a movement. Near one of the flowering bushes halfway down the garden, a small creature had moved. The creature was dressed in a green that almost perfectly matched the grass.

A female woodelf began to walk towards them. She carried a weed tray that she deposited on the ground on the far side of the bridge.

The elf stopped, bowed and said, "Greetings, travellers. I am Esterin, elf of this place, and I bid you welcome."

Catherine realized that Enwys and she had not talked about how they would present themselves to strangers. Should Catherine admit her status as High Queen, or should she simply describe herself as a human?

Before Enwys could speak, Catherine said, "Catherine, human of Palindor, and this is my companion, Enwys the Huntress."

"You don't look much like a Huntress to me," observed the elf; and it was true, for Enwys' garb was an ill-fitting suit of dirty brown quite unlike the green vestments of a Huntress.

"Don't stand there gabbing. Invite them in."

Catherine and Enwys looked towards the house in surprise at the sudden intrusion. An old woman was leaning from a dilapidated window that looked dangerously as if it might break at any moment. "The tea is just made and the honeybread is almost ready for eating," the old woman continued. "Come on in, you two; you look like you could do with a bite to eat."

Enwys and Catherine exchanged glances. The question of how they would explain themselves to the old woman and the elf — now, that was something very strange: an old human and an elf living in the same house — battled with the attraction of fresh tea and warm honeybread. The tea and honeybread won.

"We'd love to, thank you," said Catherine. Esterin led them towards the house.

"Here; come in the back way," said the old woman, indicating a door around the side of the house. "Then we can talk in the kitchen while I'm getting things ready."

The elf led them into the house through the side door, and they found themselves in a ramshackle old kitchen.

Despite its not-altogether-pristine appearance, the kitchen was warm and friendly. The smell of baking bread filled the air, causing the newcomers to salivate uncontrollably. There were two fire grates along one wall, and both held piles of glowing coals. Above one pile was a kettle that the old woman had been filling from a pump at the sink as the visitors had entered; now it swung from a tripod as the water inside was heated for tea. Above the other pile of coals was an oven for baking, and it was from here that the smell of the bread came.

"The bread and tea will be ready shortly, but I expect you'd like some scones or something while you're waiting," said the old woman.

"I'll get them," offered Esterin.

Standing on a stool, she removed a large container from a cupboard. She took a number of scones from the container, putting them on a large wooden plate that the old woman produced for the purpose.

"Take a seat, you're making the place untidy," the woman said, and the two sat at the table.

The scones were made with smoothberries, and it was impossible to eat just one. As the woman busied herself taking the honeybread from the oven and preparing the tea, Catherine and Enwys ate three apiece. Then a plate of fresh honeybread and mugs of steaming tea were added to the table.

"Don't often have visitors," said the old woman.

"It's been busy lately, though" said the elf and was immediately rewarded by a stern glance from the old woman.

Enwys did not notice the look, her face being wrapped around a thick slice of honeybread at that moment, but Catherine saw it, and wondered what it meant. She began to get the uncomfortable feeling that there was something more going on here than met the eye.

There was a sound from the kitchen doorway and everyone looked up to see a second old woman enter the room. She sniffed the air in a disapproving way. Her eyes alighted on Enwys and Catherine.

"More strangers."

Catherine introduced herself and Enwys, but the woman, instead of reciprocating, stalked up to Enwys, placed her nose close to her hair, and sniffed. She recoiled in horror.

"Couldn't make out what that awful smell was." She sniffed at Catherine's clothes. "It's you two. You both need a good bath. You especially." She looked accusingly at Enwys.

"Call yourself a Huntress? I'm surprised the animals don't smell you a hundred paces off and run the other way. I know I would. And you," she continued, turning to Catherine, "call yourself...."

"Now, now," interrupted the first woman. "Don't take on so, Harsforn. Remember they are our guests, even though they haven't said exactly *where* in Palindor they are from."

Her tone was accusatory, and she looked at Catherine as if Catherine was trying to hide something, which of course she was.

"Oh, just here and there," Catherine said absent-mindedly. "I've spent most of my time in Carn Toldwyn." She was trying to remember where she had heard Harsforn's name before.

"Huh!" said Harsforn, screwing up her eyes suspiciously. "Smells more like Carn Goblin to me. But I suppose you know your own business best."

"Tea, dear?" offered the other old woman, smiling sweetly as she poured the steaming liquid into a mug.

"Don't mind if I do. There's never a bad time for tea." To Catherine's relief, Harsforn fell silent as she began to drink.

"If you would each like to take baths, you're more than welcome," offered the other woman. "But don't feel like you have to."

Harsforn mumbled something that sounded like "Tell 'em it'd be an honor; then they'd feel obligated" into her mug but Catherine could not be sure of her words, and Harsforn did not repeat them.

"Yes, we'd love that, wouldn't we?" said Catherine.

Enwys nodded dubiously, as if she were not exactly sure about taking a bath in such a strange house. "It would be nice," she eventually admitted.

"That's settled, then. We have hot water inside the house, you know, my dears. It's quite clever, really. The pipe runs past the fires to keep the water warm, you see. When you're ready. No rush now."

Catherine went first. Esterin led her upstairs to a small bathroom in which a large tub stood next to a pair of pumps. The elf showed her how to use the two pumps to get the water to the right temperature, and then left the room so Catherine could bathe in private.

When she came downstairs half an hour later, Catherine was clean and refreshed. The elf and Enwys were talking, and there was no sign of the two old women. Enwys departed to take her turn with the bath.

"If you'll excuse me, I ought to get back to the garden," said Esterin, and she too left the kitchen, leaving Catherine to her own devices. She poured herself another cup of tea, and had almost finished it when the unnamed old woman returned. A frown corrugated the woman's face.

"Now that we're alone, I hope you won't mind my asking," said the woman, "but shouldn't you be in Carn Toldwyn or somewhere, helping with the rebellion instead of wandering the Third Land with a young Huntress?"

"What rebellion?"

"Ah! So you don't know. That explains it. I wondered why a High Monarch would be wandering around smelling distinctly of goblin and in the company of a Huntress dressed in the most unHuntresslike garb I've ever seen, instead of being with the others in Carn Toldwyn. Of course," the woman added off-handedly, "in my younger days I would have understood it all without being told."

And then Catherine remembered.

"You're Iadron and Harsforn!" she exclaimed. "The seer and the healer. It was Harsforn who saved me once when I was cut by a dark blade."

"Couldn't have done it without me," grumbled Iadron. "She gets all the credit, but she would've refused to help at all if I hadn't persuaded her otherwise."

"Well, I need to thank you both. I would have died without you."

At that moment, Enwys entered the kitchen. Unfortunately, the odor of goblin still clung to her clothing. Even so, the improvement was distinctly noticeable. A few moments later, Harsforn also came into the kitchen.

"There now, that's better," said Iadron to Enwys, her conversation with Catherine apparently forgotten. "Now, if you'll follow me, there's someone you need to meet, Huntress Enwys. She was badly wounded, but Esterin has nursed her back to health and I think I heard her go out into the garden a few minutes ago."

They trooped outside. At the far end of the lawn, Esterin was pruning a tree. With her was someone else, a young Huntress to judge from her attire. The Huntress and the elf were so engrossed in their work that they did not notice as the group approached. No more than half a dozen paces separated them when the elf and the Huntress looked up from their work and Enwys came to a startled halt.

"Gwynedd?"

The young Huntress stared at Enwys for several long seconds. She frowned, but said nothing.

"Don't you recognize me, Gwynedd?"

"Enwys? No! It can't be. You're... Enwys!" shrieked Gwynedd, and she dropped the pruning shears she had been holding and, ignoring everyone else, ran to her sister and held her tightly.

"How did you get here?" Both Huntresses asked the same question at once and the two dissolved into laughter.

"Let me look at you," said Enwys, holding her sister at arms' length. The two grinned at one another, each unable to believe what she was seeing.

"You look pale," said Gwynedd.

"It's a long story," sighed Enwys.

"And your clothes are atrocious. And that smell."

"As I said, it's a long story."

"But you're alive! You're alive!"

"Indeed I am."

"How? What happened? We thought you were dead. But... I'm sorry. This is so hard to take in."

Just then, the sound of horses making their way through the forest interrupted the reunion.

They all turned to watch as several mounted Hunters came to a halt on the far side of the little bridge.

In the lead was Gwain, sitting tall in his saddle, and leading a second horse by the bridle. Behind him was his wife, Heth. They were accompanied by four other Hunters. Gwain began to dismount.

"Father," yelled Gwynedd, and she ran away across the grass towards the bridge. Enwys gave chase and passed her. She dashed across the bridge and flung herself straight into Gwain's arms.

"Father! Mother! I thought I'd never see you again."

Enwys turned and hugged her mother, who was speechless as tears coursed down her face.

Introductions were made, and the next few minutes were full of joy.

No one could quite believe that Enwys had been restored to them after all this time. And Gwynedd seemed fully recovered from her awful wound. For a while the sounds of joyous laughter echoed around the valley floor.

But then Gwain became serious. "Your Majesty," said Gwain to Catherine, "much though I wish we could all stay here and celebrate this glad day, I am afraid that your presence in Palindor merely confirms how desperate the situation is."

"Desperate?"

"Said so," smirked Iadron quietly to no one in particular. Everyone ignored her.

"Aye," continued Gwain. "There are Dark Knights abroad. Even in Carn Toldwyn itself. We cannot stay here. We are needed in Carn Toldwyn. All of us. There's no time to be lost."

"It's Malthazzar; I know it," said Catherine.

"Possibly," said Gwain. "But if so, we don't know what he's up to. The invaders are led by a woman; although we know from the old stories that it could still be Malthazzar — he has taken a female form before."

"Don't remind me," mumbled Catherine, staring at the ground, her thoughts momentarily far away.

"From what we hear, the captain seems to spend all her time in the castle. She lets two of her aides, a man by the name of Odrian and a woman by the name of Diana, do her dirty work for her."

"Diana?" Catherine's head jerked up.

"Aye. Strange name, is it not?"

"This Diana, describe her."

One of the Hunters accompanying Gwain said, "Young. Tall. Longish hair, not at all in the Palindoric style. It's obvious that she's not from around here. Carries herself imperiously. Speaks a little strangely."

Catherine nodded.

"It's her," she said. "And you are right. There is no time to lose. Come on, we must not waste another moment. I don't know what plan the captain has in mind, but whatever it is, it must be stopped."

XXIV Confrontation

The Dark Knight, still astride his massive black horse, advanced toward Hewyn. Diana hovered in the background, watching. Hewyn swallowed with difficulty: something seemed suddenly to have stuck in his throat. He wondered how he could possibly have been so stupid as to challenge a Dark Knight.

Hewyn peered at the Knight's visor and wondered what manner of creature was inside.

Still the Knight came closer. Another few steps and the horse would be towering over the dwarf, the Knight would raise his sword, then bring it down in a single, killing swoop.

Suddenly, Hewyn seemed to wake from a dream. He drew back his arm and threw his axe at the oncoming figure with all his strength.

It all happened so quickly that afterwards it was difficult to reconstruct exactly what happened. The horse was no more than five paces distant when Hewyn loosed the axe, which hurtled through the air towards the Knight. But before it could reach its target the horse reared high in the air. Its rider was thrown backwards; he lifted one arm for balance while grasping the rein with his other hand.

The axe buried itself in the horse's flesh. A doomladen shiver passed through the animal. It crashed to the ground, dead.

The Knight scrambled to his feet. He stood, sword still in hand, looking at Hewyn.

The Knight began to advance on foot, and Hewyn turned to run. But in turning he twisted his ankle and fell. Before he could recover, the Knight was standing over him.

"You will go to Sheol for this," said the Knight, "and there you will become as I am."

He raised his sword to strike.

"Hold, Knight of Darkness. Turn and meet your doom!"

And, to Hewyn's amazement, the Knight, in the very act of readying himself to kill, turned slowly towards the place whence the voice had come.

A young man stood some fifteen paces away, at the entrance to an alleyway between two buildings. He stepped out into the street. He was wearing a light, silvery mail that Hewyn vaguely recognized. His hair was long and blond, and in his right hand he carried an unsheathed sword.

"You!" exclaimed the Dark Knight.

He stepped away from Hewyn, whom he suddenly seemed to have forgotten, and returned the gaze of the stranger who had challenged him.

"Aye, it's me, Knight of Darkness. Which one are you? Gorthewer? Hünlef? Stak-dhû of the Hordes? Pray, do tell me, before I have the pleasure of dispatching you with Den-yowŷnk and so ending your eternal journey."

Hewyn scrambled to his feet and hobbled to a nearby corner, where he watched in fascinated horror.

The Knight took a step. Unbelievably, it was not towards the young man with the sword — it was a step backwards, *away* from him.

"Answer me! I command you in the name of Olvensar! What is your name?"

A strangled cry came from the Dark Knight. He brandished his sword wildly. "That name has no power over me, for I am Hünlef, and I fear no mortal who stalks this Land, no matter the name of his sword."

Now the young man began to move closer, his steps calm and measured.

"Not afraid, Hünlef? Then you are a fool. But perhaps it is as well, for I would feel cheated if your fear instead of my hand were to defeat you. Take *that*, Knight!" And on the word "that" the young man sprang forward and brought his sword down so quickly that it seemed almost like an imagined blur.

But the Knight parried the blow with his own weapon. As the two swords clashed, a low, dull sound rent the air, as if this was a battle not of metal against metal, but of forces altogether deeper and more powerful.

"Ha!" ejaculated the Knight, and the battle began in earnest.

Hewyn watched as the two fought desperately. The Knight was much larger than his opponent, but his size and heavy armor made him slower. Surprisingly, the man in silver seemed every bit as strong as the massive Knight, for when the Knight's sword came racing down to cut off the man's arm at the shoulder, the young man successfully thrust the blow to one side.

It was perhaps half a minute before the first real blow landed. It was the Knight's, and by rights it should have ended the battle, for Hewyn knew as well as anyone that the sword of a Dark Knight could pierce any ordinary armor, and certainly a light mail such as the one that the boy was wearing; and once the blade pierced the skin, then any mortal's life would ebb away to nothingness.

But the Knight's sword, which slashed at the youth's silvery tunic, merely glanced off it. But the boy staggered for a moment, and if the Knight had not been caught off balance, he might have followed with a rapid, lethal thrust to the boy's neck. But by the time Hünlef had recovered and thrust forward, the boy had moved to one side, and the Knight's sword stabbed into thin air.

The Knight's momentum caused him to follow the sword forward; the youth thrust out a leg, and Hünlef tripped. The Knight splayed on the ground, and suddenly it was all over. The youth stood astride his opponent, raised his blade high and then brought it straight down into the center of the Knight's back.

The blade cut through the armor as if it were cloth. There was a strangled cry from the Knight. It was not a cry of pain, but almost, Hewyn thought, one of relief. And then the body of the Knight seemed to dissolve. His black armor became indistinct around the edges; and then he too began to fade away. In moments, there was nothing left. Only Hünlef's horse remained, dead in the street with Hewyn's axe buried deep in its body.

Like Herwyn, Diana had watched the battle with morbid fascination. Until this moment, she had assumed that the Dark Knights were invincible. She had seen what their blades could do against ordinary armor and, although the sudden appearance of the strange youth had startled her, she had had not a moment's doubt that the confrontation between him and the Knight would end as had all the others she had witnessed over the past few days.

Now, for the first time, she knew that it was possible for a Dark Knight to be defeated in battle.

And with that thought, she recognized that her own position was not as secure as she had assumed. For if the boyish stranger who now turned to look at her could best a Dark Knight, he would surely make short work of her.

She turned to run, and collided with someone standing behind her.

XXV A Meeting of the Rebels

Diana's hands and feet were tied tightly by leather thongs.

Apart from the bite of the thongs against her skin, she had no complaints about her treatment. It was true that she was locked in a windowless room, but her captors visited her every hour or so to ask if she was all right, and gave her food and water whenever she desired them.

She had been in the room for several hours, and she had occupied the time by thinking carefully about what had happened, trying to see a way to turn it to advantage. And now she thought that she saw a way to do exactly that.

Her immediate surprise when she had turned and bumped into someone standing behind her was as nothing compared to her shock when she recognized her father.

Before she could react, he had thrown a leather loop over her, trapping her hands tightly at her side.

The blond youth sidled up to her and removed her scabbarded dagger; then her father took a leather bag from his belt and casually dropped it over her head.

She was led blindly through the streets until they arrived at the house in which she was now a prisoner. Once inside, she was taken upstairs and the bag over her head removed. Her hands and legs were tied by a pair of gnomes and then, apart from the periodic inspections, she had been left to her thoughts.

A key turned in the lock and her father entered the room with the blond youth.

She began to put her plan into action without delay.

"Oh, father," she cried, "I'm so glad you've come at last. I've been waiting to see you all day. You've no idea what it's been like up there in the castle. That woman, the one who calls herself Captain Malliss, I'm sure she's a witch of some kind. You wouldn't believe the things I've seen her do. She's forced me to keep order in the town. She said that if I didn't do what she said she'd kill me and eat me. I'm so glad that you've rescued me."

"Eat you?" Michael looked at her with a horrified expression.

The youth eyed her dubiously.

"I told you, you wouldn't believe what she's like. She locks anyone who won't do as she says in the dungeon to contemplate their fate. Then, some time when they don't expect it, she has them taken to a room in the north tower where their limbs are ripped off. Then... oh! I can't say it — it's too horrible."

The youth said, "What? What's so horrible that you, who have ordered death without so much as a flinch, will not say it?"

"Then she eats them. She stands in front of the person whose limbs they are, and bites the flesh from them. Then she just walks away and leaves the person to die in agony."

At this point, Diana broke into tears, and it was some time before her sobs abated to the point where she could continue.

The youth asked, "And is that what the captain threatened to do to you if you did not do her bidding?"

"Yes," Diana nodded. "I was to make sure that order was maintained in the town, and if I failed, she said she would throw me into the deepest dungeon until she was hungry."

"Why did you not escape, child?" — Diana thought this description of herself as a child most rude, for surely the youth, for all his swaggering, could not be that much older than herself — "You must have known that a rebellion would come. Not all of us are as meek as those who are willing to serve you in the castle."

"It was the Knights. I was not allowed out without at least one of them to look over me. Supposedly, they were there to protect me, but in fact it was to make sure that I didn't try to make contact with any of you."

She looked desperately from face to face and cried, "Please, you've got to believe me. I'll do anything to help you fight the captain. She'll be furious when she hears what happened. She'll probably try to rescue me simply so she can kill me. She'll take it as a personal affront that I've been captured. You are all in danger. Doesn't that convince you that I'm on your side? If I weren't, wouldn't I just sit here and wait to be rescued? She'll try; I know she will."

The youth looked at Michael and said, "Come outside; we should discuss this in private."

They left the room, closing the door behind them, but leaving it unlocked.

Once they were out of Diana's hearing, Toldwyn said, "I don't like it. I know she's your daughter, but I don't trust her."

"Why not?"

Michael wanted so much to believe Diana.

"It's all too pat. Just think what she'd be worth to the captain if we let her join the rebels. She'd find out everything we were planning."

Michael nodded. "You're right, of course. But she is my daughter, and if what she says is true...."

Toldwyn shrugged. "You're the High King, and I will agree to whatever you decide. But I have to tell you that I will not trust her until I have been given a reason to do so."

"I'm sorry; I just can't leave her locked up like this. The meeting is about to start. I would like to have her there. She may have something to contribute."

"And if she feeds us a pack of lies? Or betrays us to the captain?"

"Then, Toldwyn, you can say, 'I told you so.'"

It was late evening, and the five members of the Ruling Council, along with Hewyn, Phendric, Toldwyn, Michael, Diana and the dablik were gathered in a large downstairs room to discuss the situation. The others had been quietly warned by Toldwyn not to discuss any plans in detail while Diana was present, a limitation that Michael had reluctantly agreed was prudent, and so they had been discussing for some time the general outline of what they would do now that a Dark Knight had been vanquished and the resistance had truly begun.

They were gathered in a large circle on the floor, except for the dablik, who sat in a rocking chair in a corner of the room, rocking silently with his eyes half closed.

"Even when the Hunters get here and Andwyr returns from Samuel Ironhand's forge with the weapons, what good can we do?" Talrynth asked. "Our weapons, no matter how sharp the blades, will still be useless against the Dark Knights. Your weapon can stand up to them, Toldwyn, but even you would be overwhelmed if there was more than one, or if they caught you by surprise. And don't forget that it is one thing to defeat a Dark Knight, but quite another to stand against Malthazzar himself."

"If the captain is indeed Malthazzar — a point which has yet to be proven," interjected Michael.

"Quite so. But Malthazzar has to be involved somehow, otherwise the Dark Knights would not be here. Anyway, the point is that apart from Toldwyn and his sword, and possibly the battle axe of the good dwarf Hewyn, and now Diana's dark blade," — he nodded towards Diana, who was seated (unarmed; they had refused to return her dagger) at the opposite side of the circle — "we have no weapons with which to fight the Dark Knights. And we must remember that even those weapons might not be effective against Malthazzar."

"What about Michael's sword? He is a High King. Surely his weapon is enough to defeat a Dark Knight, and perhaps even Malthazzar himself?"

"Possibly, although that theory has never been tested," said Toldwyn. "We can't rely on it until both he and his weapon have been proven in battle." He turned to Diana. "Tell us, what do you think? Is the captain really Malthazzar in another form?"

"I don't know. I don't know much about Malthazzar, just what you have told me this evening. Obviously it is possible, because you've told me that Malthazzar once before took the form of a human woman, but I really haven't seen anything more than the obvious fact that Captain Malliss is a very powerful and merciless woman. On the whole, then, I'm inclined to think that she is not Malthazzar. But I suppose," she concluded unhelpfully, "I could be wrong."

At this moment, Myfanwy, who was keeping lookout at a window, hissed, "Shhh! I see shadows moving outside."

"I hope it's not the captain," said Diana.

A desperate "Shhh" came from Myfanwy, and a withering look from Toldwyn.

Toldwyn and Michael stood and drew their swords. Toldwyn positioned himself near the door, while Michael hid behind where the door would be if it were opened.

Someone knocked smartly on the door.

"Who is it?" called Mellow.

"The Third Land," whispered a voice.

Everyone sighed with relief at the password. Myfanwy opened the door and the Hunter Gwain marched into the room, accompanied by a human whom Michael, Diana and the dablik instantly recognized.

Myfanwy closed the door behind the newcomers.

"I have my family and several more Hunters with me, encamped in the forest east of town," said Gwain. "I also found this person, who can introduce herself."

"The High Queen Catherine needs no introduction," said Toldwyn, dropping to one knee. "Even without the jewel in her belt, I would recognize her by the peace and tranquillity that surrounds her person."

Catherine glanced around the gathering, and was momentarily dumb with surprise, for not only was Michael here, but also Diana, whom she had been led to believe by the Hunters was an agent of the enemy. Even the dablik was in one corner, his whiskers quivering in greeting.

But her shock was multiplied with the next words of the blond youth, who now said: "I am Toldwyn, warrior of the Third Land, and I present myself in your service."

"Toldwyn? *The* Toldwyn?"

"Indeed, Your Majesty. Returned to fight at the side of yourself and the High King Michael,"

"But that's impossible. Drefynt once told me that your return was nothing more than a myth."

"Drefynt, Your Majesty?"

"Even Drefynt did not know everything, Your Majesty," said a middle-aged gnome whom Catherine did not recognize and who was seated next to Diana. "Forgive me for interrupting. I am Drefynt's grandson, Phendric. Phendric, son of Benglubber, son of Drefynt, at your service, Your Majesty."

It was all too much for Catherine, meeting so many unexpected people in one place. She sat down shakily while she composed herself. It was some time before explanations were completed and the meeting could continue.

"We must fight," said Shán of the Ruling Council, seated on the floor next to his brother, Talrynth. "There are rumors that the captain has issued an edict that the name of the High Lord is to be used no more. Anyone heard using it will be placed into the dungeons."

"It is true," said Diana. "The captain told me that she wants to stamp out superstition."

Phendric grunted.

Mellow said, "And there will be retribution for the courageous acts of Hewyn and Toldwyn, of that you can be sure."

"So the only real question is: how shall we fight?" said Michael. "After what happened today, the soldiers will be sure to travel in pairs or groups. They will be merciless; there is no other way they will be able to hold Carn Toldwyn."

"They'll search the homes and take all the weapons they can find," added Dibgrín.

"Then we must strike before our weapons are taken from us," said Gwain.

"I disagree."

It was Phendric who had spoken, and everyone fell silent.

"There has been altogether too much fighting," he continued. "The whole history of Palindor is replete with violence. It is time that things changed. You say that an edict has been issued that forbids the use of the High Lord's name, just as was passed by Malthazzar when he ruled in the guise of Cerebeth" — some in the room nodded; they had forgotten that this was not the first time that such an edict had been issued — "and yet I have to ask: is this sufficient cause for violence? I think not, and for the following reasons.

"Firstly, we do not know that the edict will be enforced. Perhaps, if the rebellion ceases, the captain will relent.

"Secondly, has any one of us sought to discuss this matter with the captain? I know that a delegation went to meet her shortly after she arrived and they were rebuffed; but do we know for a fact that the captain still refuses to talk to us?

"Thirdly, the edict merely bans using the High Lord's name. Does this mean that Olvensar is no longer High Lord in fact? Of course not, and we would be exceedingly foolish to ignore that truth.

"Fourthly, are we to take it upon ourselves to exact revenge for something so minor? It is the High Lord who is being snubbed, not we, and surely He is capable of standing against any power, even that of Malthazzar.

"And lastly, I have to confess my personal feelings. Is anything so important that it is worth lifting a sword to take the life of another creature? I admit that it may well be that the captain and at least some of those under her command are not mortal, but they have enlisted help, willing or otherwise, such as that of the human Diana who graces us with her presence this evening. While some of those who stand against us may be mere forces of darkness in human form, some are our friends and colleagues and relatives.

"Palindor has seen enough fighting. I for one will not lift a weapon against these people, some of whom believe sincerely that the the strong leadership of the captain is exactly what Palindor needs.

"If this leads you to think me weak or cowardly, then so be it. I care not what other mortals think. I believe that the High Lord understands full well that it is easy to fight might with might. It is far harder to refrain from lifting a sword against one who would kill you. I know that I am neither weak nor a coward, and so does the High Lord. As for yourselves, you need to decide, each of you, what rôle you wish to play in the coming days."

An uneasy quiet came over the gathering while they considered Phendric's arguments.

Toldwyn said, "I'm sorry, but this is mere wishful thinking. I know nothing of this gnome, nor indeed of any of you gathered here save the dablik. But I know this: Palindor was forged by might, and it is to be defended in the same manner. Anyone who says otherwise is blind."

Michael stood. He bowed toward Phendric. "Good gnome, you make your case well. If it were any other who had spoken such words, I would have cried, 'Treason!' and called for them to be expelled from this meeting, but from someone who brought me back from the edge of eternal darkness itself, I have to weigh carefully the words you have spoken; for if it were not for you I would not be here now, urging the others to fight by my side.

"But I confess that I too must disagree with you. I will not call you treasonous, for surely you are not that; I will not seek to have you ejected from this gathering, for I know that you will not betray us. Neither do I call you weak, nor a coward, for, as you truly say, you are neither of those things. No creature is weak or cowardly who is prepared to stand amongst his friends and declare that he disagrees with them on such an important issue.

"Yet still I say that you are wrong, and here is why.

"You say that we do not know that the edict will be enforced, and in this you are correct. However, the matter is easily tested, and I will do so the moment that we have concluded, if that is the wish of the gathering. I will simply enter the courtyard of the castle and tell them in the name of the High Lord Olvensar that I wish to see the captain. This also addresses your second point. I predict with complete confidence that at the very least I shall be rebuffed. More than likely, I shall either be dragged immediately to the dungeons or I shall be killed on the spot. I, too, am prepared to die for my beliefs.

"You seem to take lightly the banning of the use of the High Lord's name, saying that it makes no difference because He is still the High Lord in fact. This is true; yet I have to wonder whether He is truly High Lord if some upstart such as the captain, whether or no she is really Malthazzar in mortal form, can expunge Olvensar's name from our lips.

237

"You also suggest that if the High Lord is offended, then Olvensar will right the wrong. Yet more then once Olvensar has specifically used creatures to enact His will, to be His hands and to carry His sword.

"Indeed, the very founding of the Third Land flowed from a specific command from the High Lord to Toldwyn here. I myself, and the High Queen Catherine, as well as others whose name is held in high esteem by us all, such as the gnomes Drefynt and Trondwyth, and the dwarf Gondalwyn, and the elf Anderskerrin, all these have been, at one time or another, the hands of the High Lord. And so I say to you, Phendric, and to all of you gathered here, that to suggest that the High Lord will simply appear by magic and put everything to rights is naïve to the point of foolishness.

"And lastly," — and here he turned to address the gathering as a whole — "our good friend Phendric says that he has a personal prejudice against fighting. Well, so be it. But I have no such prejudice. I believe...."

Myfanwy, who for some time had been more interested in the debate between Phendric and Michael than in keeping watch at the window, was as surprised as anyone when there was a sudden rap at the door. Michael halted in mid flow.

"Open up in the name of Captain Malliss," cried an authoritative voice.

Myfanwy looked out the window and shrank back in horror. "Soldiers! Many of them."

"Out the back way, quick," urged Mellow.

"No," said Toldwyn. "If there is to be a fight, now is as good a time as any. I will not flee."

He and Michael stood and drew their weapons.

Myfanwy raised the latch, and into the room stepped Odrian, his sword drawn. He was followed by two soldiers. Several more remained outside.

Shán, who was the closest to the door, unsheathed a dagger and lunged at Odrian, and in moments the room was filled with a mêlée. It did not last long. Two soldiers were wounded — one each by Toldwyn and Michael — as were two of the rebels. Shán, too slow to parry the thrust with which Odrian responded to his attack, was killed outright by a clean stab through the heart.

But the soldiers seemed more interested in rescuing Diana than in fighting. She took no part in the scuffle, merely moving to watch it from the safety of the stairs. Towards the end, when it was clear that the soldiers were going to win, she shouted, "Someone give me a sword," but before anyone could do so, she was grabbed by a burly soldier and bustled out the door. The whole thing was over in but a few moments, and the rebels were left staring at the dead body of their fallen comrade, while the two wounded tried to staunch their wounds.

"What'll they do with Diana?" someone asked. "They'll have seen that she was sitting with us. They'll know that she was on our side."

The answer seemed obvious. Diana might or might not tell the captain what the rebels had been discussing, but unless she was a spy as Toldwyn had suggested, she would be sent to the dungeons.

Michael looked at Phendric, who, with Catherine, had taken no part in the fighting.

There was no hiding the edge of bitterness in his voice as he spoke, for he had seen how the gnome and the High Queen had refused to fight.

"There can be no more debate. We are going into the castle. We will take this fight to the enemy, and we will free those whom our enemies have imprisoned. Those who will not fight are free to leave, but I tell you all now" — he looked around the room, his eyes settling on each person in turn — "that I will rescue Diana, or I will die trying."

"And I stand with you," said Talrynth, suiting action to the word, getting up from where he had been grieving over his dead brother.

"And I."

"And I."

Until only three remained seated: Toldwyn, Catherine and Phendric.

Toldwyn looked at Michael and said, "I too will join you, but only if I am convinced that Diana is not working for the captain. We must wait to hear what becomes of Diana from our spies in the castle. If she is sent to the dungeons, then you have my word that I will fight to the death at your side."

Toldwyn stepped forward, leaving only Catherine and Phendric.

Catherine looked uncertainly at them. Then she turned to Phendric.

"I'm sorry; she's my granddaughter." She moved to stand with the others.

For a long moment no one spoke. Michael and the others were gathered in one half of the room; Phendric, alone, stood over Shán's body. Phendric looked at the body, then at Michael.

He said, "I cannot fight. But if you will permit me to join you, I will do what I can."

"And what would that be? To stand and watch?" The words came from Talrynth, and dripped with bitterness for the fate of his dead brother.

Phendric bowed his head. He said quietly, "I will do what I can in good conscience; no creature can offer more."

"Come, then, Phendric, we accept," said Michael. "Join us. Do what you can to help us, and perhaps, in the end, you will be able to do more than any of us, eh?"

Phendric looked at Michael.

"Perhaps."

XXVI *Into the Castle*

"You're sure they believed you?"

Diana and Captain Malliss were in the captain's private quarters high in the north tower of Dynas Carn Toldwyn. There was food on the table, and Diana was chewing a hunk of braised venison while holding a slice of thick honeybread. She swallowed the meat as she nodded. "Yes, captain. They honestly thought I had changed sides. At least, most of them did. Toldwyn was the only one who seemed suspicious."

"And that story you made up about my eating the limbs of prisoners?"

"Toldwyn didn't seem to believe it, but I'm certain that the others did."

The captain laughed sibilantly. "That was a good touch. You did well, Diana, very well. And this meeting you were telling me about: how was it going to end, do you think?"

"It seems that until today the Ruling Council had been unable to agree on whether to fight. When I was presented to them, it forced their hands. They weren't all in agreement, but it was obvious that most of them are ready to fight now."

"Good. If we can make them bring the fight to us, it will be so much easier. Diana, you've done very well, but I am afraid your little act is not yet over."

Diana nodded.

"I know. The dungeon."

"Exactly. We don't know what spies they might have here in the castle. Even the fact that we are here talking privately might be reported. So in a few moments I shall call a guard and have you taken down to the dungeons. I shall see that some real food is smuggled in to you at least once a day, but you must eat it quickly, in case a spy catches you. I shall inform you, of course, of anything I hear about a possible rescue attempt. And I am afraid that you must remain unarmed, at least for now. I'll have a dagger smuggled in to you along with the food, so that when the fighting starts, you'll be able to join in. On the right side." The captain smiled.

Diana began to laugh at the cleverness of the captain's plan.

"Hush!" said the captain. "In a moment you are going to be dragged out of here while I berate you at the top of my voice. We don't want anyone to think you've been enjoying yourself."

This time the two plotters contented themselves with broad smiles.

"Guard! Guard!" the captain shouted.

Jervil and Nerwyn, the dwarves standing guard outside the door, looked at one another and then burst into the room. The captain was standing over Diana, who was sprawled on the floor, her head hidden, apparently sobbing.

"Guards! Take this woman away and throw her in the deepest dungeon. Feed her scraps that even the kitchen staff refuse."

"Ma'am?" said Jervil. "Isn't this the woman who has been keeping order in the town?"

"You question me, you fool? She's a traitor, you idiot. When my soldiers rescued her, she was seated with her captors, discussing how best to attack us. She has confessed everything. Take her away and throw her in the deepest dungeon until I have decided what to do with her. And you" — she addressed the sobbing heap — "don't expect me to make my mind up quickly. A month or two in the dungeons should show you the error of your ways. If I don't get hungry first. Now, take her out of my sight."

The captain wheeled and stomped from the room.

The two guards lifted Diana, who turned on them and shouted: "Take your hands off me, you filthy scum. I'll walk."

There was wetness on her cheeks, but her eyes were strangely bright as the guards ushered her from the room.

The dungeon was worse than she had expected.

Diana was in the deepest dungeon — the same one, had she but known it, in which the Holy Gnome Drefynt had been incarcerated many centuries before. There was old straw on the floor, an ancient, worn palliasse in one corner, and a hole in the ground for necessary bodily functions in another, but that was all.

The thick oak door had a grill on it, but the grill had a cover, and the cover was kept closed except when food was brought to her, so that the only light entering the cell came from a narrow gap at the bottom of the door.

But, as she quickly discovered, she was not alone. Her sleep was soon interrupted by the sound of hurrying, pattering feet. The noise woke Diana and she listened anxiously as a chewing sound came from somewhere near her feet. She sat up, just in time to see the scant light reflected in the black eyes of a large rat. She screamed, and the rat scurried away into a corner.

For some time she sat with her legs folded against her chest, listening to the rat chewing the straw on the floor. Every couple of minutes, the rat would become emboldened, and it would slowly approach the palliasse. She shouted at the ugly brute to scare it away; but the rat soon became wise to that, and after scurrying away to hide two or three times, it began to ignore her shouts.

Diana looked for something to throw, but there was nothing. The rat came closer, and began to chew the palliasse at the place where it had been eating when she had first seen it. Diana hung her head and wept.

Food and water arrived twice a day. The food was some sort of swill that defied definition; the water tasted of the metal from the jug in which it was carried.

They were brought by a small, wizened dwarf with a tic, who watched Diana warily and refused to be drawn into conversation. His arrival was heralded by the sound of feet in the passage outside,

243

followed by a loud banging on the cell door. Then a key would turn in the lock and the door was opened. The dwarf would enter, while behind him in the corridor stood two muscular soldiers. The dwarf placed a tray on the ground, took up the old tray, and left. The whole thing took less than a minute.

Shortly after the first of these so-called meals had been delivered, the door of the dungeon was suddenly opened without any warning. A soldier threw something wrapped tightly in a cloth, and was gone again almost before Diana was sure that he had really existed. Inside the cloth were bread and cheese. Diana devoured them greedily.

The pattern continued. Shortly after the dwarf arrived with his paltry offerings, the soldier would toss in some real food. He also smuggled in a knife, which she hid under the straw near her palliasse.

She had plenty of time to think, and she found herself wondering how Michael and Catherine could possibly have allied themselves with the rebels. Didn't they realize that the creatures who lived here were vicious and warlike? As for their theory that Captain Malliss was some sort of evil monster — that was so preposterous that she didn't know how they could credit the idea for a moment. But they were so gullible. Why, they had swallowed that ridiculous story about the captain eating her prisoners without hesitation. It seemed like they believed anything they were told.

Two days passed, and she began to wonder if the rebels would ever arrive to free her. Perhaps she had overestimated their bravado, in which case all this suffering might be for nothing.

It was not a pleasant thought.

"You're sure about everything, Jervil?" Michael asked.

Michael and Toldwyn were seated in the parlor of a house on the southern edge of town. On the opposite side of a small table was a dwarf dressed in the uniform of the castle guard. The dwarf nodded enthusiastically.

"I saw it with my own eyes," he said. "The captain called us in and told us to put her in the deepest dungeon, then she stomped out the room. She was furious. We took Diana down to the dungeon, and there she remains."

"And how is she doing? Do we know?"

"A guard who is friendly to our cause told me that she is being treated the same as the other prisoners: slops and water twice a day. But her dungeon is kept dark, with the grill closed all the time. And there are rats."

Toldwyn asked in a hostile tone, "What about the story Diana told us? The one about Captain Malliss eating people's limbs while they were still alive? Have you ever heard anyone mention that?"

The dwarf shook his head. "No. But I will tell you this. When she told us to throw Diana in the dungeon, the captain turned to her and told her she would stay there for months or until the captain got hungry. The words made no sense to me at the time, but perhaps they mean that Diana's story is true."

"There's no way you could get word to her that we're going to try to get all the prisoners out of there as soon as we can?" Michael interjected.

The dwarf looked dubious. "I could try, but I caution against it. She might give the game away. Accidentally, of course; but one of the guards might see hope in her eyes, and that would arouse suspicions. Hope is not a common commodity in the dungeons. My advice is that unless you need her to know in advance, you should let it be a surprise. You shouldn't even tell me anything about your plans."

"You're right, of course. I just don't like to think of Diana rotting away in a dungeon without hope."

Michael was silent for a moment, thinking of his daughter trapped in the castle's deepest dungeon.

Then he said, "All right, Jervil, thank you. We'd better let you get back to your work now, before they miss you. You've given us much to think about."

The dwarf left Toldwyn and Michael to discuss their plans.

It was difficult to know how to proceed, even with the detailed maps of the castle that Catherine and others had provided them. A castle, by design, is supposed to be difficult to attack. Some of the guards would be loyal to them, of course, and could be depended on to join their cause as soon as the fighting started; but others would not, and it would be difficult to tell friend from foe. And there was danger from the two remaining Dark Knights. They would undoubtedly kill any of the rescuers without a moment's hesitation.

The castle was beginning to operate under a siege mentality, for the rebellion was starting to come out into the open, and creatures now wore weapons openly in the streets, despite the ban on doing so. Soldiers went about the town in small bands, but, if they were unaccompanied by the Knights, they were harried either by the Hunters whom Gwain had brought to fight for the cause, or by the other creatures who were arriving in Carn Toldwyn daily.

But rescuing Diana was not going to be easy, and both Michael and Toldwyn were afraid that it would involve at least some loss of life; so they considered their strategy carefully, not wanting to lay hasty plans.

That evening, they shared their concerns with Catherine, Gwain, Phendric and the dablik.

Phendric said quietly, "Perhaps we can get inside without being seen."

"What do you mean?" asked Gwain. "There's only one way in, through the courtyard, and that way is always guarded."

But Phendric refused to be drawn further, saying only that if they would wait until the following evening, he might be able to present them with a way into the castle that would bypass the guards.

Next morning, Phendric appeared at the entrance to the court-yard shortly after dawn. The guards eyed him suspiciously while he told them what he wanted. He was searched and permitted to pass through the courtyard. At the castle steps, he was stopped and searched once more.

"What do you want?" asked a guard.

"To go to the library. I'm a scholar, you see, and I wanted to look at a book in the library. You have my word that I am unarmed."

"A scholar, eh?" said the guard dubiously. "Well, if I can find someone to escort you, I suppose that would be all right."

"Oh, I know the way. I've been there before."

"It's not for that reason that you will be escorted. We need to keep our eyes on creatures like you. Don't want poison in the food or a knife in the back do we?" He smiled nervously, as if he had made a weak joke.

A young page, a nervous-looking young gnome with shifty eyes, was found, and he escorted Phendric into the castle and along the corridors to the library.

Phendric knew the library well, for he had spent most of the happiest hours of his youth there, poring over old volumes, reading the words of Drefynt and those few works of the old Holy Gnomes that still survived .

Phendric knew exactly which book he wanted, but he did not make straight for it. Instead, he went to a far corner of the library, furrowed his brow and, after a while, removed a book from the shelves and began to study it. The page looked bored.

"Are you going to be long?"

"As long as it takes," replied Phendric. "The answer lies here somewhere."

"Ah, I see," said the page, and lapsed into silence.

After a while, Phendric replaced the book, took down another, and began to study that one. And so he went on, looking in book after book as morning passed and then turned to afternoon.

By midafternoon, Phendric decided that he had perused so many different volumes that the young gnome would never be able to remember exactly which ones he had looked at.

Phendric returned to the shelves and removed the book for which he had come. It was one of the few really ancient books in the library, written shortly after the founding of the Third Land, when Dynas Carn Toldwyn was being built.

It was a difficult book to read, not only because it was written in an ancient script, but also because it was written in a strange kind of code, in which the meanings of words were quite different from their ordinary usage. Once, long ago, Phendric had spent an entire summer poring over this volume and it was only after several months' study that he had understood the book's purpose.

The book appeared to be a collection of nursery stories. When he had first discovered it, he had wondered why it had ever been written, for parchment was not such a common commodity that one would use it to record stories that could be handed down orally. His interest was piqued even further by the fact that even though the book was old, its script was even older. In fact, only one other book in the entire library was written in the same script: the book that his grandfather Drefynt had been translating at the time of his death.

Now he pored over the book of childish stories, trying to remember the details of the code he had worked out all those years ago. He found the story he was looking for. The symbols of the ancient script jumped off the page: ⵝⴻ⵿ⵡ)(ⴻ⵿Sⵀⴻ ⵠⵄ ⵣⵀⴻ: *The Story of Côr and the Dragon's Treasure.*

After reading the story, he replaced the book on the shelf and spent an hour looking at two more books, just to throw the page further off the track.

Eventually, he replaced the last book on the shelf and said, "All right. Thank you. I'd like to leave now."

"Did you find what you wanted?"

"Yes, I think I did."

"And just what was that?"

Phendric turned and beheld Captain Malliss standing in the doorway. "You were with the rebels when my men took Diana back, weren't you?" the captain said. "What exactly were you looking for in here?"

Phendric bowed. "Phendric, gnome of the Palindor forest, at your service, ma'am. You are correct: I was with those whom you call rebels; but as your men have no doubt also informed you, I refused to take any part in the fighting, and I shall continue to do so."

The captain eyed him suspiciously. "You did not answer my question, gnome. What did you want with these dead books?"

"Dead books? Oh no, ma'am, there I am afraid I must disagree with you. I am a scholar, and when I was young these books were my best friends. I spent much of my youth in this very room, trying to understand what the books had to tell me. I assure you, they are far from dead."

"You try my patience, gnome. What did the books tell you?"

"The books are here for any to read, ma'am. Perhaps you should ask them yourself?"

"Begone, insolent gnome! Get out of here. And you, page, tell the guards that henceforth this room is off-limits to everyone. No exceptions."

"Yes, ma'am."

The page and the gnome left Captain Malliss staring at the shelves.

"It was all in the book," said Phendric.

He was gathered with Michael, Toldwyn, Catherine, Gwain and the dablik about a fire in a clearing in the forest east of town. It was evening. Phendric was explaining what he had learned that afternoon.

"I knew that the story was there; I just couldn't remember the details, so I had to read it again for myself."

"So what exactly did you learn?" asked Toldwyn.

"Listen to the story yourself, and see if you can unravel its meaning. It's called *The Story of Côr and the Dragon's Treasure.*"

"'Côr' is the old word for 'dwarf'," muttered the dablik to no one in particular.

"Quite so," agreed Phendric, "and so it should be no surprise to learn that the creature named Côr in the story is indeed a dwarf." And, staring into the flames of the fire, he recited the story.

In a time long, long ago (said Phendric), dragons, which now are so rare as to be almost unknown, lived throughout the great forest that covers the Third Land.

Dragons, as you probably know, are a fearsome breed of creature. They are the largest of beasts, much larger even than a bear, and when angered they attack not with claws, but with fire that belches from their mouths just as you or I might breathe mist on a cold winter's day. But fortunately dragons are rarely angered. Indeed, almost the only way to cross a dragon is to try to steal its hoard of treasure. For dragons, you see, covet gold and silver and precious gems even more than do goblins (and you know what they are like!). But unlike goblins, whose treasure is stored out of reach underground, dragons live on the surface in shallow caves.

Dragons generally dwell in caves high on cliffs or mountainsides, for they must leave their caves to eat, and when they do so they wish to be sure that their treasure is safe from attack. Since dragons can fly, such inaccessible places are no inconvenience to them. When dragons take to the air — as they do at least once a week to search for food — their enormous wings beat the air with a sound like thunder. Indeed, should you hear thunder on a clear day, you can be sure that it is a dragon somewhere not far away, taking to the sky in search of food or treasure.

When they are not aloft, dragons guard the front of their cave, protecting the treasure hoarded at the rear.

This story is about a dragon called Nyja-dryk and a dwarf called Côr.

Nyja-dryk's cave was not far from the place where Côr and his parents lived. Côr's parents were very poor, and at the time that Côr grew to be an adult they were unable to give him the axe to go in his belt that would signify that he was a grown dwarf. This naturally troubled them greatly, and one day Côr's father took his son to visit a sage who lived nearby.

"What can I do?" Côr's father asked the sage. "My son Côr has grown to adulthood and he needs a good axe, such as every warrior dwarf requires. And yet I have no money to buy one."

The sage looked at Côr's father and then at Côr himself. "Tell me, dwarf," he said to Côr, "would you like to possess a magic axe, the like of which no other dwarf in any of the Three Lands possesses?"

"Of course," said Côr.

"Then I can tell you that such an axe lies not two thousand paces from here, and it is yours if only you can win it."

"Where is this axe, that I might have it?" asked Côr.

"Why, it is in the lair of Nyja-dryk the dragon, lying beside his hoard of treasure."

At this, Côr's face fell. "But then it is impossible," he said, "for there is no way to reach the cave, and even if there were, then it would be impossible to pass the dragon."

Nyja-dryk, you see, had made his home in a cave on the western cliffs of a high tor, and it was well known that there was no path up to the cave.

"Ah, but there you are wrong," said the sage. "There is a way to reach the cave without being seen. All you need do is find it."

Côr pleaded with the sage to tell him what this way might be, but the sage would say no more.

Côr went away and pondered the sage's words for many days. Many times he went to the cliff in which Nyja-dryk had his cave, and searched for some way up the cliff that might bring him to the cave without the dragon noticing. But of course there was no such route, for Nyja-dryk was not a foolish dragon.

Then Côr began to think more deeply about the problem he had been set. There had to be an answer, for the sage had been in no doubt that there was a way to reach the dragon's lair without being seen.

He decided that because the dragon lived in a cave, then perhaps there was some other entrance that would lead to the treasure; in which case, if he could just find that entrance, he might be able to sneak into the cave from behind and steal the axe behind the dragon's back.

The tor in which Nyja-dryk had made his home was exceptionally large and tall, and around its base there were many caves, but Côr began to set about the task of exploring them all.

Eventually, he came to a cave low on the hillside exactly opposite the dragon's lair, facing due east. This cave led him deeper and deeper into the tor. It branched many times, and Côr was soon in danger of becoming lost. He became scared, and it was at that moment that he heard, far away, the gentle sound of the wind. Deciding that if he followed the sound he would eventually find an exit, he began to walk towards the sound. It took him deeper into the tor, although

251

by this time Côr was so lost that he no longer knew which way he was going.

But the sound of the wind's whistling became louder and louder and eventually he turned a corner and discovered that the sound was very loud indeed, for it was not the wind at all, but the sound of the dragon sleeping, and by following the snores he had arrived inside the dragon's lair itself.

And there on the floor, between himself and the sleeping Nyja-dryk, and beside an enormous pile of jewels and gold and silver, lay the most magnificent battle axe Côr had ever seen. Carefully he lifted the axe and placed it in his belt, and it felt as if it had always belonged there. Quietly, he turned and reentered the twisting maze of passages; but now he was careful to keep moving away from the sound of the dragon's snores and, eventually, he reappeared safely on the far side of the hill.

And that is the story of Côr and the dragon's treasure.

If Phendric had expected the children's story to elicit an instant reaction from the others he was disappointed, for they all sat and stared at him blankly.

"It's an allegory," he explained, "a story that purports to be about one thing but is actually about something quite different. In this case, what seems to be a child's simple story about a dwarf and an axe is actually about a way to get into the castle."

"So you're saying that somewhere on the hill on which the castle stands there's a cave which leads inside?" asked Gwain.

"Yes, although you must pay attention to the details in the story. For example, there are no doubt many caves on the hill. The dragon's lair in the story faced west, and the cave faced east, but the entrance to the castle is to the south, towards Carn Toldwyn, so the cave will probably be on the north side of the hill. In fact, chances are that there will be a very inviting cave that faces east, and if we were to go deeply into that cave we'd probably find ourselves in a particularly unpleasant magic trap."

"And the sound of the wind that led Côr to the dragon?"

Phendric shrugged. "I don't know. The symbolism changes from story to story. But there will be something that will lead us in the right direction once we are in the right cave, I'm sure of it."

"So someone needs to reconnoiter the northern side of the hill?" asked Michael.

"Exactly. But only one or two of us should go, otherwise we might be noticed. I propose that Catherine goes with me."

"What about the dablik? Surely he would be the best one for the job. After all, it's hardly likely that he would get lost in a tunnel."

The dablik's whiskers twitched. He said, "You are right, and that is the very reason I shouldn't be included. This entrance dates from the early days, when magic was common, and, as Phendric suggests, there could well be traps associated with the tunnel. In taking the easiest and most obvious route, I might lead the others into such a trap. No, it's better that I remain outside and let others find the route."

And so it was agreed that on the following day, Phendric and Catherine would scour the hill in search of a secret entrance to the castle.

They began early, shortly after breakfast, walking around the lower slopes of the hill on which the castle stood. As Phendric had foreseen, on the lower slopes of the hill there were many caves. Most were unpretentious holes in the grassy slope, but facing due east was a particularly obvious cave. Catherine and Phendric passed it silently, exchanging knowing glances.

They found the cave they were looking for, exactly where Phendric had said it would be, facing due north. It was a small affair hidden behind a thicket of brambles. It was so small that even Phendric had to crouch, but once inside the cave opened into a tall tunnel. Catherine snaked her way inside on her stomach; once she was past the low entrance, though, there was plenty of room for her to stand.

They stood near the entrance, listening for something to guide them deeper. They could hear nothing.

Phendric began to walk deeper into the cave, Catherine a few steps behind. Just as in the story of Côr, the cave had many branches, but the two tried to keep walking straight ahead and it was not long before they began to hear something. It was faint, and it was not the wind. It was the sound of running water.

"That's it," said Phendric. "We've gone far enough for now. Tonight we'll come back and follow the sound of the water to its source. My guess is that eventually this passage leads to the rear of the throne room, because that would correspond best to the treasure in the dragon's lair; but we don't want to explore too deeply right now in case we suddenly find ourselves walking out into the castle and having to answer some very awkward questions."

That evening, it was arranged who would participate in the attempt to free Diana and the other prisoners. After considerable discussion it was agreed that the force would comprise Toldwyn, Michael, Catherine, Gwain and Phendric. The dablik would accompany them as far as the entrance of the tunnel and remain there until either the others returned or dawn came, in which case he would try to enter the castle and discover what had happened to them.

Neither Toldwyn nor Michael had wanted Phendric to join them, for it was obvious that he would be of no use if there were any fighting to be done — the same, of course, could be said for Catherine, but as High Queen she had the right to do whatever she wished — but Phendric simply said, "I am coming as well," and, since the route would never have been found without him, that was the end of the matter.

It was shortly past midnight when they reached the thicket that hid the cave. Catherine had brought a large ball of twine so that they could mark their path. Gwain wore Diana's dark dagger as well as his own sword and dagger "as a precaution, and to use against the captain if we meet her."

Phendric said quietly, "Once we're inside the cave, we must be silent. We don't know how far sounds carry in the tunnels. There is to be no talking unless it is a matter of life and death."

He looked at the others to make sure that they understood. They nodded, and he continued, "I'll take the lead in the tunnels, and Catherine will bring up the rear, paying out the twine so we can find our way back out again if we get lost. Once we are inside the castle, Catherine will take the lead, for she knows its passages better than the rest of us. She will take us to the dungeons. Once there, we will free as many prisoners as possible, starting with Diana.

"Remember, once we are inside the castle, we must be especially alert. There will be guards in the dungeons, and it may be necessary to silence them; but if we have the choice, we should try to take the keys from them without harming them. Clear?"

They nodded again.

"All right," said Phendric. "Let's go."

"And may the High Lord be with you," added the dablik.

Phendric stooped to enter the cave, and one by one the others followed. They moved deeper into the tunnel, Catherine bringing up the rear and paying out the trail of twine.

Phendric led the way down the passages that he and Catherine had explored earlier in the day; it was not long before they all heard the distant sound of running water.

They moved deeper into the tunnels, the sound gradually becoming louder.

After a while, they came to a place where steps had been cut into the rock. They climbed the steps and almost immediately the tunnel turned a sharp corner. Phendric stopped.

A short distance ahead was a vertical wall of rock, out of which came a small cascade of water which fell down a deep hole, splashing noisily on the rock below and then disappearing through a crack in the rock. The sound they had been following came from the water striking the rock far below.

"Careful now, the path is slippery," said Phendric. "And quiet; we can't be far from the castle now."

Holding on to one another, they carefully passed the cascade. The path widened into a chamber, on the far side of which was a massive, smooth-sided, black slab. They gathered in front of the slab.

"That looks like a door. Time for Catherine to lead, I think," whispered Phendric.

Catherine leaned her weight against one side of the slab, and it began to move. It pivoted outward and then sideways, creating a doorway. Immediately beyond the doorway, the way was blocked by some sort of hanging tapestry. Catherine peeked out past the tapestry, then looked at the others and nodded. She stepped past the tapestry into whatever lay on the other side. The others followed.

As Phendric had guessed, they were in the throne room. They had entered from behind a golden tapestry located directly behind the throne itself. The room was deserted, but all of them felt a frisson of fear as they entered enemy territory. Toldwyn and Michael drew their swords. Gwain unsheathed his dagger. Diana's dark blade he left sheathed — he was saving that for the captain or one of her Dark Knights.

The throne room was on the main floor of the castle. The sleeping quarters were in the towers, some distance away. The rooms close to the throne room were generally used only on ceremonial occasions, and it was unlikely that they would come across anyone skulking in the gloomy corridors nearby. Nevertheless, they moved like shadows as Catherine led them out the room and into the corridor beyond.

The torches in the sconces were unlit; the corridor was lit only by scattered moonlight. Catherine took this to be a good sign, for it suggested that this part of the castle was unguarded.

She paused for a moment to get her bearings, then, hugging a wall, she led the others down the corridor.

There were three floors of dungeons under the castle. They were reached by way of a narrow spiral staircase that led from the main floor to the highest of the three levels. On the highest underground level there were no cells, only rooms used for storing food. Below this were two levels of cells, accessed down wide, straight staircases. It was almost certain that either one or both of these levels would be guarded. Most of the cells were on the higher level. On the bottommost level were six particularly small and unpleasant cells. The spy Jervil had told them that it was in one of these that Diana was being held.

They reached the spiral staircase leading down to the first level without incident. Toldwyn tapped Catherine on the shoulder and when she halted he stepped in front of her, silently indicating that since he was armed he would lead the way. Michael followed close behind Toldwyn, ready to strike at any moment, for if they were discovered the first blow must be struck quickly, before the alarm could be raised.

But as yet there was no need for such caution. They all descended to the storage level without incident.

The torches in the sconces here were lit, and at first everyone jumped nervously as the shadows in the corners of their eyes moved around. They made their way down one wall until they came to the staircase that led to the floor below, on which the first cells were located. They halted at the top of the staircase. Now they could hear something. The slow, rhythmic sound of deep breathing came from the level below. Toldwyn put a finger to his lips and gestured for the others not to move.

Toldwyn crept down the stairs. The rhythmic sound was suddenly ended by a short, muted thud. Moments later, Toldwyn reappeared. He pantomimed someone asleep and then led the others down the stairs, where a guard lay sprawled on the ground, rendered unconscious by a blow from the hilt of Toldwyn's sword.

Ever more cautiously they crept along the corridor. Now the rooms that they passed had small barred windows, and from beyond the heavy oaken doors they heard snoring.

The stairway down to the next level was at the far end. They halted at the top of the stairs. The sound of indistinct voices came from below. Toldwyn beckoned for Michael and Gwain to join him, and together the three of them began to descend the steps.

Halfway down, Toldwyn motioned the others to a halt.

A dozen paces away, two guards sat on a bench in the spill of light from a sconce, talking in bored voices.

"I don't care what they say, the captain's all right by me."

The other guard nodded.

"Palindor has let itself slide so much that if an army came across the border from Reglandor, they'd just walk all the way across the Third Land and wind up here in the castle without so much as token resistance. The captain will shake things up, you'll see. The rebels will realize soon enough that there's no point in fighting. You mark my words, it won't be long before we're walking into Reglandor ourselves. I've always wanted to see Pirren Glan...."

The guard stopped, his attention attracted by a sudden movement on the staircase. He looked up just in time to see a dagger glint as it flew through the air.

The dagger hit his light mail armor with a loud metallic *clink* and clattered harmlessly to the ground at his feet. It was a moment before he understood what had happened, and in that moment it seemed like he and his companion were attacked by a veritable swarm of enemies. Before either of them could even stand to draw their swords, heavy hilts smashed into their shoulders and they fell to the ground. Two more blows at the base of their skulls rendered them unconscious.

Gwain stooped and picked up his dagger. He felt the tip carefully with his thumb. "Pity. That was a good blade. Hate to see it ruined on cheap mail."

Catherine and Phendric hurried down the steps to join them. "Don't worry," Michael said to them with a note of condescension, "we didn't hurt them. Gwain's blade didn't penetrate the mail, and we didn't use the blades of our swords. They'll just wake up with terrific headaches."

Catherine hurried past the cell doors. Diana was in the last cell. Catherine opened the grill and saw her immediately, asleep on a palliasse.

Phendric handed Catherine a set of keys taken from one of the guards. The sound of the keys jangling in the lock woke Diana, and she sat up just as Catherine found the right one.

The rescuers rushed into the cell, sending rats scurrying. Diana looked at them, bleary eyed, trying to understand what was happening.

"Shhh! You mustn't make a sound," said Catherine. "We're here to rescue you. We're going to free the other prisoners and then we're going to get you all out of here."

Diana nodded dumbly and Catherine held out a hand to help her to her feet.

"Thank you, my dear. That worked very nicely indeed. I can't remember the last time a plan worked so well."

They all turned, stunned by the unexpected intrusion.

In the doorway stood Captain Malliss, brandishing a dark sword. Behind her stood soldiers with swords unsheathed. The captain strode peremptorily into the cell. All except Toldwyn moved backward, toward the far wall. Toldwyn, though, held his ground, his sword Den-yowŷnk grasped firmly, staring at the captain, a rebellious fire in his eyes.

The captain halted in front of Toldwyn. Behind her, the two Dark Knights entered the cell. The soldiers remained in the passageway.

Captain Malliss looked Toldwyn up and down.

"You will stand aside, Toldwyn. You are not worth the effort."

"Never. Admit it, captain. You are the Evil One aren't you? You are Malthazzar in human form."

The captain roared with laughter.

"My, but I see that your gall is undiminished by your long sleep. Well, Toldwyn, here is my answer to your impertinent question."

And in a sudden flash of dark lightning, the captain's sword whipped sideways and plunged deep into Toldwyn's side. Toldwyn screamed — long, piercing, agonized — as a shudder passed through his body.

He fell at the captain's feet, silenced forever.

The captain stepped over his body to stand before the others, who shrank back in horror.

It had been so utterly unexpected. Toldwyn, the great warrior who had helped found the Third Land; Toldwyn, the destroyer of Dark Knights; Toldwyn, who had slept for thousands of years only to return when he was most needed — Toldwyn had been killed with a single unexpected slash from the captain's blade.

It seemed so wrong somehow: Toldwyn was a magnificent and fearless warrior; he should have died in some noble battle, leading a desperate charge against some great enemy. Instead his life had been ended by a single blow while standing alone in a dismal dungeon deep under the castle to which he had given his name.

But there was no time to dwell on such things, for the captain now turned and beckoned to Diana.

Diana, who, in the confusion of the captain's arrival had retrieved the smuggled dagger from its hiding place in the palliasse, approached, wondering what the captain had in mind for her.

Captain Malliss smiled. "You did well, Diana. You brought them here just as we planned."

"Did you... did you have to kill him?" Diana was remembering how Toldwyn had had the courage to fight a Dark Knight. It suddenly seemed a shame to have disposed of such bravery in such a cool and detached manner.

"What? That pitiable creature? Why do you care? He was the enemy wasn't he? He has received no more than he deserved. And now you too, my dear, shall get what you deserve."

The captain raised her sword until it loured over Diana. Diana shrank from the raised blade, her eyes locked on its blackness. A sudden terror filled her eyes.

"What? Are you scared? What else did you think I was going to do with you? You were merely the bait to lure the others here. You have completed your task, and I have no further need of you."

As the captain had been speaking, Diana had been moving backward until now she was trapped in a corner, cowering beneath the captain's sword. Deperately, she flung her dagger. It clanged metallically against the captain's mail and fell uselessly to the ground. Diana turned to look at Catherine, the closest of those who had come to free her, the closest of those whom she had helped entrap.

"I'm sorry," said Diana, tears now welling in her eyes. "I didn't know. I'm so sorry."

The captain's sword drew back to strike, and Catherine drew Scalmyùt. The captain's sword descended towards Diana, but Catherine threw herself at the captain, Scalmyùt extended before her. The captain turned to meet the attack but she was too slow, and Scalmyùt bit deeply into her side.

Catherine tried to pull her sword from the captain's side, but Scalmyùt was stuck fast. The captain faced her.

There was a movement as Gwain drew Diana's dark blade. He threw it at the captain. It flashed blackly through the air, and buried itself deeply in the captain's body.

Captain Malliss smiled.

And any doubts that the captain was Malthazzar were banished.

A darkness spread from where the blade had struck her. The captain grew larger and darker before their eyes. Scalmyùt clattered to the floor, and Catherine felt herself powerless to reach for it as her eyes locked with Malthazzar's. As Malthazzar's transformation completed itself, he began to laugh with a laughter that rocked the dungeon and caused the ground to tremble.

Malthazzar looked up at the roof of the dungeon and roared: "Did you see that? Did you see that? She struck me. She broke her oath."

Malthazzar looked at Catherine with a look of lustful triumph. "And now, Catherine, High Queen of Palindor, you are *MINE*."

Malthazzar's sword flashed down and struck Catherine on the shoulder. It cut through her clothing, and then her skin, and then her body; and she was cloven in two.

Diana screamed and leapt forward, but Malthazzar simply thrust out an enormous arm, smashing it into her face. Diana dropped unconscious to the floor like a dead weight.

Slowly and with indescribable awfulness, Malthazzar's gaze fell one by one on Michael, Gwain and Phendric.

"You fools. I knew I would win, if only I waited long enough. Take Palindor. I have no use for it. I have what I want."

Yelling wordlessly, Michael jumped forward, his sword raised to strike, but Malthazzar's dark sword came irresistibly down and drove Michael's weapon spinning from his hand. Malthazzar stepped forward and thrust out his powerful arm, slamming Michael back against a wall with such force that he slumped to the ground, unconscious.

Malthazzar's gaze settled on Phendric. The gnome looked directly into Malthazzar's eyes.

Phendric said, "You have killed a High Queen, Malthazzar. Kill me, too, if you can."

"If I can?"

Malthazzar drew back his sword to swing it at the gnome; but then he hesitated.

"What manner of strange creature are you, gnome? There is more to you than meets the eye."

"Kill me, Malthazzar. Why do you hesitate? Are you afraid?"

"Afraid? Ha!"

And with that exclamation Malthazzar's sword came down one last time and smote Phendric where he stood. The gnome fell to the floor, dead.

Then Gwain watched in astonishment as all of them — Malthazzar, and the Dark Knights, and the soldiers, and the bodies of Toldwyn and Catherine and Phendric, and the unconscious forms of Diana and Michael — they all dissolved into a cloud of gray mist, which hung for a moment in the air and then vanished.

Gwain looked around the cell. He was alone.

XXVII Sheol

They were chained together in a line, each one's hands manacled
to a heavy chain that ran to the next person in the line. Catherine
was at one end. Next to her was Toldwyn, then Phendric, then
Michael, then, last of all, Diana.

Behind them was a massive, black castle, from the highest point
of which drooped a flag of maroon-listed black. Far in the distance,
behind the castle, was a low range of snow-topped mountains.

The ground was dark and friable, like lava spewed long ago from
a volcano. Before them stood Malthazzar, pacing up and down
along the length of their chain, his face a gleeful mask of triumph.
Behind Malthazzar stood a group of small, dark creatures with
pointed, ratlike faces. And behind them was a veritable crowd
of even smaller winged creatures that were in continual motion,
jumping in the air and fluttering their wings so that they only
slowly returned to the ground, when they would immediately jump
back into the air once more. The sky overhead was black, except
for the disk of a red sun.

Catherine felt a familiar feeling of despair, but she was unsure
whether it came from the air she was breathing or whether its
source was inside herself. For she knew that by striking at Malthazzar she had failed the High Lord. She had made a promise to
Him, and now she had broken that promise.

She knew where she was, of course, for she had been here before. She was in Sheol, but this time she deserved it, and she knew that, unlike last time, there was no chance of escape.

Malthazzar grinned triumphantly. He roared to the sky above, his hand raised in victory: "You can have Palindor, for I have won a bigger prize. Look at them, these miserable specimens whom you chose but whom you failed to protect. They're mine now, to do with what I will. You won't be able to take them from me this time."

He lowered his hand and drew near to Catherine. He thrust his face forward until it was no more than a hand's breadth from hers. She reeled from Malthazzar's hot, sulfurous breath.

"You know I've won, don't you, High Queen? There'll be no escaping this time."

Catherine nodded dumbly, lowering her head in shame, for she understood only too well that this time, for once, Malthazzar spoke the truth.

Malthazzar stepped back and addressed them all.

"The so-called High Queen has had the pleasure of being my guest here before, but I want to make some things clear to the rest of you. As you guessed, I am indeed Malthazzar, and I am lord of all that you survey. Isn't that right, General Shadow?" he asked a gray creature standing nearby whose shape seemed to be continually changing.

The creature nodded vigorously while a wide, evil grin split its face. The fluttering creatures became even more animated, jumping high and fluttering their wings noisily. One of them jumped and perched momentarily on Diana's shoulder. Diana screamed and jerked away. The creature fluttered away to the ground, looking hurt, as if Diana's reaction had surprised it.

"The rest of you are wondering where you are," continued Malthazzar. "This place is called Sheol, and behind you is the castle from which I reign over my domain. But my castle, I have decided, is not good enough for such *special* guests" — Malthazzar savored the word "special" maliciously. "Come, High Queen, this time you will discover the true nature of Sheol. We have a journey to make, but before we begin, I make this promise to you all: that when we reach our destination, you will wish that you had never been born."

The ever-changing Shadow rubbed his hands in glee, while all around the winged creatures set up a high-pitched chatter as they fluttered their wings vigorously.

They chanted: "The Pit, the Pit, the Pit."

"You will follow me," boomed Malthazzar. "Shadow, bring guards to keep the prisoners in line. And then... to the Pit."

Shadow went into the castle and returned with half a dozen dark figures dressed in gray habits and carrying evil-looking spears.

Malthazzar set out, striding over the friable ground, climbing a hill in the direction of the red sun. For a moment, the prisoners did not move. One of the guards came forward and jabbed at Catherine with his spear, and she began to stumble forward, following Malthazzar. The others fell into line behind her, but Diana, the last in the line, took only one step, then fell to her knees, jerking the chain and bringing the others to a halt.

One of the winged creatures approached Diana where she lay on the ground and snapped with its beaklike mouth at her face. She emitted a wordless scream, and, with a shudder, a winged creature like the others suddenly flew out of her body. It was followed almost immediately by two more, whose exit was accompanied by thrashing and moaning from Diana. The creatures immediately began to jabber with the other winged creatures in a language that none of the prisoners could understand.

Malthazzar turned to look behind him and shouted to the guards: "Stab her until she comes," then he turned away and continued striding up the hillside.

Several guards stabbed Diana with their spears. They drew no blood, but she winced and cried out in pain.

"Move along," one of them said. "It will be worse for you if you don't."

"You will make the journey anyway. You might as well do it without unnecessary pain," added Shadow.

Diana struggled to her feet. Slowly, stumbling every few steps, the disconsolate group began to follow Malthazzar.

They walked and walked. The sun fell slowly toward the horizon and then set, but it made no real difference either to the darkness or to the heat of the place. They climbed one hill and then stumbled down into the next valley, and then climbed the next hill. They were hungry and they were thirsty, but they were offered neither food nor drink. They continued miserably onward, following the massive creature who was lord of this awful place.

The sun rose behind them, but nothing else changed. On and on they plodded.

The sun moved slowly across the sky and set.

Catherine lost track of how long they walked, but it must have been for several days. The only change in the landscape was that the mountains in the distance behind them disappeared over the horizon, so that all that they could see now were the neverending hills and vales, and occasionally a stunted tree or an orange pool from which a sulfurous odor emanated.

And still they walked.

For the first couple of days they tried to talk amongst themselves, but their throats were too parched; besides, there was little to say. And so, after a while, they marched ever onward in silence.

Then, when it seemed to Catherine that there had never been a time when she was not leading the chained prisoners, Malthazzar mounted the brow of a hill and halted. When Catherine caught up to him and stopped at his side, Malthazzar pointed down into the valley before them.

"Behold, High Queen. Behold, all of you: the Pit!"

Diana dropped to the ground and let out an agonized shriek. She writhed as a veritable horde of winged creatures poured forth from her body, chattering excitedly to one another.

Malthazzar watched in evident glee as the swarm slowly subsided. One last creature left Diana's body, seemingly with great reluctance. It paused for a moment on the ground before her and stabbed her cheek with its beak. The gesture was halfway between a peck and a kiss. It drew blood — just one drop swelled and then fell to the ground, where it left a tiny circular mark of blackness as the moisture was thirstily absorbed.

Malthazzar laughed.

"You see, even they know to be scared of the Pit. They know what it means, don't you, my little ones?"

The creatures began twittering and jumping with renewed vigor — whether with excitement or with fear, it was impossible to tell.

"You may rest here for a while," said Malthazzar to the prisoners, "while you contemplate your future."

Catherine gazed down into the valley. In the center was a large... something. She did not know how to describe it. Her mind had difficulty interpreting what her eyes were seeing.

Looked at in one way, it was simply a large hole in the ground, albeit one that was achingly black and that filled her with an awe and a terror greater than any she had ever felt before. Simply to look at the Pit was to know that it was something awesome and terrible and eternal. She knew without being told that the rest of Sheol, terrible though it was, was as nothing before the sheer awfulness of the Pit. Here was something from which there was no escape — nor even hope of escape.

As she looked at the Pit, it seemed to become a boiling, raging sea, from which a thick, miasmic steam arose, filling the air above its depths with choking gray vapors.

Although there was no wind in this place, still the occasional strand of vapor made its way to where Catherine and the others watched, and when it did so Catherine jerked desperately away. It was not the smell — which was of acrid brimstone, yet of no greater degree than the sulfurous odor that pervaded Sheol — but rather it was the utter despair that came over her at the touch of the vapor. One whiff was enough to know that to approach the raging, turbulent sea was to surrender all hope of... everything. It was to know that forever more, until eternity itself came and went, one would be trapped in this place without hope, nothing ever changing.

Then, between the alternating visions of a dark Pit and a boiling sea, came fleeting glimpses of something else: of a place which was worse yet than either of these two; of a place to which Sheol itself was a mere appendage. And Catherine understood that one day even the desperate awfulness of Sheol itself would pass away, and that Malthazzar's power would be broken and ended; and yet for any creature trapped in the Pit when that day came, the day would pass unnoticed, for the Pit was something greater than Sheol, something greater even than Malthazzar.

Unlike Malthazzar, who had a beginning and, one could hope, an end, the Pit simply *was*.

Catherine felt a pull at her chains, and she turned with a strange reluctance from the sight that had held her horrified attention. The others had gathered around Diana, who was on her knees, her head bent to the ground, sobbing. The dark circle that showed where the drop of her blood had landed was joined by other marks, formed from her falling tears.

Catherine joined the others and put her arm around Diana.

Diana was shaking her head, mumbling over and over again, "I'm sorry. It's all my fault. I'm sorry."

Catherine clasped Diana tightly.

Catherine said, "That's all right, my dear, I forgive you." To say more was pointless, for there was nothing more to be said.

Comfort was equally without point, because there was none to be offered. All Catherine could do was to show that she had forgiven Diana, and that could best be done by a few words and a hug. Diana looked up at Catherine and, after a while, a weak smile showed through the tears.

"Oho!" exclaimed Malthazzar. "You find something to smile about, do you, you pitiful, wretched creature? Well, we shall soon wipe the smile off your face."

He turned to address his subjects. Now that all the creatures who had fled Diana's body were added to their number, there was a formidable array of the winged creatures, and they now became strangely silent. They cast worried looks towards the Pit; their jumps were few, their wings barely fluttering before they came back to the dark ground once more.

"Where are they going, my pretty ones?" asked Malthazzar.

"The Pit!" The response was not a roar but a whisper. And even in the mere words there was a sense of unending despair and hopelessness.

"And then what?"

There was no answer for some time. The creatures stopped moving.

Eventually, Shadow said, "Pain, and hopelessness, and eternal fire."

Malthazzar turned to the prisoners.

"General Shadow is right. Gaze down on your future of pain, and hopelessness, and eternal fire. And remember all of you — you especially, High Queen: this time there is no hope of escape. In fact, there is no hope of anything, anything at all."

He roared with pleasure.

Calming himself, said, "Now, come; it is time."

He strode forward, and the guards prodded the captives so that they formed themselves once more into a line and began to stumble wearily toward their fate.

XXVIII   The End — and the Beginning

They were gathered close to the Pit. Now that they were standing next to it, Catherine could see that there was a tall lip of dark, friable ground surrounding the Pit, so that she was spared the horror of looking directly into the churning void.

Malthazzar was standing in front of the prisoners, between them and the Pit. He loomed larger than ever as he breathed deeply of the odious odors that emanated from the Pit just behind him.

The other creatures had drawn back, distancing themselves from the Pit. Even Shadow, who until now had remained close to his master, stood behind the prisoners. The other guards and the winged creatures were several paces behind him. There was no fluttering of wings or twitter of conversation. Instead, an awesome quiet had descended. The only sound was the deep breathing of Malthazzar as he savored the exhalations from the Pit. Between Malthazzar's breaths, there was only an utter silence, as if no creature dared make any noise in this fell place.

Malthazzar looked at the prisoners. He smiled. A drop of slaver fell and soaked into the ground.

He spoke.

"So, High Queen. Did you ever think it would end like this?"

Catherine tried to be defiant, but discovered that she could not look Malthazzar in the eye. She hung her head and looked at the ground. She said nothing.

"Your miserable granddaughter thought it was all her fault, didn't she? But you know better, don't you?"

Catherine nodded.

"You wouldn't be here now if you had kept your vow not to fight. But you were too weak, weren't you? You attacked me with your sword, and now you are paying the price. Now, and for all eternity."

Catherine looked up, not at Malthazzar, but at those others to whom she was joined by the chain. They were looking at her.

"I'm sorry," she said, almost in tears. "I knew better. But I failed. It's all my fault." She looked desperately at Malthazzar. "Let them go. It's me you want; you don't need the others, and they've done nothing to deserve this."

Malthazzar roared with laughter.

"Done nothing to deserve this? Why, Catherine, how poorly you know your fellow mortal creatures. They all deserve this. You, the one who is called the High King Michael: tell me, haven't you ever done something wrong? Don't you deserve to be in this place with your mother?"

Michael nodded. "I tried to kill her," he admitted.

"But that was so long ago," said Catherine.

"So long ago?" queried Malthazzar. "But I do not forget. And neither does Michael, do you?"

Michael shook his head.

"And Toldwyn. Tell me, why are you here?"

Toldwyn hung his head in shame.

"Come on; say it."

"Pride. I was proud to have been chosen to lead the warriors and found a new Land. I was proud when I defeated the Dark Knights. I was proud to be called the friend of a High King."

"You see," Malthazzar said, "even a great warrior can be brought down by his weaknesses. And you, Diana. You've already admitted your guilt."

Diana looked at Malthazzar defiantly. Of the four of them, she was the only one who held his gaze. "I said I was sorry."

"And I'm sure that your friends have forgiven you. But they haven't forgotten, have they? What's done is done, and apologies or not, now you have to pay the price."

Then Malthazzar's gaze moved to the final creature, the one in the center of the chain, the gnome Phendric, whose gaze was not on Malthazzar, nor even on the humans, but on the lip that led to the Pit itself. He seemed barely to have noticed the conversation that was taking place around him.

Malthazzar stepped forward and stood directly in front of the gnome.

"You! Gnome!" he barked.

Slowly, as if his thoughts were being dragged from far away, Phendric turned to look at Malthazzar. Then he lowered his gaze to the ground.

Malthazzar continued, "What kind of a creature are you, Phendric the gnome? There was no need for you to be here. You are not like these others. Why are you with them? Who exactly are you?"

His eyes still on the ground, Phendric said quietly: "I am who I am, just as you are who you are."

Catherine sucked in her breath and stared at the gnome.

She had heard those same words once before, long, long ago, in a place as different from this one as it was possible to imagine. What kind of strange coincidence was it that Phendric had used them now?

Malthazzar dismissed the gnome's pronouncement. "That is a stupid and meaningless answer, gnome, and it will not save you. Nothing can save you now."

Then he said in a loud voice: "Nothing can save any of you. I hereby condemn you all to eternity in the Pit. Guards!"

The guards arrayed behind them lowered their spears and began to move menacingly forward. Only Phendric stepped forward voluntarily; the others waited until they felt the painful prods in their backs before climbing the lip of the Pit.

For one moment, they stood on the lip, Sheol behind them and the Pit before them. And then the terrible odors of the Pit seemed to reach out and embrace them.

Together they took one more step, and eternity began.

Catherine did not know what to make of it. For some time, everything was so confused that she was aware only of an intense agony to which no words could do justice, as if her mind, her body and her soul were all afire. She tried to open her eyes, but there was nothing to see, and indeed she was not at all sure that she still had eyes with which to see.

She screamed, but not with her mouth; it was not her body that had screamed, but her very soul. The torment was greater than she had ever imagined possible. And part of that torment was the knowledge that this was only the beginning, that it would continue not just for a moment, or even a span of time, no matter how long, but for ever.

Slowly, after who can say how long, she began to be aware of things around her — that she was not alone, that there were others sharing in her misery. Not just a few others, but myriads and myriads of souls, their shouts of torment merging with her own, so that the Pit was not a quiet place, but one filled with the eternal screams of despairing souls.

For a long time there was nothing else — just an agony of tortured pain and an awareness that she was just one of countless others, all eternally condemned.

Gradually, though, she began to discern another feeling, something deeper than the searing agony of fire, something that gnawed at the very center of her being. It was a feeling for which she had no name, but which she slowly began to understand as a terrible desolation of apartness and loneliness. It was as if always before, without her knowing it, she had been in intimate communion and communication with someone outside and beyond herself; and now, for the first time, that communion was no more, the communication severed. In the midst of the agonized cries, she was alone. Alone. She had never understood the word before. Terrible, lonely desolation gripped her very essence.

Somehow, this desolation was even worse than the agonies of the fire.

Ages passed. Whether it was years, or days, or just moments, it was impossible to tell.

She began to be able to identify some of the souls around her, although by what means she did not know.

There was Michael. He was fighting, trying to strike back at the pain, but filled with a despair that there was no way to defeat this enemy, knowing that he was doomed always to fight and never to win.

There was Diana, whose soul was in tears as she repeated over and over again in a neverending litany: "I'm sorry; I'm sorry. It's all my fault. I'm sorry."

There was Toldwyn, trying to stand against the agony, but whose screams were all the more terrible for the reluctance with which they were drawn from him.

And then after a long, long while, she found the last of the five prisoners. For a moment, just a moment, when she found him, she felt a frisson of... of... something — something that was so alien and unknown in this place that she could not even recall the word for it.

She tried to remember something that Phendric had said, just before they had come to this place.

Or was that just a dream? Had there ever been a time when she was not in this place? How could there have been? This was all there was. This was all there ever had been. This was all there ever could be.

Yet there was a fleeting memory of words that Phendric had used. What were they? She knew that they were somehow important.

Then she remembered — not the words themselves, but that Phendric was not the first to speak them. They had once had been spoken by an old man in a garden, æons before.

And with that memory came a momentary feeling. But she had no name for it, and the feeling was quashed almost before it was born.

Yet it did not die. She tried to cling to it, knowing that somehow, in some way, it was important to hang on to the feeling, to give it a name.

In her mind she tried to fix the image of the gardener. She tried to think of what he looked like, but could remember only meaningless superficialities and none of the details: an old man with a long beard, leaning against an ancient staff, standing in a brightly colored garden, somewhere, buried deeply in her past.

The image alternated with another that kept intruding unbidden: that of the gnome Phendric, his head hanging in abject surrender before Malthazzar, who, she now realized, was as powerless as any of them before the terrible despairing hopelessness of this place. Malthazzar was lord of Sheol; but the torment of the Pit was greater by far than anything even he commanded.

And at that thought, she remembered the word for what she was feeling. This place was filled with despair and hopelessness; but the feeling that she had felt when she recognized Phendric she could now name.

"Hope."

Somehow, she had said the word out loud, and, having done so, the feeling seemed to strengthen inside her. It started to flow out to others around her.

Like a warming sun, it began to spread from soul to soul.

Some rejected it, their despair so complete that they no longer had room for hope. But others grabbed on to the word and held fast to it, as if it held out a promise of something — although what exactly that something might be, none could say.

Without knowing how she did it, she turned and regarded Phendric.

He was smiling at her, and in his eyes was the same look that she now remembered in the eyes of the old gardener. And from Phendric flowed something else. It was not hope; it was something even stronger. It flowed outward and commingled with the hope that was now pouring forth from Catherine, and together they began to bathe those souls who gathered close by the pair.

Catherine remembered this feeling that was streaming forth from Phendric. There was a word for it... how had she once described it...? She remembered. It was like being bathed in liquid love.

Love!

That was what was flowing from Phendric, and suddenly she had to avert her gaze from him, for she could no longer bear to look. He was beginning to shine with a light that pushed back and overcame the darkness that surrounded them all.

Phendric spoke.

"Come! It is done. It is time to leave this place."

And Catherine began to feel herself rising, along with countless others, upwards and ever upwards until they burst forth from the confines of the Pit.

They were in the air, untold thousands of them, hovering above the Pit, surrounded by a bright and glorious light. She could see Malthazzar on the ground before them with his army, all of them, even Malthazzar himself, cowering in fear. The ground glowed, reflecting the glorious light that emanated from Phendric and was reflected by each of those who accompanied him.

Malthazzar was shouting up at them. "Go, leave this place; you have no business here." There was an edge of desperation in his voice.

Phendric spoke — or was it the gardener? Their voices now seemed strangely alike.

"I shall do as you wish, Malthazzar, for this is your place, not mine. I shall return where I belong, taking those who wish to join me. Will you come with me?"

"No! A thousand times a thousand times: no! Begone!"

"As you wish. But first, there is one other to whom I must offer escape."

And suddenly Malthazzar, and the soldiers, and the demons (for that is what Catherine now understood the strange, fluttering, winged creatures to be) and even the Pit itself was no more, and there were just the two of them, Phendric and Catherine, standing in a wide valley above which towered a mountain that Catherine recognized as Perilorn, the tallest mountain in Sheol. At the foot of the mountain was a cottage, and out of the cottage stepped an old woman dressed in rags. The woman regarded Catherine and Phendric belligerently.

A dark cloud of winged creatures flew out of the woman and retreated, clustering some distance away. For a moment, the old woman looked suddenly lost and confused. Then she seemed to recover herself.

"What do you want?" she asked Phendric. "This is my realm. I gave you no permission to come here."

Phendric offered his hand to the woman. "Cerebeth, I extend the hand of friendship and love and release. You once desired Life. Come with me now, and be at peace."

The old woman looked at him for a moment and a struggle wrote itself clearly on her face.

Then her expression cleared. She spat in Phendric's face.

"Get out of here," she shouted. "This is my realm, not yours, imposter."

Phendric shook his head with infinite sadness and turned away, and the vision of the woman and the cottage and the valley dissolved into nothingness.

"How could she do that to you?" asked Catherine.

"It was her decision, freely given. I am bound to honor it. Now, come, we are wanted elsewhere."

Catherine was alone, standing on a wide path that wended its way through a wood. The air was redolent with the scents of life: the biting odor of pine mingled with the earthy aroma of freshly dewed grass. Above, the sky was azure; the high sun was bright and golden. Birds chirruped noisily somewhere not far away. It took Catherine but a moment to realize that she was in the place where she had first encountered the High Lord.

She looked around, but could see no one. She began to walk down the path. As she walked, she breathed deeply, and decided that never had she felt more truly alive than she did at this moment.

The path turned a corner and suddenly the trees ended and the path opened out into a wide meadow. Small wildflowers of a myriad colors formed a parti-colored carpet, and the smell of their heady perfume filled her nostrils. But she barely registered these things, for her attention was held by a strange and marvelous sight.

No more than a dozen paces away, a small lamb lay on the grass, its head nuzzling against the flanks of an enormous, magisterial, golden lion. For a moment she was transfixed by the sight, then an urgent desire came over her to run away and escape before the kingly beast noticed her. She struggled not to move, scared that any sudden motion would betray her presence. Only slowly did she realize that the lion had already seen her and that it had no intention of attacking her. The lamb continued to nuzzle the golden coat of the magnificent animal.

"A lion and a lamb," Catherine murmured under her breath.

"Indeed," said a quiet voice just behind her. "Here the past is forgotten and all is new."

For a moment, she thought that her ears were playing an ugly trick on her, for the voice was surely one she recognized — and one that she knew she could never hear again.

She turned, and her breath was taken away. It *was* him! Tears began to trickle down her cheeks as the gnome Drefynt stepped forward and embraced her.

"Dry your tears, Catherine. This is a time for rejoicing, not sorrow. Now, come with me. Your presence is requested."

And before Catherine was quite sure how it had happened, she was walking back along the path through the woods, Drefynt at her side, casting an occasional mysterious smile at her as if he was amused by some private joke that he did not yet want to share with her.

They soon reached a clearing in which were gathered many others whom Catherine recognized.

Over on the far side were the gnomes Trondwyth and Sherna and Lorin. There also was Gondalwyn, and the elf Anderskerrin, holding the hand of an elf whom Catherine did not know, but whom she guessed to be his wife, Hervân. Closer to Catherine, dressed in garments that were whiter than any snow and wearing warm smiles of welcome, were the goblin Kalingroth and his acolyte Treneere. Next to them stood Toldwyn, who bowed deeply in her direction.

In the very center of the clearing was a small pond, and now she recognized this place, for from the pond grew a small tree, and hanging from its branches were three yellow-orange fruits.

Standing in front of the tree were Michael and Diana, looking around with dazed expressions. Into the glade walked Phendric, wearing white; his face seemed to shine in a warm light all its own, so that to look on it was to forget one's cares and to be enveloped by a deep peace.

Phendric turned to watch as one last figure walked into the clearing.

Catherine felt like running up to the old man. He carried a staff and walked slowly, knowing that there was no hurry, that nothing important could happen here without him. But Catherine restrained herself and watched the man stop beside Phendric.

There was a long silence. There was nothing uncomfortable about it — rather the opposite — and Catherine found herself wishing that this moment could last for ever.

A dark memory appeared in her mind and slowly grew, until she had to blurt out a question.

"The Pit. How did we escape? Malthazzar said that there was no escape from the Pit."

It was Phendric who answered. "And the Evil One spoke the truth. There is no escape from the Pit. But we did not escape. It was simply too small to contain the glory of the High Lord that manifested itself through me. The Pit tried to contain us, but it could not. In the end, it spat us out, along with all those who understood that to hope in the High Lord is to hope in the One who can never fail."

Catherine pondered Phendric's words. She knew that she would return to them again and again before she understood their full meaning.

She said, "But not everyone came with us."

"No. Not everyone puts his trust in the High Lord. Many prefer to rely on their own strength, which is never enough."

Diana asked, "But why does such a place exist? Why is there even such a being as Malthazzar? If the High Lord is so powerful, why does He not abolish the Pit for ever?"

This time it was the High Lord himself who answered. "There is a word, my child. The word is 'kiriàl.' It is not a word used in your own world, but it is a word that signifies the true foundation of all things. The kiriàl means that there is always a choice to be made between the two ways. The choice you make, the person whom you decide to follow and in whom you place your trust, that choice determines your destiny.

"Now, my child, no more questions. You see the fruit on the tree before you? Pick one of them. You too, Michael."

Silently, Michael and Diana did as they were bidden by the High Lord.

"Now, eat the fruit."

They obeyed, and as Catherine watched they closed their eyes in manifest delight as succulent juices filled their mouths. The High Lord tapped his staff on the ground and in an instant the ground opened, swallowing the two of them. They disappeared from sight.

Catherine looked at Olvensar. "They've gone back, haven't they?"

"They have."

"And now I suppose it's my turn. I really wish I didn't have to."

Catherine looked around at the friends who were gathered nearby, then at the one remaining fruit hanging from the tree. She stepped forward and lifted her hand to pick it, and was startled by a command that caused the ground itself to tremble.

"Halt, child!"

With her hand still outstretched towards the fruit, Catherine turned towards Olvensar.

"You may not eat that fruit. The choice is no longer yours. Look around. You have come home."

The single remaining fruit suddenly shriveled and fell into the pond, sending ripples across the placid surface.

Catherine looked at those gathered around her, and wept for joy.

The room was dark after the brightness of the wooded clearing. Diana opened her eyes as the last morsel of the fruit slipped down her throat. It was several moments before she realized that she was in her grandmother's bedroom. Grandmother Fowler was resting peacefully in the bed, her head lolled over to one side, a pale cast to her skin, a look of infinite peace on her face.

Her father looked at Diana. There was something in his eyes that she could not place. One moment it looked like joy, the next an aching sadness, the next a puzzled enquiry.

"Was it real?" Diana asked.

Her father did not answer. Instead, he gazed down at his mother as tears dribbled down his cheeks.

Slowly Diana realized that Catherine, the First High Monarch of Palindor, whose hope in the High Lord had rescued them all from the Pit itself, would never speak again.

She tried to say something, but discovered that tears filled her own eyes.

She turned to her father, and they embraced.

Colophon

The main body of the text of this book was typeset with the pdfTeX digital typesetting system. The typefaces used are mostly from the Latin Modern family, set at 11/13. The paper stock used for the body of the book and for the cover depends on the particular printer that created the book you are holding.

The VEDIT PLUS text editor was used to create the original text.

The cover was created with the Scribus desktop publishing system, in conjunction with the GIMP and Inkscape programs.

Computer processing for this edition of *Phendric* was performed on an Intel 64-bit quad-core system running the Kubuntu 8.10 64-bit distribution of the GNU/Linux operating system.